Book 3 of the award-winni

Historical Novel Society Editor's Choice
Winner of *the Global Ebooks Award for Best Historical Fiction*
Finalist in *the Wishing Shelf Awards, the Chaucer Awards* **and**
the Kindle Book Awards

'Very accomplished historical fiction.' The Historical Novel Society

'Historical Fiction at its best. Rich in historical detail, this novel brings alive all aspects of medieval life from the political undertones of the high-born pursuits of hunting and jousting tournaments, to the simpler occupations of the peasants, like bee-keeping... A superb ending.' Karen Charlton, *the Detective Lavender Mysteries*

'As soon as I finished this novel, I longed for the next in the series and can't wait to read more from this extremely talented author.' Deb McEwan, *Beyond Death*

'One of the best historical novels I've read in a long time.' Paul Trembling, *Dragonslayer*

'Evocative and thoroughly riveting. A vividly-written, historical saga.' The Wishing Shelf

'A walk through time! That is what it was like to read this fine novel. It drew me into the pages and would not let go of me until done! Bravo for a wonderful read!' Arwin Blue, *By Quill Ink and Parchment Historical Fiction blogger*

'You will not find any better historical fiction, nor a more powerful evocation of a vivid past than in Gill's brilliantly written series.' Paul Trembling, *Local Poet*

JEAN GILL

PLAINT FOR PROVENCE

1152: LES BAUX

THE TROUBADOURS
BOOK 3

Cover design by Jessica Bell

Jean Gill's Publications

Novels
The Midwinter Dragon - HISTORICAL FICTION
Book 1 The Ring Breaker *(The 13th Sign)* 2022

The Troubadours Quartet - HISTORICAL FICTION
Book 5 Nici's Christmas Tale: A Troubadours Short Story *(The 13th Sign)* 2018
Book 4 Song Hereafter *(The 13th Sign)* 2017
Book 3 Plaint for Provence *(The 13th Sign)* 2015
Book 2 Bladesong *(The 13th Sign)* 2015
Book 1 Song at Dawn *(The 13th Sign)* 2015

Natural Forces - FANTASY
Book 3 The World Beyond the Walls *(The 13th Sign)* 2021
Book 2 Arrows Tipped with Honey *(The 13th Sign)* 2020
Book 1 Queen of the Warrior Bees *(The 13th Sign)* 2019

Love Heals - SECOND CHANCE LOVE
Book 2 More Than One Kind *(The 13th Sign)* 2016
Book 1 No Bed of Roses *(The 13th Sign)* 2016

Looking for Normal - TEEN FICTION
Book 1 Left Out *(The 13th Sign)* 2017
Book 2 Fortune Kookie *(The 13th Sign)* 2017

For Claire of Colonzelle

CHAPTER ONE

If someone drinks a great quantity of wine in order to quench his thirst, he induces senseless behavior (as happened with Lot). Thus it is more healthful and sane for a thirsty person to drink water, rather than wine, to quench his thirst.

Physica, Plants

'Him.' The boy's head swivelled towards the drinkers at the far table.

'Dolt!' Geral hissed. 'What have I told you? God's body! Don't look at him. Make it natural. Just follow me – and follow my lead. Best you say as little as possible.' He sighed, stuck with the youngster as his partner, all limbs and credulity but tall enough to breathe down the back of Geral's neck as they threaded a route across the crowded inn to squeeze a place beside their target on his bench.

Their task was made easier by the fact that the man in the corner was not only alone; he reeked of misery and isolation so that all those nearest had instinctively turned their backs on him and shifted to make space. The man also stood out because he was in uniform, a red tabard, grubby from travel but nevertheless a slap in the face for the ordinary working men around him. If he'd had the presence to carry

1

the rank his tabard declared, or bought a flagon for the table, he might have found himself singing 'Marie's a-courting' in good company. Instead, he was nursing a mug, a pitcher and a black look.

'Dolt,' muttered Geral, not about the boy this time. Briefly, he wondered if the man was indeed some Lord's Fool, indulging in some off-duty misery, but if so, he would have either been out of livery or wearing the other signs of his trade. No, this was a messenger, like himself, but naïve or vain enough to adopt the new trend of wearing uniform, advertising his provenance and mission to anyone who cared to look. And it was Geral's job to look, to ensure his own message reached the right ears, unhampered by others. He knew that livery from somewhere, somewhen, and his little finger told him it meant trouble. The little finger he'd broken, when he was six and fell from the apple tree, was never wrong.

'Greetings, master,' he interrupted misery incarnate. 'Bertran here,' he waved his tankard vaguely towards the boy looming awkwardly beside him, 'was much taken with your costume and wondered how a man of your standing came to be in our drinking haunt. It being my task to educate the boy, and to take every chance of letting him hear from his betters, why, I thought we could benefit from an exchange of news while you are here and, it seems, lacking company.' Geral gave his most winning smile, a little dented by the lack of teeth on one side but usually a successful accompaniment to flattery and the messenger's magic word, 'news'.

The man straightened a little and contemplated his fellow-drinkers with bleary eyes. As he sat up, the silk of his tabard rippled a golden lion into view, its tongue and claws tipped blue against the red background.

'Aquitaine!' exclaimed Geral. 'God's bones but you're a long way from home, man. On the Queen's business, I should think, and a weary one to judge from your face.'

The other man's face set into even deeper lines, grime etching the hollows of his cheeks. 'Sit,' he gestured.

Geral introduced himself as he obeyed and clambered opposite the other man onto the bench, spreading enough to make another place. 'And the boy's Bertran. We're in the same business, you and me.'

'You wear no colours.'

'My Liege is local, not worthy of your attention.' Geral shrugged, grateful that his minor Liege wasn't there to hear him and consign him to the highest dungeon in Provence, where men learned quickly that 'deepest' wasn't always the most terrifying where dungeons were concerned. 'But I know Marselha and can perhaps save you time and trouble in your errand. All in good time, all in good time. I've a thirst on me would drain the harbour. You!' He grabbed a server, commandeered a pitcher of wine and two goblets, pouring a small amount for Bertran, and a generous amount for himself and the man from Aquitaine.

'Simon.' The man offered his name like a miser giving alms but it was a start.

'I've seen a few tough assignments in my time,' Geral confided, 'and here I am to tell the tale.' He checked that Bertran was giving proper attention and was reassured by the round-eyed curiosity. 'If this lad pins his ears back and learns what I teach him, he can take my place and welcome, when it's my turn to sit by the fire.' He spoke to Bertran with a glance now and then at Simon, to include him as a fellow-expert.

'You start by carrying the women's messages; fetch the midwife, fetch the priest, tell a man there's a boy born…'

'Aye,' nodded Bertran, interrupting enthusiastically. 'One time I took a hunting dog as a present from our Lady, a long way down the coast. Rex his name was, black tip to his tail.' He finally noticed Geral's glare and blushed his way into silence. Thank God the boy was more interested in giving the dog's name than his Lady's. Giving that information away was not part of Geral's plan, not until he knew whether it would be to his advantage or not. He suspected not.

He continued, warming to his theme, and having kicked Bertran hard under the table. 'Bad news is what gets you killed. If you're not crafty. Suppose you bring message of a death?' He watched Simon out of the corner of his eye but there was no reaction. So it wasn't a death that was worrying the messenger from Aquitaine. 'How do you break the news without a bit of your body being broken in return?' he paused, a good teacher.

Bertran's face screwed up in thought. 'I'd stand a good way back when I said the news and I'd say it fast-like, then maybe run?'

A flicker of amusement shimmered across Simon's face and he sat straighter, apparently distracted from the weight he carried. Geral sighed and shook his head. 'Think, man, what impression that would leave on some poor, bereaved human. No, no, no, you must carry the death in your person as if it's your own dog that died, like this.' And he schooled his features into his special face for 'I am the bearer of sad, sad news.'

Bertran clapped his hands with admiration. 'I must do this. Is it so?' and his own baby-faced smoothness contorted into a gargoyle around his twinkling blue eyes.

'Almost,' lied Geral. ''Tis practice you need.' He felt another lift of spirits in the man opposite him, a barely concealed twitch of the mouth, and he emptied the pitcher of wine, calling for another. Tickling a fish was ever slow business to start with and a quick catch at the right time. Timing was everything.

'And when you tell of a death, then judge the telling of it to suit the hearer. If the dead one was loved, then the death was heroic and painless – make it so. If the dead one was hated, the last moments were all cowardice and pain. And if the death was not personal but a public change...' No, there was definitely no reaction from Simon. So, the red queen was not dead. What mission was the man on that brought him so far south? 'Then you must tell it for the advantage of the hearer. Find the good in it for his status. Find a future invitation to greatness from the man who has replaced the dead one.'

'But that would mean telling a lie.' The boy's eyes were saucers.

'No indeed.' *A lie is the least of what you will do as messenger*, Geral thought, *if you want to stay among the living.* 'No indeed, for the future is unknown and it might well be that the new power will bring good to your hearer. You must just imagine it to be so, when you give the message, whatever that message may be. And remember that when one flower fades, another takes its place.' Aha! That found an echo in Simon's thoughts. The fish shimmered silver below Geral's hand and he grabbed it.

'I hear there has been such a replacement in Aquitaine,' he hazarded aloud.

'You know then.' Simon's face and tone were exactly right for proclaiming a loved one's death.

'Not the detail.' Geral reeled him in smoothly and kicked Bertran once more under the table, just to make sure.

'It all happened so quickly.' Once he'd opened up, Simon spouted like a gutter in a storm. 'First the annulment, and then as if that wasn't enough in itself to put Aquitaine at risk from Louis... I mean, we didn't want a King in Paris over us, and I'd give my life for our Duchesse without a question, but it was more difficult for everyone when she was on her own. Shows what an idiot the King is, to let the richest heiress in Christendom ride away from him, leaving him with two girl-children and nothing else but his own freedom to make the same mistake again.'

Geral untangled the news. The King and Queen of France divorced. Not unexpected but now a fact. Aquitaine at risk from King Louis' spite now that he was no longer its overlord. Shocked by the implications of this news from France, he glanced at his fellow-drinkers. The men around the messengers hadn't even paused in their drinking for this talk of kings and annulments. France was too far from Provence to matter. Geral shivered. The fiery Aliénor once more alone and sovereign power in her Aquitaine. Then he took in what Simon was saying.

'And now she's not, the risk is a certainty.'

'Not what?'

'Alone.'

Probably more round-eyed than Bertran, Geral couldn't help it. 'Not alone,' he repeated stupidly. 'She's with...'

Now he was fishing desperately, way out of his depth, but luckily

Simon filled in the gap. 'Yes, Henri damn-his-pretty-face Courtmantel, Duc d'Anjou. But two months since the marriage to Louis was dissolved, just time for her to undo every change to the law Louis ever made in Aquitaine, then she was a bride again on Whit Sunday. And there will be a war when Louis finds out.' Lapsing into gloomy silence, Simon took a long draught from his goblet.

'Don't mistake me,' he continued. 'My Lady has good reason to marry sooner rather than later, with every ambitious lord hanging his hopes on her hand.' Good reason that included bedding a man ten years younger than her, fitted well with what Geral knew of the ex-Queen of France. His thoughts raced over what he knew of Henri Courtmantel, nicknamed for his shortcoat. Self-styled heir to the throne of England, and welcome to it.

'I just wish she'd chosen one of our good Aquitaine lords. There's no lack of choice and Louis would have turned a blind eye to that but as it is...'

'War, you say?'

'Sure to be. My Lady might be floating around the countryside on a wedding progress but she sent me here, didn't she, knowing full well what was coming. She's telling the nuns at Fontrevault about her marriage and her plans for the Abbey but at the same time she's checking that Poitiers and Ruffec are provisioned and fortified.'

Geral could see the hook in the fish's mouth. So close. He nodded sagely. 'Aye, she's been to war before, has the Queen ... sorry, Duchesse. Knows the men she needs to have about her to hold steady against Louis, if – when – he attacks, as he must.'

'This marriage has combined Aquitaine with Normandy and Anjou, and a claim to England,' nodded Simon.

'And she needs her best men.' The words were out his mouth before he realised what they meant. Suddenly, Geral knew where this conversation was heading and why Simon was on an errand in Provence, from Aliénor, ex-Queen of France and Duchesse d'Aquitaine. They were both seeking the same man.

'Dragonetz los Pros,' stated Simon, as if confirming Geral's guess.

Bertran's mouth was open like the fish of Geral's imagining, about to spoil everything, when half a pitcher of wine landed in the youngster's lap.

'Beg your pardon, boy. I must've drunk a bit more than I thought. Go see the landlord and beg a change of clothes and tell him we need a room tonight. I'll settle all before we retire. He knows me well enough. Quickly! You'll give the place a bad name dripping red everywhere. Looks like a man was stabbed and died under the table! And fetch more wine!'

Ignoring the boy's aggrieved look, Geral gave every sign of having been struck by an amazing idea. 'I don't know whether you need a room but if you do, why not join us this night?' An enthusiastic assent rewarded him and Geral continued blithely, 'So, this Dragonetz is the man the Duchesse wants. You know where to find him I take it?'

Geral's last hope vanished as Simon replied, 'Aye. The Lord is holed up in a villa near here in the hills. I'll head up there tomorrow to tell him my Lady wants him, and his father the Commander of the Guard wants him, then we'll be on the road back as quick as turnaround.' *Not if I can help it,* Geral thought. 'We should be home in time for war with Louis and if we survive that, what with Dragonetz on our side too, then the best I can look forward to is England.' The cloud settled over his features again and he took refuge in another swig of wine. 'And yourself, Geral? You're from here? Not working?'

'From nearby,' Geral evaded. 'My Liege is a nobody, not like yours.' He gave an envious look at Simon and prayed that his words would never reach his Lady's ears. Then he set about misdirecting Simon with tidbits of gossip about the Bishop's salt-mines and the Comte de Marselha's amours. Geral even mentioned the forthcoming visit of the Comte de Barcelone, overlord of Provence, to his most unfaithful vassal in the fortress of Les Baux, but not once did the messenger give away his own mission.

Wearing peasant hessian, Bertran thumped sullen onto the bench, grunted that the landlord would indeed await Geral's pleasure at the close of the evening, and had kept a room for the three of them with clean, straw paillasses to lie on. The boy's morose humour changed to a look of admiration as he listened silently to Geral doing a verbal dance around local politics without ever mentioning their relationship to the Lady of Les Baux, or why the two of them were in Marselha.

Later that night, late enough to stagger a little but not so late as to court the headache less experienced drinkers would have had, the three of them took a companionable piss together in the back courtyard, then sought the landlord. 'I'll settle this.' Geral brushed aside Simon's offer to pay his share, accepting the thanks showered on him with a magnanimous 'We'd have had to pay for the room anyway so I don't see why you should have to pay.'

'I don't either,' muttered the landlord, shrewder, as his torch-boy led Simon off to the room while Geral stayed to pay his dues. 'Bertran can light me up the stairs,' he said and grabbed the boy's arm to keep him from following Simon.

'You untrustworthy sewer-rat,' the landlord addressed Geral and shook his head admiringly.

Geral removed his feathered cap and sketched a mock bow to both the landlord and the boy.

'I don't know how you keeps your face so straight-like. I couldn't do it.'

'Practice, Bertran, practice.' He looked at the boy's earnest face, smooth and shiny with sweat in the torchlight. 'But you made a good start tonight. Make no mistake; this was an important stroke of luck, us meeting Aliénor's man this night. Another inn and we'd be empty-handed tomorrow. As it is...' Dropping the pretence of being tipsy, Geral gave precise instructions to the innkeeper who was first reluctant, then convinced that it was his duty, aided by the purse on offer. If Bertran had been impressed before, he showed hero-worship in his eyes now.

'And what must I do?' he asked, his voice cracking.

'Why, be nice to our friend, if he's awake. And let him sleep well if

water and a girl. It was early in the morning for satisfying all his appetites but he had time on his hands, so why not.

By the time Simon was tucking into his casse-croute, Bertran had reached a certain villa on the outskirts of Marselha, and Geral had a watchful eye on the new establishment for taking thermal waters, in Ais en Provence.

CHAPTER TWO

In order that a woman might become very soft and smooth and without hairs from her head down, first of all let her go to the baths, and if she is not accustomed to do so, let there be made for her a steambath in this manner. Take burning hot tiles and stones and with these placed in the steambath, let the woman sit in it... And when she has well sweated, let her enter hot water and wash herself very well, and thus let her exit from the bath and wipe herself off well with a linen cloth.

The Trotula, On Women's Cosmetics

E stela had well sweated. While the minerals in the water were replenishing her essence, she let her thoughts drift with the steam. Drifting, like she'd done for months, cocooned in winter. Drifting together, she and Dragonetz, with nothing more important to do than play with baby Musca, and no-one more important than each other. Time to heal and to be together after the dangers and damage of the Holy Land. Drifting, in a tacit 'Not yet' to the world that could manage without them, would have to manage without them.

Most noble families had too many responsibilities to waste time on a child, spoiling the work of a good nurse – and Prima *was* a good nurse – but they'd been able to watch Musca take his first steps. They'd heard his babble create one clear word, 'Icky', close enough to the dog's name to be recognized as such, even by Nici himself. Most of the time, Estela forgot that they would never be a real family.

In their private haven, it didn't matter that Estela was not married to Dragonetz or that their son was officially the offspring of Johans de Villeneuve, Estela's husband, who in reality had never bedded her. The lie made Musca legitimate, which mattered very much in the world outside and when Estela was honest with herself, she knew it mattered deeply to her too. As did his true paternity.

Dragonetz himself was free to marry whomsoever he chose, within the constraints of approval by his liege lord and his parents, and in the best interests of his future comté of Ruffec.

Estela saw no solution to a problem that was never mentioned between them but that she never forgot. This was not the time to burden her lover with such questions but she must think of what was best for him, when the time came, as it surely would. Decisions could not be postponed forever and the world would make that clear to the heir to Ruffec. Not yet though. She and Dragonetz were not ready yet.

She knew that his recovery was but surface-deep. He was not ready for a fraction of what would be asked of him in the world. Just last month, he'd suffered so much tooth pain that Estela had offered to rub the poppy concoction on his gum. His brief transformation with shaking greed as he fought to say no, had taught them both a lesson. The poppy's hold was controlled by abstinence but not defeated. Would he ever be free from this demon, Estela wondered. She'd stayed away from home while their man Raoulf tied string to the tooth and drew it with the slam of a stout oaken door. Drunk, his white face swollen on one side, Dragonetz slept alone till he recovered. No-one repeated the suggestion that he take the poppy.

Time, Estela thought. Time and love would see them through such moments. Even as the thought wisped towards the domed ceiling, it wavered, falling short of the repeat pattern of blue that curled to infinity. For all her love, and her conviction that Dragonetz needed more time to heal, she herself was restless. Something in the air had changed. Since Mary's Day, the end to winter, when the peasants and serfs had red faces from 'gathering flowers' in couples, eager for the old dances, the restlessness had been palpable. Estela watched the sideways glances between man and maid, and was wilder than ever with her knight, in word and deed, but she ached for something more. Another baby? No, she thought not.

Even their music-making left her dissatisfied. While Dragonetz patiently scored the unearthly music remembered from his opium dreams, Estela scribbled fragments of lyrics and melodies that never became whole. She sang her lover's work and calloused her lute fingers to match his but she had lost her own creative spark. Who was she? What was she? Lover. Mother. Mistress. Troubaritz who couldn't write songs any more. Musician with no audience, she who'd sung and played her own compositions for queens and courtiers. The wall around their perfect rose garden did indeed keep the world outside and something was missing for Estela. Something that responded to the books Malik sent her, priceless works of modern medicine, in Arabic and Latin.

A drop of sweat trickled salt into her mouth, reminded her that she was not here to fix a wandering womb or eradicate pubic lice with steam inhalation of lavender. Nor was she here to counteract a cold temperament, although exorcising a few demons wouldn't go amiss and she intended to talk of all these matters with Dana. No, she was here to become beautiful, which meant enduring a little pain in a good cause. If she didn't concentrate, she would be in a lot of pain instead.

She sighed. Being careful not to rub the skin, or it would burn and be as attractive as a plucked chicken, she pulled at a few hairs to see if they'd loosened. The decoction of mastic, frankincense, cinnamon, nutmeg and clove had done its very expensive work and she continued with the depilation. The sequel today would be gentle massage with oil rather than the usual hammam cleansing that was a specialty of the baths.

Last time she'd visited, Estela had been scrubbed with a rag sponge until her skin frothed with grey scum. That same skin would glow pink when rinsed and then shine gold when oiled. No bath or treatment would ever give Estela the white skin she craved, instead of the golden one inherited from her mother, but Dana came from a land where golden and dark were normal. Not for the first time, Estela reflected on the way fate had brought this skilled Moorish woman into her life.

What if Dragonetz had not brought a rose-grower from Damascus to Marselha? Then his wife would still be in Damascus and her Turkish cousins would not have asked the rose-grower for his patronage when opening the Ais baths for public use. The rose-grower would not have asked his wealthy patron to support the venture. Dragonetz. Who had embraced the project with all the enthusiasm of a man who liked the thought of his lover's body hairless and polished. Somehow all Estela's thoughts came back to Dragonetz. Where he was, things happened. Even behind a wall.

'You can tell Dana I'm ready,' Estela told the black-haired girl, who was clothed in only her shift as she awaited orders, as far from the hot baths as she could manage while still being in hearing of the clients. Tuesday was designated women only and Estela had been told that it was always quieter than the men's days. Ladies were protective of their reputations, which many felt might suffer if they attended the baths. Others were worried about the effect of the water itself. Estela enjoyed the artistic freedom her talent as a troubadour gave her and was so used to being a married woman that she had almost forgotten the constraints on maidens.

Feigning polite blindness and invisibility, three other women were taking the waters in silence, spaced out like compass points, Estela thought, with a sudden memory of the ship to the Holy Land and adventures past. She stifled another sigh, which soughed into the muffling steam. Occasionally there would be a splash and gloop of water as a woman moved to a higher level of stone and hotter steam, or back down into the water. In between times, all was closed eyes, calm and heat.

Estela looped her hair up in her hands. She had told Dana that she was willing to try a concoction of Gaul blacking with the ashes of oak apples to add gloss and deepen the black but definitely not the essence of boiled lizard strongly recommended in her latest reading. The price of beauty could be too high. Estela's eyes closed again.

'My Lady?' Dana interrupted her thoughts and motioned Estela respectfully to the central stone platform, used for the scrubbing and pummelling that followed the purge of sweat. *Purgatory*, Estela had often thought, as she submitted to being rubbed with what felt like a hedgehog complete with biting fleas, *then torture and hellfires*. Led by the handmaid, a group of three friends giggled their way to the stone block vacated by Estela. They dropped their white linen towels and stepped down to sit in the water, chattering like starlings, voices echoing on stone and disappearing into vapour.

How could so much dirt be skimmed from one body? Estela wondered as she did every time she came and then she lay obediently prone on her towel as strong brown hands kneaded her body. Every time she was told 'Relax,' her body tensed instinctively in anticipation of the next assault. Dana was the gentler of the two masseurs, Estela reminded her apprehensive muscles, and at least the use of the depilatory spared her the usual scouring. Lavender, she approved, relaxing in the scented oil as Dana probed and smoothed.

'Have you made progress with the medicinal bath?' Estela asked through a corner of her squashed mouth.

'Yes my Lady, thanks to your generosity. We have stored some of the herbs we need and the next shipment from Damascus should furnish the rest of our requirements. The private bath is complete and will be kept for medicinal purpose.' A particularly heavy fist rolled into her waist kept Estela quiet for a moment. 'I like your idea. Each time a lady takes the waters, we will suggest one of our treatments for hair or skin. Then when we are applying the clay or rub, we can talk about women's health matters.'

Breathing a little heavily, Estela said, 'Next will be to give the cure and use the new steam bath. You need to progress slowly though, with care to the ladies' reputation.'

'Indeed,' Dana said. 'Ladies should keep their mystery, and bodily matters must enhance the joy of the bedchamber.'

'According to *the Trotula*, the joy of the bedchamber is responsible for many unpleasant bodily matters and we must do our best to restore the ladies' health,' was Estela's dry response.

'My Lady has found a source of new learning on the subject?'

'Several! The new works from Salerno have made me think we could heal many women's diseases by proper regulation of their monthly flowers.'

'Such was the teaching of Ibn-al-Jazzar,' agreed Dana.

'And Galen before him. But the new work from Trota gives the precise recipes for us to concoct and how to apply them.'

'And you think he is to be trusted ?'

'She,' corrected Estela, considering her response. Did she trust Trota's work? 'Yes,' she concluded. It is based on so much we already know and it smacks of practice as well as theory. When you read it, you can tell that Trota is a working physician. And working in Salerno.' *The centre of medical learning. What must it be like to be a doctor in Salerno!* 'Did you get the perforated chair?'

'Yes, and I think with a curtain between, we could treat two women at the same time, one by steam bath and one through the chair.'

Estela reflected. 'Sailcloth for the curtain. And you'd have to have compatible treatments for the steam from one not to contaminate the other.'

'This can be done.'

Dana's knowledge of Arab cosmetics and the Turkish hammam had made her an apt subject for progression into medicinal treatments, and there ensued a pleasant discussion on which sweet-smelling oils would best attract a high-roving womb back to its proper place through the perforated chair and which foul scents to administer by nose at the same time. Estela left the baths glowing in mind as well as body.

The quarter was open and safe in daylight and she'd sent for her manservant, who was no doubt on his way from a game of dice in some tavern, so Estela was merely surprised at being approached by a stranger, not afraid. From habit, she reached for the knife in her undershift, just in case.

The man was lean and rangy, dusty with travel but not ill-kempt. The extended toes on his leather boots gave a nod towards fashion but otherwise his clothing was serviceable and anonymous, tabard and hose of country colours, all faded browns. His smile was black on one side with missing teeth, making Estela wonder briefly how Dragonetz' lop-sided smile would fare in the future. Shrewd brown eyes dipped as the man made a presentable bow and addressed her.

'My Lady, I bear a message for Estela de Matin.' The use of her troubadour name prickled the hairs on Estela's neck with anticipation. Some adventure was on its way. The Pathfinder rune brooch buckling her gown nudged her, a reminder of roads crossing and choices. How was it that just when she was excited about the healing project with Dana, something else should come her way? Why was her heart beating faster at the prospect before she even knew what it was?

'Then you may speak it,' she said, 'for you have found her.' Somehow she knew that she was assenting to more than her name.

'I am Geral, envoy to Lady Stéphania des Baux, whose domain is the highest in Provence and no less in renown amongst troubadours. It grieves my Liege that of all the songbirds to have graced Les Baux, one has not yet alighted on this perch. That a troubairitz who has sung for queens should be so near and still unheard is a fault she seeks to remedy. Lady Stéphania begs Lady Estela de Matin to grace the court of Les Baux, to sing for the Comte de Barcelone and his dear wife, Petronilla of Aragon, during their forthcoming visit.'

'I accept,' replied Estela. Then she thought about it and wondered what Dragonetz might say. A little pang of guilt hid quickly behind the stronger thought, *to sing before another queen*.

And thus did Estela invite the world into the walled garden.

CHAPTER THREE

The dog (canis) sometimes has a foreboding of happy or sad events to come in
the future or already present. In accordance with its understanding, it sends
out its voice, revealing this. When the future events are happy, it is happy,
and wags its tail; when they are sad, it is sad and howls.

Physica, Animals

Throughout the ride home, Estela pondered ways of sharing her plans with Dragonetz. She imagined his excitement on her behalf and, although she would not pressure him to accompany her, if he should wish to do so, surely it could be arranged. They could not be together as a family in public but they would no doubt find private moments. And should he prefer to stay at their villa, take more time to recover in peace, she would be back with him in only a few weeks with stories to tell. Musca and his nurse Prima could travel with Estela or stay with Dragonetz, whatever the latter preferred.

Estela's mind was skittering around plans and packing as she dismounted and it took several moments before she realised that there was an unusual amount of bustling activity around the villa. Her palfrey was taken away by one of the new stablehands as the boys she knew best were all occupied in saddling up several horses, including Dragonetz' beautiful destrier, Sadeek. Nici was running in agitated circles, telling his disapproval in baritone and occasionally stopping to chase his tail. He bounded up to Estela and gave her a significant stare and was rewarded with an absent-minded caress. He then continued trying to discipline his rebellious tail.

Estela's finely plucked eyebrows met in exactly the expression she'd been warned against by her beauty advisers at the baths. 'The wrinkles will stay,' warned Dana. 'The worst kind of wrinkles,' she'd emphasised, 'frown lines.' Dana would have shrieked at Estela's facial damage as she tried to make sense of servants rushing out of the villa with packed saddlebags and wineskins.

When Dragonetz himself appeared, hurling instructions at the scurrying boys, his demeanour would have excited only approval from those same custodians of beauty. He glowed with energy and no trace of a frown line marred the newly shaven skin around his mobile mouth, which twitched into his lop-sided smile as he noticed Estela's return. He was carrying Musca in his arms and swinging the baby into chuckles as he walked.

'My Lady.' He was beside her in three strides, his mouth to her hand, shredding her thoughts to tatters. If she tried to speak at all she knew it would emerge as babble less coherent than Musca's. She'd been away less than a day. What had happened in her absence? She would never be able to read the black depths of his eyes but now they gleamed like rare pearls and she waited to hear the cause.

'Estela,' he began, leading her away from all fussing servants to a quiet corner of their garden, but not far enough to find a seat. 'I am called away. I would have liked more time for leave-taking but I must be in Arle this night to assess the Baux's primary stronghold of Trin-quetaille. Then we leave for Les Baux. A messenger called today from Lady Stéphania des Baux –'

Flushing, Estela interrupted and said, 'I was going to tell you as soon as I came home –'

Dragonetz hardly seemed to hear her and clasped her hands to gently hush her so he could explain. 'Lady Stéphania wants me at Les Baux for the visit of the Comte de Barcelone, Ramon Berenguer.'

'Who is married to Petronilla of Aragon,' murmured Estela like a well-schooled child.

'The Lady wants me to take her part should the visit turn sour. I don't have to tell you that since Stéphania and her husband tried to claim Provence by force, Barcelone has tightened his grip over the region and this truce is built on Raymond des Baux's dead body. Stéphania isn't going to forget that she let her husband go to Barcelone in good faith and all she gained was widowhood and humiliation.'

Estela was no child. 'The truce won't last. And Stéphania is really asking you to be a weapon in her war, whoever starts it.'

'To lead her forces, for the sake of her fatherless boys and for Provence. For her inheritance rights.' Dragonetz nodded and gazed at her steadily.

Her mind raced, her own news forgotten. 'But Barcelone claims right to Provence and has held it against all the local risings. The visit is supposed to be the start of the new amity, underwriting the truce.'

'Or a show of force by Barcelone, which could be an opportunity for Stéphania to strike first.'

'Not when he's a guest! And bringing his wife with him.'

'He will have more than his wife with him,' teased Dragonetz. 'Malik is among Barcelone's cohort and word from him has shown me more of the game. You won't guess.'

But Estela did. She knew him too well to miss the exuberance that could mean only one thing, especially after months of inactivity. 'Barcelone has also invited you to join him,' she breathed. 'No, Dragonetz, not again. You've played this double game before and it nearly cost your life.'

His smile turned her heart as it had always done. 'So I've had practice. And you see why I must leave you.' She said nothing so as not to have the lie on her conscience along with much else. His voice had dropped its lightness. 'This game of war has already cost the people of Provence dearly but that will be nothing to what will happen if the truce breaks. There will be blood between neighbours, between father and son, and no end in sight to the feuding.'

He kissed Musca on the top of his feathery hair. 'I will only know how to play if I see the board. And,' his tone teased her again, 'I shall be back with you in a moon, having danced, sung and put on weight.' He embraced her, the baby between them. 'I must go or it will be too hard to leave at all. And you will be safe here. I'm leaving Raoulf and of course you have Gilles too, as well as the new men.' His attention had already wandered, his eyes checking men and horses but he had not forgotten courtesy. 'Any news from the baths?'

'Just women's matters,' she replied.

Afterwards she would wonder what she could have said, knowing the dangers he was going into, but nothing was the best she could offer and hope that her parting kiss spoke for her. She took Musca from his father and stood, watching the final arrangements to leave.

In a flurry of dust, the party left, without one backward glance. Estela brushed the tears from her cheeks and sent for Raoulf to tell him that they were going to Les Baux the next day, directly, not via Arle. She would take him and Gilles, plus a small party of men-at-arms; the nurse Prima and the baby; and Nici, the dog. What Raoulf said was later repeated by Gilles in even stronger language but the two men had known their lady long enough to accept the inevitable and prepare for the journey. While the men readied weapons and chainmail, Estela shook the dried lavender out of her best gowns. The troubairitz, Estela de Matin, had accepted the respectful invitation of Lady Stéphania des Baux, known in her homeland as Etiennette.

After two days in the capital of Provence, Dragonetz was confident that he could defend Arle if need be – or of course take it. The ancient city and sea-port was riven by the mouth of the great river Ròse, which itself was split north of the city into the lesser and greater Ròse. On the left bank was the heart of the city, with new quarters to the north, the ancient stone arena in the middle and the Vieux Bourg to the south, where most of the business was conducted.

On the river itself was the Méjan and north of the commercial city was the Château de Porteldosa, a disused stronghold belonging to the Baux family, which served mostly as a vantage point to observe the comings and goings of the ferry, to which they owned toll rights. The Baux ferry was the only way of crossing the river, although remnants of towers to the north on both banks testified to an earlier bridge, rumoured to be a bridge of boats, a pontoon, dipping and recovering in the dangerous floods of the great river in spate.

Not even the Porcelet family had risked trying to replace the old bridge even though there were two rates for the ferry crossing; extortionate and Porcelet price – higher again. The rivalry between the Pons family, now known as des Baux, and the Porcelets, was as old as their presence in Arle and no-one knew how far back that went. They might form an alliance during crusades but in-between was a different story. The many Porcelet businesses in the Vieux Bourg made it their pleasure, not just their work, to recoup in trade from the Baux family what they lost on ferry crossings.

Unwelcome in the city, the Baux made their own presence felt on the right bank of the river, high up in their isolated Château de Trinquetaille. The good citizens of the Vieux Bourg could see the château at night, lit up in an extravagance of torches and fires, boasting of banquets and noble guests, guarded by its wild woods and the ferry access to the Isle aux Sables, the Isle in the Sands.

The Baux held this seigneurie by gift of the Archbishop of Arle sixty years earlier and it had become the seat of their power. They had established the city's Consulate, its prisons and its lawcourts in Trinquetaille, thereby enriching their coffers through the ferry service as well as the penances and dues that resulted from the lawsuits.

All this, Dragonetz learned from the new lord of Les Baux, Hugues, still mourning the sudden death of his father. Hugues shared his rule with his mother, Etiennette, but Dragonetz quickly revised his opinion that this must be irksome. A young man who would have been serious even without the burdens of bereavement, leadership and an uneasy truce with his overlord, Hugues measured his words in a way that made him seem dull of thought. Dragonetz soon found that behind the slow words lay a deep understanding of Hugues' terrain and his people.

'I had no idea that Trinquetaille was so important,' confessed Dragonetz. 'Yet your title comes from Les Baux?'

'Les Baux is prettier,' was the reply, 'and my Lady Mother makes it sparkle in the eyes of the world, with her court and company.' *When she is not making war against Barcelone* hung in the air. 'It pleases me mightily that Trinquetaille did not catch your attention. Long may it escape the attention of others.' *Barcelone* thought Dragonetz. And then said it aloud.

'Should the Comte de Barcelone turn his eyes this way…'

'He would remember that we were *instructed*,' the word rang bitter, 'to hand over Trinquetaille to Barcelone as part of the *truce*.' The truce that was signed by Etiennette and all four sons, in this very castle.

'And your intentions are?'

'My intentions are intentions. Not actions. I signed the truce.' The subject was closed. Dragonetz imagined the Consulate: Hugues expressing his intentions to hand over Trinquetaille to Barcelone, everyone knowing that this was not going to happen and no-one able to prove it without years going by, years that changed everything. This man's slowness was indeed going to be interesting to observe, Dragonetz told an imaginary Estela and felt the usual pang at her absence.

A pigeon, he noted mentally; *I must send her a pigeon.* Then he returned to his analysis of the Méjan, where the Jewish quarter was located, and where the ships brought goods, from wool to wood, down the river from Lion and the north, where the great river was named Rhône.

In all quarters of the left bank, Dragonetz found the noble name of Porcelet on men's lips and not just praised for modern trading acumen. One old man told him with pride that in treaties during the crusades the Moors had asked as guarantees 'hostages or the word of a Porcelet.' The Pons family of Les Baux might hold the châteaux and the title of Provence but the Porcelets held the city. And they knew it.

Outside the house of Porcelet in the Vieux Bourg hung a newly painted shield, gold background with farmyard pig in sand, and the device *Genus Deorum, deinde gens Porcella, 'First the Gods, then the Porcelet family.'* It became clear to Dragonetz that, together, the Pons and Porcelet families could unite the lords of Provence against Barcelone's claim as Comte. Divided, Pons and Porcelet would split Provence between them like the great river split the city.

Prone to flooding throughout the year, the Ròse was rising in early June to its summer high water levels. Livestock, which had grazed the brotteaux, the flood plains, in winter, had been moved to safer pastures. Access to Arle was across this river by the Baux ferry; or on the river, which was a busy trade route but a clumsy and expensive option for an attacking force; from eastern Provence, which was governed by the Baux in rebellious fief to Barcelone; or by sea. It was by sea that Barcelone would make the much-heralded visit to his not-so-loyal lords of Provence, either via Marselha or Arle and then inland to Les Baux.

After hearing all the reports from his men, garnered in taverns and shops, whore-houses and docks, Dragonetz put his final questions to Hugues in private. He did not go easy.

'Your parents roused Provence against their overlord. Barcelone has the right to exact punishment from traitors, to recall your châteaux, your lands and bestow them elsewhere. He has been generous in giving a truce, in leaving you with Les Baux, in giving you time to comply with the terms you agreed and give up Trinque-taille. He is visiting Les Baux as a guest. Why should I take your part? Why should I create a threat to Barcelone by standing at your side?'

'My mother is rightful heir to Provence, not Barcelone! But you know all this already.'

'I know that *some* believe your mother was wronged.'

'My mother *was* wronged! More than once! My grandfather had no right to leave Provence to one sister and cut my mother out, after my parents had married and there was no need to dangle a dowry. My grandfather caught his Barcelone fish well enough but now we have this outsider over us. When my aunt Dolca died, Provence should have reverted to my mother, not ended up in the hands of some Barcelone nephew!'

Dragonetz did not point out that the Barcelone nephew had taken the inheritance and his responsibility in good faith, and could hardly be blamed for how it came to him. Fairness and inheritance law would never be friends. 'But you signed the truce,' he repeated, stubbornly.

'I was too young and too shocked from my father's death to know what I was doing. You speak of the truce being generous – you haven't read it! Complete submission by serment, giving Barcelone 'all dues from land or water, sweet or salt, on the honour of Hugues who will stand hostage should the truce be broken.' That's the generosity given to a family who dares to challenge the great Ramon Berenguer of Barcelone!'

Dragonetz asked, 'The Porecelet family... where do they stand?' If he'd hoped to change to a less emotional subject, he could not have chosen worse. Hugues' phlegmatic temperament was roused to red-faced fury. 'Anywhere that shifts to suit them! They are as mean of spirit as of purse, as liable to stab a man in the back as wish him Good-day to his face; sneaking, conniving, church-loving hypocrites all of them. How they duck their dues for the ferry I don't yet know but I shall find out and then we'll see how they like metal that's not small coinage and is rammed up their...'

'They do not support your mother's claim?' Dragonetz clarified.

'They do not! They switch allegiance with the wind so who knows what side they will take from one fray to the next but they spout forth about being loyal men to Barcelone and they worship not God but rather his Archbishop in Arle!'

'Ferry dues not paid, you said?'

'I can't prove it but you know how it is when a man goads you and lets you know he has the better of you, without giving anything before witnesses that would stand in law. So it is with the Porcelets.

In all our dealings, someone in that infernal family will drop hints such as 'You should raise the ferry tolls' along with a knowing smile, or 'We do appreciate the service you offer across the river' and I know the payments do not tally with the number of times they must have crossed. But I can prove nothing! They have covered their tracks by making some payments.'

For the first time in months, Dragonetz felt a pleasurable surge of pure unleashed devilment. Estela would have recognized his smile with dread of what might follow but Hugues was as yet uninitiated. That would soon change.

'I have an idea as to how we might remind the Porcelet family of their civil duties,' was all Dragonetz said.

Hugues brightened. 'Tell me,' he said, in his innocence.

'I need red dye...' mused Dragonetz

'Madder? From the dyeworks?' Hugues' whole face wrinkled in concentration.

'No, henna powder will be perfect, and I have some in the coffer of gifts for your Lady Mother. Can you wield an oar and swim? Apart from spying, lying and wearing filthy clothes, our plan almost certainly requires getting wet. First, your ferryman has to tell us the day and time of the Porcelets' next illegal crossing.'

'The ferryman?' Hugues' eyebrows met in straight lines.

'It has to be him. Bribed or bullied. So now we convince him that we are capable of greater rewards and more lethal – and immediate – punishments, than anything the Porcelet family can even imagine. Once we know all we need, I fancy the ferryman will take ill suddenly and be replaced by his nephew.'

'He can take ill permanently! A man who can be bought back and forwards is no man of mine.'

'Agreed. But if the man's family was threatened...'

'He should have come to me.'

'Did he know that?' prodded Dragonetz gently.

The silence spoke. Then, 'Maybe not,' acknowledged Hugues. 'I have spent little time of late in contact with vassals such as he.'

'Then judge him when you hear him. Gratitude for mercy can bind a man close, if he trusts in your protection. Or you'll see the greed in his eyes and know him for a lost cause.' Dragonetz could see his words sinking in.

Although Hugues was the older by a few years, he was new to leadership and his experience was limited to Provence. There was much Dragonetz could teach him and it seemed the ground was fertile as the Ròse delta. Binding a man to you, then keeping him close, was part of a leader's armoury.

Briefly, Dragonetz wondered whether the lesson to the Porcelets would push them in the wrong direction. Then he decided that if it did, the Porcelets were never winnable in the first place. And the benefits included more mischief than he'd made in an age. 'Now, there are a few more things you need to know about the plan…'

The Consul had been hoping to pass a trouble-free year and be one of those to lose the election at the end of it. When he made the youngster repeat his message, he knew his hopes were doomed. Trouble had found him, sure enough and he could not ignore such a flagrant breach of the law, even by a family as grand as the Porcelets and even if they'd been provoked – as was likely, given that the plaint was coming from their deadly equals. It would have to be the wretched families of Pons and Porcelet forcing his hand!

'Again!' Consul Xavier told the lad but word for word was exactly the same, rattled off at top speed with no pauses but as comprehensible as it was ever going to be.

'Hugues Pons des Baux denounces Porcel Porcelet for non-payment of ferry dues on this and many occasions by evidence of the indelible red marks of thievery on the palms of him and his men that have been so marked by Hugues Pons himself who will testify with witness to the crime you may apprehend the felons from this afternoon's crossing and their hands shall betray their guilt.' The boy gulped a breath with hand outstretched for his customary coin.

'Your master can reward you from the Porcelet money he recoups in fine should he speak truth,' the Consul told him sourly. If pushed to take sides, he rode behind the Pons for the good of Provence, which – as he well knew – was why Hugues had trusted him to act on the information he'd received. However, he did not like being pushed, especially when it would mean reporting to the Archbishop that his favourite family had been found erring.

Although the Consuls had freedom of action, the Archbishop of Arle had overall responsibility for them and reporting to him was their duty. Xavier cursed and wished the whole system in hell. He'd been pushed into standing in the first place and this was what happened when you let people push you. If Pons and Porcelet hadn't been at loggerheads twenty years ago – them again! – Arle would never have followed Avinhon into this Italian fashion for Consuls, inspecting the city's business.

Xavier wished he'd not bedded Widow Clans before the election – one vote fewer and he'd not be this position. The Consuls weren't supposed to know how the votes went but everyone did, of course, and it had really been that close between him and another. Another thought struck him; if only women had no vote at all, he'd definitely not have been elected.

The popularity of his curly black hair and easy manner had indeed been his undoing, although not in the manner his mother had foretold. Among the heads of household entitled to vote were many widows and women of all walks who ran businesses in their own name, whether bakers or traders, and many of them had voted for Xavier. But there was as much chance of women losing the vote as Porcelets flying, and he must suffer the consequences of his smile. Wishing would change nothing. He sighed.

The Porcelets bore long grudges and he'd hoped to avoid being on the receiving end. But he'd been sworn in at the Assembly on Michaelmas fair-day, when he'd taken the post, and an oath was an oath, so he would go down to the river that afternoon. He sighed again. The day's promise had turned to showers and he predicted storms. Not for one moment did the Consul doubt that the information itself was accurate as he cancelled his other plans.

CHAPTER FOUR

The sea (mare) sends forth rivers, by which the earth is irrigated, just as the body of a human is inundated by the blood of its veins. Some rivers go out from the sea with a rapid motion, some with a gentle motion, and others by storms. The earth along the course of each river has some sort of grassy vegetation, unless it is too rich, or too dry, or too rough, so that from it vegetation is unable to grow. But from land which is moderate in these things, vegetation grows.

Physica, Elements

'My uncle's proper poorly. Told me you'd be coming though and that you'd paid already. I'm just to let him know how many men and how many horse, and see you safely over the river of course. I'd be fair stupid to forget that part!'

Lord knew the ferryman was no genius but his nephew-replacement made Lord Porcel of Porcelet appreciate the older man's common sense and brevity. A man named Porcel of Porcelet had learned early in life not to value imagination but he did like a businessman, and the ferryman had struck a business deal profitable to all, without wasting words. Not like this buffoon. If every unnecessary word were worth a denarius, the man would be the richest in

Provence. Porcel cut him short before another of the Porcelet cadre was tempted to violence.

'Eight men and eight horses. And we're in a hurry.' They didn't wait for permission to lift the rope across the gangway and embark. At least the oars were manned and the boat empty of any but Porcelets. He could speak freely of Barcelone's imminent visit without looking over his shoulder all the time.

Ignoring the fool nephew's constant chatter, the boat's turn and straightening as a rower switched sides, and the spitting rain, Porcelet rested his hands on the railing as he shared his thoughts with his younger brother, Bens.

'I called a favour from the Genoese and their sailors sent word this morning that Barcelone should reach Arle tomorrow.'

'Arle, not Marselha?'

'Arle,' confirmed Porcel, 'but others don't know that and we'll keep it to ourselves. I want the house of Porcelet glittering at the quay in welcome. Pass the word to the womenfolk that they shake the mothballs out of their best gowns and pretty up the children to win young Petronilla's heart. I want everyone there, with loyalty on their faces and riches round their necks.'

'We still go to Les Baux?'

'*You* go, with enough of a force to show politeness, but you go with Barcelone. I heard from the château at Tarascon that he goes there first, so he'll take the northern approach to Les Baux.'

'Go there from the north?' Bens' surprise showed.

'I know. Little more than a mule track that way but he'll catch the Pons family on the back foot. I don't think he trusts the 'welcome' he might get if people know exactly where he'll be and when. This truce is only ink on parchment.'

'But we know where he'll be.'

'Aye and he won't mind that. We've shown our colours in the last few years and we'll get our rewards. Patience, brother, patience. When you offer to travel with him, let it be seen by him as protection on a tricky road; he'll see you're willing to choose sides in public.'

And if others see you and know who's in control here in Provence, that's their interpretation. I'll stay here and mind the business. I've no stomach for Etiennette and all that château frippery. Besides, it's Arle is capital of Provence, not Les Baux, and someone should remember that!'

'Look at them black river birds like black omens of black doom,' intruded the ferryman, close enough to Porcel to force him sideways so as to escape the smell of eels and the pointing finger. Glancing briefly at the cormorants, Porcel gripped the rail tight to control his irritation and was rewarded with a black-toothed smile and another blast of eel-breath.

'Black thoughts indeed,' murmured Bens, drawing a tight smile from his brother. 'You'll put the men off their stroke.'

'You noticed, then.' Nodding his head enough to give everyone looking at him a headache, the ferryman informed them, 'New oarsman today and my uncle warned me he'd be a weakness. Started strong so I kept him port-side but now he's flagging a bit so I've moved him up-river to balance things out.'

He raised his voice, presumably hailing the new oarsman. 'Put your back into it, Roc! Pull! Lift! Pull! Lift!' His rhythm fitted into that of the man calling the moves and then left it. An imaginative man might have heard the song of the two men's voices, the dip and splash of oars, the patter of raindrops. Porcel was not an imaginative man. He spoke louder.

'By the time you reach Les Baux, Barcelone will be feeding from your hand, encouraged by his lady wife, and proof against any change of heart or real welcome at Les Baux. Drive the wedge, Bens.'

'Change sides again, Roc and Gars. We're coming into land. Stir yourselves!' Roc, the unfortunate new oarsman, wearing hide that had smelled better on the cow it came from, was crossing the deck and stumbled against Porcel as the boat rolled.

'Fool!' Bens knocked the man to the ground, where he lay as if stunned.

Porcel continued, ignoring the interruption. 'Every defiant word from the Pons family, every act of rudeness at Les Baux will seal their fate. Let Barcelone deal with Les Baux – we'll help him wipe the vermin from their holes. Rightful heirs are those who show they're capable! With Barcelone back in his home, who'll be left here to rule Provence?'

'Roc, get back to work,' yelled the ferryman, and the oarsman lurched to the empty place once more.

'*We* will,' Bens replied.

There was the usual fuss of tying up and, unusually, it was one of the oarsmen who leaped to the jetty rather than the ferryman. With his fellows, he moored the boat. All Porcel's attention was focused on the men who'd suddenly appeared to meet them, who had no connection with the House of Porcelet, and who were led by one wearing the unmistakeable red cap and robes of Consul. Porcel cautioned Bens to silence, a hand on his arm.

'My Lord Consul.' Porcel bowed low. 'This is unexpected.'

'It is indeed,' was the dry response from one of the men elected to maintain law and order, resolving disputes in Arle should any be brought to his attention. Mostly, the Lord be thanked, they weren't. However the messenger's insistence that he should meet the afternoon ferry seemed to be based on good information. One simple test should confirm this.

'May I see your hands, my Lords?'

Turning to summon the ferryman in case he should need to prove his crossing was in good order, all paid and proper, Porcel became aware of the strange quietness. The garrulous ferryman had disappeared. Not that Porcel noticed, but the new oarsman, Roc, was also missing and the absences were not unconnected with two dark heads bobbing ashore further downstream.

'Your hands,' repeated the Consul, in a tone that brooked no further delay.

Puzzled, Porcel, Bens and their men showed their palms to the Consul. The time it took to cross the Ròse had been long enough to transfer the moistened henna from the boat railing to pattern their hands like a skeleton's.

'It seems, my Lords, that you have been caught red-handed.' The Consul's face remained grave but not so the others within earshot.

Porcel had been wrong about only Porcelets being on the ferry and every man-jack of the oarsmen would tell a good tale in the Vieux Bourg taverns that night. 'You owe reparation to the Pons family,' continued the Consul, 'unless you wish to dispute this in the courts.'

Briefly, Porcel considered the option. After all, his red hands only showed that he had crossed on the ferry, not that he'd done so without proper payment. It would be Hugues' word against his. In public. With everybody in the hall knowing he lied, laughing at his red hands.

'I do not,' Porcel told him, teeth gritted and mindful of his need to greet a certain ship at the docks the next day. 'There will be reparation. *In private*,' he added glaring around him and rubbing his palms against his hose, transferring a little red but leaving the traitorous hands merely rawer in colour.

'I leave the matter with you. And will of course confirm with Lord Hugues des Baux that his honour has been satisfied.'

Barely nodding farewell he was so anxious to escape, his face redder than his hands, Porcel mounted and rode off with his men. Bens didn't quite catch what his brother said but he suspected 'Bastard' and 'pay' figured in the comment.

Meanwhile, in the nearby château of Trinquetaille, servants rushed more pails of hot water to the tub, to rid the young ferryman of the smell of eels while the oarsman paced the chamber. When Hugues had run out of oaths, he stopped pacing and asked the man sitting in the bath, 'What shall we do?'

Dragonetz ducked his head underwater, came up again and let the rivulets trace their course down his black hair. 'Ambush Barcelone's cavalcade before it reaches Les Baux,' he suggested, and ducked under again.

'You jest.' Hugues' face was still alight with their success and when Dragonetz said indignantly, 'I do not!' the third ducking was a tussle between the two men that ended with Hugues in the bath, Dragonetz out of it and more water on the floor than in the tub. Later, over a large quantity of wine, they refined their own plan for welcoming Barcelone to Provence.

Later still, Dragonetz lay awake on his straw mattress in Trinque-taille's Great Hall, listening to the snorts and snores of a hundred men. He'd turned down the luxury of a curtained bed in the solar, alongside Hugues, in order to set the tone for what was, to him at least, a campaign. The Lord of Les Baux had known his terrain in impressive detail, which should make all the difference against Barcelone's men – and the Porcelets.

His senses sharpened as always pre-battle, Dragonetz let the music of the day invade his thoughts. River and raindrops; twenty oarsmen dipping to the helmsman's beat on the small oaken boat, a galley adapted to serve the busy crossing; whinny of horses, and flare of nostrils, as the planks shifted beneath hooves; the notes played in Dragonetz' imagination and fragments of lyrics danced along the melody. Jarring tambours announced Pons versus Porcelet and clear flute trilled the victory.

Committing the pattern to memory, Dragonetz allowed himself to drift into sleep, conjuring a love deeper even than his music, comfortable in his certainty that Estela was safe at home, whatever he faced at Les Baux.

At the top of the east tower, Dragonetz smoothed feathers gently with a finger, held the pigeon's plump breast cupped in his hands, wings gently pinioned. The metal tag attached to its foot glinted in the first rays of the sun. So much had happened since this little bird had left the Moorish tents outside Damascus with its fellows, a gift to the knight, presented with a strong suggestion that he should never return to the Holy Land. Cooped up at sea, then in the loft at Dragonetz' Marselha villa, the birds had accepted their new home, as predicted.

After a month, Dragonetz had started taking birds a short distance from home to let them find their way back, ensuring food and their mates were there to meet them. Then he tried further afield, and with messages; simple with the older birds who'd survived the sea voyage and already had their Moorish breeding and training embedded. Not so reliable with the youngsters he'd collected locally but Dragonetz' newly appointed keeper noted which birds performed best and discussed a breeding programme.

This was the first time Dragonetz had used one of his pigeons on a real errand rather than a training exercise. 'God speed,' he murmured, holding the pigeon out of the narrow window and throwing it gently to the breeze. The bird faltered a second, then righted and headed like an arrow south-east, to Estela, with a message of love that only she would understand.

Dragonetz felt his heart wing home with the bird as he watched the speck vanish from sight. The Moors had told him to beware the falcons that learned to watch pigeon lofts for easy pickings but he'd judged Trinquetaille safe and so it had been. Pigeons had not been kept here as meat or messengers. That was about to change, as elsewhere in Provence. Dragonetz descended the spiral staircase to organise the ride to Les Baux.

Although he automatically registered the defensive potential of the Sarragan Pass, its gigantic rocks allowing a few men to hide and seem many, the narrow bottleneck of access and exit, these features were not what had struck Dragonetz most. He and Hugues had reached the top of the rise first, in the van of their small troop, with the setting sun behind them, gilding the grotesque white boulders, the marsh-reeded valley and the cliffs beyond.

The boulders grew leering faces and demonic familiars in the shifting light and long shadows, dropping into unfathomable blackness in the valley below and lightening again as the cliffs rose, and rose again to the jagged tips. Except that the tips were not jagged but regular crenellations, the turrets of a castle that made the small hairs on Dragonetz' arms prickle with excitement or foreboding, he knew not which. 'It's prettier than Trinquetaille,' Hugues had said, regarding the origin of their name.

'Les Baux,' breathed Dragonetz.

Hugues said nothing but his face spoke. There was a set to his jaw, a determination in his gaze that Dragonetz had seen before, in the Crusades, when a man had decided what was worth dying for. For a brief moment, the low day's-end sun caught whatever metals the castle offered; armour and flagstaff, door-hinge and wheel-hub, and the fortress caught fire, dazzling and defiant. Then snuffed out, just as suddenly. His eyes still recovering from the glare, Dragonetz rehearsed his litany of defence, but this time extending it to Les Baux itself, not just tonight's camp.

The massif was occupied by the château on the northern heights, protected by sheer cliffs on two of the sides that Dragonetz could see, and dropping through the dependent village downhill to the south, Les Baux's only access and weakest point. Gate and rampart were visible even from this distance, defending the entry.

'The access to the château from here is downhill, by the boulders, across the river and marshes, then up by the south gate into the walled city and up again to the château?'

'There is no river in the valley, just marshes. The path down is basically a mule track, widened by our use. And the caves are amongst the rocky outcrops,' confirmed Hugues. They had spoken at length of the caves the night before. Dragonetz had assumed a river from the look of the land and was surprised that a fortification of this importance had no water source nearby. Rainwater was unreliable, especially in Provence, making the castle even more vulnerable to siege. He must investigate the water system when he was in Les Baux itself.

'How do men get to the château itself?

'There's only one way to get up onto Roucas, the rock on which the citadel is built, and that's to the south. The side you can't see is sheer cliff.' Just as Dragonetz had guessed.

'There are five ways to reach the bottom of Roucas. The main route is from the south, over the pass and across the marshes. They're worst with storm rain but if you stick to the path, they're not as bad as further west when the Ròse floods. That's the way my mother would expect Barcelone to go.' Thanks to the messenger Dragonetz had sent to Les Baux, Etiennette would be forewarned of Barcelone's approach and of her son's, although innocent of the reason for Hugues' delay.

'I suppose Tarascon offers him a safe night and a chance to consolidate his hold there.'

'I think so too,' Dragonetz pondered. 'It was his base in the wars with your mother and he might need it again.'

Hugues gave his slow smile. 'He might,' was his only comment.

'And he is right to worry about his safety en route to Les Baux.'

The smile grew larger. 'It was kind of him to choose the northern route. We have the small look-out posts you saw earlier in these mountains,' Hugues continued his description, 'the Alpilles.' Hugues had made sure the men at the look-outs knew their comrades were back in their terrain and what their plan was.

Dragonetz nodded. 'We want the men there to try – but fail – to rescue Barcelone in his time of trouble. And they'll be helpful in signalling his approach, to your mother and to us. That would be the natural response, no?'

'Barcelone will be lucky to avoid a flight of arrows with a troop that size and no warning.'

Dragonetz was emphatic. Barcelone was no stripling to gift them mistakes but a victorious overlord come to demand oaths of fealty more binding than ink. 'He'll send clear warning of his approach, just before he comes. He won't risk giving excuse for bloodshed to eager men.'

'He might send a Porcelet ahead to warn the look-out,' Hugues said hopefully.

'Who might be mistaken for a brigand.' Dragonetz laughed. Even if Barcelone was naïve enough, the Porcelets were wiser. 'No, my friend, you must resign yourself to whatever fun we have in the chase tomorrow as the Pons family must be seen in public to host their guests in an honest manner, which does not include killing half their number en route! You signed a truce!'

'I know. With my father still warm in some unknown grave in

but Dragonetz was struck by the family resemblance in Petronilla's mother to a woman he knew very well. Red hair, the white skin that often accompanies it and something about the determined jut of the chin were common features to them both. But where Aliénor, Duchesse d'Aquitaine was all fire and vivacity, this woman – her aunt perhaps? – was quiet-eyed and the so-similar features composed for lumpy plainness where the niece's pleased with their symmetry.

Presumably the artist had used the usual tricks of his trade to beautify the subject, making her forehead higher, clearing the skin of blemishes and in colour, in which case Petronilla's mother had indeed been very plain. The father's expression verged between sour and saintly so in some ways the couple seemed well matched although there was no sense of connection between them. Dragonetz wondered if in the future an artist might dare to show a couple's feelings for each other, as he did when composing songs, but even the thought was unseemly. Still, a daughter's love saw beauty where art showed none.

Unseen, Dragonetz slipped the package into his pouch and returned the coffer to its place. The men secured the treasure cart once more and listed the contents to Hugues, who arranged the guards until such time the treasure could be retrieved safely.

CHAPTER FIVE

Note that when a woman is in the beginning of her pregnancy, care ought to be taken that nothing is named in front of her which she is not able to have, because if she sets her mind on it and it is not given to her, this occasions miscarriage.

The Trotula, On the Reigmen of Pregnant Women

E stela sighed over an embroidered letter M which had turned into a crooked H through no fault of her own, or so she would have sworn. Even though she used a palm protector, her left hand was pricked raw from all the moments when she'd lost concentration and the needle had found her through the fine lawn.

'Is there some nobleman with the initial H?' she asked Sancha, who sat beside her, perfecting a delicate flower in three colours and chain stitch. 'Then I need not unpick it.' They were slightly apart from the other ladies, the better to talk in confidence, but so far Estela had learned only what she knew already, including how badly she sewed.

With mouth pursed, Sancha mutely held out a hand, and Estela passed over the unfortunate letter for re-working. 'I wish you could visit the baths at Ais!'

'I don't think public baths are appropriate for me,' murmured

Sancha, head bowed over her sewing, surprisingly deft for such a large-boned woman.

Estela flashed a look at her friend, knowing full well the secret proclaimed by Sancha's Adam's apple for those who were perceptive about human anatomy. Most people saw no further than Sancha's strident gown and flamboyant headwear, her make-up and plucked eyebrows. If her voice held husky notes and her build was large, then the difference between one individual and another was sufficient reason. Estela however knew why Sancha needed privacy for bathing.

'You could use the private room we've created. It's curtained off,' Estela told her, then was struck by another potential problem. 'And it would be best if you came on the women's day. After all, you would be entering the baths in a gown, whatever you look like without one.'

'Estela!' Sancha winced at the bald, but honest, judgement and glanced around but no-one had heard. Estela was careful enough to make sure of that and was continuing blithely with her own obsession.

'That is the only thing I miss from coming here. I know that the project is advancing without me and I'm sure Dana will use the perforated chair for basic regulation of a woman's flowers but if I were there, I would test some of the more complex instructions in *The Trotula.*

When I accompanied the midwife in Die, there was a case after miscarriage where I'm sure the woman had an ulcerous womb. Now I know to check for blackish fluid with a horrible stench, and I could treat her with a diet of cold ingredients – I remember deadly nightshade and white of egg were among them but I'd have to look the others up. I would love to cure a woman in such a manner!'

'Could you give me less detail, please, dear,' Sancha said faintly as she bit through a length of embroidery silk. 'It's all so …unfeminine.'

Undeterred, Estela continued tartly, 'It's actually very feminine, like so many other horrible ailments!' She relented. 'But there are many scripts on men's diseases too…'

'No,' warned Sancha. 'I really do not want to know.'

'What I would like most of all would be to carry out surgery.' Estela's voice turned dreamy. 'Imagine, if I could repair a man's arm.'

Sancha looked at the mangled letter M on her lap, the crooked stitching already coming undone at the start. 'I'm imagining,' she said.

'Like Malik did for Nici. I watched and I know with a bit of practice I could do it too. He cleans the needle first, you know, and I would never have thought of that if I hadn't seen him do it. He uses lavender oil. If only the priests didn't fill people's heads with nonsense against Arab learning, we could help so many people!'

'Nici?' queried Sancha.

'The dog.'

'Perhaps you could practise on dogs,' suggested Sancha, grateful on behalf of the human race for the possibility. There was no way of gauging Estela's response as the friends were interrupted by a messenger, wearing red and yellow stripes.

'What is the point of wearing a master's colours if all the houses bear the same?!' Estela complained. 'Provence, Barcelone – one of them should choose something different.'

'That, my dear, is the problem in a nutshell,' murmured Sancha at the same time as the page announced his mistress' request for Lady Estela to join her in the ante-chamber reserved for the guests from Barcelone. Questioned further, the boy denied any knowledge of what Queen Petronilla might want with Etiennette's latest troubadour. Whatever her misgivings, Estela had no option but to obey and at least she had an excuse to drop her embroidery into the basket 'for later'.

Her pattens clicking on the flagstones as she followed the page, Estela rehearsed all the reasons she hated Petronilla. Born into the rich inheritance of Aragon, and betrothed to Barcelone from babyhood, what excuse could there be for usurping Etiennette's right to Provence? Land hungry, power hungry, usurper and tyrant. According to Sancha, Etiennette's lord had died 'mysteriously' on his enforced truce visit to Barcelone. In Estela's mind, there was no doubt; Petronilla was accessory to murder. In fact, the more she thought about it, the more likely it seemed that Petronilla had carried out the murder, possibly without her husband's knowledge. After all, 'mysterious' death was most likely poison, the weapon of Saracens and women. Ramon Berenguer himself might be innocent of this terrible betrayal. And if the Comte de Barcelone had been manipulated and lied to by his scheming wife, perhaps Malik's respect for the man was not completely ill-founded. To the catalogue of Petronilla's known crimes, Estela added a few personal qualities; arrogant and spiteful (or why else pay this visit, rubbing the Baux family noses in their defeat), ill-favoured and ill-mannered.

Satisfied that she had the measure of the heir to Aragon, Estela flounced through the door held open to her and curtseyed with a finely judged degree of both formality and insolence. Then she took a long, level look at the girl who stood in front of her. For she was just a girl. Plainly dressed, far too plainly Estela thought, fingering her own bright silk. Rank should be displayed or how would the rabble see the distinction between themselves and a queen?

Beetle-browed and pock-marked, Petronilla was every bit as plain as her clothing. Speaking quietly, the Queen thanked Estela for responding to her invitation (as if there were any choice!) and dismissed her entourage quietly. The ladies-in-waiting glided out of the ante-chamber without hesitation. Estela waited, as she must, for Petronilla to divulge the reason she'd been summoned. The silence stretched as Petronilla flushed, walked to the window, turned her back on Estela and finally spoke.

'My physician, Malik, told me that you had some expertise in women's matters.'

The mention of her friend and mentor softened Estela's instinctive denial to mere prevarication. 'Nothing compared to his own, my Lady.' She had to strain to hear Petronilla's words, spoken as if to the blue skies through the window.

'There are things only a woman can understand. Not just of the body. And Malik said you could be trusted in this.'

In this. But not in everything. Not when she was Lady Etiennette's troubadour. It was Estela's turn to flush but Malik had indeed taught her something of his profession. 'I have helped some women with their troubles,' she admitted, 'and the practice of medicine carries the seal of the confessional, beyond politics and beyond morality.'

Petronilla's cross glinted as she kissed it and let the chain drop back onto the tiny jut of her breasts. 'There is no immorality, beyond the sins we cannot escape of being mortal and a woman.' She turned to face Estela, sat down in the carved chair and motioned her guest to take a stool. Another of Malik's lessons had been to know when to listen and when to question, whether learning to play Arabic chords on al-oud or waiting for a patient to tell you what she needed to say. After that, you might be able to find out what you, as a doctor, needed to know.

So Estela sat and schooled her face to sympathy, which needed less acting with every new observation she made of her unexpected patient. Tiny, that jut of breast might well be, but Estela divined that it had grown recently, as, no doubt, had the belly invisible beneath the modest folds of a drab gown. Someone as experienced in midwifery as Estela recognized the small signs.

In childhood, she'd accompanied her mother often enough; as an adult she'd learned from a midwife in Die, from Malik and from the precious books he sent. Most telling experience of all, she'd given birth herself, lonely and ill-attended. She reminded herself that this was the usurper and tyrant but there was no longer any bite to the words. This was a girl asking for help.

'I think I'm with child,' Petronilla confirmed, stuttering, colouring up. Drawing her black brows together, she looked as if she'd just confessed the worst of sins instead of happy tidings. 'It is a blessing on our marriage.' The frown lines deepened and her confession was spoken so low that Estela had to guess some of the words. 'But I don't know whether I can do it.'

Set-faced, she added, 'You need not worry for the succession. I know my duty and I wrote my will as soon as I knew. It is clearly written in my hand, with witnesses, in April of this year, on the Day of St Isodore, that if I should die in childbirth, my husband is heir to

Aragon. I think this will happen, that I shall die instead of giving him a baby.'

Estela spoke softly, as to a wounded animal stranded on a cliff edge. She unreeled the safety line, word by word, testing the reaction as she went. 'You are not alone, not in your fears nor in your questions...'

She caught the flicker in Petronilla's eyes and continued, 'You sense the changes in your body...'

Another flicker. 'Your mother told you what would happen but you want to know more?'

A direct hit. Petronilla's eyes filled with tears and her fists clenched, white, but her tone was even, without bitterness, as she stated the facts in her oddly accented Occitan.

'My mother left for the peace of a nun's life at Fontrevaux, when I was three, and my father returned to his beloved abbey at the same time, having betrothed me to Ramon. They are saintly people, who did their duty by Aragon and conceived an heir.

They were too pure to commit mortal sin a second time in hope of a boy. They left me affianced to the best husband any woman could hope for and he has taken care of me, waiting the twelve years until my flowers came and he could marry me.

Now it is our turn to make the heir I was born for, the reason my father renounced his vow of chastity and put Aragon before God. This baby will be the king who unites Barcelone and Aragon and I am afraid of my body's weakness and of my ignorance of motherhood. I have sinned too much to be allowed motherhood.'

'I understand how important the baby is.' And guessed at what Petronilla's upbringing had lacked. Saints for parents were all very well in theory. 'How can I help you?'

The girl – for so Estela now thought of her – turned wide brown eyes on her saviour. 'I need a potion to stop me becoming fat so that the angels will bring me a baby boy. I am fasting and praying but still my impurity swells.'

Carefully, Estela asked, 'You know how babies grow?'

Petronilla gave a nervous giggle. 'Of course. Ramon explained it all to me on our wedding night. He sowed seeds in my garden then we prayed together that the angels would give life to a boy seed and bring it to me to show the world that we have done God's will in our marriage bed.

But I am afraid that my sins have offended the angels and they have sent me this sign, this fatness, to show me I must be better or they will take my life instead of giving me the baby. I know this happens to sinful women.'

Even more carefully, Estela ventured, 'And what made you think you were with child.'

'That was easy.' The smile was assured this time. 'My flowers did not come, which means that the angels are growing a seed for me, even if they wait till I am worthy before bringing me the baby.'

'Have you talked to your Lord about this?'

Again the knotted brows and twisting hands. 'I can't. I am a woman now, not a child, and these are women's matters.' Very quietly she added, 'And the Church teaches us how sinful women are. What if the angels won't bring me the baby? Ramon has waited twelve years for this. What if I let him down? I can't bear it!'

You will have to bear it, my sweet child, thought Estela, two years and a baby older than the girl in front of her. *To become a mother, you will indeed have to bear it, one way or another.* How could a girl grow up so ignorant? But Estela knew the answer to that, having lost her own mother so young. Questions that couldn't be asked or had mysterious answers, whose sense was misunderstood.

How was she to untangle the dangerous innocence facing her? She remembered her mother, fighting to save women's lives as they quoted the bible against her interventions. *'Work with their beliefs, not against them.'*

Taking a deep breath, Estela chose her words. 'We women all know these fears but God is merciful, and you can see from the babies all around you that the angels forgive us too. They know what we must risk and suffer to give life; that is our penance and the root of our joy.'

Petronilla paled. 'Risk and suffer?'

'The angels have done their work and have already brought life to Ramon's seed.' She hurried to answer the unspoken question before further confusion side-tracked her explanation. 'But we women have to grow the baby ourselves, in our gardens. The fatness is your baby growing.'

'No!' Petronilla's horror was instinctive. 'Get it out! I want someone else to look after it!'

'No-one else can grow your baby. This is motherhood. This is God's preparation for the love you will feel.' Estela only hoped that this would be true. Growing up with saints as parents was difficult enough but being married to one must complete the feelings of inadequacy. She sent silent thanks to her own mother, for the open-eyed preparation for what human beings really did, in work and play.

'What do I have to do to make the baby come out?'

'Grow. How many flowers have you missed?'

'Three.'

'Then the baby must grow until All Souls' Day to be complete. He will be ready to come out then.' There was no avoiding the inevitable question.

'How will he come out?'

Estela prevaricated. 'First you must nurture yourself for both your own and the baby's sake. No more fasting. There are many ways of helping your body carry its burden.' Estela sifted her recent learning and found suitable advice from Hildegard von Bingen.

'When your body gets heavy and you feel tired, the mushroom of the beech tree should be taken fresh, cooked with good herbs, boiled in water until broken down and strained through a cloth. A broth from this juice with lard added should be taken twice a day after eating and you will find ease. There are many herbs to help in growing a baby and also some to avoid.'

Estela had known as many women keen to lose their baby as to keep it, often when there were already more mouths to feed than was possible. Keeping a baby was more difficult to guarantee and accepting that, however precious the baby might be to the fate of two kingdoms, was only one of the hardships Petronilla faced. There were however ways to improve the odds.

'There are some herbs to avoid, such as goatsbeard – I will give you a list and you should make sure a trusted servant keeps these out of your food or drink.' Estela remembered only too well an attempt on Aliénor's unborn child, while the Queen of France stayed in Narbonne. 'In the seventh month, your healer should mix powder of frankincense, oil, wax and mastic and anoint you front and back.' Trota's methods could be trusted but were not for the poor. 'Malik knows all this,' she tailed off lamely.

Petronilla had not been diverted. 'How will the baby come out?' she repeated.

'Your garden is called the womb by physicians. It will stop its wandering around your body to grow the baby in your belly.' Petronilla winced at the crudeness and had opened her mouth to ask the question a third time when Estela beat her to it. 'And the angels will help you open your garden gate wide for the baby to come out, the same way the seeds entered.'

There was a shocked silence as Petronilla took in what this meant. 'This is what I must do to make an heir for Aragon and Barcelone? And for Provence, in case my nephew should die?'

It was Estela's turn to wince. She'd forgotten that this was the enemy. Time to think about that later. 'Yes, this is what you must do.'

'*You* did it.'

'Yes.'

'And you gave birth to an heir for your husband.'

'I gave birth to an heir.' The wound that would never heal ripped open again. What was Musca's status in the eyes of the world?

Still pale, Petronilla stuck out her jaw and asked, 'How can I make sure it's a boy? Ramon made sure we chose the most propitious time and he prayed beforehand to be sure that he would pass on only virtue to his son but I am just a woman and not worthy. I tried to keep my thoughts pure but,' she whispered, 'there was pleasure at the conception. There must be some way I can atone.'

Estela shook her head, biting her tongue so as not to challenge the church teaching that pleasure was wrong. *Work with their beliefs.* She explained that there were measures Petronilla could take before and during conception but that afterwards all she could do was to balance the female hot and male cold elements with diet and herbs. There was no point worrying Petronilla even more by telling the truth, that even with proper preparation for the seed, some women could only grow girls. Aliénor was likely just such a one, having produced only two girls.

Although many would blame the sinfulness of the marriage itself, in being too close a relation, Estela favoured the more scientific explanation. However, Petronilla had been given more than enough truth for one day and if she bore a boy, that question was answered.

Estela had some uncomfortable rethinking of her own to do. She could no longer join in wholeheartedly with Sancha's diatribe against the usurpers. From loyalty to her host Etiennette and from long friendship with Sancha, she found Petronilla's husband guilty of all charges, including the intimacies of marriage.

CHAPTER SIX

Steel (calybs) is very hot and is the very strongest form of iron. It nearly represents the divinity of God, whence the devil flees and avoids it. If you suspect there is poison in food or drink, secretly place a hot piece of steel in moist food, such as broth or vegetable puree. If there is poison present, the steel will weaken and disable it.

Physica, Metals

'Les Baux – people find it impressive the first time they see it!' Hugues declared loudly, as he halted to allow Dragonetz the splendour of the view.

'Indeed.' Dragonetz grinned. From the broad southern approach, the château still seemed part of the rock, a hazy illusion, but the view did not catch your breath like looking down across the valley from the Col du Sarragan.

They'd blown trumpets and hunting horns loudly enough to wake the creatures rumoured to lurk in the Val d'Enfer and certainly enough to wake everyone in the château, judging by the welcome party Etiennette sent to accompany her son and his men on the last stretch of their return home. Hugues and Dragonetz played to their new audience, much to the amusement of Hugues' men.

The eastern gate was already open for them and a scattering of townsmen had paused in their business to cheer their lord home. Hugues rewarded them with a handful of alms and glared at the man in his band, who muttered, 'Moorish gold, I bet.'

By the time they reached the castle, the gate was raised there too and a line of nobles awaited them, as they dismounted. Men and horses went to their respective lodgings and Hugues threw himself to his knees before a small woman in a grey wimple and widow's black. Dragonetz followed suit, pressing his lips to the hand offered him, a hand mottled with age and more manual work than was customary for the lady of such a house.

'My Lady des Baux,' Dragonetz confirmed, looking up at a face lined with old worries and eyes that could not hide a plea. Younger, Etiennette might have had vivacity but she had never been a beauty and there was a solidity to her now, in both physique and manner, that spoke plain.

'Courtesy will serve in the banquet-hall my Lord Dragonetz but you know why you're here and time is short. Are you with us?'

Dragonetz held her gaze. 'I serve Provence,' he told her. 'And I like your son.'

Her mouth pursed in disappointment but all she said was, 'Then that must do for now.' She raised him and included those around her with a gesture. 'Let me present my court to you. Our special guests, the Comte de Barcelone and his lady, are resting after their journey, which was not without incident –' A suspicious glance at her son was met with an innocence that Dragonetz suspected had been perfected to hide stolen cakes and kisses during Hugues' growing-up years, if his own experience of mother-son relationships was anything to go by.

Dragonetz concentrated on the names of those being introduced to him. D'Uzès, Châteaurenard, de Saint-Rémy…

Etienntte murmured, 'I believe one or two of the jewels who adorn my château are known to you already…'

'Lady Sancha,' murmured Dragonetz, bending low over a large-boned, impeccably manicured hand half-covered in peach silk, a colour that was not flattering to the over-rouged complexion of its wearer. The knight could not have cared less about her appearance or what lay beneath; their friendship was a rare treasure from the Holy Land.

'My dear boy, it is good to see you again. But you shouldn't be here, you know. Of course you know.' Another pair of worried eyes. If Dragonetz had not already known of the tensions in Les Baux, he would have realized now.

He just nodded and squeezed that big hand. 'I have some brocade for you, from Damascus. When you can spare the time to select some.'

'Ooh,' she squealed, all feminine avarice. 'What colours?'

'I thought the emerald would appeal.'

Her eyes lit up. 'I find myself at a loose end this very afternoon,' she told him.

Dragonetz bent over her hand, as if pressing his lips to it and murmured, 'Then we shall make up for lost time, my Lady.'

'Naughty tease,' she twitted him, pulling her hand away, as someone else joined the assembly, in a rustling of gown and joyful yelp of dog. A horribly familiar yelp of dog. Lady Sancha said, 'I was going to warn you…' just as Dragonetz straightened in time to avoid being bowled over by something big, white, furry and yes, definitely familiar. 'Nici,' he said with resignation, as the dog presented an ear to be scratched then shambled off, having done his duty.

'I believe you two know each other,' said Etiennette des Baux as she presented Dragonetz to the latecomer, a tall beauty with tawny skin and green-gold eyes, strands of raven hair slipping out of her demure linen coif. The baby in her arms gurgled on seeing Dragonetz and said 'Icky'.

'My Lord Dragonetz.' She curtseyed one-handed, the other holding the baby…

'My Lady Estela.' He bowed over her hand. She was married. But not to him. What on God's earth she was doing here at all he had no idea until the Lady of Les Baux enlightened him.

'We are honoured that Lady Estela de Matin accepted the invitation to perform for our guests during the stay of the Comte de

Barcelone. As we are honoured that you accepted our invitation too. I believe you have sung together. Perhaps you will do so for us?'

'Perhaps,' said Dragonetz between gritted teeth at the same time as Estela commented brightly, 'Quite a coincidence.'

He looked at her, unable from courtesy either to throttle her or take her in his arms, and knowing from the laughter in her eyes that she could read his thoughts. She should have been at home, safe!

'It seems I wasted a good pigeon,' he told her.

'You always over-rated home-loving birds,' she teased.

'Now I think on the matter, I have something new in mind that would suit your voice, my Lady. Perhaps we *should* sing together.'

No-one else would have caught the spark of desire but he did as she replied, 'Perhaps we should, my Lord. I look forward to something new.'

'Hussy,' he whispered, as he bent over her hand in leave-taking. Her smile warmed him throughout the necessary practicalities of the day before he could slip through the sleeping château to her bedchamber and punish her as they both deserved.

Morning found Dragonetz kneeling at the back of the Chapelle-St-Blaise, a small, plain sanctuary placed between the château wall and the village. Forced to leave Estela sleeping, early enough to avoid being seen in her chamber, Dragonetz had sought the peace of stone walls to prepare his thoughts for the public audience with the Comte de Barcelone later that day.

The details that Sancha and Estela had added to his knowledge of Provençal politics had merely made him more confused about what was right and what he should do. He liked Hugues and was prepared to like the forthright mother but liking should not shape the future of a realm.

Sancha's family had been among the sixty-four who backed Etiennette during the recent war rather than the sixty-three who backed Dolca's heir. Etiennette had been badly treated by her father, who had no right to make Dolca heir to Provence while the younger sister was given only Les Baux and Trinquetaille.

No-one could have predicted that Etiennette's father would be murdered and that Dolca would inherit Provence only to leave it to Barcelone. Dolca hadn't been married to anyone when Etiennette and Raymond had signed away their rightful inheritance. And the sequence of deaths had left Dolca's grandson, a seven-year-old at the time, an orphan and heir to Provence, the titular Comte, even though his uncle-guardian was Regent.

In Sancha's eyes, Etiennette should have been heir by right when her sister died, and Barcelone was usurping her realm, using his nephew as an excuse. No-one doubted that it was the Regent from faraway Barcelone who held all the power. No-one even doubted that the law was on his side – but many in Provence believed that the law was not justice in this case. They wanted their land in the hands of one of their own lords – the Pons family. Unless of course they were among the sixty-three families who would prefer some Comte from Barcelone to anybody from the Pons family.

The question of rights was complex enough but even more troubling was the question as to which of the contenders could best rule Provence. For Sancha, the stakes were high, as her family lands had been in Provence as long as records existed. In her opinion, there was little chance of peace with an overlord who could not be present and had his own fiefdom of Barcelone to maintain plus the prospect of Aragon.

With power came responsibility and at this point Dragonetz had to disagree with Sancha. No-one could accuse the Comte de Barcelone of taking his responsibility lightly. He had taken his nephew in as a son when the lad lost his father. Then, in the same year, Barcelone had defended the boy's rights against armed attack from Les Baux and all those who must seem rebels in his eyes. Dragonetz' previous patron, the astute Viscomtesse de Narbonne, was Barcelone's close ally and spoke highly of him. Their friend Malik rode with Barcelone and would not do so if he thought ill of him.

Even Barcelone's marriage showed his self-discipline. He'd

become betrothed to Petronilla, heir to Aragon, when she was a year old and he twenty-four. They'd married as planned, last year, when she had reached womanhood at fifteen. Dragonetz tried to imagine himself betrothed to someone Musca's age, watching baby grow to girl, and girl grow to wife, all to unite two realms. He could not do it, but he had to respect someone who could. Combining Aragon with Barcelone was a masterstroke, creating a power in the north to balance Castile in the south. Where power was balanced, there was peace.

Could Barcelone balance Provence? Even if Sancha was right and the nephew was merely an excuse for Barcelone to claim the region, he was experienced in battle and in government, so famed for piety and restraint that he was known as 'El Sant', 'the Saint'. Not only was he a force to be reckoned with; he was here, in Les Baux, and, according to Malik, he wanted Dragonetz among those who rode with him.

'Guide me,' prayed Dragonetz, his thoughts whirling fruitlessly. A channel of daylight came through the chapel door as three men in robes entered, passed Dragonetz in a swish of skirts and stopped to pay their respects before the altar. One was surely the Chaplain and the other two Benedictine monks, judging by their black garb. They knelt, crossed themselves, then moved to the choir and prepared their voices for song.

Dragonetz knew well the way they hummed, warmed their throats with scales, tested a high note and a harmony. Idle thoughts stopped completely when the brothers started to sing. Dragonetz felt his heart stop too, then soar, as he heard music as close to the divine experience of his opium dreams as any he'd heard before or since.

From the very first words, the Latin chant spoke to him as if each word were for him alone, and the music of the combined voices carried the words of the mystical hymn deep into his psyche.

'O ignee spiritus laus tibi sit
qui in timpanis et citharis operaris

'Praise be to thee O spirit of flame
who speaks through lyre and tambour...'

Dragonetz shut his eyes to better conjure up the spirit of flame, better hear the lyre and tambour that he would have used in performing such music. Whoever had transcribed this piece for men had surely heard the voices of angels, whether his dreams were inspired by opium or other means.

'Intellectus te in dulcissimo sono
advocat ac edificia tibi
cum rationaliate parat
que in aureis operibus sudat.'

'Intellect calls to you
with sweetest sound
and teams you with Reason
to make works of great worth.'

Dragonetz didn't know whether he aspired to works of great worth but he was open to the advice that he should build on reason in choosing between Les Baux and Barcelone. Maybe the choice would become clear; maybe there would be no need to choose.

'Tu autem semper gladium
habes illud abscidere
quod noxiale pomum
per nigerrimum homicidium profert.

Quando nebula voluntatem
et desideria tegit
in quibus anima volat
et undique circuit.'

'Sword e'er in hand
to cut out
what the apple poisons
through blackest murder.

When mists cloud the will
and its desires,
the soul takes flight
in circles, rudderless'

Blade in hand and swinging wildly! Dragonetz wanted to cut out what was poisonous to the body politic but how could he determine exactly what – or whom – should be removed? He knew only too well how the sword-bearer could turn murderer if a knight forgot his vows and lost his way, which was why he was here, praying for guidance. No ordinary sword but one of Damascene steel, it was forged with the secret skills of that city. Dragonetz had named it Talharcant, 'Bladesong' in his native Occitan, and he vowed here before God that its song would be worthy of the hymn he heard.

An awkward transition from one phrase to the next jarred on Dragonetz' ear and reminded him these were no angels. He imagined Estela singing the verses but it sounded wrong. Not just the richness of her experience, confusing the spiritual qualities. The hymn demanded choral singing. Perhaps several women... but then the sensual associations would intrude and of course, women choristers would never be permitted in any church but a convent. Boys, then.

In his mind, he replaced the deep chant with the ethereal quality of young boys' voices and smiled. One particular boy's voice blended with the others but could not hide its exceptional quality. Muganni, thought Dragonetz, remembering the little Arab boy who'd served him and saved him. By now, Muganni should be with his people in the mountains, free forever. His beautiful voice was lost to the court of Jerusalem and some might consider Dragonetz' training wasted on camels and dervishes but maybe 'God's creatures praised Him' and that was enough. Singing could be for pure pleasure.

'Tu eam citius in igne
comburis cum volueris.'

'Your fire purges all ill
as is your will'

Dragonetz nearly murmured 'Inshallah' from old habit but luckily the blasphemy stopped in his mind. Perhaps he had lived in Arabic too long when captive in Damascus, to return to unthinking Christianity. It had been a shock at first to see the human faces in a church, the Christ-figure hunched in suffering on the cross, after the purity of Muslim tesserae. So close in origin, the two religions, and yet so divided. Another blasphemous thought, unsuited to his setting!

'Nunc dignare nos omnes ad te colligere
et ad recta dirigere. Amen.'

'Gather us to you now
and set us on the right path. Amen.'

'Amen!' said Dragonetz aloud, fervently. Sometimes, asking the right questions was more important than being given answers and he now knew what he needed to find out, about Les Baux and about Barcelone, and about Provence. His intellect would determine *how* he found out. And his sword would serve its proper purpose on the right path.

When the singing ceased and the Chaplain was lighting a candle, alone, Dragonetz approached him. And so was Talharcant, the sword forged by a Saracen smith in Damascus, blessed in the chapel of Les Baux, as was the knight who wielded it.

'Bless this sword so that it may be a defence for churches, widows and orphans, and for all servants of God, against the evil one.'

The statue of St Blaise watched from his niche, adding to the blessing his skills of healing and calming wild beasts, of which there were many prowling the darkness of Dragonetz' soul.

CHAPTER SEVEN

Through the beneficial herbs, the earth brings forth the range of mankind's spiritual powers and distinguishes between them; through the harmful herbs, it manifests harmful and diabolic behaviors.

Physica, Plants

By the time Dragonetz knelt over the hand of Ramon Berenguer IV, Comte de Barcelone, Prince of Aragon and Regent of Provence, he was composed and inscrutable. Barcelone and Petronilla were holding 'informal' court in the Great Hall, ensconced in the carved chairs Dragonetz guessed were usually occupied by Etiennette and Hugues when they heard lawsuits and resolved disputes. On Ramon's right hand, stiff and stone-faced, was a fourteen-year-old boy, the young Comte de Provence, Dolca's grandson and heir. Old enough to know that he was the cause of six years' civil war in Provence but too young to rule.

The Regent, his uncle and guardian Ramon Berenguer, Comte de Barcelone, had waged war in his nephew's name and would have no hesitation in peace-time decisions. The boy had been well-schooled and watched, sharp-eyed, then accepted Dragonetz' obeisance with a dignity that gained the tiniest nod of approval from Uncle Ramon. His aunt, Queen Petronilla, flashed the boy a smile of encouragement.

Petronilla herself looked sickly and was barely older than her nephew but equally accustomed to the role she must bear. Although her white face suggested that it was just as well she were sitting, her back was ramrod straight and her accented courtesies were faultless.

It was, however, the man standing guard beside the boy who made Dragonetz' heart lurch. This was not someone he could fool with fancy word-stepping or cold courtesies. This was someone to whom he owed everything.

'Sire, with permission?' he asked the Regent, laying down his sword, and Ramon nodded.

Then Dragonetz crossed the few paces and the abyss of circumstance to take the turbaned guard in his arms. 'Malik,' he said, feeling his bearhug returned, in the more reserved manner that characterized his friend.

'Dragonetz.' The hint of a smile flickered and vanished. The warmth lingered and no more words were needed. They'd all been said. *Dearest friend of my mind* Dragonetz heard and his stomach clenched. He knew what he owed but he could not repay it nor even take it into account. Not when Provence was at stake. But Malik knew that too, with the same acceptance that would run a sabre through Dragonetz should he raise Talharcant against a Berenguer. The abyss of circumstance. Perhaps it need not come to that.

'My Lord Dragonetz.' The Regent made it clear that his patience was limited. 'Your reputation as a commander does you credit but I find you in my fief of Les Baux, without an army, in the company of those who recently led a rebellion against my true vassals. Should this worry me? Or are you willing to offer that renowned sword in my service?'

So there was to be no thrust and parry but warrior-to-warrior honesty. Dragonetz studied Talharcant at his feet. He already knew his answer but words mattered.

'Sire, you do me honour.' Which meant no. The very silence held its breath. What Dragonetz could offer was equal honesty. 'I swore fealty to Aquitaine and its Duchesse. Though I am freed from duty, that oath takes precedence over all else and always will. I have sworn no oath to any Lord but my Lady Aliénor.' Meaning, not to Hugues and not to you. Meaning, I have not decided yet.

Ramon must have understood Dragonetz' intention and yet he looked puzzled. 'You are sworn to Aquitaine?' he repeated, frowning.

'As of many years.' Dragonetz was steadfast. Ramon was silent, musing. The knight continued. 'I have an estate in Provence and care about its people. If my sword can keep the peace then we do what we were both forged for. This is my purpose here. To keep the peace.'

Ramon might be known as El Sant but he was no peaceful monk. His tone held iron threat. 'Allying yourself with Les Baux will encourage a new rebellion. And rebels lose. However good their hired swords. You may leave.'

Dragonetz flushed at the insult and merely bowed to the Regent. But for Malik, he added, 'Our hostess appreciates songsmiths. Would you be willing to share your art at table one evening?' And to make his message clearer, he sang the lines that were haunting him.

'*Nunc dignare nos omnes ad te colligere*
et ad recta dirigere. Amen '

'Gather us to you now
and set us on the right path.'

'The remarkable Hildegard von Bingen,' Malik acknowledged. Dragonetz had long ago lost his surprise at the Moor's learning. 'She is as well known for her medicine as her music, you know.'

'She?!'

Malik smiled. 'Yes, the composer is a woman. Lady Estela can tell you all about her.'

Of course, Lady Estela *would* know all about a woman remarkable for medicine and music, Dragonetz thought ruefully.

'And yes, we can still sing together,' was Malik's final word as Dragonetz bowed and left. Could such a friendship be as precarious as the truce between Les Baux and Ramon Berenguer? If so, they would still sing together while they could. And Dragonetz had to find the best way to return a precious portrait to Queen Petronilla. No doubt Lady Estela could advise him on that too. As it turned out, she could indeed.

'But we went to so much trouble to steal the cart!' Hugues was digging his heels in, as could be expected.

'And what could show your superiority better, in *your* terrain, than declaring in public that your diligent pursuit on Barcelone's behalf has recovered some of the missing goods. Everyone will know that he was robbed and helpless, while you show both good faith and greater power.'

'There are those who think we were behind the theft…'

'Including Barcelone himself.' Dragonetz let his protégé work out the ramifications for himself.

'If I announce that I've found some of the goods, that will lull his suspicions … or at least make him unable to make any such allegation, whatever he suspects.' Hugues was indeed growing in statecraft. The young man's wide grin proved so as he realized, 'He'll have to thank me.'

'Quite.'

'But he'll want to punish the thieves. It won't work, Dragonetz.'

'Of course he will want to punish the thieves. And you are so efficient, you will have already done so. You will be able to tell him the names of the offenders and the terrible vengeance you wreaked on his behalf. I'm sure your men can provide you with details of suitable criminals who've been dispatched in the last few days, preferably in villages far enough away to deter further inquiry by Barcelone. He is too astute to waste time on what can only be a wild goose-chase.'

'And I can remind the men that the rest of the treasure can safely be distributed once this cursed visit is over. It would be better if our markets were not suddenly flooded with gold coins depicting Barcelone's cursed face and some inscription in Arabic!'

'Safely and fairly,' Dragonetz agreed. 'However loyal your men, the tale you tell of the alleged thieves' deaths will serve as a reminder of your mailed fist. Barcelone is a proven general with a reputation for justice. You must be seen to match him for strength and fairness.'

'There's no justice in him stealing my inheritance!' burst out Hugues, his boyish temper rising.

'Your inheritance is the people of Provence. Ask yourself what is best for them. *Be* what is best for them.' Dragonetz sighed inwardly as he saw the young man dwell on the unfairness of his lot.

Hugues' next words, 'I don't know that my mother will like it,' confirmed Dragonetz' worst fears but he restrained himself from pointing out that Barcelone didn't consult his mother when making decisions.

'Lady Etiennette will respect your thinking,' was all he said. Then he visited his hostess to ensure that she would.

Estela was glowing with satisfaction as she returned from her mission to Petronilla. The young woman's expression when her miniature was returned, all that she had of her saintly parents, would have brought tears to a tougher onlooker. 'Hugues des Baux believes this is yours?' Estela had said, certain that she was embroidering threads in the silken web that would maintain peace in Provence. 'It was among the treasure he recovered and he wanted to ensure it was returned to you, personally.' It went without saying that Hugues could not have presented it in person, given the delicate relationship between Barcelone and Les Baux. Even an innocent like Petronilla would understand that the gesture, although through an intermediary, was conciliatory. Not the word that came to mind in any dealings with the formidable Lady Etiennette. Maybe the next generation would find a way out of the impasse. Even if the gesture had in fact been concocted by Estela and Dragonetz.

It had been a good morning's work and Estela was humming as she tripped along the flags between Petronilla's ante-chamber and the window bay where she'd arranged to meet Malik and Dragonetz to practise some new material for evening entertainment. She felt creative again, had an idea for a lyric and wanted help with the melody. She'd wanted to include some of von Bingen's work in the repertoire, if the two men were willing to sing plainsong with her. They blended well, Dragonetz' bass and Malik's lighter tone, and all three knew each other so well that they could feel the pauses for breath without any signs.

To Estela's chagrin both men had vetoed von Bingen's work as inappropriate for entertainment. Sacred music could only be sung in church. Estela's frustration was no less because she knew they were right. 'But I can't perform in church because I'm a woman! Not unless I join a convent! Perhaps I should go to Alsace and sing with von Bingen herself. She has more freedom than I do.'

'I can't sing her work in public either,' Malik reminded her quietly. As a Muslim he couldn't – or wouldn't – enter a church (Estela wasn't sure which). But sing it in private, they could and did, the words carrying them to that other world they shared, where God and Allah were but two faces of some eternal truth.

'O ignee spiritus laus tibi sit
qui in timpanis et citharis operaris'

'Praise be to thee O spirit of flame
who speaks through lyre and tambour…'

When the music stopped, Estela could feel the tension, the choosing of opposite sides that lay between the three of them, but in singing there was only the old harmony. They all needed that respite. And this morning she felt optimistic about finding that same harmony in the greater world. Provence was beautiful in the slanting summer sun, hazy blue through the arrow slits.

Peasants would be harvesting spelt and the first of this year's honey had already reached table. It was still early enough in the day for the dairy farmers to sell their fresh cheese at the castle gate. Soon they would have to pack up and ride home, hoping to peddle their wares after hours to buyers willing to risk cheese rancid from heat if they could save some coin or bartering power.

Longer-lasting products such as grain or flour could be sold on to the regrators, middle-men who would store goods as long as they could afford and sell when the price was highest, winter or famine. Estela had grown up a castellan's daughter and was accustomed to the way the hinterland contributed to the community within the walls.

Perhaps she would saddle up and explore the valley after practising her music. What was it Bernard of Clairvaux had said? *'Stone and trees will teach you a lesson you never heard from the masters in school.'* Stone and trees had always taught Estela more than masters; being a girl, she had taken schooling where she could, from her healer mother and from shadowing her brother.

Most of all, she'd been taught by Gilles, who taught her how to choose and use a dagger, how to ride and care for a horse, and how to read stone and trees so she could always find her way home. He'd saved her life and paid with his right hand. He was all the protection she needed to ride out with her, to escape the walls for an afternoon. Nici could run alongside. Dragonetz would no doubt be busy with Hugues' guard, with sword drill and tilting but she would have all the protection she'd ever needed. All was as it should be.

Perhaps not quite all, she amended. There were always minor domestic concerns. Estela had caught the wet-nurse rubbing red eyes with her wimple when she'd thought herself unobserved. Prima's care of the two toddlers, her own and Musca, was faultless.

They thrived and slept well, despite the love games of Musca's parents on the other side of the chamber's damask curtain, and the whimpering dog dreams of Nici, guarding the threshold. With a guilty pang, Estela had wondered whether Prima slept less well beside the babies and behind that same curtain but when she asked Prima what was troubling her, noisy bed-neighbours weren't mentioned.

With some reluctance, Prima confessed. It was no secret that Dragonetz' gruff man-at-arms Raoulf had enjoyed the nurse's favours.

Indeed, the two of them had lived like a family, protecting Musca in a hideaway while his parents were in the Holy Land. They had even looked after Nici, although the dog would probably give a different version of events, if he could speak.

It seemed that the change in domestic arrangements had made Prima less available and the ever-fickle Raoulf had happily found his pleasures elsewhere. Not that Prima had expected fidelity from a married man above her station but she hadn't realized how lightly he took her until she saw how lightly he left her. She had even hoped that she might bear him a child and keep his affections where others had failed.

All Estela could offer were sympathy and security. And privately she thanked the fates that Prima was not pregnant. Raoulf's bastards were numerous, his generosity to them impeccable – unlike his begetting of them – but Musca needed his nurse's full attention. Prima was young and would get over it and Estela saw no other clouds on her horizons. The day was too fair to worry over her wet-nurse's amours.

The door to the Solar was ajar as Estela passed and although the voices inside were low, she was so attuned to one of them that the words reached her clearly and stopped her in her tracks.

'My Lady, you do me great honour.' Dragonetz, saying no. But what was he saying no *to*? She knew he was speaking to their hostess even before she heard the other voice. She also knew that it was despicable to listen like this, that Dragonetz would tell her the whole conversation later in the day. She remained rooted to the spot.

'I am not asking for an answer now, Dragonetz, just asking you to consider my proposal. Since my Lord was murdered, I have taken his place as best I can but I know my weaknesses. I am but a woman and, as you have shown me, my sons are not yet the men they need to be against such as Barcelone.

You are young in years but old in experience. You are a man. A man with rare talents. A man who has already been more of a father to my son in a month than he has ever known! I offer you Les Baux. Marry me and be Lord of Les Baux. Chase Barcelone from *your* land and keep its people safe.'

Estela waited for Dragonetz to say it was impossible, that he loved and was loved in return, that he had a child, a family. She had to remember to breathe.

'Hugues would not accept me as Lord of Les Baux.' Twin points of anger reddened Estela's cheeks and it took all her self-control not to march into the chamber and slap 'her' knight.

'You would win him round. And I do not ask that you love me or renounce... other commitments. I could perhaps surprise you...' the tones furred and Estela envisaged grey hair being loosed, the robe unlaced seductively, ageing fingers stroking Dragonetz' jaw and neck. She felt sick. 'We might find solace in each other and I am not too old to bear another heir, another boy. Just think on it, Dragonetz.'

'My Lady, I did not expect...' *Neither did I!* thought Estela. 'I think you underestimate your own strength, without any man's help.'

'But I want a man.' Lady Etiennette could sound every bit as petulant as her son. 'And you are my first choice!' *Good Lord!* thought Estela. *She has a list!*

'Then I must indeed consider the matter seriously.' There was no mistaking Dragonetz' meaning – he was taking leave. Estela picked up her skirts and scuttled out of sight before she could be caught eavesdropping. She too needed to consider matters very seriously. Suddenly, the day clouded over.

CHAPTER EIGHT

Primrose (hymelsloszel) is hot. All its vital energy is from the sharpness of the sun… whence it checks melancholy. When melancholy rises in a person, it makes him sad and agitated in his moods. It makes him pour forth words against God. Airy spirits notice this, and rush to him, and by their persuasion turn him toward insanity. This person should place primrose on his flesh, near his heart, until it warms him up. The airy spirits dread the primrose's sun-given power and will cease their torment.

Physica, Plants

Had she not overheard the conversation, Estela would not have noticed that Dragonetz was a little abstracted in their practice, a little too easy to convince of changes to phrasing or tempo. He hid it well but his thoughts were elsewhere and it didn't take a genius to guess where. She too fumbled a line, missed a note, was less than her best, while she wondered, *'Is he thinking about it? Lord of Les Baux? Is that why he's backing Hugues and his mother? Provence and legitimate heirs? And who would blame him! What do I offer instead, that won't turn to dust?'*

'Will you sing with me in the Great Hall one evening?' she asked. 'Lady Etiennette would like that, I'm sure.' She kept all inflection out of her voice and watched anxiously for his reaction. Maybe there was a slight tightening of the jaw. Maybe.

'I'm sorry, my Lady. It might be misinterpreted.' His gaze was steady, telling her to trust him, but the ink-black of his eyes was fathomless. *Misinterpreted as open support for Les Baux? Wasn't he already showing that? Or misinterpreted as showing his love for Estela and rejecting Etiennette's proposal?* 'We'll talk later.' She flushed at the tone, the one he used with his men.

And they didn't. In the days and nights that followed, they made love and they sang together, and they spoke of Musca and Prima but they didn't talk. The closest Dragonetz came to opening his mind was to repeat, 'There is justice in both claims to Provence but one must cede. I will do what must be done to make a lasting peace.' *Even marry Etiennette?* Of which nothing was said, by either of them.

Estela threw herself into composition, knowing full well that entertainment must perform the same balancing act as all else in this fortress. She'd been invited by Etiennette to entertain the widow's guests, so her audience would take for granted her sympathies to Les Baux. In which case, she would please everyone with some reference to history further south, to the lands of Barcelone, Aragon and Zaragoza.

Playing the gracious hostess would win hearts and remind all of Les Baux's nobility and largesse. In sheer courtesy, Barcelone had already been forced to thank the son; now he would be forced to thank the mother. At the same time, perhaps he could be moved by the words of the song, by love of a land, to understand Les Baux.

Perhaps Estela could play her own part in Dragonetz' private war; the balance that kept peace. It would take a very careful lyric though, something from the past that spoke to the present day, that woke every man's love of his terroir and that crossed barriers in friendship. There was only one way of finding such a lyric: she would have to compose it herself. And only one person could tell her all she needed to know.

Every time Dragonetz excused himself from their musical interludes, Estela interrogated Malik on his past and on his homeland. Her

Arabic was not as fluent as Dragonetz', nor anywhere near as good as Malik's Occitan, but she wanted to improve and it seemed fitting to hear Malik's stories in his own tongue. All of them used Latin with ease, as was civilized.

'Why do you wish to dwell on the past, my Lady?'

'I want to understand,' she told him.

Once he started talking, Estela was lost in a world of dry mountains and magical gardens, scimitars and poetry.

'My grandfather, Abd-al-Malik, the last Huddid King of Zaragoza, fought alongside Aliénor's grandfather at the Battle of Cutanda. You've heard tell of it?'

Estela shook her head.

'So fierce it was that there is a saying in my country 'Peyor est quam illa de Cotanda'; 'This is even worse than Cutanda.' They won a hard victory and sang together in celebration, each of them a noted troubadour in his own language. As a token of brotherhood, the King gave Aquitaine a rock crystal bottle, multi-faceted like their alliance but holding the most precious substance of all – water, the life-giver.

As you know from your reading, crystal is made from air touching cold water when it coagulates into a solid, as if it were the heart of water. It has many healing powers. Perhaps William of Aquitaine thought of this and wished to balance too much heat in Aliénor's nature when he presented it to King Louis of France, for their wedding gift. But it was not enough.'

'No,' agreed Estela, thinking that it would take more than a crystal bottle to dampen Aliénor's combination of ardour and ambition. Medicine could only work so much change on a person's given nature.

'When we were in Narbonne, I made inquiry. In one of his many acts to gain forgiveness from the church, Louis gave the bottle to Archbishop Suger and it now resides, cold and useless, in Saint-Denis Abbey.'

Hearing the song of the crystal bottle, Estela murmured, 'Where once there was love, an empty place. Old alliances and pledges replaced with … with what?' She pictured the bottle on a shelf in the abbey reliquary, dust dimming the sparkling treasure that had crowned a friendship, sealed a marriage. She had never even seen a crystal bottle but if she were ever given something so beautiful, so rare, no-one would take it from her. And if it commemorated her marriage to Dragonetz, she would set Nici to guard it! If only...

'And, though my grandfather lost our kingdom, he became Imad ad-Dawla, the pillar of the state, to Alfonso the Battler, and there is no shame on his name or on the Banu Hud for serving our land as well as we can.' *As I do.* Estela heard the words as if they'd been said aloud and thought of her knight, his love for Provence and the way such warriors could fight harder for peace than some men did to grab lands and riches.

'But if you want a story, my Lady, you should hear of the Christian El Cid of Castile. Falsely accused and banished from his homeland, El Cid was alone and rejected everywhere he sought shelter. Men were too frightened of reprisals from Castile to welcome even such a proven warrior.

Until he was found, ragged and dying of thirst, by the knights of al-Andalus who served King Yusuf ibn-Ahmad al-Mu'taman, my great-great grandfather. Zaragoza and its king welcomed the outcast and, in return, El Sidi, as we call him, served my homeland as a loyal general for many years.

When El Cid needed protection for his daughters against the treachery of his enemies, he turned to his loyal Muslim servant, Aven-galvon, who took in the girls and guarded them as his own for the love he bore El Campeador, the Warrior.'

'Which are you, Malik? Are you El Campeador or the Pillar of the state?'

'A man can be both, my Lady, a master and a servant. But I do not seek to acquire lands that are not mine, nor even win back a crown that my grandfather ceded; not when the ruler is just.'

Ramon the Saint. Estela sighed.

'Castile could not let El Cid and his army continue to grow more powerful so Alfonso offered to reinstate the hero, with Valencia as his reward if he could take it, and so Zaragoza lost its famous general.'

Estela listened spellbound to the many legends of El Cid, noting what might fit her purpose in composing a lay and what might engage her audience for its own sake. She knew the part that would catch Dragonetz by the heartstrings.

'When he came of age, Rodrigo, the young Sidi, was taken by his godfather, the monk Pedro, to the place on the mountain where a herd of Andalusian horses were grazing and he was told to choose a foal to be his warhorse,' Malik had told her. 'Rodrigo made his choice, a white foal and earned a cuff and a curse from his godfather, who called Rodrigo 'Babieca', 'Stupid.' Estela could feel the story finding its right threads, the parallel of her own story with Nici, the dog who'd also been named 'Stupid' in the language of his region.

'And Babieca – for so Rodrigo named his horse – grew up to be the white stallion, El Cid's warhorse, the most feared horse in any battle, with legends of his own. He carried his master's dead body into battle, strapped onto him, and they defended Valencia together one last time.

The besiegers were so terror-struck they fled and so Babieca won the day, just by his presence. He lived to see his fortieth summer's grazing and in the two years after El Cid's death, no man rode him. No man could take El Cid's place.

When his spirit left this world, he was buried by his master's request, beside El Cid, at the monastery of San Pedro de Cardana. There, they were later joined by Rodrigo's courageous lady wife Ximena.'

If only… a family burial: Dragonetz, Estela, Sadeek and Nici, at the end of a song worth singing. A foolish thought. Estela swallowed. Thought instead about Malik's ancestors, kings, philosophers and – so Dragonetz had told her – renowned mathematicians.

When the three of them were together, the two men would some-times lose Estela with their discussion of mathematics. She could understand most of what applied to music but knew nothing of the pure Arab disciplines. Dragonetz would tease his friend, suggesting that he should continue with his ancestor al Mu'tamen's geometry proof, compete with his ancestor for pride of place in Maimonides' update of the 'kitab al-Istikmal', 'the Comprehensive Treatise in Mathematics'. Malik would respond in kind, saying that he fully intended to do so in the time left from serving his Prince and mentoring ill-disciplined Christian musicians.

Listening to their banter, Estela realized how far their friendship had come, that Malik could appreciate such humour at all, never mind respond. He had always been self-contained, reserved, mistaken for mute on many occasions. To let his guard down in such a way was a gift, a treasured moment for all three of them. *Should we let our guard down as we do? Can anyone be trusted completely?* Estela wondered, newly sensitive.

How did Malik feel about the castle's Saracen Tower, built as a look-out when Moorish armies were invading from the south, pushing ever further into Occitania. One battle different and the language of Les Baux and its songs would have been Arabic. If there really was Moorish treasure in the caves, it belonged to Malik.

Wasn't he tempted to search for and claim what was his by right? As heir to the Banu Hud, he had as much right to Zaragoza as did Les Baux to Provence. And yet here he was, commander and physician to the Christian Prince who had conquered his homeland, accepting whatever fate brought his people and himself. Was that the way to live well: acceptance? Or was it better to fight to the death for what – or whom – you loved?

'Estela,' Malik broke into her reverie, which Dragonetz seemed not to have even noticed. 'You have been treating Petronilla. How do you find her?'

With an easy smile Dragonetz told them, 'If you two are going to discuss deer-hide belts and dried crane's blood, my delicate sensibilities are better off shouting at men who hack when they should parry.' He excused himself as if a proposal of marriage happened every day and he had more important matters waiting his attention.

Equally light in tone, Estela chivvied him. 'Dried crane's blood is indeed recommended to aid childbirth, by von Bingen herself, but I won't tell you where it should be put...'

'No...' Dragonetz crossed himself and left quickly.

His absence was a relief, allowing Estela's mind to cease its self-torture and discuss the care of a pregnant woman with a physician who knew so much more of medicine than she did but who might learn from her insights all the same. It would be better for Petronilla if she learned to trust her Moorish doctor, even on women's matters, as Estela would not be there when the Regent's progress ended.

Her mind skated over where exactly she would be if Dragonetz married Etiennette and war erupted. Even if Dragonetz didn't marry Etiennette, what if war recommenced, with Dragonetz leading Les Baux and Malik commanding Barcelone's men? Turning her thoughts resolutely away from the possibility, Estela assumed peace, Barcelone secure and the entourage returning home after the display of force. Indeed, the sooner that happened, the better for the chances of an heir being born without mishap. Travel would be safest between the fourth and seventh month, agreed the two healers.

'Has she told him yet?'

'I fear not,' Estela replied, sighing. 'I have encouraged her to but she finds the evidence of her sin difficult to speak of, even though she knows Ramon longs for an heir. There is only one way to cut through this tangle of ignorance and church teaching.'

Malik nodded. 'You have told me nothing I did not observe myself so you've broken no oath. I have not been asked to treat her for this so I break no oath if I tell my Lord that I am wondering whether the signs suggest… he is wise enough to say the words for her and let her tell him in such a manner.'

'What is he like, Malik? I cannot imagine a man who'd plight his troth to a baby, bring her up like his daughter then marry her for the sake of two kingdoms.'

Malik was silent. 'I have only known one other man be Ramon's equal as a general. He will not lose.'

'Even if Dragonetz leads Les Baux?'

'It would be my duty to take down Dragonetz.' It was just a fact. 'And there is no-one of any stature behind him. I have Ramon behind me and his reputation was not gained from pretty games in mountain passes.' So they knew the truth of the ambush. Of course they did.

And if Dragonetz continued on his present course, war would mean one leader against two.

Not just any two leaders either. Could Dragonetz really make peace or was he just diving headlong into another crazy fight, one that he could only lose. She knew her man well enough to know that he would give his life rather than surrender and she felt a surge of anger at his lack of concern for her and for his son.

'I can do nothing, Malik,' she told their friend frankly.

'I know. He must be himself. Be patient. Allah's will is not clear to any of us in this matter.'

'But as a man, what is Ramon like?' pursued Estela.

'Not as you imagine.' Malik smiled indulgently. 'Petronilla is his meaning in life; he was twenty-four and she was three when he accepted her as a sacred charge, betrothed her to protect her. He was there when she read her first verse, was father, mother, brother and mentor as she grew. They played hoops and ball together, read Latin together, danced courtly steps together. By law, he could have married her when she was twelve but he waited till her first flowers.

He is her entire world and she is the reason behind his every act. He refused to call himself King of Aragon for fear he would forget that the land is hers and their son's. He is the same way as Regent of Provence: he holds it in trust for his nephew and will stand down the moment he feels he can. There is an integrity in him that is rare. He is nicknamed El Sant with reason. He weighs his acts to decide what is right by his God.'

This was not what Estela wanted to hear so she sniffed and thought of Lady Sancha's opinions of the usurpers. And of Petronilla, surrounded by saintliness. Much good had it done her! But then again, she didn't want to hear too much praise of Lady Etiennette's indomitable spirit and fierce pride in her inheritance, not at the moment.

'Provence should have belonged to Les Baux.' She made one loyal attempt to defend Dragonetz' stance.

'*Should have* is not law, my friend. Provence *does* belong to the young Berenguer and so to his uncle Barcelone, as regent. By decree of the Holy Roman Emperor, Conrad, who holds jurisdiction over the province.'

'But it's not fair. These people know nothing of Provence. Conrad's never even been here.' Unwittingly, Estela echoed Hugues.

'You want things to be fair, don't you.'

Estela gazed at him mutely. The need to judge fairly *should have* been obvious.

'Much hurt lies that way. Sometimes you cannot make things be as you wish.'

It was as if he'd read her heart and Estela's eyes brimmed with unshed tears.

Malik quoted the poet al-Mutannabi.

'Al-haylu wa-l-laylu
Wa-l-bayda'u ta'rifu-ni
Wa-s-saifu wa-r-rhumhu
Wa-l-qirtasu wa-l-qalamu.'

'The desert knows me well
The knight and the mounted men
The battle and the sword
The paper and the pen."

Inshallah,' he said softly and left her.

CHAPTER NINE

Nutmeg (nux muscata) has great heat and good moderation in its powers. If a person eats nutmeg, it will open up his heart, make his judgement free from obstruction, and give him a good disposition. Take some nutmeg and an equal weight of cinnamon and a bit of cloves, and pulverise them. Then make small cakes with this and fine whole wheat flour and water. Eat them often.

Physica, Plants

Days turned to weeks, and Estela lost any hope that she would be told about Etiennette's proposal to Dragonetz. The sun still shone. Dragonetz still stepped over Nici and came to her bed each night, leaving before dawn to protect her reputation. As if there were anyone in that court who didn't know they were lovers!

They rarely touched in public but when they did, the contact lingered a second too long, the alchemy too evident. They circulated among Etiennette's guests at opposite sides of the hall and still invisible ties linked every word they spoke. Even the way they avoided catching each other's eye exposed their feelings to the most casual observer. When their eyes did meet, there was no-one else in the hall.

No, Estela could not accuse Dragonetz of loving less. Her fears were more practical. She was no green girl mistaking ballads for reality. A man like Dragonetz could have as many lovers as he chose and he chose her. But he had to take a wife. The one thing she could never be to him. If she really loved him, should she not encourage him to accept the proposal? If he spoke of it, perhaps she could find the strength to encourage him. He didn't speak of it. He threw Musca in the air and tickled him. He stroked the muzzle of the great white dog, who blocked the entire doorway to the chamber but only snored when Dragonetz made his night visits. He sought peace in her arms from whatever troubled him by day and Estela held nothing back but her thoughts.

The sun always shone. Blistering brains with relentless heat. What it must be like for men practising sword-strokes, wearing armour, Estela could only imagine. She sought refuge in the cool stone interior, with the other women at their sewing, or in the Lesser or Great Halls, as required for hearings and meal-times. Amid the usual tenant disputes over land and legitimacy, was a steady flow of land-owners, lords and castellans come to pay homage to their liege. Although they'd been summoned by Les Baux to kneel to Barcelone in public, their private allegiance could be detected in the way they spoke first to Etiennette and Hugues, or held hand to hilt.

That same impartial observer who would know that Dragonetz and Estela were lovers, would know that Etiennette was summoning her supporters, a few at a time, to surround her Barcelone guests with carefully chosen company. Moustier and Avignon were among the old guard who'd resisted Barcelone back in their fathers' time. From the recent wars came the Baux supporters; de Simiane, de Cabannes, de Trinquetaille and de Beaufort, all bending the knee to Barcelone and then ranging themselves beside Etiennette. Her cohort grew daily.

Not all the guests were chosen by Les Baux however. Porcelet was quick to spot the growing partiality in invitations and he sent out a few of his own, on Barcelone's behalf. Etiennette could not veto them so she graciously welcomed d'Orgon and de Rochebrune, de Trans and de Volonne, gritting her teeth. The Comte de Toulouse was busy with a convenient local insurrection but would send lesser castellans in his stead.

Toulouse had his own lands bordering Provence and everyone knew that he had greedy eyes on the whole, so his support for Etiennette would be tactical and temporary. But it was still support. The same could be said of Forcalquier, the third ruler of Greater Provence, who held the north as far as Savoie.

Let Barcelone and Etiennette weaken each other enough, then Toulouse and Fourcalquier would be quick enough to divide the remaining spoils. Support the weaker now and clean up afterwards. Etiennette knew this well but it was still support for her, now.

Ermengarda of Narbonne was also unable to attend in person but sent her oath of loyalty to Barcelone (who was unlikely to doubt her support, given that he had rescued her from an inappropriate marriage to Toulouse when she was four years old). Estela was relieved that Ermengarda was not coming: Dragonetz' love life was complicating her life enough without without having to take into account the sophisticated and beautiful Viscomtesse of Narbonne. Although it would have been theoretically interesting to match Ermengarda against Etiennette, not just as political opponents. At one time, Estela could have said so to Dragonetz and they would have laughed. Not now.

If this were peace, Estela thought, then maybe war was preferable. The sun beat down, the pressure built up and still more local lords filled the castle with their demands for food, beds and stables. Etiennette had to send ever further afield for the wagons of spelt flour, mutton and poultry, lard for cooking and wax for candles that were needed to meet the needs of a fortress bursting at the seams. And still she sent for more people.

This was not so much peace as the drawing up of battle lines and when the storm broke, the lightning would strike without discrimination. Sancha on one side: Malik on the other. Dragonetz slipping down his see-saw towards Les Baux. And as for herself? She had a pregnant woman to look after. Usurper and bearer of the King of Aragon sounded very fancy but Petronilla was just another scared girl about to have her first baby, and Estela would give her all the care she could, regardless of sun or storm. Estela's own personal storm was still merely distant thunder and had not yet crashed through any illusions of security that she retained.

It was easy enough for Dragonetz to avoid being alone with Etiennette in the most natural way possible: by spending time with her eldest son and heir.

In that, as in most of her observations, the Lady des Baux had been astute. Hugues was responding to training and the harder he drove himself, the more his men loved him. From a ramshackle band of vassals, the men of Les Baux had become an army. Each day as the new guests brought their followers to the fortress, Hugues slipped away from the court protestations of loyalty and forged rather different ones with swords and sweat.

Dragonetz demonstrated Sadeek's paces in the hastily constructed manège, pole fences forming a corral over scorched summer earth. Only those knights who'd been on crusade to the Holy Land had ever seen such tricky horsemanship, and never from a Christian knight. Trained by Damascan guards, Sadeek and Dragonetz formed a new being, a centaur, side-stepping, reversing, capable of turning on a penny.

At first, men leaned on the fence and laughed at the dancing horse but then Dragonetz donned armour and still Sadeek twisted and turned. The man instructed to run at him waving an axe, fell flat on his face in the space where the horse had stood, while it was Dragonetz' turn to laugh. And, this time, men laughed with him.

Without hesitation, Hugues joined Dragonetz. Les Baux's sturdy mare looked stolid beside the black destrier but was soon proving her master no dullard in horsemanship. Soon, Dragonetz had volunteers being schooled in the manège and a waiting list eagerly watching. It was not an activity for mid-day sun but neither was war, and endurance might prove to be the supreme decider, whatever the men's skills. So they worked and sweated.

As the days went by, Dragonetz delegated more of the training to Hugues and watched the young man's confidence grow alongside his men's respect. Leaning on the fence-posts, one eye on the movements in the ring, Dragonetz swopped stories with the other onlookers. He made them laugh at the punchlines and learn from the apparently incidental details. As did he.

A red-faced man with broken nose and hands like hams argued with his friend. 'Nay, that would be Groms, the best armourer. Wilmen at Aurenja will charge you lands, wife, and horse with them, but for all that his chain has weak links. I'd not trust my life to his mail.'

'Where did you get your sword, my Lord?'

Dragonetz unsheathed Talharcant, passed it round so men could admire the balance, the blade and of course the Damascan filigree, like watered silk along the steel. 'I brought the swordsmith with me from the Holy Land. He has a smithy in Marselha if any man has the coin for his skills. Say Dragonetz sent you and you'll get a fair price.'

Envy warred with the reality of their budgets as the men reluctantly returned Talharcant to its master.

'Don't be like the Castellan of le Caylar ,' Dragonetz warned them with mock-severity.

'I've not heard that one.'

'What did he do?' Scenting a good tale, the men round Dragonetz prodded him to continue.

'Beitz, his name was.' Dragonetz shook his head at the tragic fate of poor Beitz. 'A knight fond of his armour, very fond of his armour. He wanted to make a good show in all he did. Some men can't resist a neat ankle on a woman ... well, Beitz couldn't resist the shine of a new mail shirt, or a hawk reputed to be the keenest, or a horse with good breeding.

Every smith and armourer in the Causses, every knight wanting to reap some coin knew his weakness and, if he were visiting, the prettiest, most expensive goods were on display.'

'Ay, that's the way Wilmen at Aurenja plays it. And they're not always the best goods, neither. Just polished up a bit and set in the light.'

Dragonetz nodded. 'So, with his pretty armour and weapons, Beitz was bound to win in any contest, wasn't he. Or so he reasoned. To pay for all these purchases, he'd bet one of them against another.

He bet his hawk would drop the rabbit before another man's and he lost his prized hound. He bet that he'd win against all-comers in duel and he lost his helm.

Then of course he'd seek better accoutrements, convinced that he could win it all back if he bought better armour. He grew deeper and deeper in debt, gambling all he had and sometimes winning.

This only made him bet more and lose all. In his cups, and he was often in his cups, he'd place a bet on which duck would rise first from a lake or that a certain maid would smile at him.'

'This will go ill with Beitz,' the men predicted, with knowing smiles.

'And so it would have ...' Dragonetz teased them. 'But as it turned out, his debts grew smaller. His favourite sellers told him he was such a good customer that they would wipe out his debts for the sake of future custom.'

The men laughed sceptically. 'I thought you were telling a story of this world not the next!'

'Would that such a miracle came my way!'

'Ay, Wilmen would break out in boils at the very thought!'

'Nevertheless,' Dragonetz insisted. 'So it was. From then on, when he saw goods he wanted, he was pleasantly surprised at how little they cost. He gambled less now he no longer had heavy debts and he found the same excitement in betting trinkets that he used to have in larger stakes. You are wondering how this came to pass?'

'Nay. We *know* it couldn't happen,' was the blunt reply.

'I should tell you that there had been a ten-fold increase in the flocks grazing the Causses during this time.'

'They were Beitz' flocks?' hazarded one man.

'No, or he would have bet them too.' The men were stumped for answers and waited for the solution to the riddle.

'Beitz had one treasure that he never wagered. His Lady was neither fair nor young but she was shrewd and loved her Lord, for all his faults. Unbeknownst to him she had acquired flocks of sheep and with good husbandry, they had multiplied.

She paid his debts from her flocks and allowed her Lord to enjoy his habits without either of them suffering from the consequences.'

There was the silence then sigh of satisfaction that follows a good ending to a story.

'Would that I had such a wife.'

'I'd rather have a sword like my Lord's.'

'Or both. A good wife *and* a sword like my Lord's.'

Dragonetz let them indulge in good-natured banter and the word 'wife' merely skimmed the surface of his thoughts, reminding him of the widow's proposal. He had promised his sword to protect widows and orphans but his own person was not available.

He'd evaded offers of marriage before and Les Baux held less attraction than Tripoli or Antioch, either of which could have been his if he'd accepted a widow's hand. Etiennette's marriage plans for him added a complication to the balance in Provence but nothing important. The place of a wife in his life was taken and he smiled at how good it felt, to trust and be trusted. Then his attention returned to what was most important for Provence; the training of these men.

Hugues was looking to him for the next instruction. 'Now with spears,' Dragonetz called to the two men taking their turn in the manège. Their squires ran out to them and equipped each with a spear. 'Show me the first position.' The men continued wheeling around the ring in the same direction but giving each other enough space to avoid harm. 'Jax – arm out further. That's it. Feel the point of balance. Remember you're going to strike under the arm.'

Dragonetz checked the grip of each knight, right arm extended, carrying the spear. 'Second position,' he shouted and the knights switched to over-arm.

'Third!' The arms went back, ready to use the spears as projectiles.

'Good. Take the spears to the far end and practice one at a time with the target. From a stand then moving left, then moving right. Increase the difficulty as you get better. Next two – in the manège.'

Dragonetz nodded to Hugues, knowing that the younger man was eager to take over again, now he knew the drill. Dragonetz headed off to the weaponry. He had an idea for improving the design of their lances.

CHAPTER TEN

Agate (achates) is born from certain sand of water which extends from the east to the south… every night before a person goes to bed, he should carry a clearly visible agate through the length and then the width of the house, in the pattern of a cross. Thieves are then less able to exercise their wills and so profit less in thievery.

Physica, Stones

W hat Dragonetz had not taken into account was that, unlike the widows of Tripoli and Antioch, the Lady des Baux was frequently within touching distance and determined to have her way. However irritated he might be at leaving the training-grounds, Dragonetz had no choice but to wait on Etiennette when summoned.

He couldn't help but notice the overwhelming scent of violets, laced with sweat, which emanated from the matriarch. She wore her full array of jewels, in her snood as well as sewn into her bodice, her stately figure stiff in the crusted fabric, neither her physique nor her attire suited to the sweltering heat. Her lips rouged, her eyes bright with belladonna, Etiennette had made every effort to remind Dragonetz of the woman she was and the girl she had been.

She was too shrewd to remind him of her proposal in words but it lay in the air, cloying as her perfume, any time they were alone together.

'Have you seen these?' she asked him, passing a gold coin to him, with a cross stamped on it. 'The Arabic is nonsense! Meant to impress like the long title – and meaning nothing. Like a monkey imitating its owners and understanding nothing.'

Dragonetz waited, wondering where this tirade against the coin of Barcelone was leading.

'You're an Aquitaine man.' Nodding seemed safe. 'And you have your own coin there.'

A nod. 'With the face of Charles the Bald,' Dragonetz risked adding.

'And the Tours currency is strong, with the monasteries controlling it.'

Now Dragonetz was really interested. 'You are better informed than I, my Lady.'

'My face is better than Charles the Bald's,' Etiennette stated.

'I –' began Dragonetz but she cut off the expected compliment before he got any further .

'And so is my son's. I want Les Baux coins. We must move with the times and, everywhere you look, trade is conducted with coins these days, even at market. I wish we could go back to honourable barter – you can't forge sacks of flour! – but the river does not flow upstream. I've even had to accept these confounded new bankers' notes, with promises to pay, guaranteed by the Knights Templar. Thank the Lord, we are still untainted by moneylending, apart from those heathen Jews, of course.' Dragonetz saw no need to explain how helpful he'd found a loan from a Jew. 'We have authority for a mint in Arle and I want Provence to have its own currency, with its own sovereign pictured. And I want you to make it happen.'

'I have no experience with metals and mints. And who will train the men?' Dragonetz demurred. *So, this is war against Barcelone with money as a weapon and the winner's vanity tickled.* If he'd read Barcelone correctly, neither would worry the Comte. In which case, there was no reason why Etiennette shouldn't win her money war. Maybe it would prevent casualties in a real one. However, it was unlikely that the council of Arle would accept a mint in their city without demur.

'You don't have to be there all the time, just set it up,' Etiennette told him airily. 'And there is a man can tell you all you need to know about making money.'

'The authority to set up a mint comes from…?'

'The Holy Roman Emperor, Conrad,' confirmed Etiennette. 'When he confirmed our rights in Arle and 'our own territories', he also documented permission for us to set up a mint.'

Dragonetz had served alongside Conrad during the crusade and had little respect for him or his ill-disciplined Germanic troops. His attitude to his vassals Les Baux and Barcelone during their war had been to make ambiguous statements supporting both sides and to let them get on with it. However, he hadn't declared against Les Baux and it seemed that he had given documented permission for a mint at Arle.

Anything that distracted Etiennette from her dual aims of war and seduction was worth pursuing. And he couldn't deny that he was curious. He was always fascinated by the manufacturing process and even though his paper mill had come to naught, what he'd learned in engineering and chemicals could be applied to new projects.

'Who is the man I should speak to?'

'The gaoler will tell you,' Etiennette shrugged her satin shoulders, dismissing the very idea of remembering the name of such a man. 'He's in the dungeon accused of forging coins. This is his work.' She gave Dragonetz the Barcelone penny. 'Very good, I'm told. If you judge him as good as they say, free him and make him Mintmaster. But you'd better hurry; he's a commoner so there was no mitigation. He's been branded and pilloried. He's due to be boiled alive today, I think. They tell me that's the process used for counterfeiting billon so that was the judgement. But if you think he could be useful, you have my leave…' She waved an airy hand, dismissing both Dragonetz and the man's fate.

The knight bowed and left for the dungeons without pausing once, not even to appreciate the view, which was surely as beautiful as any man condemned to death could wish. From the heights on which the fortress was built, the view stretched across the marshes and limestone rocks to the sea. Whether the blue horizon was sea or sky could not be determined for the heat haze but a fanciful man might imagine the white sails bobbing and changing into clouds as they sailed to heaven.

Dragonetz was not in a fanciful mood. He was mindful that dungeons over an abyss put the fear of God into a prisoner quicker than thumbscrews. He knew full well that the quickest route off Les Baux for a criminal was over the edge. But the moneymaker had not been offered a quick route. Dragonetz quickened his pace and reached the cages. If the bars had not indicated their use, the smell would have done so; fear and urine, blood and bones.

As was gaolers' wont, this one carried his bodyweight in keys and a face that no man would wish to be his last sight on earth. Broken teeth and nose testified to past altercations, probably with inmates or their kin, or both. He lumbered to his feet from the stool he'd leaned against a wall.

'My Lord?'

'Dragonetz.' One look at Talharcant, even sheathed, was enough to establish credentials in the gaoler's eyes but a penny added goodwill to the transaction. The gaoler bit the coin and nodded, happy that it was true. 'Show me to the moneymaker. I wish to speak with him. Lady Etiennette thinks he might be useful.'

Horrified, the gaoler said, 'My Lord, you can't go in there! Your boots!' He looked down at the polished brown leather, a little dusty from the dry earthen paths but otherwise unscuffed. 'I'll bring him to you.'

If the man had only seen the state of 'my Lord' and his boots when camped on Damascan soil or crossing the desert by camel! Dragonetz reminisced idly while waiting. He did not lean against the wall, which was oozing moisture and green with lichen. *Did you get used to this?* he wondered, the smell already diminishing from his immersion in it. And then the gaoler appeared, leading by chain something which might be human underneath the filth, and Dragonetz' stomach revolted anew.

'He was pelted right well, my Lord,' asserted the gaoler, torn between pride and apology. 'A good crowd came to the stocks and they'll bring their friends back for the boiling today. It's not the usual, a boiling.'

Dragonetz studied the unfortunate topic of conversation but there was no reaction at all. The forger had gone beyond thought and feeling as men did when tortured. Nature's kindness, professional torturers called it, and they would allow a pause to maintain life, to let feeling return – as it always did – so they could recommence their work. Without pain, their work was wasted.

In this case, neither feeling nor pain were necessary, only speech and, in Dragonetz' case, some fresh air. He motioned the gaoler to drop the iron ball and the prisoner to follow him, dragging the chain. He was barely up to the height of Dragonetz' shoulder and further bowed by his treatment, so each step pained him. He breathed in ragged fits, hobbling as best he could. As soon as they were outside, away from others' hearing and not close enough to the cliff edge to risk a premature end to the conversation, Dragonetz posed his questions.

Although the forger had made pennies of billon, silver alloy, it seemed he did know how to make true silver coin and even gold. His strange accent was explained when he told his story. He had once worked for the Royal Mint in the barbarous north, in England, which he claimed made 'the best money in Christendom.' English sterling was weighed and true, carefully controlled.

'The King's head means you know the money is good,' he declared proudly.

The irony was not lost on Dragonetz. 'The money you make is clearly not good so how did you come to this pass?'

'The wars between the Queen and her brother,' was the terse reply.

'Matilda?'

'And Stephen, aye.' Dragonetz noted that Stephen was not dignified with his crown, whereas 'the Lady of England' was given one.

'While they were warring, every Baron in England wanted his own head on a coin and I had a family.' There was silence. There were many forms of torture. 'I had no choice but make coins for this lord and that lord, as the battles turned for and against each one.

Such a collection of noble heads is rarely displayed from pikestaffs and battlements but I take no pleasure in it.' In the circumstances, the man's gallows humour had a certain style, above his station. 'Stephen won. I had nothing left to lose but my life and that was wanted, so I escaped. Travelled south where no-one cares about English wars. Fell into another one instead.'

He'd searched for employment but soon realized there were no official mints in the region and before he could head south or west, he'd been approached and offered work, producing Barcelone billon. 'And here I am,' he finished with a tremulous attempt at what was probably once a cocky smile. His eyes still carried the knowledge of his sentence.

'Who sourced and funded your material?'

'I don't know names. Intermediaries hired me, set up the foundry, brought the silver needed. All I know is that they were Genoese.' Yes, it would be the Genoese, who could only profit from fake Barcelone money. If it went undetected, they could spend it. If caught, the blame could be placed on Les Baux, as part of their war. 'They came stealthily to Arle by ship, took money from me and left enough that I could live,' continued the forger.

'The foundry was at Arle'

'Aye.' A little illegal counterfeiting to discredit Barcelone coin would be a neat move. So neat in fact that it could never have been dreamed up by the guileless Pons but Barcelone would not have known that. It could however have easily been dreamed up by another wealthy family, with connections to Genoese trade. Dragonetz had learned enough when in Arle to smell a Provençal rat behind this forgery. Porcelet would benefit even more than his Genoese allies if – or rather when – the forgery came to light.

'How were you caught?'

'I can tell you where, my Lord, but how, I'll never know. That coin is as good as the real thing, I swear on the life of Mary mother and all the saints. The Genoese told me to use my coin around the province and I heard there was Barcelone coin in plenty round Les Baux so I thought it would blend in well here and I could spend more than usual.

'I was buying sausage in the market when Lord Hugues' man cried 'That's the man! Forger!' and the guard brought me before Lady Etiennette. Smoked, with garlic,' he added. 'The sausage,' he clarified, wistfully.

'So the foundry is still untouched?'

'As far as I know.' But not for long. If Dragonetz was right, the moment the Porcelets knew that the forger was caught, they'd be trumpeting that Les Baux were behind the counterfeit. Not only would Barcelone be forced into punitive action but the lords of Provence would react against Les Baux. Forgery was a despicable weapon, unworthy of any liege and would cost Les Baux supporters. Even those loyal would feel shame by association. And the only man who could prove the accusation false would be dead.

'A forger may prove what's true,' Dragonetz murmured.

Wisely the other man held his tongue, no doubt hoping beyond reason that he might keep that same organ and other parts.

'Do you have a name, Master Forger? In true coin, now,' Dragonetz warned.

'Men called me John Halfpenny.' Eyes the colour of mud fixed on Dragonetz like a starved cur's when he sees the meat on a market stall.

The knight nodded. He felt he had the measure of the man; billon by force of circumstance but could be recast yet as sterling.

'Well then John Halfpenny, good luck has come your way.'

'That was my exact thought when I woke at dawn, my Lord,' was the dry answer. Then Master Halfpenny saved his breath to drag himself back to the gaol.

Another penny sealed the gaoler's speedy co-operation but

nothing could compensate for his disappointment – nor, he warned, that of the crowd – for the loss of their afternoon's entertainment. 'I'll have to find a whore to strip for the stocks', he muttered, 'and they won't be happy.'

Unchained but still shuffling, the forger followed Dragonetz, who paid no attention to men's stares but headed directly to the training-ground with his unlikely companion.

He knew before he reached the men that something had happened. He knew from what was missing; no banter, no movement among the onlookers beside the manège, who were all focused intently on whatever was happening in the ring. The tension was palpable as Dragonetz approached and a space cleared automatically for him to see what everyone was watching.

CHAPTER ELEVEN

...where the fiery power that flows in water penetrated the earth, the fire of the water transformed the earth into gold. Where the purity of the flooding water penetrated the earth, that purity transformed itself and the earth which it suffused into silver.

Physica, Metals

As always, there were two men in the ring, practising steps and weapon positions. The difference was that one of the men was Ramon Berenguer IV, Comte de Barcelone, Prince of Aragon, Regent of Provence and the very person these men were being trained to fight against, even if no-one was stupid enough to say so.

Dragonetz breathed again once he realised that the other man was not Hugues des Baux. A direct contest of any kind between Barcelone and the heir to Les Baux could only have led to bloodshed, whoever won. Watching the elegant steps of Barcelone's al-Andalus mare, and the ease with which the seasoned warrior switched hands with his spear, there was no doubt in Dragonetz' mind as to Hugues' chances against Ramon. He weighed up his own chances, and was within one curt order of taking Sadeek into the manège and putting them both to the test, when he realised what Ramon was doing.

Barcelone was not demonstrating his superiority. In fact, a trained observer could tell that he held back some of the fancier moves of which he and his horse were clearly capable, in favour of repeating the ones his partner in the ring could copy. He was training the man! And, by observation, he was training all those who watched.

A flick of his gilded helm in Dragonetz' direction indicated that Ramon knew exactly who was in the audience. Of course he did. Yet he continued, patiently, drilling and demonstrating, praising and construct-ing. The other man was nobody; or rather someone chosen because he wasn't in the political game but a member of this army. Ramon was here to win hearts like the brilliant general he was reputed to be.

The other man, representing all his fellows, was now someone very important and when Ramon called, 'Another man?' those gath-ered around looked at Dragonetz, waiting to know what he would do, what they should do. Hugues was nowhere to be seen. The golden helmet faced Dragonetz, also waiting, delegating the choice, neither challenging nor backing down.

Dragonetz acknowledged the Prince with a bowed head, made his decision. 'We are honoured, Sire,' he called, loud and clear. He yelled at one of the men glued to the railing. 'Bavex. You've been wheedling to put that over-fed barrel-on-legs through her paces. Get in there and learn!'

It was a popular choice and the men relaxed into bets on whether Bavex would drop his spear trying the fancy new hand-switch or whether the horse would balk at a scarf being thrown in front of her. Three of the men had been appointed as 'irritants' to simulate the unexpected events that might spook a horse. With a brief nod in Dragonetz' direction, Ramon acknowledged his new partner courte-ously and set to work.

As the atmosphere lost its edge and men returned to comments on the quality of al-Andalus horseflesh (perfection) and armour (girlish), Dragonetz asked quietly, 'My Lord Hugues is not training this morning?'

'Summoned by his mother. Turn her! Shield her eyes at the side!' yelled his neighbour as Bavex's mount stamped nervously by a silken banner weaving snake-like in the dust. 'Needs a hood on that mare,' he told Dragonetz. 'Something at the side will always spook them – any boy knows that but Bavex always thinks that pudding of a beast is too placid to react.'

'Confuses her with hisself,' agreed another.

At least there had been no confrontation between Hugues and Ramon but Dragonetz felt a stab of irritation. Damn Etiennette! Did she realise how it looked to an army when their leader was called to heel by his mother? He remembered another boy whose mother had withheld the power that was his birthright 'until he is capable of wielding it'.

And now that little boy had his mother trapped in the city of which she called herself Queen. Little boys grew up and widowed mothers who didn't let them, paid dearly! Unlike the Queen of Jerusalem, Etiennette still had her son's respect but she was abusing it daily. Dragonetz half-wished Hugues would stand up to her as Baudouin had to Mélisende. That would be better than hearing a man whisper, 'Barcelone doesn't wait on his mother's permission...'

Dragonetz chose two of the guard. 'Take this man. Get him washed and dressed in clean clothes, then bring him back here.' Their disappointment at missing the display in the manège showed in their eyes. 'When you come back, when the Prince has had enough, we'll train together, the three of us. Make sure you're saddled up and ready.'

Their smiles were all he needed to know. They were still his men. But there was so much work to do to make them Hugues' men and only Hugues could do it. Frowning, he fetched armour and weapons, saw Sadeek prepared for the ring and then, like everyone else, he enjoyed the show.

Finally, the Comte de Barcelone declared, 'Enough,' and dismounted. His boots scuffed and dusty enough to enter a gaol, he strode towards Dragonetz in the bow-legged, heavy walk of an armoured man. He removed his helm and his whole face still glowing with exhileration, he spoke, soldier to soldier.

'Well done, my Lord Dragonetz! I had no idea the men of Les Baux were so skilled!'

'My Lord Hugues has trained them well,' Dragonetz replied, loudly.

Ramon let it pass, with another nod of respect, one leader to another. 'I would they were better equipped as to horses. What say you to some southern stock joining you?' The men's spontaneous cheer spoke for them and Dragonetz could only try to benefit from their pleasure not disappoint them. 'I'm sure my Lord Hugues will be delighted.'

'I'm sure he will.' Ramon's usually severe expression was beatific, his eyes dancing with excitement. El Sant was in his element and the coup de grâce was his modesty. 'If I can help others improve, then I do God's work. As Regent of Provence, I take The Lord of Les Baux and his men under my care, as much as those of Barcelone and Aragon. Of course I knew of your training. I find it's even better than I imagined, my Lord Dragonetz. I am only sorry...'

His eyes lost their sparkle and Dragonetz read into them a renewed request for them to ride together. He saw the moment he needed for his own request. 'Sire, I seek a boon.' Scrubbed and dazed, the forger was on hand, flanked by Dragonetz' two guards.

Serious, deep brown eyes met his. 'Speak.'

Dragonetz gestured and the forger was brought in front of the Prince. 'My Lord, this is one John Halfpenny, a master minter who was wrongly convicted of forging coins of your realm.'

'You intrigue me. Pray continue.'

John Halfpenny seemed equally intrigued but had enough sense to look down at his boots and keep his mouth shut. Dragonetz presented the forged billon penny to Ramon, hoping that the forger was as good as he said he was. 'You can see, my Lord, that this is true coin, and envious mouths secured a false conviction.'

'It does look like good money,' Ramon agreed reluctantly. 'I'd heard there was a sudden influx of Barcelone coin into this region at present.'

Dragonetz looked suitably puzzled. 'I had not heard, my Lord? Be that as it may, this good servant of Provence and Barcelone is highly skilled and could be put to good use.'

'Indeed? I have heard of your penchant for lost causes, my Lord, projects and people. Is this another such?'

The hit went home but Dragonetz had too much self-control to show how aware he was of his failures.

'There is a royal permit for a mint at Arle and Lady Etiennette begs your indulgence in allowing your Mintmaster to set up his forge there, under her surveillance, so that your province might have its own currency.'

'My Mintmaster?' Barcelone queried.

'Evidently,' Dragonetz confirmed, indicating the Barcelone coin produced by the man.

'So I sanction the... Mintmaster... to commence coin making in Arle, for Lady Etiennette.'

'If it please you, Sire. Provence would be appreciative of such an honour, especially it being your own Mintmaster and a coin specially created for this noble region.' The last was said on a note increasing in volume, guaranteed to draw the cheers of the men standing around. Dragonetz could have said, 'mmm, mmm, PROVENCE!' and the men would have cheered, as he and Ramon both knew well.

Ramon's lips twitched but he played the scene well and announced for all to hear, 'Be it known throughout the province that my man John Halfpenny shall be Mintmaster in Arle, tasked with the setting up of a new mint for the money of Provence, under surveillance of the lords of Les Baux.'

'Thank you, Sire.' Dragonetz' words were barely audible above the weeping of John Halfpenny, whose bravura cracked. He knelt to kiss the hem of Barcelone's surcoat. The knight laid his hand lightly on the forger's head as he added, 'If you would make a point of telling Lord Porcelet, personally, that Master Halfpenny is under your protection and the mint authorised, it would be much appreciated, Sire. I think old rivalries have clouded some judgements in this matter and in the interest of the truce with Les Baux...'

'Ah.' Ramon mulled over the implications. 'My Lord Dragonetz, I think you have magicked some faux monnaie into my purse but with such skill I can only admire the magick and spend the coin. Rise, man, you've watered me enough.'

So addressed, the little forger rose, new minted. 'Your Highness,' he whispered, 'the silver I make will be the mark of true coin in the whole of Europe, weighed and stamped to but one standard. I swear by all that's holy.'

'Possibly,' Ramon replied. 'But I suspect it will have a double face, and neither of them mine.'

CHAPTER TWELVE

The best grain is spelt (spelta). It is hot, rich and powerful. It is milder than other grains. Eating it rectifies the flesh and provides proper blood. It also creates a happy mind and puts joy in the human disposition. In whatever way it is eaten, whether in bread or in other foods, it is good and easy to digest.

Physica, Plants

The horse's movement gave the illusion of a breeze and Estela breathed in the scents and sights of Provence in summer. Heat had its own smell and shimmer, skies hazy or blown sharp by the mistral, that wind which etched the white-stone mountain crests to whetted blades and which drove men mad or made them poets, so said the legends.

Today was still and hazy, perfect for an escapade. Nici didn't need asking twice to come out for a run, his plumed tail waving enthusiasm as he tracked and backtracked alongside the two horses. Gilles had been more reluctant but well aware that his disapproval was water off a duck's back. Estela knew perfectly well that her man wouldn't let her ride anywhere without him and he knew she wouldn't change her mind. She really needed to escape from Les Baux. Her finger was callused and sore from plucking chords for a melody that she could hear but not capture; her eyes ached from penning the words to her ballad.

She could have visited Petronilla again, and listened to the girl's unworthiness until boredom lulled her to sleep. She could have taken needle to cambric in whatever monogram was the choice of the day in the solar with the ladies but, in addition to her hatred of chain stitch, her eyes were tired of close work, and conversation with Sancha drew more blood than the needle. Estela could not listen to the demonization of Ramon and Petronilla any more than Sancha would hear of their rights.

If Sancha had been interested in healing or music, they might have found safe ground, as did Malik and Dragonetz, but Sancha was ready to faint at the mere word 'swelling', never mind naming of parts. If ever Estela wished to torture her friend, she only had to read aloud parts of Trota's 'Treatments for women.'

Sancha preferred romances, tales of unattainable ladies and their gallants. From personal experience, Estela found the whole business of sneaking around bedchambers to protect a lady's reputation rather tedious. Even the perpetrator of said sneaking seemed of less interest to Sancha than in the past.

When Estela mentioned Dragonetz, desperately seeking a topic on which she and her friend could agree, Sancha was interested in a friendly way but without the more tender feelings she'd shown in the past. Something had changed in Sancha and the only passion aroused by mention of Dragonetz was over his support of Les Baux, which was exactly what Estela did not want to talk about.

As for music: Sancha had the voice of a crow with the ague and as much appreciation of the finer points as she had dress sense. Estela caught herself short, ashamed. She knew full well why Sancha shaved her forehead too high, cluttered her garish robes with clashing lace furbelows and ribbons, wore shoes so pointed they were lethal weapons.

Estela also knew why she was indulging in this spiteful line of thought. She felt guilty. And she'd really had enough of being torn apart by Provence's civil war. *If it was like this during a truce, what would happen if the killing started again? Friend against friend; brother against sister; vassal against liege.* She dug her heels in savagely and startled her placid mare into a few quickened steps. *And for what? Both sides are in the right and neither of them can see it!*

'My Lady?' her man Gilles queried anxiously, pulling his mount into step by her side. The pathway south curved downwards, opening up once they'd left the citadel and the rocky passes.

She couldn't hide much from someone who'd known her since childhood so she didn't try. 'This truce is wearing,' she acknowledged. 'Every day, new lords come to swear fealty to Barcelone and some do so with their hearts; others with their fingers crossed behind their backs. God might forgive them but Ramon won't.'

'Dragonetz is no oath-breaker, my Lady.'

'At the moment, he's no oath-*maker*! He trains Hugues' men, he kneels to Lady Etiennette in her ante-chamber,' *and the less said about that the better!* Gilles showed no awareness of Estela's more personal anguish at the latter fact and she continued quickly, 'and yet his respect for Barcelone grows each day. I can feel how torn he is and I am worried he will break in two. All he will say is that he has chosen already and his choice is Provence. Whatever will keep the peace. But it doesn't feel like peace!'

'No, my Lady,' agreed Gilles. 'It feels heavy and the storm must break some time.'

'Well, I'd rather it broke when my family was five hundred miles away!'

Gilles pointed out the obvious but it was good for Estela to hear it said. 'That is not Dragonetz' way. If there's a storm, he'll be the lightning. And you wouldn't want him any other way.'

'I know,' she conceded, 'and I will listen and love, and say nothing to shake him from whatever he decides. But I need a moment out of that atmosphere. Come, let's see what it is that all these lords are squabbling over. Let's see Provence!'

They rode in companionable silence. Nici disappeared after scent trails and reappeared ahead of them, checking on where they were before following his own distractions once more. Estela listened in the way Dragonetz had taught her, reaching for the song that was always there for those who were open to it.

Cicadas pulsed shrill with summer urgency; house-martins and swallows swooped their joyous loops; a skylark's solo soprano rose to heaven. Birdsong was replaced by the work-songs and shouts of peasants threshing the spelt, their jointed whips flailing at the cut sheaves. Estela couldn't see the golden grain falling onto the threshing sheets but she knew the precious harvest was there. Behind the men, the fields were scythed stubble, dry and golden under relentless blue skies.

'Stop!' she told Gilles, whose instinctive protest turned into a sigh. He had indeed known her a long time. He dismounted, caught Nici and attached him with a length of rope to the peasant's cart. They would not be popular if a giant dog joined in the threshing.

Careful to keep her mare from straying onto the threshed spelt, Estela called to the nearest men. 'Good-day.' Reluctant to break their rhythm, the men nevertheless recognized her rank and paused. Sweat glistened on their shoulders and in the V of their leather jerkins and Estela flinched from the memory of another young peasant in leather, the smell of sweat and straw, and the terrible harm her young ignorance had caused. Such memories helped no-one but served as a reminder that her rank carried responsibilities. Any words she spoke would have the weight of her standing. Her deeds would take on a life of their own.

'I mean no harm,' she said quickly, stupidly, prompted by the past instead of the present. One of the youngest there laughed and was immediately clouted by his fellow, at the same time as Gilles threw his reins to Estela and dismounted, the better to draw sword with his one good hand. 'No!' she said. 'There was no disrespect meant.'

'No my Lady, no disrespect,' said one of the older men, glancing at her quickly as the boy who'd laughed was shoved roughly behind his elders, away from Gilles' half-unsheathed sword. If he still smiled, it was from nerves.

'I serve Les Baux,' Estela told them, stumbling on, 'and I wanted to know how the harvest goes? What preparation should be made at the castle for the winter? And for our people? For all of you.' As she spoke, Estela felt her mother's presence: the visits they'd made together, checking on flocks and grain, vines and babies. This was grain and vine country, some goats but not sheep. 'The spelt has ripened well and you've got the harvest in while it's dry and without storm damage but I wondered whether the quantity was down because we've lacked rain this springtime?'

This time the man looked at her with genuine respect and more warmth. 'Aye my Lady, that's it, exactly. Good in quality and none ruined but growth was stunted and not as much grain as some years. Middling, I'd say.'

'Too early to say for the grapes,' she mused aloud. 'If the storms bring hail, there's always a risk.'

He nodded. 'Till the last moment there's a risk.'

'The grape harvest here is in two months? Three?'

'Aye, thereabouts, depending on the weather. End of August.'

'And your goats are milking well?'

Another man spoke up. 'You won't find better milk or cheese anywhere my Lady. My daughter's the goat girl and she'd fight that Barcelone army single-handed to protect the village well and her goats. They get water before we do.'

'That's a fact!' the others agreed.

The goat girl's father said, 'By your leave, my Lady,' and, watched closely by Gilles, he went to the pouches piled together and pulled out an object wrapped in dried leaves, which he presented to Estela, saying 'You don't have to take my word for it, my Lady. This be for your break fast.'

Picking open a leaf, Estela studied the contents. Her home region produced exceptional sheep cheese, both the strong blue-veined from the caves and the soft creamy white, but this was a small, firm round. She sniffed and approved. Just a tang of goat and the look of crumpled parchment. The neatness of its form, a perfect round nestled in its carefully interleaved protection, told of a cheese-maker who took pride in her work.

All eyes were on Estela as she evaluated the gift. And found it beyond price. Her eyes glistened as she spoke. 'You speak truth. Surely, there can be no better cheese than this, for it was made with love and skill, and given with the true spirit of hospitality to a stranger. No money could buy what you have freely given me but please do me the honour of accepting a gift for the goat girl.' Gilles followed Estela's quiet instructions. From the saddle-bag he pulled out the silk scarf and linen wimple she'd abandoned there once out of sight from Les Baux, and he took a penny from the purse.

Estela cut short the effusive thanks with one last question. 'Do you have enough for yourselves, for the winter?'

Honest men, they told her that they could pay their dues without fear of starvation – this year – as long as there was no more war. Fighting would mean fire and destruction, with grainstores and barns the victims, whichever side won. Estela understood. In war, the peasants never won. She nodded, apologised for the interruption and rode on. Gilles walked his horse back to where Nici, sullen, watched from a tethered distance. He'd already started chewing through the rope. With only one regretful look at the men working, he bounded after his mistress and Gilles, mounting, followed suit.

When they were hungry, they found a copse, tied their horses to a tree and sat on the grass together, as they had when Estela was a motherless little girl and Gilles her only protector in a cold household. She broke the cheese and gave him half. He sliced the bread and the dried sausage with his knife. They shared the wineskin. It was the best meal Estela could remember eating in days and she spoke with her mouth full of goat cheese. 'This,' she mumbled, 'this is what Dragonetz is fighting for. And it's worth it!'

After lunching, they lay in the shade, pleasantly sleepy with wine and full stomachs, a long way from court formalities. Stretched out in a most unladylike way, eyes shut and idly masticating a dry grass blade, Estela murmured, 'Do you remember teaching me how to choose a dagger.'

'Mmm. Your brother never did understand. But you, quick as a fox with a rabbit.'

'I still get it wrong,' she confessed. 'Petronilla. She's not a pretty one. But she's strong and true.'

'Ay, a man's eyes can never be trusted. But the second lesson is the more difficult, once you've learned the first.'

Estela sighed. 'Pretty *can* be strong and true. Like Talharcant. And Dragonetz.'

'And you, my Lady. Beware men's eyes, especially those who've not learned the second lesson. '

Estela instinctively felt her side, the leather sheath a hard lump beneath her kirtle. 'Don't worry. You taught me to look after myself. And I have you. And Nici.' The dog opened one eye at his name but saw no reason to get excited and drooped back into his sprawling doze.

'Maybe one day I will have my own lands and fiefs,' Estela mused aloud. 'I will oversee the harvests, protect my people, heal the ailing and help the women birth their babies. I will supervise the accounts and ensure that the coin is spent for the good of all. Our land will have the best markets in the whole world. I will hire the goat girl and we will have the best cheeses! Musca will grow to be a man in the sunshine of his people's love. And of his parents' love for him and each other.'

'You would like that, my Lady.'

'I would like that. Yes, I would like that very much.'

After lazing an hour or two in this manner, they pursued a circular route that would take them back through the plain, with its fields and vineyards, to the narrow canyon that took them back to Les Baux. At the point where fields changed to rock, a bizarre figure set Nici barking.

'A scarecrow?' Estela wondered aloud but no scarecrow stood straight beside a stone wall, then bent over, walked a few steps with the aid of a stick, and repeated the movement. The creature was swathed from top to toe in what looked to be a bundle of random cloths, all brightly coloured. The human inside was well hidden and as the riders approached, they could see that the face too was covered, but with mesh, like fishing net. As they grew closer and recognised the clouds of insects making angry protest round the invader, the figure's purpose was clear. Six niches in the stone wall each contained a wicker basket.

'A beekeeper! Gilles, take Nici further on and I'll get us some honey.'

'My Lady, you'll get stung!' was spoken with the resignation of a man who expected to be ignored and Gilles was already leading horse and dog into the canyon when Estela called out to the worker. 'Good man. Do you have honey I could buy?'

She thought the man hadn't heard her as there was no change in his rhythm. He put the lid back on the basket beside him, waved the smoking torch along the wall. Estela was close enough to hear the enraged buzzing change to mere irritation and she stored the sounds in her song of the day, along with the stream bubbling nearby and the man's strange chant in a foreign tongue. Then she realised from the voice that this was no man.

The female beekeeper walked slowly and steadily, towards Estela, leaning on her stick, lumbering and anonymous in her protective clothing.

'I have been waiting for you, my Lady,' she said. 'Please, be my guest. I have comb in my shelter. Follow me. You may bring your man and hound. They will come to no harm.' She remained veiled and Estela followed her own curiosity and the strange woman, into the canyon, where Gilles and Nici accepted their mistress' madness, and followed too.

CHAPTER THIRTEEN

*The honey bee (apis) is from the heat of the sun... For anyone... who has had
some limb moved from its place, or who has any crushed limbs, take bees that
are not alive, but which have died, in a metallic jar. Put a sufficient amount on
a linen cloth, and sew it up. Soak this cloth within, in olive oil, and place it
over the ailing limb. Do this often, and he will be better.*
Physica, Birds

The beekeeper motioned them to follow her and disappeared
into solid rock. When Estela looked more closely, she could see
that the fissures gave the illusion of solidity and behind the façade of
rock lay an unmagical cave entrance, narrow but tall enough to enter
on horseback. Was this where Dragonetz had hidden Barcelone's treasure? No, surely not. First impressions had been of how spacious the
first cavern was overhead but the flickering torch showed that it was
small. The roof of the passageway from there into a back cave grazed
Estela's head if she forgot to stoop. The beekeeper's home was
adequate for one person's basic living conditions but would not have
hidden a treasure cart.

The torch was slotted into a sconce and by its light, Estela saw two
further tunnels, narrow and forbidding. Estela felt no compulsion to
extend the day's adventures beyond whatever she might experience

within these walls. A mattress and cover, a cushion, a chest that served for table. A pitcher full of water stood beside plate and knife on the chest.

She rested her hand lightly on her skirt, just where the slit allowed her to reach the hidden dagger. Gilles was rubbing his head where he'd bashed it on the rough ceiling of the tunnel. Nici had refused to enter the cave at all but would no doubt wait for them somewhere round the entrance, peeping in at the horses from time to time.

'Honey,' Estela said. 'We would like to buy some of your honey. I think you were collecting it.' *I have been waiting for you, my Lady. What did the woman mean?*

'You shall have your honey, my Lady.' The beekeeper unwound the cloths from her head and the mesh attached to them, revealing an ancient face, skin weathered to walnut, eyes rheumy with age and shadowed in the cave-light. She unbound her hands and removed some of the outer layers but those she revealed were just as bright and ill-assorted, cotton and cambric, fustian and hessian. She reminded Estela of someone but the memory was fickle as torch-light in a cave.

The woman suffered a coughing fit, doubled over, hacked and spat. Estela could not tell the colour but would not have been surprised if the flux was bloody. Straightening, the beldame addressed Gilles, nodding at the stump where once his right hand had been. 'Does that hurt?'

Estela winced at the lack of courtesy but Gilles took no offence. 'It was well cauterised but sometimes I feel it still,' he confessed. It had never occurred to Estela that he might feel hurt where there was no longer a member.

'Too late for honey on the burn,' the woman mused in her strange accent 'but there will be dead bees aplenty as I smoke them out for harvest. Mustn't harvest with thunder in the air tho'. Bees turn evil. Kill if they're poked. Do you want them? Dead bees?'

Estela jumped at the question, aimed in her direction. She would like dead bees very much! She could add them to the little collection of potions she had stored on a shelf in a cold chamber beside the kitchen.

'Yes, I could use them,' she replied. 'And if it might ease Gilles' dolour, I have a recipe to soothe such with cloth, oil and dead bees.'

'I read only people and lives, not books.'

There seemed no fit response. A different thought struck Estela. 'How will you have honey again if the bees die?'

'There are always new bees, my Lady. It is nature's way. I will catch six more swarms in the tree hollows next spring and bring them to my skeps in the wall.'

Estela felt a sudden sadness that the bees died to make her honey. 'Do they have to die?'

'All creatures serve us, my Lady, each in his own way. As sheep give us meat and wool, so bees give us honey. The bees themselves have order and rank. I have long watched my bees and they have a king, just as we do, his soldiers who do his work and the females who produce young. All have their place in the bee world as we do in this one. Those who give their lives now while I harvest the honey, will be replaced in the spring. There are always more bees.'

Estela had no option but to accept the woman's obvious expertise but she thought stubbornly that if she ever kept bees, she would at least try to keep them alive. Maybe honey harvesting *could* be like getting milk from a sheep, taking only a portion.

'There's fresh comb for you, my Lady.' For the second time that day, Estela was given treasure from the terroir of Provence, this time in a pot.

'Gilles, a coin for the beekeeper?'

'Two, my Lady,' demanded their host.

Estela was so taken aback by the effrontery, she merely repeated, 'Two?!'

'You don't recognise me, my Lady, do you.'

'Should I?' Estela managed a haughty tone but her heart was pounding, acknowledging something. *Where? When?*

'One coin for the honey and that's generous of you, my Lady. But

Dame Fairnette needs her palm crossed for a true reading and that's what you're here for, lovely. You just don't know it yet.'

'What trickery –' Gilles began, drawing his sword.

'The Gyptian!' Estela realised, remembering a late-night escapade in Narbonne, Jewish mystics and a Romani fortune-teller. What had she been promised? Or rather threatened. Something about a man's death. She took the coins from Gilles. 'Leave us,' she told him. 'I know this woman. I will come to no harm with her and I wish to hear what she has to say.'

'Then you can hear it with me stood here,' declared Gilles, sheathing his sword but not his frown. 'You shouldn't meddle with dark arts, my Lady.'

'But she already has, hasn't she, my pretty.' Dame Fairnette's sing-song voice addressed both her hearers and neither. 'For all your fierce words, I see love in you, fierce man.'

Gilles snorted but maintained his guardsman stance, feet apart and firmly planted on the hard earth. 'Not just for my pretty Lady, no, that takes no second sight. No, the love in your heart for another is what I can see.'

Estela couldn't see Gilles' face in the cave's wavering light but she could feel the slight hiccup in his breathing, the tell-tale stillness in the atmosphere. Silence did not keep secrets, not in this cave. The voice chanted, 'Be bold, Gilles Lack-hand, and she will turn to you in her need. She sees you now whereas before she could not look. You will find each other.'

Rather than risk being dismissed again and having to obey, Gilles kept firmly silent but his relief was apparent when the fortune-teller turned her attention to Estela.

'Remember now, my lovely? The red-headed Queen is moving ever closer to her tower prison; the golden ruler of Narbonne is about to meet her troubadour. The cards cannot lie. And I recognized you straight away. You were Nobody, remember?' She cackled at her own joke.

Estela did remember when she was nobody. She frowned and spoke sarcastically, even as she accepted the invitation to sit on the rough bed-cover while Dame Fairnett sat cross-legged on the cavern floor, drawing a pack of cards from one of the floral fabrics around her hips. 'The 'golden ruler of Narbonne' had already met her troubadour, so you are mistaken.'

The Gyptian shuffled the cards while replying. 'But that wasn't *her* troubadour, was it, my pretty. *That* troubadour was the one in your cards, wasn't he. And when I told you someone would not survive the *knowing* of you, I was right, wasn't I. Oh yes, she knows I was right, doesn't she.'

Estela was glad of the dim light that hid her flushed face and sore conscience. She took refuge in a counter-attack. 'Why are you all alone?' she demanded. 'I remember you were with a band of your people. You had some holy mission to a place by the sea. Why are you living in a cave near Les Baux? Did they cast you out?'

Dame Fairnette hissed through her teeth. 'She remembers now, does she, but she's got it all wrong. The Gyptian mother is always on a mission for her people. They're by the great salt wash, waiting for the Maries and Black Sarah but I had to leave them because of you.' The direct address was like a slap. 'You and your Lord Dragonetz. Not even the Saint Maries are safe from what you *great lords* do in Les Baux. So I am here and so are your cards.' The cards waited on the table, promise and threat, neutral. The patterns on them reminded Estela of the mosque in Jerusalem.

'Where did you get those cards?' Estela asked. 'I have never seen their like.'

'A Mameluke gave them to me, in the days when I could dance a man's blood to madness, before the trek over land and seas to shape our people's future. The cards talk to me but no-one else hears them. Goys see the four suits, and the number of cups or coins on a card, but they don't know the Malik from the Na'in and Thani Na'ib.' She moved three cards around as she named them and Estela could see that each belonged by its symbols to one of the four suits but had a different, distinct design.

She knew enough Arabic to understand that her friend's name also meant 'king' and the other two titles, lesser courtiers. Their designs of intersecting circles and triangles could be taken by a fanciful observer for a child's drawing of a person, and each suit had its three courtiers. 'The Malik of Les Baux must come to me himself if he would know his origins,' muttered the Gyptian, retiring the card she named, one painted with stick symbols. 'The cards will tell you what they want you to know my pretty.' She placed the Thani Na'ib of the cup suit, on its own, face up and held out her hand, waiting.

Mute, Estela passed the silver coin three times over the outstretched palm and watched it disappear into a fold of skirt. Then the fortune-teller laid out three rows for the reading, as she had done the last time.

'No nasty Pathfinder blocking this time.' Estela had indeed left her runic brooch back in her clothes chest, needing no clasp or extra weight in the heat. 'There you be, dark lady.' She placed one card alone. 'Pathfinder lies still, watching your path tied to another's. Choices... there are always choices... but so faint this time. The road runs straight. If you be yourself, you'll choose the straight road.' Lost in trance, real or feigned, the woman frowned, studying a card.

'That can't be,' she complained, 'that has already been.' She fixed an angry gaze on Estela as if blaming her subject for the impossible card. 'But the reading is clear. Someone will not survive the knowing of you.'

'Dragonetz,' breathed Estela.

'No. I see his path, the one you're tied to, the Oath-breaker.'

Estela jumped to her feet, enraged. 'He is no oath-breaker! He is a true knight.'

'So you say, my Lady, but the seven cups is beside the Na'in of swords, your Dragonetz.' She pointed to them 'I see a man despised, a man who's broken the promise that makes him knight. Sit, if you would hear more. Or go. The cards don't care.'

Estela sat and the voice continued. 'And I see a different man, his path a shadow bound to yours. It will happen again. A man. Flesh of your flesh and dead because of it.'

Estela felt sick and felt for the reassurance of her dagger. 'I would kill any man who tried!' she said, 'so there might well be dead men but not… the rest. It's not possible. What else?'

'A straight path,' Dame Fairnette repeated, 'until you cross the sea.' She pointed at a card picturing six swords. 'Inversed,' the fortune-teller murmured, 'so not into calmer waters but into more troubles. Seas or troubles… real water, I feel it. Then you will use Pathfinder to help make your choice. I see gold… no, not for you directly. Your lord should beware gold.' Her eyes focused and her voice snapped back to the present. 'Enough. I'm tired.' She added as an afterthought, 'my Lady.'

Estela made light of the prophecies, 'What, no handsome husband? Not even sons like you promised Queen Aliénor?'

'The cards do not lie, my pretty one.' Estela could see white whiskers on the woman's chin and she longed to pull one out.

'So that means I won't have a handsome husband and lots of children,' Estela persisted, with brittle flippancy.

Dame Fairnette cackled. 'You'd like that, wouldn't you. But the cards don't care what you'd like. They don't say all that is, they don't say all that isn't.'

Estela breathed out heavily, controlling her diaphragm as she'd been taught, modulating her voice. 'Well you won't make much silver that way, Dame Fairnette. You must be getting old and have mixed up our fortunes. Here's Gilles all set for romance and me for exploring the world Oltra mar. My days on a boat are over!' She rose, smooth and graceful. 'Thank you for the honey and I will let Lady Etiennette know that you are harvesting.'

With the help of her stick, the Romani also got to her feet, muttering to herself again. 'Honey for the castle, happy to oblige the lords, happy to live in the caves with the guardian beast, keep the treasure from the wrong hands. If my Lady comes to the Val d'Enfer at night, she won't like that, no she won't.'

Gilles shook his head. He was right. Whatever sense there had been in Dame Fairnette was losing the battle. Estela clutched her jar of honey and followed Gilles into the tunnel's darkness, then towards the light of the outer cavern, to the horses. Nici patrolled outside, noted they were back and bounded off.

'She is going crazy,' Estela stated. 'She never used to talk to herself like that, or about us as if we weren't there.'

'Gives me the creeps.' Gilles shivered and crossed himself. 'Makes you think burning might be right for one like her.'

'Gilles! It's just foolishness. Anyone living here would know the names of people at court, like me and Dragonetz. Peasant gossip. Les Baux has been at war for years so it's all got muddled in her head with the legends of her people. And the rest of it is market-day twaddle. 'You'll find love, big choice to make, beware gold... foolish jabber to please or frighten young girls – and old men-at-arms. Lucky in love, eh?' she teased him and this time she could see the colour in his cheeks.

'Mind your step,' he warned her and Estela smiled as her mare picked a delicate, precise route over the stones. It had been a lovely day and she wasn't going to fret over the words of a crazed beldame. As if she would cross the sea again!

Dragonetz lay in the circle of Estela's arms, his shelter from the world outside. He remembered that he wanted to tell her something before giving in to sleep. He started to speak and so did she, at the same time.

'You first,' she whispered.

'Lady Etiennette made me a proposal,' he told her. She moved away from him, leaned on her elbow to study him as she spoke, looked at him intently and waited. 'She wants me to oversee a mint, at Arle.'

There was silence. When they sang together he could read her very breathing and he was surprised by the quality of this silence, its wrong note.

'And?' she asked, her usual self.

He must be over-tired from all the politics around him to see complication even in the bedchamber, he chid himself. 'I'm tempted,' he admitted. 'The workings of a foundry intrigue me. And I have a mintmaster.' He told her the strange and wonderful tale of John Halfpenny.

Contented, in her arms again, he asked drowsily, 'What did you want to say?'

'Nothing important. A matter of cheese and honey, a ride in the sunshine.' And clouds, she thought. Black stormclouds. But she said nothing more as she cradled her knight to sleep.

CHAPTER FOURTEEN

If the devil should incite a man to love a woman so that, without magic or the invocation of demons, he begins to be insane with this love, and if this is an annoyance to the woman, she should pour a bit of wine over a sapphire three times and each time say, 'I pour this wine, in its ardent powers, over you; just as God drew off your splendour, wayward angel, so may you draw away from me the lust of this ardent man.

Physica, Stones

Wine and chatter flowed liberally and no-one would have guessed the hatred Les Baux felt for their highborn southern guests from looking at the High Table. The most civilised of hosts, Etiennette and Hugues exchanged pleasantries with Ramon and Petronilla. Each evening at meal-time in the Great Hall, Les Baux demonstrated to their visitors just how civilised their court could be, how exquisite the food and the entertainment. From the conger eel in green garlic sauce to the honeyed figs, no expense was spared.

Seated at one end of the High Table, Dragonetz thought cynically that, whether he knew it or not, Barcelone was being entertained at his own expense. Les Baux could afford to be lavish at table, knowing that most of the Barcelone treasure cart remained in reserve. The knight surveyed the assembly, lords red-faced with wine and the flickering torchlight, relaxed and replete, their ladies glittering. One such lady caught his eye. She was taller than most, wearing large paste jewels that dazzled the onlooker as she hid her blushes behind a demure hand, in response to what were clearly outrageous suggestions from a gallant pressing his suit.

Dragonetz smiled. Those who didn't know Lady Sancha might dismiss her as vulgar and featherheaded but his friend was as astute in gathering political secrets as any minister to the crown. It was a comfort to him that his current path met her approval but he knew their agreement grew from different roots. Sancha's loyalty to Les Baux was deep and unshakeable; should Etiennette declare war once again, Sancha would rouse for the righteous cause. Dragonetz wanted peace. He'd had more than enough of righteous causes in the Crusade, especially when he could see no clear distinction between the two claims.

It didn't look as though Sancha's current activities had much to do with politics, however. Never had Dragonetz seen his friend play the fluttering, giggling girl as she was doing now. He had certainly never seen a man encouraging her to do so. Not since the moment Dragonetz rescued her from a Holy Land battle-field, had he seen Sancha vulnerable and he suddenly realised why her feelings for him had changed. It had nothing to do with Estela or with his own indifference to anything other than friendship. Sancha was in love with someone else and from the exchange of glances and laughter, a hand kissed and an anecdote sketched in the air, it seemed that the someone else returned her feelings.

'God's breath,' swore Dragonetz under his breath, drawing a surprised look from the courtier seated next to him, and prompt topping up of his cup with wine by the attendant page. Taking a large swig, Dragonetz wondered whether there could be anything other than hurt come of this sweet romance. Surely Sancha could not hope to find another husband who would accept the body she hid in skirts?

His sense of foreboding weakened with another draught of wine. It was none of his business, anyway, and he had more than enough to worry about. At table, every man should put down his troubles;

enemies became host and guest, protected by the most sacred trust and by all the gods.

The warmth in his belly increased as, with a smile in his direction, Lady Etiennette's celebrated guest troubadour picked up her oud, an Arab lute, and made her way from her end place at a lower table (carefully chosen to allow room for a large white dog underneath) to a clear spot, lit by a wall sconce, where she could perform.

When Estela began to sing, the chatter died to whispers and then to silence and Dragonetz was lifted once more to the realms they inhabited together. Her voice had matured, gained range and emotion but kept the sweetness that hit a man's soul. Where once she would have trilled the joy and milked the tragedy, now her judgement removed all artifice. There were no barriers between the listener and the music as Estela lost herself in storytelling.

When she announced her new work, his heart lurched with anxiety but she smiled at him again. She knew from experience that an audience never liked a new song. But, if it was good enough, the second time they heard it, they would applaud and the third time they would be humming along. After that, they would request that very song and be disappointed if it wasn't in the programme. It was always this way.

From the first verse, Dragonetz knew who the song was for, with its tale of El Campeador, a misunderstood hero and his Moorish friend. When had his lover become so skilled at sending him a private message of support in such a public way? He was almost jealous when he realised that each man there felt the same way, felt that the song was specially for him. When had she learned how to win hearts and minds with her own lyrics and melody?

'Wild and free roamed the horses of al-Andalus
on the world-edge where plains met sky
where a boy chose with his heart,
the white one who called to him
in a mane-toss and a dance.'

Or *the black one*, thought Dragonetz, seeing himself as the boy Rodrigo and Sadeek as a foal in his homeland. They would have known each other, however leggy and awkward the colt might once have been. As Malik had known, gifted and named Sadeek to be friend of his friend.

'Babieca' spat the godfather-priest
despising the young and their ignorance but
'Babieca,' announced the boy to his horse
in the naming that seals the future
in the bond that would never break,
not in the blood of battle nor the
shared grave of their old bones.'

As Dragonetz's vision blurred, thinking of Sadeek, so did every man there imagine his own horse, companion in travail and danger. All present were caught up in the story of Rodrigo, El Sidi. Dragonetz began to understand how many stories Estela was telling in her masterwork and his respect grew. She sang of the hero's dishonour, exile and near-death; his rescue by the King of Zaragoza and years in his service.

There were gasps in the hall at the idea of such a hero being in the employ of Saracens and many eyes turned towards the Prince of Barcelone's lieutenant. Turbaned and inscrutable, Malik sat at the High Table, listening to the story that was also his, of the time when his people ruled his kingdom.

Is he thinking of the time before that, wondered Dragonetz , *when his people could have been rulers in this very hall? How easily the wheel of fortune could spin and stop at a different place. How clever of Estela to make her audience think this way without having to draw their swords.*

When Estela sang of Ximena's courage in strapping her dead husband to his horse and defying an army, the Queen of Aragon, descendant of that same heroine, lost her self-discipline enough to clap her hands and call, 'Brava, Ximena!' Her own, reserved, stern husband took her little hand in his own and kissed it, murmuring softly to her. Ramon, too, claimed El Sidi in his ancestry, through the couple's daughter Maria, and the song could only remind Barcelone of what he and Petronilla represented, the unity of two kingdoms and the balance of power between north and south.

Balance, thought Dragonetz. *Peace is all about balance and the only justification for war is to restore balance.*

As the applause died, one voice carried along the High Table. 'Perhaps your troubadour would do us the honour of celebrating my grandfather in song. 'The word of a Porcelet!' would make a rousing chorus, would it not.'

'Very rousing,' agreed Etiennette drily, while her son glowered at the Porcelets.

Dragonetz glanced at the Lady of Les Baux, picking out barbs as to the manner born. He wondered how she really felt about the glorification of her hated guests' ancestors; not to mention the triumphant performance of her troubadour, his lover. That one glance at Etiennette put his mind at rest. She glowed, the supreme hostess. For the first time, she had established her superiority over Ramon and Petronilla and her magnanimity radiated along the table, basking in the pleasure of her guests. Tonight, Les Baux had lived up to its reputation as the most civilised court in Provence.

Estela swept her final curtseys, her oud tucked under one arm. She observed every formality, with grace, but her eyes found his *and always will,* he thought, *across hallfulls of people and hell itself.* Then he shivered at his own blasphemy. *Careful!* warned his old superstition that he endangered those he loved. *Don't let jealous gods see how blessed you are.*

There was no such fear in the troubadour who'd just played for another queen; Estela went to pay respects and receive compliments at the High Table. No matter that Petronilla was younger than Estela had ever been and struggling to enjoy such a banquet in her condition: she was still Queen of Aragon and Estela made her the reverence due, without limit this time.

In response, Petronilla ceremonially unclasped a bangle from her wrist and offered it to Estela in appreciation. Not to be outdone, Etien-nette gave her troubadour a golden hairnet, studded with jewels. Estela returned to her place a wealthy woman. Dragonetz remem-bered the first time Estela had sung in public, beyond her childhood home. The prizes at that tourney had been sword-belt and armour, on the assumption that a man would win. And yet, his then protégée had charmed the Prince of Orkney so much that the gold Pathfinder brooch had found its way onto Estela's cloak instead of Dragonetz'.

Another man could claim his share of pride in tonight's music, perhaps the lion's share, Dragonetz acknowledged. He looked along the table and saw Malik offer his praise to Estela. Some prizes were worth more than gold and his lover deserved every word from such a master of their art. They were linked the three of them, deeper than circumstance, stronger than alliance. Whatever this warlike-truce demanded of them.

Only one person on the High Table remained aloof from the joyful atmosphere. Hugues des Baux lolled back, brows lowered, frowning and drinking hard.

'My Lord Hugues,' Dragonetz called to him along the bench. 'I need your thoughts on new training for the men.'

'Not now, Dragonetz,' was the petulant reply.

'It would be a pity to go ahead and find that you'd authorised something you mislike when you see it...'

'Tell me here and be done with it, man!'

Dragonetz gave an exaggerated look of distrust at the backs of the two guests between himself and Hugues, who were politely leaning forward to facilitate the conversation. 'Not here, my Lord,' Dragonetz said with so much emphasis he could almost feel Ramon smiling at the other end of the table. Barcelone would know full well that any secret announced in such a way was not one he need worry about. Hugues was such a boy!

'Very well then! But be brief!' Hugues elbowed his neighbours with no apology as he scrambled to extricate himself back over the bench and accompany his knight past the crowded tables, the attendant page-boys, the scrounging curs and out into a night so black they were blinded at first.

'Where's the justice?' ranted Hugues, letting off drunken steam somewhere safer for himself than in the hall. 'He's a murderer! I don't see any punishment though... son of a whore has everything! I could have killed him where he sat! I owe it. I owe it to my father. '

For once, Dragonetz was grateful for Etiennette's hold over her son. 'For your mother's sake, my Lord, it would not do. Your Lady Mother showed the world tonight that the hospitality at Les Baux, in *your* castle and *your* land, is second to none. Would you undo her reputation by breaking the duty of a lord to his guests?'

'No.' Was Hugues actually chewing his lip? 'But it's not fair that *his* ancestors – and *her* ancestors – have stories and mine don't!' Dragonetz knew better than to enquire about Les Baux's ancestors. The very fact no-one knew who they were told its own story. 'Even Porcelet has a blazon and we have none!' It was true that more families were putting personalised devices on their shields.

'I think you can do better than a pig for device, my Lord.' That raised a laugh and Hugues was beginning to sober up in the night air, which was still warm but fresher than the smoky hall. 'What's this training idea Dragonetz?

Luckily, there had been time for Dragonetz to think of one and the mention of blazons gave him another. 'The men need to practise their skills, in the field,' he said, adding hastily, 'but not in a real battle. We should host a tourney, to train the men and to entertain our guests.' *And to defuse the growing urge to kill each other.* 'In two teams so we would need two devices that distinguish one team from the other.'

The idea sparked a ready-laid fire. 'I would lead one team and Barcelone the other!' His face glowed at the prospect of a duel against his enemy.

'You should indeed lead one team, my Lord,' Dragonetz agreed, 'and we need time for you to discover the blazon for your house, such that the women can make many; on tabards for the men and cara-paces for the horses.'

As to who should lead the other team, Dragonetz refrained from saying that he'd rather have his fingernails pulled out one by one than see Barcelone and Hugues pitted against each other. However, discussions with key players were needed before Dragonetz could enable Hugues to think up the arrangement that would, by then, already be agreed.

As he told Estela that night, 'I don't suppose it matters what device or ancestors he comes up with and the work will keep him out of harm's way for a while. If only he could grow up more quickly!'

Turning onto her side, Estela had murmured, 'The Malik of Les Baux... she meant Hugues... I know who can tell him his origins... I'll take him there.' She was asleep before he could ask what she meant and he'd forgotten by morning. But she hadn't.

CHAPTER FIFTEEN

A certain kind of serpent (quoddam genus serpentis) is very hot and is able to live on land and water. It has diabolic arts for ambushing people. This serpent is hostile toward human beings. It sends out its breath, which is full of deadly poison, toward a person.

Physica, Reptiles

For once, Dragonetz and Estela were fulfilling their court duties in the same place. Their hostess had asked both of them, separately, to attend the morning's judgements in the Lesser Hall as part of her entourage. At least she had heeded Dragonetz' advice to build up Hugues' standing in the eyes of the people, and he was seated beside her.

After each suit was presented, Etiennette turned to her son, held a whispered discussion and made it seem that the judgement came from the two of them. On Etiennette's right hand, Dragonetz could hear the content of the whispers and was grateful that others could not. At least she was making an effort for appearance's sake.

It was not enough, weighed against the Prince of Barcelone's power, but it was a start. And it would never do to underestimate the power of the widow herself, displayed in the people surrounding her now. Dragonetz was not the only knight on duty in full armour, his hands crossed formally on his unsheathed sword.

Estela occasionally moved close enough for him to smell her perfume but maintained her public discretion. She had come straight from rehearsing her songs with Malik and had her precious oud under her arm as she wove in and out among the other ladies, exchanging whispered gossip or observing the lawsuits. A whisk of white fur made its appearance from time to time as Nici checked on his mistress, then disappeared.

Sometimes the details of a plaint caught Dragonetz' attention; two men were accused of transporting Christian Slavs from the far north down through Provence to Muslim al-Andalus, where Christians could be legally kept as slaves, as was the case for Muslims in Christendom.

This case raised some of the finer distinctions between fiefs, freedmen and bondsmen but the conclusion was inevitable. Slavery of Christians was against the laws of Provence and God; no matter that one of the men was Jewish, he would forfeit his life by Christian law. The men's pleas for mercy fell on deaf ears. They were sentenced to be placed in cages overhanging the cliff, there to die of thirst and starvation as an example to others.

When removed from the hall to the dungeons, they were still shouting of the unfairness that their partner in crime was free and wealthy in al-Andalus. It sounded like a tavern tale mused Dragonetz, of a Jew, a Christian and an infidel. The best stories were always true.

He knew of one very profitable business in Marselha run by a Jew, a Christian and a Moor so that they could open during all Holy days as each of them respected different ones. The inter-faith laws on property and finance could be applied very flexibly where there was a solid business partnership.

The next suit had no such wide-ranging implications. A baker accused of fraud was allowed his supporting witness, who said nothing for or against the alleged crime but waxed lyrical about the quality of the loaves produced. Every man present began to think on his next meal, salivating as the list of bread products grew longer and more literary. Etiennette grew impatient at 'manna from heaven, yellowed with saffron' but ended the paeon abruptly at 'rolls rosy with rosepetal like a virgin's cheeks'.

'God's blood,' swore Etiennette, 'if I hear one more dough-related metaphor, I shall have your sweetbreads butchered!' The silence following this remark was impressive. 'Now, tell me what this man's crime is, other than bringing the most boring poet to our court that I have heard since Brother Lan sought to improve us at Lent!'

The accusers, a band of four, two women and two men, looked at each other anxiously, each afraid to speak first, then they all began at once.

'We took our dough...'

'... down to Baker Cam like every Tuesday...'

'... boy under the table!'

'We've been cheated!'

'One at a time!' roared Etiennette, red-faced. From a more controlled version of the story, Dragonetz gathered that the villagers had taken their dough as usual to the bakery, where it was placed on the moulding board for a final shaping by the baker.

A servant-boy had been hidden by the pretty yellow curtain round the table ('I don't need to know what flowers were on the curtain!' interjected the long-suffering Lady des Baux). The boy had pulled pieces of dough from each loaf, through a trap-door in the moulding board, to make extra loaves for his master at the villagers' expense.

'The servant-boy?' enquired Etiennette.

'Ran away.'

'But we got this, my Lady. Bring it in, Mord,' he called to someone at the back of the hall and like runners carrying a palanquin, four more villagers rushed into the hall carrying the offending table.

'Yellow,' observed one of the witnesses smugly, pointing out the curtain. When the drape was whisked dramatically aside and the trapdoor opened, the route between top of table and a boy's greedy hands was clear.

The baker tried feebly, 'That's not my table...' but a glare stopped him making any further protest.

Etiennette made play of discussing crime and punishment with Hugues, then pronounced, 'For selling underweight bread, Baker Cam will be carried through the town on a hurdle. Lace one of his measly loaves round his neck so all shall know that he's a cheat.'

Subdued at the prospect of a day tied to a horse-drawn cart and being pelted at will by jeering onlookers, the baker was led out, to be replaced by the next plaintiff.

Although his body maintained its military discipline in pose, Dragonetz' thoughts drifted away. When Halfpenny reached Arle, it would be the ideal opportunity to test a pigeon from the loft he'd established in Les Baux. He now had communication lines between Trinquetaille, Les Baux and his own villa in the Marselha region. Each time a man Dragonetz trusted was dispatched to an ally's castle, he could send pigeons; to carry messages to Les Baux and to breed homers for that Lord. Gradually the network would expand, under the watchful eye of the man in charge of Hugues' loft.

The pigeon-keeper had been quick to learn; competent in the politics of messagery and far more skilled than Dragonetz in pigeon husbandry. He'd been an apprentice falconer, recommended by the Master of Hounds as one who knew his hounds and his hawks. It was a relief to train him up and hand over the responsibility. Although Dragonetz had been entertained by his project at first, the daily realities of animal care and breeding had lost their appeal and he'd spent enough time on pigeons. Now he was more interested in using the communications he'd set up.

It was his daily habit to mentally review each of his activities, analysing progress and disappointments, incorporating changes and new plans. The men's training? Good in that their skills had improved immeasurably and Barcelone's input could only benefit them. However, the cohesion and loyalty to Hugues was diminished by their admiration for others; first Dragonetz himself, however hard he'd tried to show Hugues at his best; then Barcelone, whose experience and presence left their mark on men. Etiennette was not helping;

her strength only made her son look weak and she didn't even notice the effect. What else could he do to make Hugues look good? To fuse a bond between him and his men?

The sooner they could hold the tourney, the better. Dragonetz remembered a demonstration, himself and his Muslim guards scything silk scarves, wheeling on desert sands. Blood and death. No, he wanted to avoid blood and death. But men liked risk, his split self persisted, arguing the case. Danger created bonds. A little danger. The pretence of war might lance the boil of hot tempers turning putrid. The heat didn't help, the lack of breath and a storm brewing, that never came.

As for a leader bonding with his men: for the sake of Hugues' men and Provence, he'd neglected his own lieutenant, Raoulf and his own men. Maybe he could put that right at the same time. He'd also neglected his old friend, Lady Sancha, although at least they were of the same mind, which could not be said of himself and Malik. He sighed as his guilt accumulated. Estela and Musca were last on his mental list. He could trust her to understand why, to know that if Provence went to war again, their lives were endangered too.

There were some risks men did not like. But what if Estela felt neglected? She had reacted strangely when he told her of Etiennette's proposal. Probably afraid he would go to Arle, which he certainly didn't have time for, however much he'd have enjoyed making money. He dismissed the thought. Women had such moods, such moments. He dismissed the guilt. A leader had no use for guilt outside the confessional. If penance must be done, so be it, but making any decision was better than making none at all.

With that comforting conclusion, Dragonetz' attention was jerked back to the hall. An angry white monster carved through the crowd to stand growling, hackles up, beside his mistress. Estela had her fist curled round a handful of Nici's neckfur, whether soothing him or restraining him, Dragonetz couldn't tell, but even from this distance, he could see how the colour had drained from her face.

His sword half-unsheathed, he moved towards her but she caught his eye and shook her head. She stood ramrod straight and still as a carved saint, Nici tensed by her side, as a new party of nobles made their way towards Etiennette and Hugues. Any plaintiffs slow to make way for the newcomers were knocked aside.

Dragonetz had seen many of the local lords and castellans coming to give their oaths of allegiance to Barcelone – and to the Lady of Les Baux, not necessarily in that order – so it was no surprise when the man dropped to his knees in front of Etiennette and his lady curt-seyed. The Castellan of Montbrun, for so he was, looked much older than his wife, with a grizzled beard and hardened features, scored deeply with bitterness. It was as if any trace of ageing had been trans-ferred to his face from his lady's, which was smooth pearl with a cupid's kiss for lips. Wayward tendrils escaped from her jewelled hairnet and glittered sunshine blonde.

She satisfied Dragonetz' curiosity by meeting his eyes as she rose from the most graceful of curtseys and her lips parted in a sponta-neous smile that lit up her eyes. Fascinated, Dragonetz held her gaze, responding to its blue, round-eyed innocence. Her colouring was unusual in Provence but her fragile beauty would have attracted attention in any company. The instinct to protect her was so strong that Dragonetz felt guilty, remembering his first meeting with Estela and the way she had affected him. This was very different but, even so…

Before he could speak and break the spell, the Lady of Montbrun had acknowledged his attention with a little nod and turned away from duty to her liege and was focused on someone elsewhere in the hall. As she swished away, Dragonetz was treated to a back view of long neck, slim shoulders beneath silk that revealed rather than concealed every movement of her delicate frame and a hint of neat ankle above the tiny red boots. He licked his lips, his mouth suddenly dry. Montbrun? He should know the name but could not recall the context.

'The sooner Lord Montbrun takes his wife back home, the easier his life will be. Let's hope he is lusty enough in bed to keep her out of others' – or that he's brought key and shackles. You would rather *that* were your marriage prospect, my Lord Dragonetz? I fancy your hesitation would be over.' Lady Etiennette's cynical words brought Dragonetz out of his reverie, guilty on all counts: not only for looking longer than he should, at a married woman, when he had sworn to be true to his own lover; but also for offending the Lady of Les Baux. He had to choose his words carefully.

'My Lady,' he said, for her ears only, hoping that Hugues had not heard or had not understood his mother. 'Nothing and no-one could be a more beautiful bride than Provence herself. I swear to you I will do all in my power for your Provence, as if I were her husband.'

With that, Lady Etiennette had to be satisfied because all eyes were fixed on Lady Montbrun, who had stopped in front of Estela, her husband trailing behind her. The court hushed, sensing a confrontation brewing. Nici continued to growl and held still, quivering with barely suppressed rage. For the first time, Dragonetz heard Lady Montbrun speak and he shivered, his own hackles rising as he realised who this beauty was.

'It seems we've found our little lyre.' The word was drawn out into two syllables, the insult stressed. Costansa de Montbrun, Estela's stepmother, stepped forward, braved Nici in one swift motion and grabbed Estela's oud. She stepped backwards quickly enough to evade both snap and slap. Estela was rooted to the spot, her hand grasping a handful of fur tightly, as if she'd fall down without Nici's strength.

Costansa's words were dagger sharp, spoken as if to her husband and yet piercing every ear in the hall, leaving no doubt that she wanted all to hear her. 'And our own dog too. We'll take this,' she shook the instrument like a rattle and Estela winced, 'and our livestock back home with us when we go, won't we, my Lord.' That she spoke for both of them could be judged from the still, silent presence of her husband.

'I believe you have one of our men here too? I'm sure we can find some use for even a one-handed servant. There are latrines to clean out. And you should learn that no-one steals what's ours. I think the man has learned but you need another lesson. Shall we take her back with us, my Lord?' There was no answer and none was expected as

Costansa fired some more barbs. 'I'm sure you could chastise her into a daughter but not one you would want. Perhaps we can leave the whore here, to count her rather attractive blessings.' The sideways glance at Dragonetz left no-one doubting what she meant.

With no discernible change in his furrowed cheeks, Montbrun's deep voice rang out. 'She's no daughter of mine. Aye, we could do with the man. He's paid for his crime and owes us service. And we'll have the dog she stole. Let's hope breeding plays truer in the bitch we find for him than with your mother!'

Dragonetz' hand was to his sword but he held back, knowing instinctively that Estela would not thank him for intervening. Etiennette placed a hand on his arm, reminding him that Talharcant was under her orders in this court and he stood, helpless, watching. Estela looked large and clumsy, sallow and coarse, beside the tiny figure spitting venom at her.

'It's a lute, an oud,' she said, struggling to speak at all but still restraining her dog.

'Lute, lyre...' Costansa shrugged her perfect alabaster shoulders, enjoying the chance to insult Estela again. She leaned in close enough to say something that Dragonetz couldn't hear and then she added, loudly. 'You haven't asked after your brother.'

'How is my brother?' asked Estela, like a prisoner on the rack who hopes the torture will end if he gives the words required from him. The last Dragonetz had heard, Estela's murderous brother had been left unconscious by a hearthfire.

'His face isn't as pretty as yours, with half of it burnt away after your man left him for dead. It pains him. He doesn't like to go out as much as he used to do. He feels a little... bitter. He'll be pleased to see the cur again.' How could such a pretty mouth deliver such a sadistic laugh? All sweetness turned to poison as Costansa spoke and yet the timbre was light and tinkling, musical, if you didn't listen to the words.

'Honey,' stammered Estela, no doubt quoting one of her favourite authorities on medicine. 'Flaxseed in water, dip a linen cloth in and place the cloth over the area of the burn. This draws out the burn.' It was as if reciting the recipe returned her to adulthood from the frightened child she had seemed when first confronted.

'No, Nici,' she told the great white mastiff. And the dog went quiet, looking up at her, clearly unhappy with her decision but willing to go along with it. Estela's voice rang out louder and stronger. 'I call on everyone here gathered to witness that this is my dog. Should this lord and lady wish to challenge my rights, let them ask me to loose the dog and judge who is master by the way he behaves.'

There was a silence

'No?' asked Estela, coldly. 'You do not want me to loose *your* dog, for him to come to you?'

Costansa recovered her poise and retaliated. 'The brute needs his jaw tied but that won't stop him siring useful pups. You stole him and turned him into a monster. That doesn't make him yours. We'll see what the court says. My Lady,' she addressed Etiennette. 'We would like to present our case to recover our goods and have this thief suitably punished. It's not the first time she's stolen from her own family – after all we did for her!'

The Lady of Les Baux enjoyed taking her time to whisper with her son before pronouncing her decision. Dragonetz considered whether he could demand trial by combat and what impact on the future of Provence it would have if he killed a man for the sake of a dog – or if he were killed.

Fortunately for Provence, it looked as if Costansa would pay for flirting with Dragonetz. 'I am sorry, my Lady but you can see we have a full hall today and I'm sure you are weary after your journey so we will arrange another day for your hearing, if you can't find a private agreement before then.' Her tone left no room for challenge and the prettiest lips in the hall straightened in frustration then delivered a parting shot.

'He has an eye for the ladies, your knight, doesn't he. You might be advised to look for a more secure position for a whore.'

Dragonetz shut his eyes, knowing from personal experience when Estela had been goaded beyond fear.

'Like yours?' demanded his black-haired fury. 'It's difficult some-times to tell whether a woman is wife or whore when she does the same work!'

Dragonetz feared for the oud as Costansa waved it around while she struggled for a witty reply. Estela clearly had the same concern for her lute and, though her voice still shook, she was calm as she spoke to her father. 'My Lord Father, this instrument was my mother's, given to me in her name and in all conscience you cannot take it from me. Please, I beg you, for all that you once held dear, think on this, my sole legacy. I claim no other and never will. May God and the assembly here gathered be my witnesses.'

The solemnity of what she renounced echoed in the silence of the hall but still the grey, furrowed Castellan of Montbrun said nothing, a pillar of stone behind his animated wife, whose tinkling laugh shat-tered the moment.

'Ever the performer, Roxie.' Estela winced at her own Christian name as at a stone flung. Dragonetz had only known her under her troubadour name, her own choosing. 'We will settle this by the law. Meanwhile, I suggest you chain that dog up where he can't hurt anyone. We know how to deal with ill-disciplined curs. Come, my dear, I am weary. My Lady.' She curtseyed to Etiennette and stalked out of the hall, followed by her grim lord. This time, Costansa did have the last word. Estela said nothing as the party left and no-one risked a kicking by being in their way. There was a collective sigh of relief before the next suitor claimed his place.

'My Lady, my neighbour Venter has been fouling the river north of my farm and two of my goats have sickened and died from his spite.' All was back to normal and Dragonetz endured a long succession of trivial plaints before he could offer support to his lady, who remained still and solitary – unless you counted the presence of a large white dog.

When the Lady of Les Baux finally called a halt to the session, Dragonetz rushed to Estela's side and escorted her out of the Hall on his arm, glaring at anyone who risked staring at them. As soon as they were somewhere private, he asked, 'What did she say?'

Estela dropped onto a window-seat and looked out at the plains merging blue in the distance to the haze of mountains and sky. 'She said she carries the heir to Montbrun. She said, 'Don't get fond of your bastard. Toddlers die so easily, smothered by their pillows or choked on their food.' That's why I renounced my inheritance.' Her voice shook. 'I tried to buy Musca. I tried to buy our baby.' The tears came, despite her efforts and Dragonetz folded her in his arms, heedless of reputation. 'She will try to kill him and he will never be safe,' she whispered. 'What are we going to do?'

CHAPTER SIXTEEN

When a woman brings forth an infant, from the time she gives birth through all the days of its infancy, she should keep a jasper on her hand. Malign spirits of the air will be much less able to harm her or the child… Also, if a serpent sends out its breath in any spot, place a jasper there. The breath will be weakened, so that it will be less harmful, and the serpent will stop breathing in that place.

Physica, Stones

Estela laughed for the first time since she'd seen her stepmother. 'You'd have faced trial by combat? For Nici?' The dog wagged his tail.

'No.' Dragonetz stroked her face. 'For you. I'd do it for you.'

'And Gilles.' Estela's smile died. 'And Musca. If only we *could* put that woman on trial and let God decide!' A pause. Flat-voiced, she said the hard words. 'You found her attractive, didn't you.' It was not a question.

He didn't insult her, or them, by lying. 'Until she spoke, yes. I didn't know who she was.' It was not said as an excuse. Facts, reactions existed, regardless of whether they were embellished.

Estela felt like a child again, gawky and desperate to please this angelic being who'd come into her father's life. Nothing and no-one

139

could replace her mother but surely this vision of sweetness would help her grow into someone prettier, more confident – like Costansa herself. 'I felt the same,' she told Dragonetz. 'Until she spoke, lied, got my father to whip me. She'll kill Gilles for helping me escape, now she knows he's happy. She won't let go until her prey is dead.'

There was no chance Costansa would give up and the longer Etiennette postponed a lawsuit, the more rumblings of discontent there would be among the minor nobles. Unfortunately, the law was on Montbrun's side in everything except Estela's inheritance. She knew that she would be laughed out of the Hall if she told the truth.

Who could look at her stepmother's frail beauty and believe what she had done? Even Dragonetz probably thought Estela was exaggerating. She shivered. Only Gilles, her rock since her mother died, knew what it had really been like at Montbrun.

She rehearsed what she could say in front of her judges in the Lower Hall to prevent Costansa claiming Gilles, Nici and the oud. 'The woman my father married (she could not bring herself to call Costansa any kind of mother) had me falsely accused of theft. After getting my father to whip me (she would not show the scar that still remained) she hired a murderer. Gilles, my mother's loyal servant and mine, helped me fool them, let them think I was dead, so that I could escape with the oud, the lute my mother passed down to me while still alive. The dog was no good with the sheep and he ran away too, followed me. They cut off Gilles' right hand for theft he never committed. She did that. So he followed me too.'

Even in her imagination, Estela could hear the laughter, see Costansa's victorious smile. Nobody would believe such vicious schemes weren't the invention of a jealous stepdaughter. The worst of it was that, were she judging the case, she would find against herself.

Since her mother's death, Gilles was a bondsman of the Lord of Montbrun, who undoubtedly owned Nici (though he had no chance of mastering the dog!). There was no chance of reaching her father's conscience. He had long believed everything Costansa told him and doted on her – what man wouldn't!

The law and justice were very different matters; Dragonetz and

Estela were united in choosing justice. They quickly agreed on their immediate action and help came from an unexpected quarter. After consulting Malik, Ramon was sending Petronilla back to Barcelone while her pregnancy was in its safest stage for the journey. On the surface, this was merely a husband protecting his wife and child.

In the power game below the surface, it was an interesting move. Although this would split his army, it would strengthen his position, should there be armed conflict. No general fought better with his pregnant wife on the battlefield.

Bringing her with him had been a declaration of peace; sending her home, however good the excuse, left him ready for war. The nobles summoned to make obeisance at Les Baux could be asked to show exactly who their allegiance was to, without Petronilla tempering Ramon's response.

If there was an extra wagon accompanying the Queen's party, with a one-handed man-at-arms who knew how to use both sword and dagger, so much the better from Barcelone's point of view. Nobody need ask any questions about the others in the wagon, nor why they would all leave the main party north of Marselha.

'Won't you go with them?' Dragonetz asked her, for the third time. 'I would feel happier knowing you were safe.' Like Ramon, better able to wage war if need be, thought Estela. But she was not Petronilla. The girl-queen had also pleaded with Estela to accompany her, not realising what extra motives the troubadour had for being tempted. To go south with the mother-to-be, away from these tensions and beside her own toddler, free as a peasant. To leave Dragonetz and run away from Costansa.

'No. I won't leave you and I won't run away.'

'You're making it more difficult for me!'

She had a twinge of guilt but not enough to become someone else, a scared girl on the run with only her oud and a large white dog. She didn't even have her oud! But she was not that girl any more. She summoned a smile for him. 'I must fight my own battles, my Lord, but I own it's good to have Talharcant guarding my back.' She could say no more, crushed against him.

'At least Musca will be out of harm's way,' he murmured. 'And Gilles will be only too pleased.'

Estela struggled out of his embrace. 'How so? He has a lady-love here so I can't imagine he wants to go back to our villa. I thought it might be Lady Sancha,' she confided. 'I don't know what to say to him if it is!'

Dragonetz laughed freely. 'You are backing the wrong horse completely – Sancha *has* found the man of her dreams but it's not Gilles. Nor does Gilles lust after her.'

'Who then?' Estela reflected quickly. It must be someone in Petronilla's train because Dragonetz had said Gilles would be happy going with them. Someone with them... then it dawned on her.

'Prima!' she exclaimed.

'Quite,' Dragonetz teased her. 'You haven't noticed the dalliance going on right under your eyes, with your own child for witness. Tsk tsk. Hardly the perfect mistress, are you.'

She flirted a glance under long lashes. 'That's not what I've been told, my Lord. But God's body! Prima! That's not such a bad thing, you know.'

'No,' he agreed cheerfully. 'We'd have had the devil's own job to get him to leave you otherwise and it's still going to be hard. Won't you...?'

'No!' she said but somehow her heart felt lighter. Whatever came, she and Dragonetz would stand against it, together. Musca, Gilles, Prima – with her own son – and, of course, Nici, would be safe and happy in the villa. All that remained was for her to be suitably astonished on hearing that her manservant and her dog had taken flight – and to announce that the child had taken colicky so he and his Nurse had withdrawn to healthier air.

'Isn't that the truth!' observed Dragonetz. 'And you can borrow my lute,' he promised as he kissed her.

As predicted, Gilles did not want to leave Estela. He accepted the need to protect Musca but was fiercer than Dragonetz in challenging her reasons for staying at Les Baux herself. The notion of her supporting Dragonetz was ridiculed and Estela could visualise her lover nodding in agreement as Gilles lectured her on how she would be a hindrance, a woman in a war zone; how Ramon had more sense; how Etiennette no longer counted as a woman because her death would be irrelevant – she couldn't fight and her four sons were man enough to make their own lives. Unlike Musca.

Estela smelled the toddler who wriggled in her arms, his black hair warm, rosemary in sunshine. Sleepy with milk, Musca snuggled into her breast, contented and safe. She would do anything to protect this love child: die, kill – or leave him go. She could not tell Gilles that she had to prove something to herself, that she could not run away from Costansa a second time, that she was an adult now.

The last thing she wanted was for Gilles to feel that *he* was running away, however sensible that might be, given his status. She wanted him and Musca hidden far away from the woman who'd married her father – and, however feeble it might be to care, she wanted Nici safe too. The dog had been her friend when she had nobody, when she *was* nobody, and he had never let her down.

She could just give him the order but she owed Gilles the courtesy of an argument he could accept. 'She will find me, Gilles. You know she will. If Musca is out of sight, she will concentrate all her hate on me. You can keep Musca hidden and safe but no-one can hide me any more.' It was true and Gilles knew it. Roxie de Montbrun could have hidden but not the troubairitz, Estela de Matin. The more acclaim she received, the more her movements would be public knowledge, easy to track.

'Raoulf accepted this, when my brother tracked us down,' she reminded him, 'and Dragonetz' man is no coward, nor disloyal to me.' She paused, let him think about the last time, the attempts on Musca's life that all too-nearly succeeded, then she delivered the coup de grâce. 'If you really don't feel up to defending Prima and Musca, I can send Raoulf instead.'

'I'll go,' he said instantly and she tried not to smile. The thought of Raoulf and Prima thrown together again, like a family, had obviously clinched matters. *Thank you, Dragonetz!* 'Thank you,' she said aloud. 'Make as little fuss as possible in departing. Just blend in with Petronilla's train. I must say goodbye now so as not to draw attention to you. And you'll need a leather muzzle and rope.'

'I remember,' Gilles said grimly. 'That's something Raoulf can help with.' This time, Estela did smile, remembering Musca's birth and Nici's reluctance to leave his mistress. She left Gilles to make his arrangements while she made hers.

On finding Prima, Estela gave her sleepy child to the nurse and picked up his foster-brother for some attention. She might have to act like a noblewoman in bringing up Musca but she saw no reason to deny simple affection to the little peasant who'd shared his milk from birth.

Little Primo had benefited from the comforts in which Prima lived and he was chubby-cheeked with health. Anyone might have mistaken the two boys for blood brothers and watching Primo cuddle up to Estela, the affection for both mothers would have left doubts as to who had birthed which child.

Prima still looked a bit peaky but she didn't dislike the idea of going back to the villa with the children. The further away from Raoulf the better, judged Estela, hoping that the whey-face wasn't a sign of being with child. That was a complication they could all do without, Prima included.

There would be a last chance to hold Musca again at bedtime but after that Estela would let go, without drama. She was a wise enough mother to know that the more fuss she made, the more likely she was to upset the child. The more ordinary the day seemed, the more relaxed both children would be.

There was one more adieu to say and Estela couldn't resist burying her face in the deep, white fur, then running her fingers along the side of Nici's face as she whispered in his ear the same words she'd used once before, the time her dog had saved her son's life: 'Take care of Musca for me.'

As long as Costansa thought there would be a trial and that she could hurt Estela – and Nici – more by taking him back to Montbrun, there would be no attempts at poison or 'accidental death'.

Nici was allowed one last evening under the trestle table, scavenging for scraps and titbits. Then he lay snoring, peacefully replete, while his mistress sang of a heroic horse called 'Stupid' and defiantly plucked her borrowed lute, in front of an audience that included her father and her stepmother.

Constansa's attempts at spiteful comments during the song were shushed by her neighbours and even she had to accept that she was outnumbered. The best she could manage was a noisy exit in the middle of an emotional verse but the audience closed ranks behind her as if she'd never been in the hall, and she wasn't missed.

Dragonetz was the only one in the hall who could hear the change in Estela's singing and playing when Costansa had gone; every breath in the right place, the phrasing natural and every note true, of voice and lute – a victory song.

He'd had a minor victory of his own during another meal that filled the eye and stomach to bursting. A word with Etiennette had made sure that the Montbruns' suit was scheduled for three days hence and he'd informed her that the subjects of it would be long gone by then. With disarming generosity, Etiennette had given support to her troubadour, within the letter of the law, while, at the same time, letting Estela's lover know that the offer of marriage was still open.

The Lady of Les Baux could not have judged her throw of the dice better; Dragonetz owed her a favour and she'd shown that marrying Provence did not mean losing Estela. To the contrary: Estela was benefiting from Les Baux's protection and doing what she loved best – performing in front of one of the most refined audiences in Christendom, earning praise and honour.

Etiennette's unspoken message was clear: *'Marry me and your lady can only profit. I accept and I will respect your mistress, with no jealous fits. Marry me and you lose nothing. Marry me and you save Provence.'* Every exchange between Dragonetz and Etiennette led to this conclusion.

But it was her conclusion, not his, so he said, 'Perhaps an entertainment, outdoors, is in order? One that will keep the ladies amused as well as their lords?'

Eyes narrowed, Etiennette looked at him and waited.

'I believe Les Baux prides itself on the finest hawks in Provence? Why don't we test them? Offer the Comte de Barcelone some distraction after his wife's departure? And afford entertainment for those ladies who have accompanied their lords to what must be some tedious business of oaths and fealty.'

Etiennette nodded, her eyes sparkling with understanding. A way to keep the Montbrun woman too busy to vent her rage over a cancelled lawsuit.

Dragonetz turned to Hugues, who was nursing a full cup of wine, not his first. 'My Lord, what say you to a hawking expedition this week? Show the Comte de Barcelone the quality of your mews?' according to Dragonetz' source, his pigeon-keeper and ex-falconer, hawking was one of the skills in which Hugues would show to advantage, especially on home territory.

The young man's eyes brightened instinctively at the prospect then chilled, sullen once more. 'As you wish,' was his curt reply. No doubt he was chewing over some insult from a Porcelet. Although constrained by larger politics (and probably by orders from Ramon and Etiennette) petty acts of spite between the rival families were a daily occurrence: horse dung on a sword hilt or flies in a wine goblet. Like Ramon and Etiennette, Dragonetz turned a blind eye and just hoped Hugues could keep some sense of perspective.

Undaunted, Dragonetz put the proposal to Ramon, who accepted the invitation with a ready smile. Shrugging off Hugues' mood – he had so many! – Dragonetz withdrew into his own thoughts. Although he knew how to busy himself, he could not forget that his son was leaving the next day; leaving for safety, yes, but that didn't prevent the absence aching. For the last two months, his nights had been accompanied by the chirrups and bubbles of babies' sleep noises.

He and Estela had the luxury of watching over their son together, hearing his vocabulary expand from 'Icky' to 'Mar', 'Par', 'Pweem' for Prima and of course, like every small child, 'volt' for 'want.' Sometimes, these distractions from the importance of his task had irritated Dragonetz, although he knew Estela had tried her best to spare him domestic trivia and Prima was an excellent nurse.

Now that the children were leaving, Dragonetz knew that he would miss the daily treasures they had offered him: Estela singing a bedtime song of love and nonsense as she rocked Musca's cradle; the smile of wild pleasure on his son's face when thrown in the air; the appearance of black hair and dark eyes that promised a true baby Dragon.

What would his grandfather make of the boy? As Aliénor's Commander, Lord Dragon was no doubt busy in Aquitaine. Dragonetz had been too busy himself to wonder what problems his liege lord and his sire might face. More thoughts to be dismissed. He was still too busy.

The next day, he would oversee the departure of Petronilla's expedition. It was safer if Estela went nowhere near the company but nobody would give a second glance if Dragonetz gave last minute instructions to John Halfpenny, who was heading back to Marselha accompanied by three crates of pigeons; one for his own use. Nobody would know if Dragonetz lingered in adieus with those who shared Halfpenny's wagon.

God willing, he would be able to reassure Estela that all had gone smoothly and then he would spend time at the stables. The hunt would need careful planning for horse, hawks and hounds, just the thing to lift Hugues out of his doldrums. It might even draw him close to Ramon, in an enthusiasm where they could both show expertise without having to compete. Dragonetz would then be able to build on any complicity between the two leaders in his plans for the tourney.

Costansa would certainly accept an invitation and Estela would not be given one. His mood was almost light-hearted, smug at outwitting Costansa, protecting his family and keeping the storms at bay in the castle but he should have known from experience: every victory has its price.

CHAPTER SEVENTEEN

Nature established a certain purgation especially for women, that is, the menses, to temper their poverty of heat. The common people call the menses 'the flowers', because just as trees do not bring forth fruit without flowers, so women without their flowers are cheated of the ability to conceive. This purgation occurs in women just as nocturnal emission happens to men. For nature, if burdened by certain humors, either in men or in women, always tries to expel its yoke and reduce its labor.

The Trotula, On the Condition of Women

After her lover left, early in the morning as usual, Estela went back to sleep. She was so heavy-headed she barely stirred as Prima took the children and their boxes, hushed them through the door. Nici had already been secured in a stable, ready for the journey.

Hooves thundered, pounding babies to dust, and the elfin woman laughed, tinkling, evil. Her ringed fingers glittered as she pulled on long silk scarves, floating, attached to the limbs of a shadowy hulk.

Jerking into movement as the woman pulled her scarves, the man came after Estela. She ran and ran but he was always in front of her. She turned and he was behind her.

She turned again, felt a touch on her neck, cold as death. She would not look... but she had to face him, had to. The touch squeezed round her neck, another scarf, blood red but she turned anyway and as her life ebbed she saw the man's face, flames licking up blackened skin, a hole for a mouth, a hole through which his tongue forked at her.

'Sister,' he hissed. 'Knowing you gets people killed. Whore.'

And Estela started awake, sweating. She began to shake. Her teeth chattered and the chill spread through her bones, making her back and neck ache. She felt nauseous and her head span as she tried to self-diagnose. She couldn't even think of the right word. 'Balance… cold…' she murmured, 'but no fever.' Surely there was a remedy among Nicholaus' compounds but first she would have to decide what she was treating. 'Poison?' Waves of shivering racked her body. If poison she didn't have to think to know who was to blame. 'Vergichtiget,' she suddenly remembered von Bingen's term for someone in whom the humors had become unbalanced, someone who was falling apart mentally and physically, someone who needed help.

Teeth chattering, she wrapped the bedcover round her and staggered to the door. She must have looked a madwoman, barefoot on the flags, peering into the darkness, but she didn't care. She spotted a page at the end of the corridor and stuttered, 'Boy, I need a message taken.' Well-trained, the lad came to her and followed orders.

Within minutes that seemed like hours, Malik was at her bedside with his precious box of herbs. He pulled her winter rabbit-skin cloak out of the trunk and added it to the coverlet, wrapping her in warmth.

'Poison,' she said, in between waves of shivering, 'need to know what… can't help otherwise.'

Malik felt her forehead, looked at her eyes, asked her as one healer to another, 'How long since your last menses?'

'I don't know,' she stammered. 'Not so long as to think I'm with child but probably a long month.'

He nodded. 'Too long for the extra strain you're under. You need to be purged. This is not physical poison but imbalance.'

His eyes were full of pity and his physician's voice was soothing as he told her, 'You have used up all your heat to be strong in mind and your body cannot fuel this mental battle any longer. You need to stay in bed. You need sleep. You need to bleed the excess cold away. If your menses do not come soon, naturally, then we should draw blood.'

'Nature will bleed me, I know she will. I can feel the churning inside that I always get beforehand. I'll take a draught, sleep but please, Malik, not the poppy.' Estela struggled to say why not but she didn't have to. Malik had been with her when Dragonetz had been at his lowest from addiction.

'Valerian,' Malik reassured her, 'and herbs for heat.'

She was too cold and tired to even ask him which herbs but still she struggled against this confinement. 'I'm not afraid of her! I'm not Roxie any more!'

'You have proved that, Estela, in front of a hallfull of witnesses. You sang in front of her and she couldn't bear your success. You don't have to keep proving yourself. Your body says 'enough' and you must obey.'

'She'll think I'm afraid.' Estela could feel the tears about to come and she knew it wasn't about what Costansa would think. She *was* afraid. She had failed. She would always be little Roxie.

'She will think you have an ague because that is what we will tell her.' Estela squeezed her eyes shut but she felt the trickle running down her cheek to dampen her pillow. 'Fear,' said Malik softly, 'can save a man's life in battle. As your general in this battlefield, I order you to rest.'

Whether it was the valerian or her own weakness, Estela gave in. The bed was downy soft; the smell of warm furs made her feel as if she was wrapped up in Nici's protection. No need to be brave any more. Just lie here and cry when she felt like it, let her nose and eyes turn ugly red. No more pretending. The chamber echoed with the absence of baby-snuffles and dog-snores.

'I will send a friend to sit with you.'

'No!' Estela struggled through the fog, trying to raise up on her arms. Nobody could see her like this. Nobody.

'Sancha,' said Malik.

Yes, Sancha. No need to pretend with Sancha. 'Yes,' she murmured aloud, sinking back down onto the pillow. 'Not Dragonetz. Tell Dragonetz... ague, too dangerous for him to be ill, Les Baux needs him, stay away till I'm better.' Then Estela abandoned self-control completely and sank into dreamless oblivion.

Drifting in and out of consciousness, Estela was aware of a hand smoothing her forehead, re-arranging her coverlet to keep her warm and placing water within reach. The rustle of silks and tenderness awoke old memories. 'Mare,' she murmured but even as she said the word she knew the scent of over-sweet violets could not be her mother.

'Sancha,' the gravelly voice replied. 'I'm here. Ask me for anything.' And the rustling silks arranged themselves gracefully on a stool by Estela's bedside, a large hand extended to squeeze Estela's briefly, then tuck it carefully under the rabbit furs.

Large it might be but that same hand was more dextrous with crewel and wool than Estela's would ever be. Through half-closed eyes, Estela could see the flash and dive of the needle as Sancha's neat stitches worked a flower, a purple iris, the kind that grew wild in Provence. There was a song in that too, Estela mused, every bit as important as knights and battles; the rhythmic glint and stab, artisan beauty that calloused the hand and offered wayside flowers to the heart... lilies of the field... why did the banner of France use lilies? Not royal, lilies... and her eyes closed again.

'How is she?' whispered a much loved voice from the doorway.

'She sleeps,' Sancha whispered back.

'She's much better, thank you!' Estela informed them. 'But don't come nearer! I don't want you catching it!'

Across the distance between bed and door, she could feel his relief. 'Petronilla has gone. There were no problems.'

'I gave her a list, herbs for her women to give, things she should do. There will be healers when she gets home.' Estela let go of her responsibility for her patient. Others closer to her heart were more at risk.

Astute as always, Sancha asked, 'Do you want a private word?' Their political disagreements hung in the air.

'No,' said Estela, and the air cleared. Three old friends, who had been through hard times together, shared some more.

'He blew a bubble for me and cooed like a pigeon,' Dragonetz informed them.

Estela smiled weakly. 'Yes, he would.'

'Nici was in a furry sulk and Gilles had much the same expression, for the same reason. They'll be fine.'

'I know.'

'Gilles promised he'd send word when he's home.'

'Pigeon.' It was a statement.

'Told you those birds would be worth it.'

She didn't have to open her eyes to see the mischief in his grin. 'Nothing would make up for the smell of bird droppings all winter!'

'Get better.'

'I'll be fine. Go and do things with men and swords.'

'Horses and hawks,' he corrected.

'It's tomorrow?'

'The day after. The day the hearing should have been.'

'When will *she* be told the hearing is cancelled, that they've gone?'

'The morning of the hunt. Give her no time to think about it or look for you. Etiennette doesn't want that sort of trouble stirred up in her court by guests. There's enough for her to deal with.'

'I'm sorry. I brought this mess and you're the one dealing with it. You and Etiennette. Thank you.' Estela was too weary to say more.

Dragonetz just shook his head, blew her a kiss, repeated, 'Get better,' and left them.

The next time she awoke, Estela felt hungry and once she'd started on the goat cheese, her appetite returned. If the goat girl only knew, she could add it to the praise sung by her father in the fields. Wayside flowers, cheese and goat girls. Would they exist at all without the protection of men and swords? Avoiding that line of thought, Estela looked at the woman nursing her, tried to remember her first impressions of Sancha but they were lost beneath the inside view of friendship.

When Estela looked at her friend, she saw a mother's tenderness, a friend's loyalty and a feminine sensibility that she herself lacked. How long had it been since she'd known a woman's touch, other than that of a maid? Not since her mother died, she admitted. A decade then. She struggled to talk like women do.

'You don't mind about Gilles?'

Sancha looked up from her embroidery, her overplucked brows already arched in permanent surprise that could not be heightened. 'Gilles? Leaving, you mean? To protect him I suppose. Why would I mind?'

'I thought, maybe, you... and he...'

'I think Gilles has given his heart elsewhere.' Sancha laughed. 'And there is compensation in his journey, I take it.'

'Everybody seems to have noticed but me,' grumbled Estela. 'I thought you were behaving... as if some-one were making love to you.' *Skittish, idiotically distracted, not interested any more in Dragonetz,* was what she didn't say. 'Looks like I'm wrong again.'

Was Sancha really blushing and hanging her head, being – there was only one word for it – sheepish? 'You are not wrong.'

'I don't believe it!' Estela sat bolt upright, dropping crumbs all over the coverlet. 'You have a lover! And you love him!'

'Is that so hard to believe?' Sancha asked, coy, frowning at her crewel work.

Estela feared for the flower. She hesitated. 'I know you were married. I know you are warm, and talented and so much more lady-like than I am but not – as other women – in body.'

The rest came out in a rush. 'I don't know how a man would react to knowing you, fully. Whether it would be a shock.' It was her turn to blush and Sancha's to hesitate, while the needle regained its sureness and rhythm. Estela blamed her medication. Had she really just asked Sancha to explain the mechanics of her carnal relations?

'I was born into the wrong body,' Sancha stated simply. 'Once I accepted that, I put it right, on the outside. Became a story that my family told, of a brother dead in the Holy Land and his sister who came back alive. If any remembered that there had never been a sister, nobody was fool enough to say so. They never knew the man I married Oltra mar.'

'Dragonetz told me,' Estela said softly. The last thing she wanted was to make her friend relive the manner of her widowhood.

Sancha nodded. 'He makes me feel like a girl again.'

'He?' Estela prompted gently.

'Lord Vinse.' Sancha flushed beetroot as she pronounced the name.

Estela frowned. 'I don't want you to be hurt. Is he married? If he is, you shouldn't dally with him. If he isn't, he'll want a good alliance – I suppose you offer that, with your lands in Provence – and he'll want heirs. You can't marry him without letting him know… Sancha, you just can't! Imagine your wedding night!'

Her friend guffawed in a most unladylike manner. 'Now who sounds like whose mother! You sing of it all the time but it has never crossed your mind that a man and a woman might enjoy courtship and courtesy, favours and kisses, knowing that it can never be anything more?'

Estela considered the matter briefly. 'No,' she decided. 'One or the other will always want more. Usually both.'

Sancha laughed again. 'Then we must prove you wrong, my troubadour sans romance. I am very very happy with my knight's attentions and if he enjoys languishing as much as he says, then we are well-matched and may last longer as a couple than many who sate their lust.'

'We shall see.' Estela could feel her mouth pursing and knew she sounded more like a granddam than a mother but she couldn't help it. Romance indeed. There had obviously been another sleeping draught in her water because a wave of weariness took away any impulse to argue further.

'Sleep,' suggested Sancha, taking away the plate and cup,

arranging the coverlets, returning to her embroidery with a little smile that owed nothing to her care for Estela.

Black enfolded her, the next time Estela woke, and she panicked at the shadows until her eyes adjusted and the husky voice soothed her, 'It's all right. I'm here. I can light a candle if you wish?'

'No need. It would be a waste. But you must sleep too.' Estela felt the panic rising at the thought of Sancha leaving the room, leaving her alone with burnt men in shadows. She could not bear the thought of being left alone, nor of a servant, some stranger witnessing her weakness. Least of all did she want Dragonetz distracted by worries over her, not after all she'd said to persuade him to let her stay.

'Share my bed,' she said. 'Stay with me and sleep. There is room for both of us.' There was also room for love that was not romance nor desire but the simple comfort of friendship. Estela woke a few times in the night, with that same moment's anxiety, but her friend's breathing, regular as a needle through linen, kept the fears at bay.

One time when she woke, she sensed Sancha was awake too. The night favoured the sharing of truths that the day preferred to stay hidden. 'It doesn't go away, does it,' Estela whispered. 'You think you've grown out of it, that you've become strong but there's always part of you that's a scared little girl, when you see the person who did it.'

'No, it never goes away.' The disembodied voice in the dark was heavy with its own memories. 'Do you know how pearls are made?'

'Pearls? No.'

'Dirt gets into a shell and alchemy turns it to a thing of precious beauty. The dirt changes.'

'Will it take long for the magic to happen?'

'No, child. Anyone who sees you knows the magic has happened. You just don't know it yet.'

Then they slept side by side, comfortable and warm, while, alone and awake in his chamber, Dragonetz fretted over the weight and hunger of a hundred birds of prey.

CHAPTER EIGHTEEN

The hawk (habich)... knows other birds and understands their nature.
Following what it knows about them, it traps and seizes them... The feathers of
the hawk are not good for beds or cushions. If anyone were to lie on them, he
would sleep deeply only with difficulty.

Physica, Birds

The switch from bright sunlight to dim mews was made even more disconcerting by the shuffling of a thousand feathers, the click of talons on wooden perches, the stink of carrion and of regurgitated pellets dropped on sand. As his eyes adjusted to the dark, Dragonetz could see the ranks of hunting birds, organised in some combination of size and good neighbourliness that was no doubt carefully monitored by the man who came in behind him.

A harrier was on his shoulder, presumably still in training, for his eyes were sealed. The falconer loosened the thread as he moved the hawk from his human perch to the wooden one and deftly fastened leash through the jess rings. The harrier peeked through half-closed eyes and then relaxed in near-darkness amid the shifting chirrups of familiar voices.

'She'll be a good 'un,' was Moisset's verdict. 'Took her through the streets all morning and she only bated twice. Once was some fat wife with lungs like a bugle. Second time was at the church bells. She'll be unstitched within a week if I get another two days walking her in crowds.'

'How is she on horseback? Did she bate at first?' Dragonetz knew exactly how a man's shoulder would ache after a bird that size panicked and tried to fly, ripping and tearing its perch-turned-prison, even with padded leather between flesh and talon. He might have been tempted by the harrier had the bird been further on in training but he already had his mind set on a different hawk.

'First time, yes. First time with dogs too. Depends on her handler now. Any bird will bate at something new but if'n she's well-trained and fed right, once that bird is tied to you, she should accept 'most anything if her perch is there and food comes after she works.'

Fed right was the crux of the matter. Moisset had not been happy with two days' notice of a large hunting-party, including Les Baux's finest lords and guests. His pride at stake, he'd explained at length to Dragonetz how he couldn't suddenly starve his birds but they'd be lost for good unless they went out hungry. Not to mention the fact that the birds were only just past the moulting season, when everyone knew it was rash to fly them.

Knowing when a bird was in yarak, the right weight and condition to fly, was a fine judgement that came from years of experience. After enough compliments to smooth his ruffled feathers, Moisset had promised fifty birds – but which they'd be, he'd need time to judge and to discuss with the falconer. Moisset himself was an austringer, specialising in the hawks of the fist rather than the hawks of the tower.

'I might put this one to the crane.' Moisset nodded at the harrier. 'We've broke the legs of one ready for training up new birds. Might be a bit soon but you can't always get the heron or crane to practise on. And if they don't build up confidence with one that's weakened and bloodied with liver to stir up their spirits, they'll never go for one in the wild.'

'I've heard no man is your equal in the training.'

'I know a trick or two. Too many austringers forget the dogs. If you don't train hound and hawk together, work with the Master of Hounds, you've but half a beast. As long as they're steady below hawks, horses are just mounts in our work, not like in hunting deer or boar.' Moisset cricked his neck back and forth to ease his shoulder after its weight-bearing exercise. 'Where did you hear that? About our mews being a fine example?' he asked, preening.

'Ais, Marselha… the hawks here are known.'

'Not just hawks. We have gyrfalons, peregrines, mostly female but some tiercels – all bred here. My Lady and my young Lord have sent as far as Nice to get a bird for the bloodline. And if some noble wants to make amends for a wrongful act, he knows exactly what will help Les Baux understand his plight and show mercy. We had a lovely little merlin just this week that solved a disagreement over land boundaries and helped my Lady judge what was fair.'

'And you've managed to bring enough birds to weight? In the time?'

'It'll maybe do but it wasn't easy.' Moisset shook his head. 'And another time I'll be pleased to have more warning for those sort of numbers, my Lord! Most of the mews in Christendom would still be stuck with moult so you're lucky to be with someone who can do the impossible!' Dragonetz looked suitably repentant. 'But yes, they'll be ready for the morrow, after noon. The ones ready are all on these perches.' He pointed to the left hand side, his moves measured from habit, no sudden gestures to startle his hawks. He flashed the knight a shrewd look. 'And you're the day before everyone else to choose your own bird, no doubt.'

'You have me.' Dragonetz laughed. 'And I have chosen.' Without looking, he could feel orange eyes fixed on his, a sheaf of white feathers in speckled; bigger than the harrier. 'I want her.' He walked to the one goshawk, sleek and deadly, on a right hand side perch.

Moisset's eyes narrowed. 'A goshawk's below your rank, my Lord. And she's not at weight. Why not a saker? This tiercel?' he indicated a male falcon smaller than the female I have one that flies sweet and straight, would suit your Lordship perfectly.'

'She seems perfectly at weight to me.' The goshawk gave a tiny shiver of pleasure as Dragonetz drew one leather-clad finger gently down the white breast, then again, and again. Her feathers fluffed out as she relaxed. 'We're river-hunting, not in the open. I don't want a bird that suits my rank; I want the best hunter. And I know this is the best one. I know because she's yours, isn't she.'

Moisset mumbled something that was probably an assent, however ungracious. He made one last try. 'What about a gyrfalcon?'

'You flatter me.' Dragonetz smiled. A gyrfalcon, fit for a king. 'But I'd rather have that goshawk.'

'Vertat,' muttered Moisset, giving in, 'she's called Vertat.'

Truth thought Dragonetz, admiring the goshawk again. She looked back at him, unblinking, deadly. Truth indeed.

'And how many others will be wanted?'

'About two hundred in the party but a hundred birds will be enough. They'll be collected before mid-afternoon tomorrow. I'll take Vertat tonight, let her get to know me.'

'She'll want a morsel before sundown then nothing.' Moisset was obviously reluctant to entrust care of the goshawk to Dragonetz.

'I'd let you do it yourself but you'll have your work cut out here.' Dragonetz had a sudden inspiration. 'Bran was your apprentice before I took him for pigeon-keeper. What if he looks after the goshawk while she's with me?'

The relief was evident in Moisset's face. 'Aye my Lord. He's a good boy. That would be better...'

Dragonetz grinned at the lack of faith in lords. 'What about my Lords of Baux and of Barcelone?'

The man bristled. 'My young Lord's falcon is well out of sight, my Lord! You might have netted my goshawk but no man will fly Lord Hugues' saker but himself! And the Prince of Barcelone – God curse him!' Moisset swore automatically and spat, then made the sign against the devil, '—he knows a good bird when he sees one.

Lord Hugues brought Barcelone to the mews and made a choice for him that nobody would refuse who knows his birds. Fit for his station too.' He glared at Dragonetz who was unabashed at the implied criticism. He was also pleasantly surprised at Hugues' mature courtesy to his guest. Perhaps there was hope for him after all.

'He'll be singing the praise of Les Baux hawks after tomorrow, that's for sure. As shall I,' Dragonetz demurred.

'That's as may be.' Tight-lipped. 'But Barcelone's and my Lord's are well away from prying eyes and no man else will have them,' continued Moisset, who apparently saw no contradiction between hating Barcelone on principle and providing him with a fine hawk.

'You do your Lord proud,' Dragonetz told him, 'both in your loyalty and your skills. I'm sure you keep abreast of modern methods. What do you think of this Jewish notion for silvered talons?'

The chance to talk of his passion brightened Moisset's eyes and loosened his tongue. 'I've heard of it,' he began. 'There's a Jew in the north –'

'Rabbenu Tam,' nodded Dragonetz.

'That's him. For all he's a heathen, he knows a thing or two about hunting. What I've been telling the apprentices is that everything comes at a price.' He was obviously launching into a well-rehearsed speech but Dragonetz could always find the patience to listen to someone who knew his craft. Amongst the parts he knew would always be something he didn't – and which might prove invaluable in the future.

'A great hunter never wants to let go. If we've trained 'em right then trading ready-meat for prey will do it most of the time but when you get a big one like a goshawk, and she has a mood on her, she just will not let go. Then what, I ask them? And the man that can answer me shall have my job for I'm sure I don't know!

But then this Jew, Rabby-whomsoever, says try gloves on the bird itself. Not just any gloves but silver ones. Never tried it myself but they say it lets the hawk catch prey but not dig its claws in. Now that would be useful! And keeps the Jews happy too. They have right funny laws about food, you know.'

A sudden horrible thought struck Moisset. 'Saints preserve us – there's no Jews in the party is there?'

'No,' Dragonetz reassured him, well aware of the complications that would bring.

'You never know these days.' Moisset shook his head. 'You can't even tell them apart from us in the street. Everywhere, they are, come up from the south – and not short of moneybags. Easy enough to recognise the Moors though!' He laughed. Then reflected. 'That Moorish lieutenant of Barcelone's – will he be wanting a hawk?'

'He might well be. And make sure it's one of your best. Do this right and you'll get enough silver to make and test out those talon covers.'

As discussion rambled round training (the best in Provence if not Christendom) and the quality of apprentices (not up to the old days), Dragonetz ensured that sufficient jesses and bells were neither fretted nor rusted. He checked that sufficient pouches with meat scraps would be prepared.

Then he took his goshawk on his shoulder and left for the kennels, where he had a similar discussion, but this time involving running-hounds and spaniels, beaters and dog-boys. It was also a chance to test Vertat's stress levels amidst a kennelful of barks and scuffles.

Only the three lymers remained silent, the tracker-dogs, trained to keep their noses to the ground and their thoughts to themselves. No need for lymers on a hawking expedition but Dragonetz was pleased to see that the quality of kennels maintained by Hugues was a match for the mews. Ramon might have better horseflesh but otherwise Les Baux could offer princely sport.

Dragonetz was also pleased with his hawk's indifference. If Vertat's presence tended towards brooding, then that made two of them, he thought. There was something oddly comforting about the weight of Truth, like the guardian angel in an allegorical painting – or of course like the demon familiar depicted on the other shoulder. He would summon Bran, arrange a perch and the goshawk could stay in his chamber that night, where they could both dream of hunting.

The morrow would show Costansa she had no power at Les Baux and the afternoon's entertainment would keep her away from Estela.

There was no doubt his lover would recover from her illness sooner if left in peace. As long as Hugues continued to play the role of good host and the game was plentiful, a fine day's sport was in prospect for all.

All morning, hawks and falcons toured the cobbled streets of Les Baux on human perches, either with servants or, in the case of real afficionados, the masters themselves. Dragonetz had worn Vertat like a cloak brooch since dawn, talking softly to her, learning her foibles.

Typical of a yeoman's hawk, she was solid amid noise, even sudden shouts or clanking: less steady visually. A sudden downpour of slops from a window startled her and a swirl of a silk cloak flicking at her side caused her to bate. The full weight of anxious hawk, digging heels into his shoulder and beating her great wings in an attempt at flight was a bruising experience. Even more than a horse, she saw movement so far around that it was behind them, out of Dragonetz' periphery.

'Later girl, later,' Dragonetz soothed, and she calmed to his murmured compliments. He could sense the muscle and hunger, in perfect yarak. Moisset would have approved her preparation.

The minuscule portion of bloody meat which Dragonetz gave her, supervised by Bran, was just enough to take the rawness off her famine but not enough to dull her for the day's work. She would be ravenous by the afternoon and his own senses heightened as he focused on his hawk. In the castle walkways with pages scurrying, in the crowds of street vendors, there were only the two of them. He felt her heartbeat quicken and slow.

He visited the stables, made sure Sadeek would be readied for him, met the lad's hesitation and understood. He even did the stable-boy the courtesy of an explanation. 'I know. A destrier for a hawking party is like wearing cloth of gold to till soil. But Sadeek is Arab bred, knows hawk as well as he knows fancy footsteps and has no more fear of bog than of battle. This is a pleasure outing with no risk to my friend.' He stroked the arch of satin neck.

The boy's eyes shone, reminding Dragonetz of another boy, in another land, his protégé Muganni. A pang of loss and regret. Perhaps he should have brought the boy with him instead of freeing him to rejoin his tribe of Hashashins. Few were born with such a voice and even fewer came through a man's changes to find their new voice pleasing. The fleeting sweetness of youth...

Shaking off his nostalgia, and earning a reprimand from Vertat, Dragonetz left the stable, happy with the encounter between hawk and stallion. As fully prepared as he could be, Dragonetz broke fast and rested in his chamber, not alone. The room's dark filled with another's breathing and heartbeat, a stir of feathers, a small 'chuff' of complaint and whenever he looked her way, the orange eyes of the goshawk stared him out.

What were the hunting verses of the Moorish poet Abu Nuwas? Horse, hawk and cheetah. There would be dogs instead of hunting cats but Dragonetz thought the poet would approve of Sadeek and Vertat, who looked every bit the 'demon spirit' of the Arab verse. Through darkness and closed eyelids, Dragonetz sensed the orange glare from under the furred eyebrows, as he fell asleep.

A light breeze offered some relief as the party rode through the great gate, confined to three or four abreast by the rocky path, as they rode south, down towards the marshes. Scarves fluttered and spurs glinted. Final numbers were well over a hundred horse and as many beaters, peasants taking time off their usual work to earn an extra penny.

Moisset had no doubt received a stream of visitors all morning to judge by the variety of hunting birds perched on every third person in the throng. Ladies had responded in force to the invitation, some riding pillion behind their lords, others riding astride, with falcons on their shoulders. The most seasoned huntresses wore duller, forest colours and serviceable circular skirts but there was no shortage of bright silks, sported by those who placed entertainment above sport.

The Master of Hounds had done his work too and Moisset grunted approval at the mixed pack which accompanied the beaters. When Dragonetz asked for spaniels, the fewterer had shaken his head at the failings of the breed. 'They're the best at flushing but the most quarrelsome. And they're as like to chase chickens around a cottage as head for the woods with you. Keep them leashed! After you've started up the game, you'll need something steadier to follow through and retrieve. With spaniels, game is the word! All's a game to spaniels! Take some running-hounds too.'

Dragonetz could see the three breeds; the bouncing vivacity of the liver and white spaniels, always ready to play; the tireless lope of the greyhound pairs, elegant and ready for work; and the rugged terriers. Beside him, in the vanguard, Hugues sounded his horn and the signal was conveyed back along the line, a simple 'onward' that made the heart beat faster and had the hounds yipping in anticipation.

Once out of the rocky ravine, riders regrouped, following beaters and hounds, spreading out across the marshland. Dragonetz identi-fied the various lords and was pleased to note the Porcelets splitting off with lesser bands. Although they might gain followers, that possi-bility was probably less dangerous than if they stayed near Hugues and Ramon. Les Baux wouldn't take much sparking to catch fire and a hunt always roused the blood. With less pleasure, Dragonetz noticed that Costansa had stayed with the royal party. If there was to be mischief, she would doubtless be its source.

Although hawking lacked the dangers of more manly hunts, Hugues and Ramon were both proud enough of their skills to have donned coarse garments in muted colours. Like Dragonetz's own jerkin, theirs had well padded shoulders and with reason. As they rode easily towards wherever the beaters chose to stand, the marsh creatures paused to stare. This was a new beast but not one that frightened the small beasts of field or scrub: the hunting trinity, man riding horse and hawk riding man, aroused no fear, unlike a man on his own two legs. The three men rode easily, in silent communion.

Dragonetz noted the qualities of the two sakers with approval. Hugues had indeed paid tribute to his guest and deserved respect for his fine taste. If Malik had flown a bird, it would doubtless have been a saker, as his people generally prized these falcons above all other hunting birds. Although smaller than the goshawk, both sakers were large females and the combination of speed and strength made them formidable hunters. They were also less prone to bad temper than goshawks.

As if reading his thoughts, Vertat shifted her weight from one foot to another, reclaiming his attention, reminding her perch that a goshawk could match a saker. Sadeek kept to the walking pace required, but with a hint of spring in each careful step. Horse and hawk tolerated each other, and neither balked when spaniels scampered too close. Horse, hawk and hounds. How could a man not thrill to the power of earth harnessed between his legs, and the power of air on his shoulder, ready to loose like an arrow, to recall like a familiar demon? This was true lordship, reading track and fewmet, acknowledging your own animal nature and controlling it. Loosing death as part of the great cycle of nature that was both man's pleasure and his responsibility.

'My Lord Dragonetz?' Etiennette's interruption made him frown but he recovered his courtesy instantly. Like her son, she was dressed more for practicality than for decoration, unlike the Lady of Montbrun. Costansa could have modelled for a Psalter illumination, an allegory of Love Divine.

Her golden hair was caught in a glittering net with a silk scarf fluttering. Her robe might have had a full skirt for riding astride but no man would have described it as practical. Royal blue and flimsy, the hem floating above a neat ankle, neckline deep and hinting at more than the lace beneath.

If she'd told the truth regarding her condition, then it added no more than some becoming curves to her delicate frame. Everything about Costansa suggested a summer butterfly, about to alight on a man's hand. Only her serviceable boots and her shoulder padding suggested that she was no novice in the sport of hawking. To judge from Hugues' gaze, hawking was not the sport foremost in his mind as he acknowledged the ladies.

'Mother. My Lady de Montbrun – your Lord is not joining us?' Dragonetz and Ramon exchanged glances, a shared smile, at youth, at lack of subtlety. Etiennette was not smiling.

'My Lord is fatigued and prefers to rest,' Costansa replied, reining in her grey palfrey beside Hugues' solid brown mare, and neatly forcing Sadeek to step further away. 'He has suffered a deep disappointment today and needs to recover.'

'I am sorry to hear that. We must ensure that you find solace in the day's sport.' Hugues' sincerity was unmistakeable.

'How could I not, in such company? But you are dressed to chase the hart, my Lord Hugues. I fear I have mistaken the game.' Costansa's meaning was equally clear, as the couple put enough distance between themselves and their entourage to allow privacy for a conversation that occasioned much mirth.

'You told her?' Dragonetz took the chance to speak to Etiennette.

'Aye. I sent word to the two of them. She and her puppet-husband were informed that the hearing is cancelled, with no grounds, given that the servant and stock have vanished without trace.' It was strange to hear Nici referred to as livestock and Dragonetz was surprised at how far he'd come to think of Estela's dog as a personality. It wasn't as if the dog was even a gentleman's breed like a greyhound. But of course, stock was the exact term – and stock belonging to Montbrun. 'Apparently she slapped the messenger – gave him a nose bleed.'

Another trill of girlish laughter reached them from the couple in front and Etiennette winced. 'I'm worried about Hugues.'

'You're his mother. Every young man grows beyond his mother.' Dragonetz felt a twinge of conscience, thinking of his own, of all she did not know, of Estela, of her grandson. He spoke with extra firmness. 'A dalliance is normal.'

'Not with her,' muttered Etiennette. 'And it's not just that. There's something more, something wrong.'

'Your men do you proud. This is as fine an expedition as I have ever seen' Ramon pulled his little al-Andalus mare up beside them. 'Where did you find your falconer?'

The compliment was irresistible and Dragonetz left the pair to discuss the staffing and provision required for top quality mews and kennels, where the debate could be more equal than over horses and stables; in equine matters Ramon had little to learn.

The beaters and dog-boys were spreading out under the capable direction of the Master of Hounds. Dragonetz recognised another familiar face and sighed. Another boy who wanted to be part of the day's excitement.

'Bran!' Dragonetz summoned the boy, who started his excuses in mid-trot.

'...you might need me for Vertat.' He lowered his voice. '... and you need have no worries. I left a boy in charge of the pigeon-loft, a good boy. He knows what to do if one of yours comes home.'

A message. Dragonetz' heart thumped. Yes, he was expecting a message. And then he need have no worries. 'Be off,' he told the lad, 'and if I need you, I'll call.' He smiled at the thought and at the exuberance of the small figure running back to his work.

As the small groups re-formed, Dragonetz was joined by Barcelone's lieutenant.

'How is she?' Dragonetz asked Malik.

'She will be well. The sooner these Montbruns leave the court, the better,' was the verdict.

'It's over now,' said Dragonetz. He was wrong.

CHAPTER NINETEEN

The sparrowhawk (sperwere) is hot, and happy, and quick in flight... A man or woman who burns with lust should take a sparrow hawk and, when it is dead, remove the feathers and throw away the head and viscera... The man should anoint his privy member and loins with (the unguent created) for five days. In a month the ardour of his lust will cease, with no danger to his body. The woman should anoint herself around the umbilicus, and in the opening of the belly button. Her ardor will cease within a month.

Physica, Birds

The young heir to Provence was a cipher to Dragonetz, silent and observant beside his uncle, the Regent and Protector. At fourteen, Berenguer the younger carried the weight of a province that was unsure whether it wanted him. For all Ramon's care, the youth must miss his father. He might as well be motherless too, as the widowed Béatrice had abandoned her son to his estate and taken her dowry of Montgeuil to a second marriage and a new life. No wonder that Petronilla had shown her affection for him, given all they had in common, including Ramon as a father figure.

It was also easy to understand why the boy's default expression was solemn, cold and reserved. It was therefore with some surprise that Dragonetz caught an expression of pure glee on the youngster's face as he pulled his horse up beside Malik and murmured to his sparrowhawk in southern dialect. He sat his horse as could be expected of one trained in Barcelone, controlling his lively mare as if by instinct. Malik's deeply lined features softened as the boy spoke to him.

'Is it far to the stand, Malik?'

'I don't think so. My friend, Lord Dragonetz, knows the terrain.'

A flicker of uncertainty dimmed the enthusiasm for a second but didn't prevent young Berenguer addressing Dragonetz directly, stammering a little and flushing. 'My Lord, I've seen you training the men and I wish I had your skills!'

His voice cracked into a squeak as he spoke and Dragonetz understood the real motives for the boy's silences, wondered once more what had happened to Muganni, the boy with an angel's voice. Maybe he too had reached the change. Better that than pay for that voice with his manhood, in the Arab way. At least Dragonetz had spared him that. And given him the diamond that ought to make the boy's future secure. The instinct to cross himself shook Dragonetz back to the present and this other boy, with a quite different future.

'We are nearly there,' he confirmed. 'We've left the four other parties behind so they won't set off our game, and our dog-boys and beaters will stand behind that copse.'

'Of course we have spaniels and greyhounds,' young Berenguer observed. 'But I've not seen hounds like those blues.'

'Terriers of local breeding,' Dragonetz told him. 'Sturdy running dogs though not as fast as the greyhounds; obedient and with the courage to aid the hawks at a hard kill. That blue-black coat is waterproof, makes them tough.'

'My uncle says all-black dogs are bad,' squeaked the boy. 'For dogs are warm and dry and in black dogs their colour is burned to naught, allowing of only cold and moisture, in which lie cowardice and evil.'

Surprised by the maturity of thought, Dragonetz reassessed the ruler-to-be. How easy it was to be misled by the surface, glittering like the marsh waters or dull as the dried reeds, when so much was going on below. 'Malik can better debate such matters than I.'

'As can the Lady Estela de Matin,' Malik reminded his friend.

Dragonetz felt a flash of irritation, as if he was being criticised for not giving sufficient credit to his lover's studies. Because of course he had not. Then he let his surroundings wash away such trivia.

The brackish water glinted among the reeds as the horses picked their way through shallow marais. The spaniels were leashed more tightly and their handlers tried to control the yapping exuberance but had more success with the braces of greyhounds. Making the most of what cover the wind-stunted trees offered, Hugues drew their party to a stand and they spread out enough to fly their hawks without tangling jesses. In the quiet of anticipation, the horses' snorts and the jingling of the hawks' bells mingled with the babble and squawk of birdlife. Not till the predatory silhouettes filled the skies would the alert be sounded across trees and water and by then it would be too late.

The riders eased past the copse where the fewterer signed instructions to dog-boys and beaters. The strange tripartite beasts formed of horse, human and hawk could advance further into the shallows, without causing alarm.

The hunters could even exchange words, laugh, without being perceived as human. Maybe they no longer were so, but rather part of the natural world, their animal selves to the fore. The more he listened, the more Dragonetz heard. Burbling of frogs in summer second mating frenzy; territorial squawk of a duck; soft splashes of vole or even otter; occasional bubble and rise of fish; a skylark rising.

He breathed evenly, channeling his thoughts along every ripple and splash, noting the song of the marshes, as yet only melody. The words would come later, when he was alone. Not alone, Vertat reminded him, shifting feet, heart pounding beneath speckled white feathers. What did she hear?

The moment before the hunt hung on the air. Even Costansa and the spaniels were quiet. Time stopped. It was like the moment in battle when you took responsibility for bringing death, the moment of

Truth, each man accepting his part in the greater workings of destiny. It was that place in each man beyond thought, a communion with bird and beast.

Von Bingen's words fitted themselves to the song of the marshes

'The will rises from here
gives flavour to the soul
and kindles the senses.'

Dragonetz heard the long-legged splash and stab of heron or crane as it speared fish; the huge beat of swan wings dropping to a clumsy landing. He opened his eyes and caught the splashing rise of a cormorant. It gulped down a slithering eel, into a throat that snaked double with its prey, lost the tail, then swallowed the whole. Dragonetz removed Vertat's hood.

Hugues signed to Dens and the spaniels rushed the covert, yapping and squabbling. They flushed a flurry of songbirds to the air, three partridges toddling and bouncing along the ground, some bobtails of rabbits scattering to holes and one hare. The disturbance carried a warning to the water, where the smaller birds, shelduck and water rails scudded to a rising flight. The hunters unloosed the lords of the air.

The falcons sped high and fast, beyond sight, diving like stones to take lark and thrush, ducks and all that flew in their path. The hawks took the ground prey, dispatching confused partridge with ease and chasing rabbits. Dragonetz walked Sadeek further into the water. He whispered words of blessing on the goshawk, his sword of air, then he flung Vertat out above the rippling water to do death's work.

The greyhounds were unbraced to help the birds at the kill, especially with the bigger prey, while the spaniels reverted to chasing each other round the scrubby bushes.

Concentrating on Vertat, who had perched as high as she could on a drowned tree, surveying her options, Dragonetz had little time to spare for observing others. He did however note that Hugues' saker had its claws in a crane and was bringing the huge bird into submission with help from a marbled blue setter. The young Comte de Provence was red-faced and bright-eyed, swinging the lure to recall his merlin, which carried a small brown bird, perhaps a lark, between its claws. There would be pies a-plenty at Les Baux the next day.

With a triumphant 'ark' Vertat claimed all Dragonetz' attention and his heart stopped, realising the goshawk's target. A lone swan swam kingly, ignoring the melée all around, far enough away to discount the threat as irrelevant. Like a quarrel from a crossbow, Vertat hit before the swan even realised the danger. As the hawk screamed and sank its talons into the swan's back, Dragonetz called 'Dens!' and the fewterer sent a speckled black terrier and a greyhound splashing to the bird's aid.

The greyhound reached the struggle first, snapped and ducked under the vicious beak while Vertat kept her perilous perch and prevented flight. Then the marbled terrier arrived, as furious and determined as the hawk.

Had Dragonetz trusted too much too quickly? He walked Sadeek closer to the flapping swan, saw it pecked to madness in the goshawk's implacable grip: walked closer to the blood-crazed hounds, which dodged two beaks while launching their own attack with teeth and claws. There was a real danger that the dogs would kill both hawk and swan – or die in trying. Dragonetz focused all his will on the goshawk, calling with his mind; with words, in a voice she had known for only one day; and with the outstretched gauntlet offering the only reward Vertat wanted: blood and bone. Marrow of crane and strips of chicken.

And she came. As suddenly as she'd struck, Vertat dropped the swan and came to her master's glove in a majestic swoop that did not go unnoticed.

'Bravo, Dragonetz!' cried the Comte de Provence, his little merlin back on one shoulder, hooded and leashed.

Hugues and Ramon, equally satisfied with their own hawks' performances, added shouts of congratulation, as Dens sent another hound to finish the swan and help retrieve the prey. Hunters were recalling their birds and praising others', satiated and yet also disappointed that the chase was over.

Dog-boys were retrieving dogs and game, bagging fur separately from feathers, tying the sacks to poles, ready for bearing back to Les Baux. Hugues blew the formal notes of hunt's end to let the other parties know they should wind up too. Dens gave the hounds their share of the catch, the curée, which the ladies watched, torn between horror and fascination. Dragonetz saw only the latter in Costansa's parted lips and gleaming eyes as she watched the dogs tear into the bloody innards.

Moisset and Bran were organising the pairs of beaters, carrying poles, and the dog-boys with their leashed hounds, when Bran suddenly looked skywards and yelled, 'Hood all hawks. Keep them tied and tight!'

Hugues reinforced the shout with the horn notes for 'Call in hounds and hawks', two short notes, three long, and then three longer. Those with horns repeated the message and those without shouted it along the group from one person to the next.

'Pigeon,' Bran shouted the one word of explanation and it too was passed on, as the hunters followed the falconer's gaze. Sure enough, a lone pigeon was winging a weary route overhead, easy target for any of the hunting birds, even those who'd worked hardest.

Dragonetz was the first to understand, then Hugues. They didn't need to see the tiny cylinder attached to its leg to realise what Bran, the pigeon-keeper had spotted. It was one of their pigeons returning to the castle coop, and, whatever the message, it was definitely both precious and private.

Batting tired wings, the carrier pigeon made its heavy way over the marsh, watched by all below. Most of the watchers must have wondered why anyone was interested in a pigeon, given the size of bags from the afternoon's sport.

White-faced, Hugues made an attempt to sound nonchalant. 'We use them for messages.'

Ramon was no sluggard. His tone had lost all the lightness of sport. 'From Trinquetaille perhaps.' He might as well have said *Full of treason and plotting against your Liege Lord.*

'Yes,' admitted Hugues, unable to do otherwise. So much for their secret line of communication.

'Oh dear, I am sorry.' A woman's voice dripped honey at the same time as a bolt dropped from the sky on the pigeon. Dragonetz didn't need to look at Costansa to know her shoulder was empty, her falcon loosed. If, as he suspected, the message was from Gilles, Costansa would have all the evidence she needed to pursue her lawsuit again.

Estela would face charges herself, as well as lose Nici and Gilles, and their fate didn't bear thinking about. Vertat was unhooded and flung to the attack quicker than thought. The peregrine had already gripped its prey, savaging the pigeon with its curved beak, when the heavier hawk slammed into the falcon, making it drop the wounded bird to the ground. The peregrine spiralled to gain height and attack the goshawk with its characteristic high-speed dive but the larger bird countered in clumsy swoops that disrupted the elegant arc.

'I wager ten denarii on the falcon,' cried out the Comte de Provence, radiant with excitement, unaware of the tensions around him.

'You'd lose.' Malik's deep tones supported his friend, understood more than a battle between birds.

'In the air, maybe,' contributed another lord, intrigued. 'The gentle falcon has the advantage of speed and impetus. But on the ground, I don't know. Goshawks lack nobility but their brute strength in cover might win the day.'

'Surely,' continued the Comte, in his untrustworthy squeak-and-bass of a voice, 'nobility will always win over commonality.'

Not this time, prayed Dragonetz, whose personal experience suggested that tactics were more useful than nobility in any battle. He wished it were only his money riding on the outcome here.

'Bet on the pigeon,' was Ramon's harsh advice to his nephew. 'He's going to die. No!' he ordered Bran, who was all set to wade out with a dog to retrieve the fallen pigeon. 'My nephew wishes to see how this ends.' Nobody moved. All eyes were on the battle in the skies. The peregrine caught a current and sped upwards but the same capricious breeze took her close enough to be clipped by one of Vertat's wings. With a massive effort the goshawk gained the upper position, dropping all her weight on the smaller bird. Down they fell, the goshawk covering the peregrine, pinning it until they hit the ground. Though cushioned by the falcon, the goshawk was dazed and lay still for long enough that Dragonetz thought her dead, then she hopped groggily towards the pigeon and claimed her trophy with a scree of triumph.

An equally shrill, 'No!' escaped Costansa as Vertat gathered strength and flew, the pigeon firmly in her claws.

Steady orange eyes found the voice and outstretched glove that meant ready food and she flew, true as her name, onto Dragonetz' gauntlet, trading the pigeon for a strip of liver, swearing in irritation as she settled onto his shoulder. He hooded her, the easier to attend to the pigeon. Though mauled, the messenger was still alive, would probably pull through with Bran's care thought Dragonetz as he removed the capsule.

'My Lord Dragonetz seems over-concerned with the contents of the message,' Costansa observed. 'Maybe he doesn't want it made public.' Hugues' gesture of irritation warned her that she could alienate her own young prey if she wasn't careful and she adjusted her line of pursuit.

'I know! Why don't I read the message aloud, so you may all be reassured there is no treason in it.' Her smile at Dragonetz promised that she would find harm for him in the contents, whatever the message actually said. Hugues was infatuated enough to have relaxed at the proposal, probably assuming that, as Montbrun was his mother's ally, any message from Trinquetaille would be suitably translated for Barcelone's ears.

Costansa was drawing up beside Sadeek, one hand stretched out to claim her prize when someone else beat her to it.

'My Lord.' It was not a question and Ramon's outstretched hand demanded the tiny scrap of parchment that Dragonetz had extricated but not unrolled.

Conscious of Hugues' white face, and his own suspicions as to the contents, Dragonetz hesitated, then he let fate decide and passed the message to the Comte de Barcelone, Regent of Provence, Liege Lord to Les Baux.

Ramon studied the note for an eternity, his face giving nothing away. Finally, he said, 'It is good news. It is indeed from Trinquetaille.' His steady gaze at Hugues made it clear that there were to be no more secret pigeons between the two fortresses of Les Baux. 'Let me read it to you. *All arrived safely.*' Then Ramon smiled. 'My wife,' he clarified, 'and all her party, have arrived safely in Arle. Thanks be to God.'

'Allah be praised,' echoed Malik, with a sideways glance at Dragonetz.

Ramon's expression hardened again and he looked down at the bird which had battled wind and predator to reach its mate, and now lay still but breathing, nestling in his soldier's hands. He wrung its neck and dropped it on the ground. 'I don't gamble,' he stated, passing the message to Dragonetz. Then he rode off without a backward glance.

Dragonetz re-read the message, every word as Ramon had relayed them. Except for one. The message was signed *Gilles.* Enough to tell Ramon that the pigeon had not come from Trinquetaille but from Dragonetz' villa and that those safe were a man, a dog and a baby. Enough to condemn Estela for theft and collusion if Costansa had got her hands on the message or if Ramon had read out the name.

The Comte had spared Dragonetz' family, given Hugues a warning and killed a pigeon. A lesson for his nephew? Or for them all. Dragonetz shivered, as the exhileration of the day's sport turned to chill foreboding. He was suddenly glad that Estela had not come hawking.

Hugues blew his hunting horn loud and clear, the long one, then two, then three note sequence that signified the return. The hunt was over.

As the party rode back to the castle, the black cloud of Ramon's displeasure lifted, the ladies tootled their hunting horns in all manner of conflicting calls; the indefatigable spaniels were allowed to scamper freely; and the swaying bags of game returned everyone to good humour.

The camaraderie of the hunt took on an edge of licentious banter as couples rode together, with talk of chasing the hart and finding a sweet deer. Costansa let Hugues coax her back into good humour after her loss of the falcon and it was obvious the young man was enjoying his role of protector. A cynic would have observed that Costansa recovered her good humour quickly enough to adjust her neckline becomingly low over bare shoulders. Hunting roused a man's blood.

Perhaps it should not have come as a surprise to Dragonetz when a soft knock came at his chamber door that night. His own blood was aroused, his heart still pounding from the sport and he had deliberately stayed away from Estela for fear the sight of her would tempt him against his better judgement. She needed rest, not a lover who wanted carnal acrobatics. Just the thought of her lying there, hair spread out over the pillow, topaz eyes drawing him in... the knock on the door gave him hope. Perhaps she was well enough and seeking him for the same sweet purpose he desired. He opened the door and invited in the woman who stood there, her tunic showing underneath a cloak thrown on roughly.

'A little après-hunt sport, my Lord Dragonetz?' teased Etiennette, younger by candlelight, her hair loose and showing strands of silver. She swayed into the room, her eyes large with wine and belladonna, her breasts swinging free beneath the thin tunic. 'What harm could it do?' she murmured, her hands small and tender on his shoulders, her mouth reaching up to his, a flower opening to him.

'It has been so long,' she whispered, pressing against him, curves fitting in all the places he wanted to feel curves. He couldn't hide his response and he stepped backwards, clumsy with sleep, lust and darkness. He'd forgotten the perch. Stumbling against the wooden block at one end, Dragonetz aroused the demon.

Vertat bated, squawking expletives, flapping huge wings with intent to kill, lashing out at Etiennette with her beak even though she could not see where to aim. The widow of Les Baux jumped out of range at the hawk's first movement and the wooden perch was now between her and Dragonetz. He donned jerkin and gauntlets, picked the pouch from the floor, extracted a strip of raw meat and soothed the hawk.

'I'm sorry, my Lady.' He didn't look at her. 'I need to calm the hawk and she'll tolerate nobody but me when she's in this mood.'

'A jealous bird, your hawk,' observed Etiennette, keeping her distance and making no sudden movements.

'Aye, my Lady. I'm afraid she is.'

A flash of anger. 'No doubt my son's hawk will be more obliging!'

'Your son is young and has made no promises to his bird.' Dragonetz looked up then, saw the double chins, deep crevasses into sagging breasts – and looked back into the eyes of the woman who was the wrong one for a reason more important than all her body's flaws; she was not Estela.

Etiennette pulled her cloak tight round her, grasping it closed high at the neck. But she remained the Lady of Les Baux, and she met his gaze, head high. 'This is your final answer then?'

'I am sorry... But it changes nothing.'

Her silence spoke. Then she told him, 'I'm not putting up with it. That whore leaves tomorrow.'

For one terrible heartbeat, Dragonetz thought she meant Estela. Then he understood. 'Hugues won't like it.'

'He will learn that we can't always have what we want. At least he's had one night's fun.' Her self-mockery pinched the heart but pity could only worsen the rejection so nothing was said, no gesture made. 'Good night, Lord Dragonetz. I expect you in court tomorrow.' Her exit was dignified, which was more than could be said for a semi-naked man protecting his genitals as he squeezed past a highly irritated goshawk. They both swore loudly.

CHAPTER TWENTY

Likewise, an excellent powder for provoking the menses: take some yellow flag, hemlock, castoreum, mugwort, sea wormwood, myrrh, common centaury, sage. Let a powder be made and let her be given to drink one dram of this with water in which savin and myrrh are cooked and let her drink this in the bath... Or let there be made another pessary in the shape of the male member and let it be hollow, and inside there let the medicine be placed and let it be inserted.

On the Conditions of Women, The Trotula

E stela was feeling quite recovered from the dizzy sickness but the ache in her belly, as if she'd been kicked by a horse, was only too familiar. Her menses would start some time soon and she just wished her body would sort itself out so she could get on with her life. She still felt reluctant to face any public situation so she intended to take refuge behind her 'illness' for a few more days. Not even to herself did she name the individuals she couldn't face, represented by 'public situations'.

When the knock came on her door, her badly-behaved heart skipped a beat but, as Sancha was absent on other duties, Estela forced herself to take the normal action of opening the door, seeing who was there. How did all these fears take root? She watched her own hand as it turned the door handle. She felt her heart pounding as she tried not to picture the unknown behind the door.

The more she tried not to picture someone the more convinced she was that Death had come for her, a skeleton in a cloak, a skull for a face. Only when she'd given in to her day-mares, when she accepted that if it be Death, then whatever God willed would happen: only then, in total acceptance, and after a third attack of knocking, could she open the door.

Where a page stood bearing a large bundle wrapped in sackcloth. As was the way of young boys, new to their position, he delivered his message at full sing-song speed with no inflexion whatsoever as if it might be the receipt for orange preserve rather than a matter of any moment.

'Roxane once of Montbrun know this that the Lord of Montbrun casts you off you are no daughter of his nor heir to his lands and you renounce all such rights for yourself or your ungodly offspring as you swore in front of witnesses should be...' the boy took a breath and continued, '... the case if you should regain the object alleged to be a legacy from your dam which is hereby given to you to seal the contract his dearest wish is that he never see you again and they leave Les Baux this morning the Lady Costansa de Montbrun says it is not over and she has given you token also...' another breath '... thank you my Lady if you are satisfied with my delivery please to remember that a boy needs to eat.'

Estela felt like clapping at the end of such a message, almost distracted from its content by the unique form of delivery. She fetched a penny from her pouch, was rewarded by genuine thanks and a huge grin, then she took the parcel from the boy and he skipped off along the corridor.

After checking, twice, that the door was firmly closed, Estela put the package on the bed and unwrapped it carefully, afraid of her step-mother's parting shot. Her father's word counted for enough still to guarantee that the oud would indeed be inside the sackcloth but Costansa was perfectly capable of breaking the instrument.

Not until she had examined every inch of the oud did Estela

believe that she really had her precious lute back unscathed. She exhaled with deep relief, her thoughts singing 'leave this morning', telling her that the Montbruns were gone, out of her life. She placed the oud on a stool, her fingers itching to pluck the strings, find a new melody, create the song of a freed cagebird.

Absent-mindedly she started to shake and fold the sackcloth wrapping, when a tiny chirp arrested her. Maybe that was the sound that had suggest birdsong to her troubadour's senses. It was no doubt a cricket, hopping on to warm fabric and getting caught up for the ride. Not wanting to harm any living creature on a day that promised fair, she unfolded the cloth again to rescue the little insect – and jumped back as black claws clicked shut where her hand had been a second earlier. The unmistakeable arched back and clicking claws of the black scorpion continued their small threat, then scuttled off the bed, across the floor and into a crack in the stonework.

Costansa's parting gift – a scorpion bite. No doubt intended to be fatal. Except that she'd sent the wrong kind of scorpion. Even if it had bitten Estela, the black scorpion would have caused no more pain than a wasp sting. If Costansa had been brought up by a wise woman, as had Estela, she'd have known that the brown scorpion might look less offensive but was far more likely to kill. Costansa! Always judging by appearance – and hoping that others would do likewise. And the worst she could think of was to send a chirruping black scorpion to say 'Boo!' Estela could think of a million far worse things to do to Costansa! However, all of a sudden, she no longer needed to; Estela de Matin was somebody who did not need to prove herself. Roxane de Montbrun did not exist any more.

Collapsing onto her clothes-coffer, Estela started laughing. Once she'd begun, she couldn't stop, whooping until tears came. She was still chuckling to herself when Sancha returned and rushed to her side, concerned at these signs of hysteria.

'I'm fine, fine.' Estela told Sancha she was on no account to fetch Malik and concluded, 'but I have started bleeding, by the bucketful in fact.'

It was Sancha's turn to collapse, pasty-faced with shock.

'For the love of God,' snapped Estela, earning another reproachful look for such blasphemy, 'act like a woman!'

'Just the thought of blood makes me faint,' confessed Sancha, perched on the stool beside the oud, swaying precariously.

'Be careful with that!' Then Estela started giggling again, just at the thought that her oud might be destroyed by her friend after surviving Costansa's spite. 'All I need is for you to take a message not to look at...' Sancha gave her a pleading look. 'Send me a maid, one of the reliable ones, with clean cotton rags. If I can use pessaries for medication, I can use them to soak up blood...' but Sancha had already rushed for the door muttering 'maid, cotton rags' and she bolted before the end of the sentence.

Light-headed, perhaps from loss of so much blood, Estela closed her eyes while she waited for the maid; saw a cage-door opening, heard a bird sing.

'They've gone,' Dragonetz told her, hovering in the open door, his eyes assessing her state of health. 'How are you?'

Estela was propped up on the bed, her oud beside her. The note-book Malik had given her, in which she recorded her songs, was on her lap. She'd been working. 'I'm bleeding,' she told him.

'I know.' He grinned. 'I guessed from the way Sancha turned green and avoided in any way telling me what ailed you except to say that you 'would be better in a few days'.' His eyes softened and he hesitated. 'Are you disappointed?'

'If you are.' She met his question, straight, no games.

'There is no rush for more babies. It's enough work to look after the family I've got!'

She smiled weakly. 'I'm glad they're gone.' Her not-family.

'Do you prefer me to stay away for a few more nights?'

'I'm bleeding,' she repeated, stupidly.

'I'm not Sancha.' The lop-sided charm of his smile made her insides lurch and she suddenly felt weepy again. To be held in her

lover's arms, soothed and stroked was all she wanted. The Montbruns, Les Baux, Barcelone and the whole of Provence could go hang
themselves!

Dragonetz read her face, came into the chamber and closed the
door behind him. He placed a stool against the door, moved the oud
and the notebook, and stretched out beside her. She found her place,
head tucked under his chin, into his shoulder.

'Your training,' she murmured.

'Can wait. We're preparing for the tourney. Hugues can manage.
Give the boy something to think about that doesn't wear skirts.'

'Wear skirts?'

He didn't answer and she was too contented to pursue the subject.
Other people's amours were of no interest. Her own folded her in his
arms and she stayed awake as long as she could, to better enjoy the
long fingers stroking her hair from tip to waist. Then again, and
again, in the slow rhythm of comfort as he murmured in Arabic the
words of the poet Ibn Faraj.

'All night I lay by water
thirsting like a muzzled camel,
her bounty flooding my senses
with fruit and flowers.
No wild beast, I would not take
A garden for a pasture.'

CHAPTER TWENTY-ONE

Sanicle (sanicula) is hot... One who is wounded by a sword should squeeze out the juice of sanicle, pour it into water and drink it after a meal... It purges the inside of the wound and gradually makes it well.

Physica, Plants

Two mares, a grey and a roan, were saddled ready for the outing. 'My Lord Hugues,' Estela greeted her host with all courtesy, showing no sign of her inner doubts. Never again would she be afraid of ghosts and threats. As a scientific, she could study such curiosities, and as a troubadour, she could turn them into song. A black scorpion was just a natural phenomenon and the Gyptian's words had lost their sting. She intended to prove this to herself by taking the Lord of Les Baux on a quest to find his ancestry. He had readily accepted the invitation to visit the wise woman of the caves, famed for honey and soothsaying, who had promised to shed light on the matter. Estela just hoped that any light shed would shine as brightly as El Sidi and remove the permanent scowl from Les Baux's face.

Although her sympathies still leaned towards Barcelone, Estela had not visited the Barcelone quarters since Petronilla left, and her status as Etiennette's troubadour required her support for Les Baux.

Loyalty to both Sancha and Dragonetz also made her bite her tongue when faced with a sullen Hugues, bearing his ill-treatment by the world in brusque manners and furrowed brow.

'My Lady,' he grunted, checking the girth and stirrup before mounting his roan mare, without any thought of Estela. A stable-hand rushed to her side and offered her a boost. She had not seen any need to let Dragonetz know of the expedition as he would have fussed about her security, insisting on her bringing one of the men or – heaven forbid! – on coming himself.

The last thing she wanted was for her lover to hear the old woman's pronouncements on oath-breaking and infidelity. He had more important matters to worry about. If she could find some glorious past for Les Baux to include in his blazon, that would help Dragonetz in his plans for the tourney but there was no trusting the Gyptian.

Estela would have brought Gilles and, of course, Nici but her two guardians were safely in the Marselha villa. Her insides gave the usual contraction that went with missing her son but the word 'safely' steadied her. Les Baux was anything but safe, whether Costansa had left or not. She could have brought Raoulf, Dragonetz' bear of a lieutenant but he was Dragonetz' man to the core and whatever was said in the cave, Estela preferred to rest with her – and with Hugues, who was unlikely to take an interest in anything that didn't apply to him.

So Estela sighed and accepted that she must make the best of a bad-tempered young lord, and hope that what they heard in the cave would brighten his day – and hers. Whatever happened, she would bring her remaining fears into the light of day and see how pathetic they looked.

'It is but a few minutes' ride, my Lord.' Estela used the same tone with which she rallied baby Musca when he was teething and it had as much effect on Hugues. He made a noise that could be construed as an acknowledgement. Then they rode in silence.

She'd sent a messenger to the cave the day before so was not surprised that when she called into the cave, Dame Fairnette's voice answered, echoing from the tunnel, the hoarse croak of age even more apparent than usual. Would she too grow old enough to lose her voice, Estela wondered. No, of course not. She would never be old. Hugues tied and hobbled the horses outside the cave entrance then escorted her into the dark cavern, apparently remembering some chivalry as he ushered her forward, his hand on his sword hilt.

All was as before: the tallow candle and rough furnishings; a chill after the warmth outside that felt pleasant for a few seconds, then seeped into the bones with the damp of marsh-fever. Estela felt goose-pimples along her arms from the contrast.

'So she's back and she's brought the great Lord of Les Baux. We knew she would. Sit there, my Lord Hugues, sixth of the line Pons of Les Baux, and tell Dame Fairnette what you want of her and what you'll pay for it.'

Estela couldn't decide whether she was irritated or relieved at being ignored. She stayed in the shadows, standing, watching as Hugues reluctantly took the stool, moved it further away from the smell of aged dame, sat on it and stretched his long legs to find some comfortable position. His back gave nothing away but his shuffling and the way he cleared his throat testified to his unease. The shadows flickered across the fortune-teller's face and she shut her eyes, frowning in concentration, as if to see him more clearly in her mind.

'Well?' she prompted. 'Or you can buy honey and go.'

In his haughtiest tone, Hugues said, 'I was told that you knew Les Baux family history. Beyond my grandparents. If so, you are to make this known to me.'

'I am to make this known to you,' mocked Dame Fairnette, imitating his tone, her eyes still closed. 'And why would I do that?

'Because I demand it as your liege.'

'He demands, does he? Nobody told him that truth must be paid for in good coin or what he gets will be fair payment, base for base. But he knows now, doesn't he... so what will you pay for my story, Lord Hugues?'

'Barcelone gold morabitani,' whispered Hugues, 'and the story be true and good.' He opened his purse and put a golden coin in the clawed hand. The dame put it to her mouth, bit it and said, 'True coin but not enough for what I can give you, my Lord.'

His hand hovered, tempted, by his sword hilt but, instead, 'What do you want?' he asked.

'A promise,' she said opening her eyes, fixing him in her stare, unblinking. 'My people are waiting on your lands that fight the sea, where the dunes meet the saltwater pools, where the Maries and black Sarah will make their sacred landing. This will be a meeting-place for my people, wherever they should roam in this world of Goys and I want safe passage from Les Baux from this day forth, through all time, or may your house die barren and forgotten!'

Still whispering, Hugues said, 'Along the salt-marshes by the coast? Permission to camp and safe passage through our lands? Nobody shall have the right to turn them away?'

'For this shall be their rightful meeting-place each year, forever. Swear it!' The clawed hands gripped Hugues', squeezing the coin against them.

'I swear.' Hugues spoke the oath as one brought up by Etiennette. 'I swear that safe passage shall be given to the Gyptian peoples and the right to meet by the salt-marshes from this day on, by Les Baux now, and of every generation, or may our house fail. May God be my witness!'

Dame Fairnette relaxed her grip and hid the coin in a fold of her multi-coloured layers while Hugues rubbed his right hand. The imprint from the coin of what could only be Barcelone's image showed red on the back of his hand, so tightly had the dame ground it into Hugues' flesh. A strange bargain. Estela prayed no harm would come of it.

The fortune-teller shut her eyes again and hummed, then started her story. 'I will tell this only once so listen well or lose your way.' Hugues no longer fidgeted and Estela was a pillar of stone, not wanting any noise or movement to interrupt the strange sing-song recital.

'All men know of the three magi who brought gifts to the Christ-child but my people lived in their countries, can tell of their sons and their sons' sons who were blessed for all generations. It came to pass in the time of the Roman Emperor Theodosius that the ruling Bautasar left his land of Ethiop.

He took his wife, his children and his treasure in the service of Theodosius, and travelled over land and sea until he reached the city of Lion. Yearning for a place to call his own, Bautasar heard tell that in all the Province there was nowhere fairer than an eagle's perch among the white rocks, a day's ride north of Marselha.

He came to the rocky heights and had a vision of a citadel there, raised to the glory of God. And so it came to pass that Bautasar of blessed line gave his name to the citadel he had built...'

'Les Baux!' breathed Hugues.

'Les Baux,' confirmed Dame Fairnette, 'where the rocks stood guard against all the evil without and where the sons and grandsons of Bautasar continued to receive God's blessing, from one generation to the next.'

In the awed silence that followed, Estela thought of Etiennette's father being murdered, of young Barcelone's bloodright and wondered what the definition of 'blessed' might be. There was no doubt, however, that Hugues was caught up in the story, *his* story, with a saint for an ancestor. Another scientific observation struck Estela: belief comes readily when we are told what we want to hear. Medical study was indeed a way of thinking, not just of healing, and part of her remained detached, watching, analysing, no longer scared.

'Chance,' murmured Hugues, 'by hazard, the divine Bautasar founded my line and my citadel... By hazard his ancestor, *my* ancestor saw the star that led him to his destiny, to sanctity...'

'What a man calls hazard, God calls His plan,' prompted Dame Fairnette.

'Au hasard, Bautasar!' Hugues cried out. Then again, quietly, liking the sound of it. 'Au hasard, Bautasar.' *Into hazard, Bautasar!* As if thinking aloud, he continued, 'For a blazon, what should I have to honour Bautasar. Gifts. He brought a gift for the Christ-child? Myrrh, that was it.'

Myrrh, thought Estela. Precious ointment, treatment with aloes against worms, or for a cold stomach if mixed with olive bark and pine resin. A good blazon for a healer. But Les Baux were not healers and Hugues asked Dame Fairnette, 'Show me! You *know* what must be!'

Her answer was to reach for his hand once more. She shut her eyes and on the back she traced the four compass points in a cross. Then Estela found it hard to follow the pattern but it made her think of more compass points, as she'd seen in the navigation of ships. Then Dame Fairenette paused, as if the final pattern was clear in her mind and in fluid movements she traced lines and points, to end where she'd begun.

'The star! It will be like the sun with sixteen points, like the compass of our house, showing us the way forward. White light, blinding, on a blood red field.' He clasped her hand tightly, rough in his exhileration. When he let go, her hand dropped like a dead chicken, its neck wrung, and the fortune-teller seemed to shrink. Another coughing fit started.

Hugues didn't notice but stood up, eager to leave, talking half to Estela and half to himself. 'We must to the armourer straight, to order shield and the tailor for a standard. I want them before the tourney.'

Hoarse but insistent, Dame Fairnette said, 'Go and wait at the entrance. The girl must do the thing that she came for.'

Gathering his manners, Hugues looked to Estela, awaiting her decision. She nodded and he left, barely containing his impatience to let the world – and particularly the Porcelets – know of his glorious heritage. Alone with Dame Fairnette in the flickering candle-light, Estela suddenly felt the dampness chill her bones. Medicine and music escaped her as she remembered the words that haunted her in the middle of the night, when she couldn't sleep. Oath-breaker, unfaithful…

She prepared to hear those words again but instead was told, 'Not much time… go down the tunnel and take what is yours, but *only* what is yours. Payment is always taken…'

'I don't understand,' Estela stammered.

Dame Fairnette cackled, coughed again and spat on the earthen floor. Estela could see the dark stain that confirmed her previous suspicions: blood.

'I can get you a potion,' she offered.

'Too late for potions.' More coughing and cackling. 'As if the girl could give me anything better than I can prepare myself. No, no, no the girl can't do what's needed for me but I know those who can.' More incoherent chuckling. 'The tunnel. The girl should know what she came for. Even though she doesn't know yet what she came for. Family.' The cloudy eyes, pupils large, fixed Estela. The Gyptian was indeed taking potions already. 'You should know where you're from.'

Was there never armour strong enough to keep words out? Just when she'd accepted her disinheritance, she was being taunted with it. Estela gritted her teeth, picked up a candle in its holder and said coldly, 'Very well. One more game and it's over. I shan't pay you as this is not of my choosing. This tunnel?'

'Nevertheless, payment is always taken…' repeated the Dame, nodding towards the black mouth at the back of her cave-dwelling.

Estela held out the candle in front of her and entered the darkness. She had to stoop to avoid hitting her head and, even so, she felt the sticky brush of insect threads, something crawling on her head. She shuddered, her skin crawling even where nothing touched it.

Silly goose, she told herself. This was just like the passages in Montbrun after her mother died, when the servants did as they pleased, which amounted to very little. At least her stepmother had ensured the castle was cleaned. Estela's nerves steadied as she imagined the orders Costansa would give regarding the tunnel – brushing, strewing with herbs and a sconce midway with a pitch torch would arrange matters nicely. Having conducted a full tunnel-improvement plan, Estela felt a change in the air before she saw the cavern opening up ahead.

Only when she let it go, did she realise she'd been holding her breath. She took a few seconds to enjoy the extra space then she held the candle up to explore, section by section, clockwise. She hugged the wall to get her bearings as she couldn't see the far walls of the cavern and was afraid she'd lose her way if there were further tunnels.

Rock wall met her hand and eye, yellowish-white in the candle-light, as she counted her paces in case she should need to retrace her steps. She thought she was probably walking round in a circle but she couldn't be sure.

After fifty-eight paces, the shadows in the distance showed some kind of heap covering the dusty earth and a black tunnel-mouth inter-rupting Estela's route along the cavern wall. Estela's imagination sparkled with all the local legends about Moorish treasure and she quashed every possibility that, if the treasure was real, so was its guardian, the Devil Goat. 'Touch only what is yours,' the Gyptian had warned her.

'Nothing here is mine!' Saying the words aloud was supposed to make her feel bolder but, instead, the echoes of 'mine, mine, mine!' eroded her confidence with the deep voice of dark places. Why place such a hoard to block a tunnel? Unless something was in the tunnel…

The candle shook and wavered in the dank current of air from the tunnel. That would be just perfect, if the candle went out! Estela put it down, to one side, safe from the breeze but further than she'd have liked for visibility. She bent down over the heap of objects, confirming her first impression.

Metal, shiny cups, a buckle. She moved the topmost goods to look deeper in the pile. Pottery: plates and pitchers. A flute. She lingered over this. Was the instrument meant for her? She moved the cloth that was covering half of the flute and saw the cracked mouthpiece. As she looked more closely at the other objects, she realised that they too were broken and worthless. Someone's inheritance, battered by time to a heap of rubbish. She laughed softly, trailing the fabric through her fingers, feeling its embroidered surface, expecting moth-holes and finding none. Perhaps she could use it for rags if it was good cloth. She gave it a strong tug and it didn't come apart, so she tied it round her neck.

She shrugged. There was nothing here for her. She bent down to pick up the candle and her makeshift scarf dangled into the light, revealing a pattern that she knew by heart. Arabesques and interlaced points embroidered on silk brocade. Surely this was merely a similar design to that on her oud, similar to so many to be found Oltra mar. But no, this was the exact same design; three circles, each with its symmetrical patterns and in one corner an embroidered signature in Arabic.

A noise from the tunnel behind the heap startled her and when she looked into the black depths, she saw yellow eyes with square pupils, fixed on her from behind the heap of objects, getting closer. A stone slipped, shifting the pile in a clank of metal and the noise disturbed the black ceiling of the cavern into a flurry of mouse-faces and tiny wing-beats.

Bats! The rousing above her freed Estela's feet and she didn't count her steps as she ran back the way she'd come, protecting the guttering candle as best she could. Once in the low tunnel, she was forced to slow or fall, and as she sensed the return to roost of the bats behind her, Estela's heartbeat settled to merely frantic.

The torchlight grew larger as she approached Dame Fairnette's niche and Estela was relieved to find it empty. The Dame had no doubt gone to tend her bees. Yet another cryptic conversation was not what Estela most wanted and she would be very happy to get out of these caves, find Hugues and return to Les Baux. She was eager to compare the design on her oud with the fabric and consider in private what this might mean.

Gripping her skirt tightly, Estela blinked in the daylight outside the cave, blinded. The first thing she saw was that the horses were still tethered. Then she realised that Hugues was staring at her. She probably looked a fright after scrambling around the tunnels. She smoothed her hairnet to brush off any cobwebs.

At the same moment she realised what such a look from a man might mean, Hugues grabbed her wrist and pulled her after him off the path, between rocks and into some bushes. Not a day for chivalry then. If she screamed, her own reputation would be called into question. With her free hand – the right, Hazard be praised! – Estela found the slit in her riding-skirt and grasped what lay beneath it.

Heart pounding, her instincts screaming for blood, she tried to think of actions and consequences. After all, this was the Lord of Les Baux dragging her into the undergrowth. She would try talking first but then… and she didn't dare leave it too late or she might not get a second chance.

Presumably satisfied that they were out of sight and earshot, Hugues stopped and pulled her to him, forcing wet lips on hers. She fought the urge to wipe her mouth and spit, struggled free enough to say, 'My Lord! Stop! You are confused!'

His hand spanned her neck. A hunter's hand, big enough to break a neck or strangle a silly goose. 'Little tease. You knew what you wanted when you came out alone with me. The seed of Bautasar.' His voice was thick, beyond reason, hands exploring everywhere but where the danger was.

She made one last attempt, using the one word that might bring him to his senses. 'Your mother…' she began but he cut her off, maddened further.

He held her face as in a vice, too close. Was this the look in a man's eyes after battle? Hate and lust, a hardness that raped and killed? 'My mother.' Such bitterness. 'We owe them this, your Lord Dragonetz and my mother. They can marry and swive but we will do this first and spite them both!'

Numb, with no time to think, Estela let his words pass into a pocket of her mind, closed it, left it for later. She felt the surge and heat of his body, recalled her anatomy books and considered what would hurt enough without maiming forever. He was the Lord of Les Baux after all.

As he reached to untie and drop his leggings, she pulled close to him as if amorous, close enough to feel his leap of response. She put one arm round behind him and stabbed him hard in his right buttock. The worst pain was always as the weapon was pulled out and she was quick. Gilles had taught her well. While Hugues yelped and lost concentration, she fled.

Stumbling back through the undergrowth, hoping the bloodletting would bring Hugues back to reason but not risking the consequences if it didn't, she untied his mare, the faster of the two. Hands trembling, she mounted and kicked the horse to a pace that was dangerous on the stony path – but not as dangerous as being caught. All the way she imagined hooves behind her but she rode into the citadel alone.

At the stables, she made up some story of a girlish bet and Hugues' indulgence, told them their Lord would soon arrive on her palfrey and they were to tell him she was tired after winning and thanked him for the outing. Not until she collapsed on her own bed, did she feel safe. As her breathing returned to normal, the sealed pocket in her mind spilled out all the day's events and they rushed around her head like bees in smoke. Patterns; ancestors; Dragonetz marrying Etiennette; brocade; her mother; Hugues' assault; her foolishness in going unaccompanied.

As she tried to order her thoughts, two things became clear to her. She could not tell Dragonetz about anything other than the legendary ancestor of Les Baux, or the balance of Provence would be threatened by her own stupidity. If he didn't mention the marriage with Etiennette, then neither could she. 'Au hasard, Bautasar!' And if Estela were to have her own blazon, it would be a brown scorpion, for she seemed to be forever drawing poison.

Later, but not enough later for Estela's taste, she was surprised by a messenger knocking at her door, the same boy who had not yet learned to breathe *and* recall a message. 'The Lady Etiennette says will it please you to use your medical skills with her son who has taken a cut in training and might need some balm she would like your opinion of his wound and thanks you I will take you to him now.'

One huge gulp of air followed, just the time for Estela to decide that she could not ignore the summons and must accept this fabrication. She collected her box of medicines, vowing that she would not be gentle if she was forced to place hands on Hugues. She had faced everything else that the last few weeks had thrown at her and she was not hiding from a man with a sore arse.

Chin up, Estela followed the page to the chamber in which lord

Hugues was lying on one side, in his cot, ashen-faced. He did not meet her eyes but mumbled, 'You may go,' to the page.

'I'd rather he stayed,' Estela told him clearly. 'It is more seemly that we have an observer. And I'm sure there will be nothing unsuitable for a boy to see.'

Hugues reddened but nodded.

'Your Lady Mother told me you had received a wound in training. Where does it hurt?' asked Estela, barely disguising her glee. Let people make what they would of a 'training wound' in such a place.

Hugues rolled onto his stomach, bared his behind as requested and Estela looked objectively at her handiwork. A neat thrust and withdrawal – not quite the one Hugues had hoped for. The blade had been sharp and clean, and the blood was already coagulating. 'Perfect,' she said aloud. Nobody asked her what she meant.

'It will heal well,' she pronounced, 'but we don't want it closing too quickly.' Von Bingen warned against wormwood as too speedy in healing the exterior, leaving the interior to putrify. Estela reflected for a moment, then gave the prescription. 'A potion of sanicle each day to heal inside and a soothing poultice twice daily. There is no need for me or another doctor. One of your attendants can prepare the drink and apply the salve.'

Hugues said nothing, which was probably safest.

'Meanwhile, avoid putting pressure on the sore part. No riding and if you must sit, try placing a cushion underneath.' Her healing habits got the better of her urge to make him suffer. 'If you have a hole cut in a cushion to make a ring, you will find that more comfortable.'

He pulled his tunic back down and rolled onto his side again, risked a glance in her direction. 'Will you tell Dragonetz?'

'That you came off badly in training?' mocked Estela. 'No,' she said. 'I will not tell my Lord. But women do chatter. And if I hear that any girl wishes you'd learned from this lesson in training, my Lord Dragonetz will be the first to hear the full story. Do we understand each other?'

'Yes. I'm sorry.' Hugues looked so sheepish that Estela found it hard to feel as angry as she knew she ought to. He directly looked at her, no trace of the earlier madness. 'But is it all right if the girls are willing?'

Estela chewed the inside of her cheek to prevent herself laughing. 'Yes,' she said gravely. 'If the girls are willing.' The relief in his face tested her self-control severely. 'You are not a camel!' she told him and left, leaving him to make of that observation whatever he would.

CHAPTER TWENTY-TWO

Since birds are lifted by their feathers into the air, and since they dwell every-where in the air, they were thus created and positioned in order that the soul, with them, might feel and know the things which should be known. And so, while the soul is in the body it extends everywhere, elevated by its thoughts.

Physica, Birds

Dragonetz was disappointed in Estela. Her incomprehensible refusal to share a bedchamber with Vertat left him no option but to return the goshawk to the mews at night. Her notion that she'd feel spied on and inhibited in her love-making made no sense at all. 'Jealousy!' he explained to the bird on his shoulder. 'She ought to be above all that.' Vertat shifted her feet and swore in bad-tempered agreement. If 'manning' meant being accustomed to human company and social situations, then Vertat was as thoroughly manned as a hawk could be – despite her recent exile from bedchambers.

'And this business with Hugues is badly timed. What idiot gave his lord such a wound in training? Though it is noble in Les Baux to hide the man's name. That will gain him credit with his men, maybe even outweigh the indignity of his injury.' Dragonetz heard the warning shout and automatically side-stepped a bucket of slops being thrown out an upper window; continued along the cobbled street that led to the training ground, still thinking aloud. 'Hugues *must* lead a side in the tourney if I have to strap him to the saddle like El Sidi's corpse! Getting him to agree to that will be less of a problem than getting him to see who his team-mates must be... and what to do with the Porcelets? The dratted family goad like gadflies, a dangerous distraction.'

As they neared the training ground, Dragonetz hooded Vertat, who was unruffled by the noise and movement that greeted them. Ramon was leaning on the fence, concentrating on the manège where four riders put their mounts through some simple paces. Not so simple when done in unison. And nothing was simple when one of the riders was the young Comte de Provence, perfectly at ease on horseback, taking instructions from men who would have killed him a year ago, during the war.

Under the watchful eyes of Ramon Berenguer, the Protector, Hugues' men stepped up the pace, gradually, working together, watching what the lad could achieve comfortably and not testing his limits. Banter from the onlookers was soldier-crude but without malice and turned to cheers when the youngster was allowed to finish on a flourish. He reined his steed to a snorting two-legged stand, catching Dragonetz' eye as he came back down to earth.

Ramon turned to follow his nephew's gaze, nodded, as the boy rode towards them both, face glowing from exercise and praise. 'My Lord Dragonetz, did you see me in the ring?'

Vertat's weight steady on his shoulder, comforting, Dragonetz answered the boy truthfully. 'I did. I am impressed. Your uncle must be proud of you and your training.'

'Uncle?'

The grave, rare smile broke through Ramon's reserve. 'I am. My Lord Dragonetz is right. I am very proud. Of you...' he raised his voice, 'and of the men here who have trained hard and let you work with them. May their families see the benefit of such work.' A word to his aide and it was clear to all there that some Barcelone gold would find its way to the men who'd pleased Ramon with their conduct.

'And you'll let me ride in the tourney?' asked the Comte. 'Uncle?'

Heavy eyes, lined with responsibility, gazed unblinking at Drag-onetz. 'That is not my decision,' Ramon said, giving Dragonetz yet another complication.

The desperation of youth to prove itself, the belief in its own immortality. 'Please, my Lord Dragonetz?'

'It's not my decision, either,' replied Dragonetz, earning an amused twitch from Barcelone, quickly controlled. 'It is my Lord Hugues' tourney. I am just organising practicalities for him – and it is on exactly that matter I wish to speak to your uncle.'

Not completely bamboozled, the Comte persevered, 'But you will speak to him. He listens to you, I know he does.'

'I will speak to him – but I make no promises.'

'I will keep practising – tell him that!' Shining eyes said that a hope was already a certainty. Youth. 'Vertat is magnificent!'

Dragonetz was sure the hawk fluffed up its feathers, maybe sensing his own pride. 'Thank you,' he said simply.

'Your horse needs rubbing down,' suggested Ramon and the boy obeyed the thinly disguised order, as did Dragonetz when asked, 'Shall we walk?'

Their path followed the cliff edge along the earthen promontary, at one side of what was to be the tourney field. The view stretched far south, across fields and vineyards to the white mountains and a glimpse of blue sea, but neither man stopped to gaze outwards. Drag-onetz made his proposal. Ramon understood what lay behind it but asked anyway then kept silence while he considered the answer.

At the furthest point away from the keep, before they must round the head and walk back, Ramon seemed to reach a decision. 'Will you let Truth fly?' he asked. 'If she comes back to you, I will do it.'

The place was not good to hunt with a goshawk. It was exposed, windy, lacked cover. The prey would be down on the cliff-face and Vertat might overreach the distance he could feel their connection. He had not intended to fly her and she had eaten, not enough to satisfy but more than she should have. He might lose her.

'Yes,' he said, unhooding the hawk. He stood at the edge of the cliff, stared down at the black fissures in the rock with the eyes of a hawk. Vertat stiffened at the same time as Dragonetz spotted a slight movement, bird or vole, he knew not. Too high and steep for rabbit. He picked up some pebbles and gave them to Barcelone. 'Throw them there, where the shadows look like sheep, when I give the word.'

A moment's concentration on the hawk, her anger, her desire to kill, her wildness and then Dragonetz ordered, 'Now!' loosed the jesses and flung her into the wind.

Ramon shied pebbles at the rock face, disturbing a scurry of greyness with feet. Vertat rose, shrieked and dived, taking something with her that wriggled, had a tail. She perched on a ledge far below and the bubbling scream told of her kill but that only mattered to the hawk, not to her master. Getting her back was what mattered and had to be done quickly, before she wondered what it would be like, to keep eating, to keep flying, to become unmanned.

Dragonetz pulled a strip of meat out of his pouch and whistled, cursing the wind that stole his breath and mocked him. The hawk cocked her head, heard and ignored him, renewed her drilling into the squirming prey. He cupped his hands round his mouth and the whistle was louder but gained even less of a response from the hawk. He could almost feel her disdain. What did he offer that was worth coming for?

Provence. War. Brother against brother and blood on every man's hands. What did that matter to a goshawk? Out of the corner of his eye, Dragonetz sensed Ramon putting down what was left of his pebble collection, one careful stone at a time. One last time, Dragonetz called his hawk, but not by whistling. He cried out, 'Vertat!' in the voice that had lost a siege and survived; battled nightmares and been helped back to himself; won the only woman he'd ever loved. He put everything he was into calling his hawk and all his attention into the tie between them. And she came. Fierce and proud, she flew to his glove and snatched her reward. He took the mangled creature and fed a bit to her, threw the rest off the cliff, leashed Vertat.

'So it's yes,' he stated.

'Yes,' said Barcelone. They walked back to the training ground in silence broken only by a goshawk's complaints. Then Dragonetz went to visit Hugues in his sickroom.

As predicted, Les Baux was determined to lead a team in the tourney, despite his inability to sit up in bed, never mind ride a horse. 'A week, Dragonetz! Give me a week and I'll be mended!'

'I don't know... Estela said the wound went below the surface and would be sore for some time.' She'd sounded oddly satisfied at the thought too, perhaps pleased at having prevented infection. For the umpteenth time, Dragonetz demanded, 'How in God's name did you get such an injury in training?'

Hugues' flush could only be genuine. 'I told you – these things happen.'

Dragonetz sighed. He respected Hugues for loyalty to his men but found it odd that no gossip between the men themselves had hinted at the miscreant. 'Are you sure there was no foul play?'

Hugues flushed even redder. 'No,' he said shortly. 'I deserved it.'

'Well I only hope you have the defence prepared for another such duel.'

Hugues frowned and returned to more interesting matters. 'Fix the tourney for Saturday week, so we have no complaint from the church, and I will be ready. My shield has been painted with the star of Bautasar and my standard will be ready by then. I suggest each of my team wears a red scarf around his arm.' There was no mistaking his satisfaction with his newly-discovered ancestor and livery. 'I have given thought to the teams while I've been lying here. Do you have the names for me? Of all who enter? Barcelone will, won't he?'

'He will, my Lord.' Dragonetz was dismayed by a sudden thought. 'He'd never agree to serve on your team as your lieutenant. That's what you had in mind wasn't it?'

Surprise washed over Hugues' face, quickly replaced with his usual stubbornness. 'You don't think I can get people to do anything, do you. I'm the Lord of this citadel and Barcelone is my host. If I invite him to be on my team, he cannot in all courtesy refuse. I shall ask him tomorrow and you will eat your words. Or shall we have a wager on it? His eyes brightened at the prospect.

It was Dragonetz' turn to wince. 'No, my Lord, please, no wagers. I've had enough gambling today.'

Hugues laughed aloud, then winced as he accidentally rolled on his sore parts. 'Threw dice with Cam and Moran, did you?'

'Something like that.' Dragonetz gave a wry smile. 'The sort of day I'm having, I wouldn't be surprised if you ask me to head up the other team!'

Hugues sat bolt upright, startling Vertat. He grunted with pain, made himself comfortable and said, 'That's a splendid idea! You must lead the other team.'

'My Lord,' protested Dragonetz weakly, 'I can't fight against you, even in sport.'

A shadow passed over Hugues' face and the laughter died out of his eyes. 'I can fight against you, though.' There it was again, the wrong note, something sour between Hugues and Dragonetz. Surely he hadn't drilled Les Baux too hard, trying to make a leader of him? Had Hugues seen the easy respect his men gave Dragonetz? Respect for which Hugues had to work so hard? Dragonetz gave up trying to discover the cause. Whatever it was would work its way out in the tourney.

'My Lord,' he sighed. 'I will do as I'm bid but I don't like it. And you still have to get Barcelone on your side. He's the obvious leader for the second team.'

'You've heard my decision. So, let's talk about who we'll each have.' The enthusiasm came back into his voice as they traded team members, taking turns in choosing from the list that Dragonetz reeled off. Assuming that Hugues would have Barcelone, Dragonetz chose Malik. After that, they competed for the strongest fighters, approving each others' choices with 'He can turn a horse on a denarius!' and 'He's a good man with an axe!' until they reached the Porcelets, whom neither of them wanted.

In the end, Hugues took the three of them, on the grounds that it would cut them down to size being under his leadership. Dragonetz hid his satisfaction at placing the irascible family where they were least likely to harm Hugues under cover of sport.

They tallied up to find that Dragonetz was a man short.

'I'll ask a Porcelet to stand down,' suggested Hugues.

'Can't. We invited them to enter their names for tourney so we dishonour anyone we don't accept.'

'I don't mind dishonouring a Porcelet.' Hugues grinned and Dragonetz was tempted but shook his head.

'Then we must add someone. There must be someone else who wants to join in the sport.'

Dragonetz bit his lip, not naming the someone else.

Hugues picked the name from his mind. 'The young Comte,' he said with a sneer. 'He's man enough to inherit my province, to hunt with hawk and I bet he's been training in the manège. He'd follow you, wouldn't he?'

'Yes,' said Dragonetz, quietly. That was exactly the problem. But if he said no to Hugues des Baux, the young heir would make a liar of him by pestering Les Baux personally to join the tourney.

'Perfect.' The light of battle was in Hugues' eyes. 'And your team will wear what colour?'

'Blue,' said Dragonetz, remembering Estela's blue scarf fluttering, wearing his colours with no idea how he felt about her. Suddenly, he wanted to find her. Vertat could go to the mews.

'I'm tired now,' declared Hugues. 'I think we've organised everything rather well.'

'Yes,' agreed Dragonetz, 'I think we have.'

Estela was in the solar, dutifully stabbing white lawn with a blue silk trail of what could have been broken arrow-heads or duck footprints. Blue, Dragonetz' colour.

'My Lady Estela?' As if she'd conjured him, there he was, framed in the doorway, dark and intense. 'We need your healing skills. One of the men is fevered, crying out that he's a thirsty camel and only you can help him. Could you leave your embroidery to do a work of charity?'

Estela lowered her eyes demurely to hide the laughter in them as she sought permission from Etiennette to quit her task. 'My linen thanks you for the reprieve, Lord Dragonetz,' the Lady des Baux told him, as Estela secured her needle and dropped the sorry excuse for decoration into the work basket. Sancha looked up from stranding an iris petal, in silks graded from pale blue to purple. 'Camels,' she said. 'He does sound in a bad way. You will no doubt require all your skills. And your box of medicines.' She smiled as she returned to her delicate stitches.

'Box of medicines,' repeated Estela, flushing. She'd been ready to run out of the hall and skip along the corridors.

'And riding skirt,' suggested Dragonetz. 'We'll ride there. Meet me at the stables. I'll get the horses saddled.' He vanished.

'Ride. Yes,' stammered Estela, rushing out of the roomful of women and along the corridors, as would be natural when called to an emergency ailment. Another doctor would have diagnosed her condition as having little to do with a sick man. Her blood thrummed in anticipation. She had missed this!

Glossy black in the sunshine, Sadeek snorted, eager as Estela for an outing. His master was waiting, his hauberk and Talharcant glinting silver, his hair and eyes dark as his horse. Estela's usual dappled grey mare had been saddled and a stable-hand hovered. He moved to help Estela mount but Dragonetz was there first. He stooped and cupped his hands for her. She was pleased that even in the rush, she'd chosen her new blue boots with purple favours on the side and a toning skirt, running Sancha's iris shades in broad, ragged stripes. It was all rather fine for riding but some days were meant for finery, high days and Holy Days. This promised to be a high day.

As blind to the stable-boy as if the lad had been a goshawk in the bedchamber, Dragonetz captured one booted foot in his long musician's hands, holding it long enough for her to feel the pressure of his warm fingers through the goatskin sole, before she was released and boosted into the saddle. His fingers circled her ankle, opened and played three chords on her calf.

Estela looked down at him, laughed, sang the opening line of a duet they had performed many times and chid him. 'Sadeek grows impatient, my Lord.'

'As do I,' he told her, leaving her side, mounting in one fluid movement, saying, 'Follow me!' As if there were any other option. She would have followed him, anywhere, Oltra mar across churning seas or to the depths of the devil-goat cave, while this fire burned between them. He led her up the steep southern path, past the cave where the ambush had taken place, past the look-out posts on the hillside, where Dragonetz exchanged passwords and pleasantries with Les Baux guards. At the top of the ridge, Sadeek picked his way off the path and through the garrigue, between white rocks four times the size of a man on horseback. One looked like a crouching ogre, another a hunched vulture.

Dragonetz rode on until a craggy lion couchant seemed to meet his requirements and he dismounted, tied Sadeek to a rock outcrop and came to Estela's side. His hands spanned her waist as he helped her dismount and she breathed in, hoping he wouldn't notice the loss of girlish slimness since she'd had Musca. From the way his eyes and hands lingered, his thoughts were not critical. A wind-sculpted pine tree offered another tethering post. After securing the mare, Dragonetz gave Estela his full attention.

Unhurried now, he freed her plaits from their coif, unbound them, loosed her black hair, let it swing around her waist. He twined his fingers round some strands and gently combed through them, stroking her back through the curtain of hair, murmuring a quotation in Arabic that she suspected had nothing to do with camels.

'Are you thirsty?' she murmured.

He laughed, black eyes gleaming. 'I brought water,' he said and laid her on earth that smelled of pine needles, thyme and summer savory. When she closed her eyes, she could still see azure skies spinning, dizzy with sunshine, burning blue.

How could anyone think this was wrong, she wondered, holding him as he slept, both of them clothed only in her hair. A buzzard krie-kried overhead and cicadas rubbed their summer chorus, over and over. A lizard stretched out on the stone, taking in heat. Wise lizard, she thought, knowing its cold nature and finding what it lacked. Like her and Dragonetz. Perfect harmony. Heat and cold. Fire, water, earth and air: no element missing. 'Nobody will ever come between us,' she murmured.

'Nobody,' he agreed sleepily, rolling over and kissing her again.

Then they talked, far from the castle's ears, where he could speak of the tourney, of his hopes that the ties begun in hawking would grow in the sport of a tourney: that idle men's rivalries could be harnessed: that Ramon Berenguer, Comte de Barcelone, had the skills to bring des Baux to his glove while playing the inferior role. He spoke of his fears too.

No such sport was without danger. He had lost men in training exercises before, through careless use of weapons or through delib-erate use of the opportunity to settle scores. There would be no shortage of scores to settle on this mock-battlefield. He had to hope that Malik could protect his team-mate, the young Comte de Provence, but that would leave Dragonetz only Raoulf whose loyalty was without question.

Estela listened, asked good questions, offered reassurance. Her heart screamed, 'Let's go home, where you'll be safe,' but she loved a warrior and knew the cost. He must be himself and she must be a fit helpmate. Lying on the pine needles and scorched earth, she nearly asked him about Etiennette, nearly told him about Hugues, but she knew that none of these revelations would help him carry the burden he had taken on.

She collected the clothes strewn around them, shook off the earth and pine needles, winced at the creases in her riding-skirt. They dressed and he plaited her hair, tutted as he picked some dry grass blades out of her coif. She checked his apparel and passed it as acceptable for view from a distance. Then they mounted once more, touching hands from the saddle as if it was too soon to return to one body each.

Neither of them was in a rush to return to the citadel and they stopped on the ridge as the view opened up. Provence lay spread below them, Les Baux turning blue and gold in the sunset at their feet. 'Even Provence is blue,' she told him. 'Your colours.'

'Sing for me tonight.'

'I always do,' said Estela.

CHAPTER TWENTY-THREE

When a wolf first sees a person, the airy spirits accompanying it weaken the person's powers, so he does not know that the wolf sees him. If the person sees the wolf first, he holds God in his heart, and by that effort both the wolf and airy spirits flee.

Physica, Animals

From his seat at the High Table, Dragonetz watched Estela as she performed for the court. Elegant in blue silk and sapphires, her black hair disciplined into a net studded with periwinkles, she looked queenly and unattainable. It seemed impossible that such a woman had been wild and naked in his arms, smelling of pine needles and summer herbs. Impossible that she was here, in public, wearing his colours and glancing in his direction, making mischief with the lines of a song that meant more in private than any other listener could know. How could anyone in that hall look elsewhere? Her fingers running over the oud plucked at his heart-strings and her sweet voice made a man believe in angels.

While Estela sang, all was right with the world. Hugues' absence, laid up in bed, removed the glowering tension from the High Table, where Etiennette would always be too proud a hostess to let politics destroy courtesy. Ramon was more than her equal and could not be

faulted as a guest. Though they would kill each other on the battle-
field, they would never trade insults. The same could not be said of
the Porcelets and lesser lords – nor of Hugues himself – but Dragonetz had high hopes of the coming tourney. Discussion with Malik
and Raoulf had clarified their strategy, so that the event should purge
men's frustrations without turning a blood-letting into a bloodbath.
Dragonetz could trust Malik and Raoulf with what meant more than
his life, his honour, and he felt whole again at the very idea of such
men being at his side. And such a woman.

The pause between songs allowed a newcomer entrance to the
Great Hall. Dragonetz was vaguely aware of the shuffling and
murmur as someone entered, made way along the tables, past the
seated guests and busy servers but all his attention was on Estela as
she picked up her instrument for the last song.

He was apprehensive when he recognised her transposition for a
lute and one voice of the von Bingen song that had so moved him in
the chapel. However, as she put her soul into the words and sang for
him, his very being sang with her. He'd underestimated her and what
a woman's voice could bring to this heavenly music. 'Praise be to
thee, O spirit of flame,' she sang, and he shut his eyes to concentrate
better.

> *'Intellectus te in dulcissimo sono*
> *advocate ac edificial tibi*
> *cum rationaliate parat*
> *que in aureis operibus sudat.'*

> 'Intellect calls to you
> with sweetest sound
> and teams you with Reason
> to make works of great worth.'

This was his life's work, in the words of a song, and he could
already hear the next verse in his mind, describing Talharcant's
blessed mission, when another voice chimed in, adding an unmis-

takeable male tenor to Estela's soprano. The blend chilled Dragonetz, every word become a deadly irony. Poison indeed. He opened his eyes.

'Tu autem semper gladium
habes illud abscidere
quod noxiale pomum
per nigerrimum homicidium profert.'

'Sword e'er in hand
to cut out
what the apple poisons
through blackest murder.'

The singer was weaving through the courtiers towards Estela. A knight, muscular, and fresh from travel. He was still wearing mail shirt, the hood cowled round his neck and revealing tousled gold-brown locks. His leather britches were serviceable and no doubt stained, hardly meant for a court appearance. He'd no doubt left his sword with the weapons at the door but Dragonetz would bet he was armed – a dagger in both boots probably.

Estela had faltered in surprise but picked up the next verse and they completed their duet. They bowed and curtseyed to the audience, smiled silly grins at each other. The knight made obeisance lingering long enough over Estela's hand to make Dragonetz' sword-hand itch beyond bearing.

'Who is it?' whispered Etiennette.

'Geoffroi de Rançon,' replied Dragonetz. The knight who'd tried to murder him in the Holy Land. The knight who'd wormed his way into Estela's good graces, posing as Dragonetz' best friend. The enemy Dragonetz could not kill or even unmask without losing Estela. And the only other person who knew de Rançon for what he really was had been banished; Gilles would be no help this time. Aloud, Dragonetz said, 'One of Aliénor's men, an old acquaintance.'

Beaming, resting on de Rançon's arm, Estela brought the knight to the High Table, no doubt to introduce him to Etiennette and re-unite him with his best friend. Swordless, Dragonetz willed himself to be Damascan steel, fine and strong, honed and meet for purpose.

'Dragonetz, my friend!' the man hailed him, with evident delight at renewing their acquaintance. He threw his arms round Dragonetz in a manly hug, his hauberk catching on the linen tabard, pinching the skin underneath. 'At last!' De Rançon's eyes were what people remembered of him, all colours and no colour, gathering and reflecting light, hypnotic, hypocritical.

'My Lord de Rançon.' Dragonetz could not feign a matching warmth and felt Estela's disappointment. *Already,* he thought. *It begins.* He didn't have to wait long for the first hit.

De Rançon's expression shifted to the solemnity appropriate to announcing a death in the family. Dragonetz waited, impassive.

'Would I had found you under other circumstances...' began the newcomer. Estela looked from one man to the other, her smile fading.

Stammering in his embarrassment at the errand but loud enough to be heard by everyone in the hall, de Rançon said, 'I have been charged by our Liege,the lady Aliénor, Duchesse d'Aquitaine and Queen of England, to declare you Oath-breaker, exiled from her protection and her presence, hencewith.'

Estela gasped, murmuring, 'It has begun!' as if she'd read Dragonetz' own thoughts.

Through gritted teeth he said, 'This makes no sense. There is some misunderstanding.'

Sadly, de Rançon shook his head. 'No my friend. She sent a messenger to you telling of the threat posed by King Louis after her marriage to Henri Courtmantel, Lord of Anjou and King of England. She summoned you to her side and you were oath-bound to obey. She did not believe you had not come but the evidence of her own eyes could not be denied. And as soon as the battle with Louis was over, and she was victorious – without your support – she sent me to proclaim your dishonour to the world. I begged her to send someone else...' he tailed off, broken-voiced looking down.

'I received no such message. I knew nothing of the Queen's

danger or need.' *Why* did he know nothing, Dragonetz wondered. He looked along the High Table, caught the pity and guilt in Etiennette's eyes, the calm judgement in Ramon's and he understood. They had known.

When he'd knelt before Ramon and spoken of his fealty to Aliénor, Barcelone had known full well that all Aliénor's men were at her side. But he'd said nothing because he'd wanted Lord Dragonetz for himself. Etiennette had known and said nothing, for the same reason. And he had played with pigeons from the south, caring nothing for events in the north, thinking nothing of the lack of news. What a fool he'd been and how de Rançon must be enjoying himself.

'This is a grave mistake. No news reached me or I would have gone to my Lady's side. I am no oath-breaker.' His voice rang out in the silence of the hall and the word 'Oath-breaker' echoed, lingering.

'The Queen will have you killed if you go within a hundred miles of her,' stated de Rançon. That, Dragonetz could believe. He'd been on the receiving end of a red-headed temper more than once. If he couldn't get to see Aliénor, he could never redeem himself.

'There's more,' de Rançon declared solemnly, his face the picture of pained sympathy. 'Your father...'

Dragonetz' jaw ached from gritting his teeth during the dramatic pause but he managed to keep silent.

Clearly struggling to say something so difficult, de Rançon continued, '... your father, Lord Dragonetz, is shamed to have given birth to you and disinherits you. He says you are no son of his and Ruffec is barred to you.' Apologetic eyes looked frankly into Dragonetz' own, man to man. 'He bade me say this to you, word for word.'

I bet he did! Dragonetz took the gaze as he was trained to do with a sword through the guts; noting the pain, knowing he would have to feel it later, disciplining his body and speech. 'I need to take some air,' he said. 'Please excuse me, my Lady. My Lords.' A nod in the direction of Etiennette, Ramon and, of course, de Rançon, sufficed and he could make his escape. He had to pass the infernal man within touching distance and the latter took the opportunity to give friendly solace, whispered but loud enough to reach Estela. First mistake, thought Dragonetz grimly, even as he reacted helplessly to the new thrust.

'This must be hard for you. I have brought the medicaments that gave you such strength in the Holy Land. Just send me word if you should need a little help in sleeping…'

Dragonetz felt the instant craving that returned if he did not keep busy and out of temptation at all times. All he had to do was send a messenger to de Rançon, any time he felt overwhelmed and the poppy would let him sleep, would do more than that – would give him such dreams… He stumbled against a courtier. 'Excuse me', he mumbled and headed blindly for the door.

Behind him, he heard Estela's angry, 'No! I am in charge of any medicaments here.' He had the impression she was following him out but he was too churned up to look, as he reclaimed Talharcant from the pile of weapons and fantasised about driving his sword through de Rançon's smug face. Part of Dragonetz' mind registered that Estela knew the impact de Rançon's parting words would have and that her angry reaction played against the enemy.

She caught up with him outside, took his arm, held on tightly as if he would float up into the sky if she didn't tether him. He laughed at himself, bitter. Poppy-thoughts already.

'He just thought to ease your mind after such a blow,' Estela put the best interpretation on de Rançon's words. Of course; she would. 'He doesn't know what we went through, what you went through.'

Dragonetz leaned against a wall, breathed deeply, shut his eyes. 'Oath-breaker,' he said. 'What is my fealty worth now?' She moved into his arms and they clung to each other.

'Nobody will come between us,' she murmured. *Why would she say that again? Was it because somebody might? Somebody who'd found them, here, in Les Baux.*

'It seems we are both orphans,' he told her, digging deep for a lighter tone and gently disengaging from her embrace. 'But there is a bigger field of battle to consider. I need some time to think.'

She nodded and said nothing. He left her standing at the entrance to the Great Hall, and strode off, blind to the guards he passed, the giggles of girls giving night exchanges until he reached the chapel.

The great oak door swung open, offering sanctuary, and Dragonetz knelt before the altar, in the candlelight, the cross of his sword a focus for his thoughts. Any attempt to empty his mind and allow something greater to direct him merely dropped him to base need. Those who'd given him the poppy had known full well the life sentence they had given him.

His hands shook and the demon on his shoulder whispered, *'Just one message. Send a boy to de Rançon and pain will cease. Oh and the dreams will be beautiful, this world as it should be, as it could be, paradise itself...'*

He missed Vertat's weight and claws, suddenly angry with Estela for banishing the hawk. If Vertat were with him, he'd be fine!

Poppy thoughts, he told himself, as a cloaked figure appeared and knelt beside him. He didn't have to look to know that Estela had followed him, was keeping him company.

Another surge of anger – she was watching him to make sure he didn't succumb to poppy temptation. She didn't trust him.

As suddenly as the anger came, it went, and he knew her presence was a silent message of love. He also acknowledged that he didn't trust himself.

For an eternity, they knelt in silent communion. As Dragonetz prayed and fought his demons, he was visited by memories of his greatest battle with the drug, and of the people who'd helped him. He could not distinguish between the living and the dead in that battle. He knew that Estela and Malik had tended his body's needs and fought his unreason. He knew that his dreams had taken him beyond this world and there too he'd found friendship from beyond the grave; Arnaut had walked with him in that otherness, fought for him as he had when alive.

The worlds had fuzzed and fused, worlds in which Dragonetz was not alone, but staunchly defended in his weakness. Even the boy, Muganni, had crossed worlds with Malik, saving Dragonetz' mind as once Dragonetz had saved the boy's body.

In his mind, Dragonetz could hear the perfect voice of that little Arab boy, singing for the Queen of Jerualem. Before he'd been set free, with a diamond in his pouch.

'Sing for me,' Dragonetz murmured.

Shocked, Estela said, 'Here? A woman sing in a church?'

'Von Bingen and her nuns sing.'

'But that's in a convent. The priest here wouldn't like it.'

'He's not here. Sing it again for me. *O ignee spiritus.*'

Standing, so as to breathe correctly, and facing the altar to do reverence, Estela's voice filled the corners of the chapel with the words that echoed in Dragonetz' heart. His insides clenched as she sang the verse he'd last heard in duet, then eased as he let the words and voice touch him, heal him, cleanse the dirt de Rançon had left on the music.

He let the message reach him, released in the purity of his lover's song. To poison what was good and what was beautiful would always be easier than to proclaim it. But poison only worked if the body allowed the toxins. Once the poison was identified, it could be purged. And Dragonetz had no problem identifying the poison.

Estela sang on and Dragonetz watched the candlelight flare on Talharcant, the sword consecrated to fight evil. He saw a fallen angel, eyes sparkling with many colours, falling from the tower of pride. He understood what he must do. All that remained was to decide on how.

> '*Quando autem malum ad te gladium suum educit*
> *tu illud in cor illius refringis*
> *sicut in primo perdito angelo fecisti*
> *ubi turrim superbie illius*
> *in infernum deiecisti.*'

'When evil draws its sword on you,
you turn it back into its black heart
as you did to the fallen angel
in the beginning
hurling his tower of pride
down into hell.'

CHAPTER TWENTY-FOUR

Certain people are malicious, either by nature or because of the devil, and express nothing willingly. When they speak they have a harsh look and at times they nearly go out of their mind, as if propelled by madness. They then quickly return to themselves. These people should often, or indeed always, place a diamond in their mouth. It is of such virtue and of such great strength that it extinguishes the malice and evil in them.

Physica, Stones

In the morning, once she was sure Dragonetz was deeply asleep, aided by a potion which owed nothing to the poppy, Estela sought out the one person with whom she could share her fears. 'You know how he is,' she told Malik. 'He has so much self-control in public and then, to deal with all *this* in private! Of course he is tempted to seek oblivion.'

A slant of sunshine grooved the furrows in Malik's face even deeper. Estela had never thought about his age before and, suddenly, she noticed how much older he looked. Could age sneak up on a person like this? Could she be ambushed by furrows and grey hairs? Would it be worse to find herself suddenly old or to notice each little change as it happened? She shivered.

Still frowning, Malik asked, 'Who is this de Rançon?'

'He didn't know the effect that mentioning the poppy would have. Most people don't know what the poppy does. Dragonetz only knew because Muganni told him. And we know because we saw it.' There was no need to remind Malik of what they had seen when they'd imprisoned Dragonetz to purge him of the drug.

If anything, Malik frowned more deeply. 'He knew the likely effect of calling Dragonetz Oath-breaker.'

'He had to. Aliénor commanded it and you know what she's like. It would have been even worse from someone else.' She answered the earlier question. 'He's Dragonetz' childhood friend. They were brothers-in-arms in the Crusade and then last year de Rançon took me to the Holy Land to rescue Dragonetz, when he was in trouble. He saved Dragonetz' life. Gilles was there.'

She didn't mention the details Geoffroi had given her, which reflected badly on Dragonetz. How de Rançon the elder had been dismissed as Aliénor's Commander because of Dragonetz: had returned home with his son, disgraced; had been replaced by Dragonetz. And how Geoffroi had forgiven his friend for all the mistakes and damage caused.

Estela preferred not to dwell on Dragonetz' past, nor to remember that Gilles had warned her against her lover, after listening to de Rançon's stories during their journey. Gilles had come round once they'd met up with Dragonetz again and bygones could be left as bygones.

'I will tell him,' she said simply. 'Geoffroi. Not to mention the poppy or let Dragonetz have any, even if he asks for it.'

'No,' was Malik's judgement. 'We should hide our friend's weakness, not shout it to anyone, not even to another friend.'

'Then what should I do?'

'Tell de Rançon that all medicines in Les Baux are distributed by you or by me as part of the enlightened view that practitioners should be licensed, so if he wishes to make the poppy available then he should place it in our hands. That you are the dispenser for Lady Etiennette and her vassals, and also for Dragonetz.'

It was Estela's turn to frown. 'That's what I said in the Great Hall.'

'Then make it so.'

Suddenly Estela knew where all her studies had been leading. 'That is what I want! To be like Nicholaus of Salerno; to note and list the ingedients, administer medicines. To be a chemist. I don't want to be a surgeon at all!'

Some shift in the light made a flicker of what could almost have been relief cross Malik's face. 'You excel in such work,' he told her.

'I will speak to Lady Etiennette too! If she makes it more formal then Geoffroi will naturally turn to me for advice rather than speak ill-advisedly to Dragonetz!'

'Let us hope so.'

'We shall keep Dragonetz safe and healthy. I am not letting him go through that again!' She realised what she was saying and sighed. 'Healthy then. There's no keeping a man like that safe. I'm worried about this tourney too.'

Malik's eyes gleamed. 'A man takes the risks he must.'

'Do you think he's right? I know he's behind the choice of leaders and sides.'

'I think his purpose is right. He wants men to form bonds through dangerous sport, as they do through his training methods. My Lord Ramon is a peerless warrior and his support for Hugues on this play-battlefield will give that young man a taste of what it would be like to ride with Barcelone instead of against him.

Dragonetz and I working together might be able to shape this tourney to our ends but much will fall to him as I have the young Comte to protect. It is worth a throw of the dice I think but the outcome will be as Allah wills.'

The words 'our ends' reassured Estela. If Malik and Dragonetz were on the same side in their intentions as well as in the mock-battle, surely good would prevail. 'Inshallah,' she echoed.

'You said there was another matter?' he prodded gently.

'I'd forgotten!' Estela unrolled the fabric she was carrying. 'Can you read this?'

An hour later, Estela hurried to her duties with Lady Etiennette, none the wiser about the origins of her Moorish treasure. She had learned much about the symbolism of Arabic swirls and how a pious artisan would remain anonymous in his work. None of this explained what looked like a signature beside the same pattern that was engraved on Estela's oud. Nor did it explain how Estela's mother – or rather her forebears – had come by the instrument in the first place.

All Estela remembered being told was that the oud was a family heirloom and that she would be the first in many generations to do it justice. How typical of the Gyptian to add another puzzle into Estela's life! When Estela found time, she would make another visit to the cave and squeeze all the information she wanted out of that sour old malediction.

As if there wasn't enough to occupy her thoughts in the news from Aquitaine – and its impact on her knight. What had the old woman said about him? 'I see his path, the one you're tied to, the Oath-breaker.' Estela's retort had been true – Dragonetz was no oath-breaker! – and yet, he'd been named so, publicly. Perhaps the evil words about Estela herself would find some twisted way of being spoken, without being true. Perhaps the world would believe her unfaithful to Dragonetz. How could she fight against words that wriggled into the core of her life, worms in the sweet fruit, waiting an innocent bite?

When Dragonetz finally awoke, his head was heavy with some vague presentiment of doom. Then he remembered the events of the previous night and understood that it was no presentiment. A knock at the door brought further confirmation of his shame via a messenger bearing a saddle-bag.

Alone, Dragonetz took the missives out of the saddle-bag, one letter with Aliénor's seal, one with the dragon seal of his ex-domain, Ruffec, and a short note in his mother's own hand, unsealed. No doubt de Rançon had enjoyed the blurred letters where tears had fallen, the hope that an explanation would bring forgiveness and most of all the unspoken hurt that her son had shamed the family name.

There was no such bewilderment in the letters from Aliénor's notary or his father. Legalese in one, and penstrokes like swordthrusts in the other; both cast him off formally. Dragonetz let his anger burn to white, controlled, the cutting edge to his purpose and then he sought out his first target.

She came at once to his message, an admission in itself, and she waited for him to speak first.

He offered no title. 'You knew of this and said nothing.'

The Lady of Les Baux said, 'I knew nothing when I sent for you except that there was bound to be unrest with Aliénor courting the self-styled heir to the English throne. The alliance between Aquitaine and Anjou, with England as the golden apple just within reach, threatened France. Louis was bound to challenge Henri's increasing power in the north. But this,' she shrugged, 'was common knowledge. And you were still in Marselha. I thought news would have reached you and if you chose to remain in the south, it was for your own reasons.'

My reasons. Still weak from the poppy, recovering, spending time with my lady and my child, far from the world and its madness, knowing nothing of Aliénor's machinations and caring less, Dragonetz did not say. 'We had withdrawn from the world. And I received no messenger but yours.' He was letting her off the hook and she knew it. The atmosphere lightened. *Too easy* he thought and added, 'You kept news from me, here, didn't you.'

Her turn to concede a point. 'I always hear messengers in private but no, I did not discuss their news with you for fear you would go north. I need you. Provence needs you. Aliénor has others, as does Henri Courtmantel.' She turned her plain features towards him, fully lit, guileless. 'I received neither message nor messenger for you personally, only my own men with news.

You care about Provence! You don't care about the north and you certainly don't care about England, that mud-bath of a barbaric island! If Henri does take his much-vaunted inheritance away from his Uncle Stephen, he'll waste all his men and time fighting the heathen Welsh!'

'Maybe. But Aliénor is – was – my Liege Lord and I was honour-bound to obey her command.'

'The command which never reached you. God's will be done.'

'Lady Aliénor prefers God's will to coincide with her own.' In that, the two women were alike, thought Dragonetz, studying the ruler of Les Baux. He knew her well enough to believe what she was telling him and in truth, he could not blame her for the outcome of her small evasions. His ignorance of events was his own fault.

'Nothing has changed,' she told him. 'You are the solution for Provence'

'Everything has changed,' he replied, bowed and left.

Then he sought out the second person he must charge with the same accusations, prepared this time to gain no satisfaction. He was not prepared to be received in formal court, with Malik standing guard on his lord's right hand and de Rançon on the left of the young Comte, who sat in state beside his uncle. Dragonetz gritted his teeth and knelt to Ramon Berenguer, Comte de Barcelone, Regent of Provence.

'Rise, my Lord Dragonetz,' Ramon ordered. 'You are always welcome in my court.'

'You welcome oath-breakers?'

'Even El Sidi had a time in exile, riding with those he had previously fought against.'

'When you asked for my oath of allegiance and I told you Aliénor was my liege, you knew I should have been at her side, that she needed me.' The accusation drew a shift in posture from Barcelone's guards, ready to act if required. Malik tensed. *To stab him or save him*, wondered Dragonetz.

He focused on Barcelone, ignoring the dancing eyes of Aliénor's popinjay and the round eyes of the young Comte, who had surely never heard anyone challenge his uncle in such a manner.

Ramon stood up and the ring of steel half-drawn echoed in the hall. Slightly shorter than Dragonetz, he held the knight's gaze. 'I was surprised that you did not go to her,' he said, his tone calm, measuring. 'I judged it unlike you to hold back from duty to a liege. I was right, was I not?'

Dragonetz looked down to avoid being unmanned by words that both let blood and applied salve to his wound, in one deft move. He understood why he had been received in public. It was so that Ramon Berenguer could declare Dragonetz an honourable knight, no oath-breaker, in front of the whole gathering, in front of de Rançon.

'And now things have changed and you are free to choose your allegiance,' Ramon continued.

Dragonetz' every muscle ached. This was the moment he would be backed into a corner, forced to swear to Barcelone or insult him for Les Baux's sake. Which would he do?

'And you have time to think on your changed circumstances.'

Dragonetz looked up, faced the ruler who could have taken his sword but chose instead to wait until it was offered. He could not speak but knelt and kissed the hand that was offered before Ramon returned to his chair.

'Can I tell him now, Uncle?' asked the young Comte, his eyes shining. He barely waited for Ramon's nod before continuing. 'We have one more for our team. Hugues des Baux has allowed us to have an extra man, given my youth. Of course, he is wrong and I shall deliver the worth of a full man at the tourney but I shall not fight over a decision that gives us such a knight for our team.'

'This is good news,' said Dragonetz gently. 'And who is this warrior we have gained?' He already knew the answer.

'Your friend, my Lord de Rançon,' revealed the youth with pride, while de Rançon looked every bit the humble, flattered vassal.

'That is indeed great news.' Dragonetz hoped his enthusiasm was every bit as convincing as the slap on his back delivered by 'friend Geoffroi'. He suspected that he would never be the other man's equal in dissimulation but now was a good time to start practising. Even

Malik looked pleased at the 'great news'. Dragonetz swallowed his bile and smiled.

'We have a battle plan,' the young Comte informed his team leader, 'but I can't tell you in front of the enemy.'

His uncle smiled. 'The enemy is worried,' he said. 'And we have our own battle plans.'

'In Dragonetz we trust,' declared de Rançon.

'Inshallah,' murmured Malik, his hand now relaxed on his sabre-hilt.

Dragonetz looked at his ill-assorted team members: the boy and knight alight with the prospect of action, his Moorish friend, calm and seasoned. Barcelone was the still centre, indulging the enthusiasm of his opponents-to-be.

It was Barcelone, his enemy, who had raised Dragonetz above the waves of personal doubt, reminded him of who he was, and it was to the Comte that he spoke. 'To meet such opponents in the field can only bring honour to all, whatever the outcome.' He bowed in homage, then addressed the youth. 'I fear we are already outshone in finery. Have you seen Les Baux's banner?' A shake of the head. 'My spies tell me of a magnificent banner, a star and a saint to support our enemy.'

The young Comte's smile wavered. 'But we have a banner too, don't we? And colours?'

Suddenly, Dragonetz felt the rush of blood he needed. Action! 'Oh yes,' he said, 'we have a magnificent banner. And enough blue ribbons to join the windows of Les Baux to your castle in Barcelone.' Ramon nodded. Yes, they shared the same goal.

Dragonetz continued speaking to the young Comte. 'Tell your lady-love to pin blue ribbons to her sleeve.' The youth looked sheepish. 'If you can't choose between, then tell *all* your lady-loves,' Dragonetz teased him. 'I swear we shall win any tourney in ladies with ribbons.'

'Unfair, my Lord!' protested Ramon. 'My Queen has gone, and her ladies with her.'

'I think you'll find my Lord Hugues can help the cause,' countered Dragonetz.

Finally, he turned to de Rançon. 'Let it be a fight that men speak of in years to come. A fair fight with honour, that earns only renown.' He was not speaking of the tourney. De Rançon nodded, a glittering cypher.

CHAPTER TWENTY-FIVE

If a person, man or woman, eats or drinks a love enchantment, then plantain
juice, with or without water, should be given to him to drink. Later, he should
take some strong drink, and he will be purged inside and be relieved.
Physica, Plants

At last, Estela had completed her duties and could seek out her old friend, to catch up on all the news he brought. She pricked a pattern of holes in a doomed piece of linen to look busy while she waited in a window-seat, her attention straying out of the window-slits. Below, the marketeers were packing up their goods into carts while donkeys waited patiently. So patiently in fact that they showed no interest in moving once the carts were laden. The routine curses and thwacking of sticks followed and then the train started off towards the gate, heading out of the town.

Estela imagined the farms and settlements in the countryside where the traders milked goats and cows, grew vines, kept sheep. What would happen to them all if Les Baux went to war against Barcelone once again? She knew from Sancha the damage caused before the truce, each side burning crops and killing livestock to stop the other profiting; peasants and tradesmen being taxed by both sides to pay for soldiers, armour and weapons. Bleeding the land. Not a healthy purge in her professional opinion but a cause of death if not stopped.

And yet, Sancha was willing to see such carnage again, for the sake of the Baux 'right' to Provence. Sancha, who fainted at the thought of blood, never mind the sight of it, wanted war. It made no sense. Was this the proper way for a lady to think? To cheer her knight on to war from the sidelines of a sewing-room like a spectator at a tourney?

She stabbed the linen again, noting that the pattern was like that on her oud and would be very pretty – if Sancha did the embroidery. But no lady could stay in the sewing-room if there really was war. Sancha must know that too. War for ladies meant taking on the management and defence of the stronghold if the lord was out in the field; making the most of the old men, women and children, who were the only people left to carry out that defense; bearing arms yourself if you could; and of course in defeat, everyone knew what would happen to a lady! Sancha most of all! No, it made no sense that anybody would want war.

'My Lady? I'm sorry to keep you waiting so long – Barcelone detained me. It seems everybody wants my news.' De Rançon bowed low, the double imprint of his lips warm on her hand. His rueful smile suited a face that was still boyish, northern in its regular features, framed by honey-brown curls. And those eyes. Rings of clear colour, no colour, changing colours; sparkling like a magical spell in a fairy-tale. Even when a girl had spent months with him as a travelling companion, had camped in a forest and shared secrets with him, those eyes still held a glamour. Especially when her lover's best friend looked at her with such devotion. As was due to Dragonetz' lady, of course.

Estela remembered that she was annoyed. She did not need to be polite or careful with somebody who'd witnessed her seasickness. 'You shouldn't have offered the poppy to Dragonetz! It's hard enough for him to forego it without the temptation being put under his nose when he's had such a blow! And couldn't you have told him such news more privately?!'

The rueful expression deepened and the eyes dulled. 'You know Aliénor. She charged me with the message, to be given in public – made me swear an oath. All I could think was that it would be better from me than from somebody else, who might twist the words. And then I would be here to help him, afterwards.'

Estela did indeed know Aliénor, guessed at what de Rançon was too proud to say, that he'd been threatened with disgrace himself if he disobeyed. She imagined Aliénor's rage and de Rançon being the nearest target. Mollified, she contented herself with, 'Yes, I know Aliénor, and I can understand that you were under orders.'

'I don't understand what you mean as to the poppy. It's a medicine. I thought he might need a calming potion for sleep after such bad news.'

Estela sighed. She herself had been just as innocent in the past, before hearing from a young Arab boy what the results of regular use would be, before witnessing those effects in Dragonetz, before fighting for his life – against Dragonetz himself.

She gave de Rançon a summary of the poppy's dangers and asked him to give her his supply, so she could lock it away with the other poisons. Of course, he agreed, clearly impressed by her status as physician. The matter concluded to her satisfaction, Estela interrogated him about the news from the north.

'So Aliénor has married Henri of Anjou.'

'The King of England,' corrected de Rançon, twinkling.

'Do you think he will be? What manner of man is he? How does he compare with her last king?'

'You're worse than Barcelone and Etiennette combined!' laughed de Rançon, fending off the battery of questions. 'Primo, yes, I think he might get his wish – and live to regret it. Henri is fiery, a fighter with his own men and now all of Aquitaine to back him. Stephen's star is fading. He cannot fight off Henri forever and the claim is good; he's Stephen's nephew, the Empress Mathilde's son and strong in his own territories. He owns more Frankish land than King Louis does!

So yes, I think we shall see Henri King of England and Aliénor Queen.'

He raised a second finger. 'Secundus. He is as red-headed as she and there are sparks. It is a good political marriage but not a cold one. Becoming king is an obsession. He needs Aquitaine but he's happy to have Aliénor too.'

He ticked off the third answer. 'Tertio. Aliénor has more satisfaction of her new husband than her old.' He glanced at Estela, teasing again. 'But I can't give you more details.' She flushed. That wasn't what she'd meant. Was it? 'Whether she births another girl or gives him the boys they need, we'll see.'

Boys, thought Estela. Plural. A man needs boys. Her insides twisted into a knot. 'Aliénor has always wanted to be mother to a king,' she said, 'to rule through her son.' A memory stirred, back in Narbonne, the Gyptian studying Aliénor's cards, prophesying kings, a tower… Well, if de Rançon was right, Aliénor already had her second king lined up! Aliénor, married to Anjou.

Another thought jumped into her mind. 'England might be more comfortable than Anjou,' she observed. 'Is it true that Aliénor was once closer to Henri's father than is seemly?'

'Swived him you mean?' Accompanied by a dazzling smile, that filled his eyes, De Rançon's crudity was amusing but also disconcerting.

'Do tell,' prompted a familiar voice.

'Dragonetz,' Estela stammered. 'I was asking for news of Aliénor.'

'And getting an interesting response, my love.' Her lover stood, something of the goshawk in his pose as he loomed over the couple perched on the window-seat.

'So serious, Dragonetz, and quite right too! Finding us snug in our little corner, looking like a pair courting, anybody would think I'd been kissing your irresistible lady.' The very words tinged Estela's cheeks with a memory that flitted into view, slight as a butterfly but brushing against Dragonetz as it flew. As surely as if he'd spoken, Estela saw him make the connection and realise that she *had* kissed de Rançon. *Once*, she told him silently. *And you were so far away, for so long*

'And did she?' he asked, patiently, just the slight tightening of his jaw telling someone who knew him well how angry he was.

De Rançon pursed his lips in comic judgement. 'Possibly,' he concluded, 'though I'd wager more on the uncle in Antioch as a certainty. You know Aliénor.'

Dragonetz just nodded. He reached for Estela's hand, kissed it and asked, 'My Lady? When you have finished your gossiping, perhaps you would care to ride with me?'

Estela just nodded, the trace of lips burning her treacherous hand. She didn't take in one further word spoken by de Rançon before she excused herself and donned her riding skirt.

This time, the ride was silent and their love-making fierce. Estela met her lover's urgency with her own fire but when she lay in his arms afterwards, what she felt was guilt. That was when he asked her the question that was not a question. 'He kissed you.'

She confessed into the black hairs of his chest, 'No. I kissed him. Once. On the voyage to the Holy Land. He behaved as your friend should, with courtesy, and escorted me back to my cabin – the only cabin on the ship.'

'Once is too often.' His arm remained around her, steadier than his voice.

She said, 'And you?' They both knew what he had done in the Holy Land.

'That's different.'

Is it? she thought. *And would it be different to marry the Lady of Les Baux? How far would 'difference' take a man?* She rolled out of his arms and straightened her clothes.

'I will sleep in my chamber tonight, keep Vertat with me,' he told her. 'I need to think.'

Instantly, her thoughts flew to a locked cupboard. He read her face. 'No,' he told her gently, taking both her hands in his. She could feel the musician's calluses on his long, tapering fingers, as surely he could on hers. Twin souls. He wiped the tear that escaped her control. 'No, I will not seek the poppy.'

'I made de Rançon give me his store and it is locked away where

you cannot reach it without robbing Malik's dead body for the key.'
There had been a time he would not have hesitated to do so.

He smoothed her hair back from her face, putting the strands back
under her coif. Then he cupped her chin, tilting her face up so she
must meet his eyes. 'You did well. It is hard for me not to kill him,
you know.' He ran his fingers over her mouth then kissed her. She
knew he didn't mean Malik. She had been right to hide Hugues'
assault from her lover. If he reacted this way to a kiss, what would he
do if he knew his host had behaved with such discourtesy? For a
moment, Estela weighed the power she held over Les Baux and
Provence. But she was no Helen of Troy.

'It was my fault,' she repeated. 'He did nothing wrong.'

'Let him keep it that way,' Dragonetz said, with Damascan steel in
his tone.

'Then you'll come to me tonight?'

'No.' Still gentle. Most dangerous when gentle. 'I do need to think.
It has been a difficult couple of days.' His tone lightened and he
squeezed her. The first sign of play. 'And you are most distracting, my
love. When a man needs to plan his tactics for a tourney, a goshawk is
a better aid in focusing the mind.'

'Should I be jealous, my Lord?'

'Never,' he told her. 'But make sure that *I* am not.'

When Estela found a posy of bright flowers on her bed, she knew all
was well between her and Dragonetz, even if he kept his nights to
himself. Like the smiling faces of young maids-in-waiting, the multi-
coloured pansies gave her their message.

'Thoughts,' she mused aloud. 'Thinking of you, bright colours,
happy thoughts, heartsease.' The hours spent in ladies' company had
not been wasted and she could speak the language of flowers as well
as she could identify their medicinal properties.

Von Bingen had no use for pansies but Estela's mother had made
tisanes of the wild tricolour flowers to soothe coughing. A good

choice from Dragonetz, she decided, and the flowers did indeed ease her aching heart. She was surprised he hadn't chosen blue flowers, his colour, but otherwise the gesture was perfect.

She pinned one pansy to her gown, to show appreciation, and pulled the petals off all the others to use medicinally. She tied them into a square of muslin and took them to her dispensary, where she boiled some water and added the muslin bag. She added some of her precious stock of sugar as sweetener.

Since Aliénor had brought sugar back from the Holy Land to Narbonne, Estela had taken to the white substance and often used it instead of honey. In fact, she liked sugar so much that she wondered whether it had qualities like the poppy and she was becoming an addict.

Her train of thought led her back to Dragonetz and his problems. Was he really as strong as he claimed? He'd survived all manner of horror in war and capture but his reputation had always been untarnished. Dragonetz 'los Pros', 'the brave'. Did men now call him oathbreaker behind his back? Surely he must be wondering the same thing.

'Mother Mary and all the saints!' she swore as the pot frothed brown on the crucible. She grabbed a gauntlet stuffed with rags, that she kept for the purpose, and moved the pan onto the cold stone in the fireplace, where the mixture sizzled and spat.

Stirring with the wooden spoon and cursing her lack of attention, Estela watched the bubbles die back and the brew settle to a clear liquid. She lifted the spoon out of the goo and let the liquid drip back, drop by drop. Except it didn't. They drops hung like tears, like dew, like pearls but they stuck to the spoon, dangling. All very interesting.

Estela put a spoonful onto a platter to let it cool quickly. Then she tasted it, briefly wondering what Dragonetz would say if she died during one of her chemical experiments.

'It's good! May I be turned into a scorpion for basil-sniffing if this isn't the best tasting potion ever!' Wondering how long the miracle would stay syrupy in consistency, and, if it did stay syrupy, how long such a product would keep, Estela started planning further experiments. She couldn't wait to tell Malik.

This was a sign that she had made the right decision; she was meant to be an apothecary, maybe even an alchemist. The change of base metal to gold must be similar to what she had just seen; bubbles and magic.

CHAPTER TWENTY-SIX

... there are some dirty and corrupt prostitutes who desire to seem to be more than virgins and they do make a constrictive for this purpose, but they are ill-counselled, for they render themselves bloody and they wound the penis of the man. They take powdered natron and place it in the vagina.

The Trotula, On Treatments for Women

Occasional storms had punctuated the summer heat for weeks but the heaviness never quite cleared. It was as if the pressure outside gathered inside her own head, thought Estela as she worked in her dispensary or practised her lute, far too busy for embroidery. She saw Dragonetz in passing, a glance, a fleeting touch. She could see how busy he was too, now that the date for the tourney was fixed, but he was never too busy to send her flowers, speaking in the language all lovers knew. Marguerites, with their delicate suggestion that she was 'a pearl' among women, had been followed by roses and more roses, passion and more passion. A promise.

Still a surprising lack of blue in his choices but no lack of fervour. Surely he would send a blue flower for her to wear at the tourney? If not, she could pin whatever it was with a blue ribbon. But would that seem ambivalent to others if she had a red rose and a blue ribbon. On tourney day of all days she wanted to wear her lover's colours.

Not that she anticipated he would be in any real danger, with Malik and de Rançon to watch his back and do his bidding. He was too fine a commander to come to harm in play-fighting. There would probably be more damage to the men from heat-stroke in all that armour than from the mock-battle itself! But the body of soldiers needed blood-letting as much as did any human corps. Good health for the body politic would follow.

She thought of her own blood-letting and how effective it had been in calming the hot humours of the Lord of Les Baux. If only she could tell Dragonetz who'd inflicted Hugues' irritating wound, the cause of all these delays in the tourney. She smiled to herself. Hugues was on the mend and if his pride still felt the prick, so much the better. The tourney would take place, Ramon would win Les Baux's alliance if not allegiance and then Barcelone would return home, where Petronilla was in the last months of pregnancy.

Afterwards, the story would be worth singing and Estela was part of it, but she longed for home, for Musca and Nici. When Barcelone left Les Baux, Dragonetz would be free to leave too, for his mint project in Arle. Estela refused to consider the idea that he might choose to stay in Les Baux as its lord. Hugues was wrong and that was all there was to it. There was no reason why she and Dragonetz should not return home in a couple of weeks, he to his various projects and she to the baths at Ais, where she could make the most of her new chemical expertise.

In the meantime, she had her studies, her experiments and her singing. She had been too busy to see much of de Rançon but, when she had, she'd been mindful of Dragonetz' feelings, however misguided they might be, and had steered conversation away from the most titillating gossip. He had accepted her lead and proved, as always, to be a paragon of chivalry in her company. It was normal to enjoy the company of an attractive man, she told some silent challenger, with a flare of irritation.

Perhaps in response to that inner voice, she had ducked de Rançon's suggestion that they sing together and also changed her programme of songs. She'd prepared some of the northern ballads that Dragonetz loved so much, lays of King Arthur's knights that had reached the court of Aquitaine by way of the Welsh bard, Bledri. She was proud of having acquired some of the original songs, as well as some Frankish versions, and she planned to surprise her lover with the new repertoire.

Gallant knights and beauteous ladies made for stories that touched the heart but somehow she didn't think Dragonetz was in a humour for Lancelot and Guinevere, the perfect knight and his best friend's wife. Estela was neither Helen of Troy nor Guinevere but she *was* a troubairitz with a certain reputation. Growing older and wiser merely seemed to constrain her subject matter beyond bearing! Frowning, she added an extra dose of sugar to the bubbling pot and noted the quantities. At least here, in her scientific domain, there were no people to consider!

She ignored the knock on the door at first but it was persistant, if not loud. The quickest method of making it go away was to answer. She sighed, yelled, 'Wait a minute!' at the door in a manner more suited to the apothecary than the lady. The mix of blackberries, water and sugar boiled and clotted to her satisfaction. She removed the pot from the heat and, red-faced from working, went to see if anybody was still standing at the door.

Patiently waiting on the other side, was a girl with long, black plaits, a demeanour that suggested she was a servant but clothes richer than such a station would allow. Estela sniffed. She knew what her mother would have said.

'Come in,' she said, 'and don't touch anything. I expect you have coughing fits or some such thing.' Or the pox, she thought, wiping her hands on her sackcloth apron.

The girl flinched at such a brusque reception, eyeing Estela like a rabbit with a rabid fox.

'I'm sorry. I was busy with my work.' Estela wiped the sweat from her forehead and remembered that she'd tied another bit of sacking round her head, to protect her coif and hair. No doubt she had traces of soot on her face too. Sackcloth and ashes. She must look like a pilgrim on the last step of a thousand mile atonement for murder. She laughed.

'What must I look like!' She moved 'Antidotarum Nicholai' onto a clean flagstone and liberated a stool for the girl. 'Sit yourself down and tell me all about it.'

Hesitant at first, the girl – Maria – opened up with more confidence as Estela prompted gently. She'd heard such stories a thousand times and however often she had to turn down the requests for love potions and abortificants, she felt that it helped girls like this just to unburden themselves. So she listened, waiting for the moment Maria said what she'd come for. Estela schooled her restless spirit to patience, to the observation Malik had taught her.

The patient's eyes? Bright with clear whites, so healthy. Not over-bright, pupils not dilated so this was not a digitalis-user. Not unlike Estela's in colour but more hazel than golden. Black hair shiny and well-oiled. Skin the olive tones of the region, smooth but not always protected from browning, although the patterns of sunlight were faded. This was a girl who had only recently started to take care of her appearance.Her hands gave her away, as was always the case. Just as Estela's said 'lute-player' so did Maria's hands show manual work. In the past, no doubt. Perhaps even washing clothes. River-water and wringing clothes on stones, in all weathers, coarsened hands.

'He has asked me to come to him and I have said I will, tomorrow night,' Maria was saying. 'I know he is too much above me for me to hope for marriage and yet, I think, if I please him enough, he might keep me by him as his mistress...'

'So you want help in pleasing him enough?' Estela helped her, awaiting the inevitable.

'I know exactly *how* to please him,' was the unexpected reply, 'but it's physically impossible.' Estela ran through the many and varied sexual problems detailed by Trota, along with their cures, and waited.

'I need to become a virgin.'

'Ah,' said Estela, not very sympathetically. 'I take it you have lain with another.' The situation was common enough as most men expected a maiden in bed on their wedding night and many men preferred virgin whores or the illusion thereof. Many a good marriage had been founded on reconstructed virginity and many a renowned whore had remained a professional virgin.

In her current humour, Estela was critical of all this hypocrisy. At least she could say she'd never tricked her lover, whatever her nagging conscience might say about enjoying dalliance. So she was not in the mood for indulging such a request.

'It's not as if you're hoping for marriage,' she said bluntly, 'and if this noble lord expects a virgin to come to him when he snaps his fingers, he doesn't seem very admirable to me! If he cares about you, then he should accept you as you are.'

'My Lady, maybe such a one as you could behave so but not an ordinary girl like me. I worked hard to become a servant in the castle, I was hoping to be a lady's maid one day, maybe even marry and have children. To be chosen by a knight like my Lord, you couldn't know what a chance this is for me. He says he'll give me a ring,' she declared with pride. 'Every girl is after him but he's chosen me. And I love him. I will do anything to make him happy. And he has told me how. One night and he will be mine. But I have to be a virgin!'

There was silence as Estela considered how to phrase her refusal. 'I can pay you well,' Maria offered. 'My Lord has been generous.'

Payment in advance, was Estela's cynical response to my Lord's generosity. Then a thought struck her. Could he have recovered enough to be back to his old ways already? Ignoring her threat? By God, if he was, she'd tell Dragonetz everything and Provence could go to hell!

'Is it Lord Hugues?' she asked. 'This fancy lord of yours. You can tell me. A physician is like a priest and shares nothing with others. And I would do nothing to hurt you. I swore an oath that I would do no harm.' Except to that rutting lordling, who needed more blood let than she'd thought!

Maria's startled expression showed the words had hit home. 'How did you know?' Estela nodded grimly. 'It was my Lord Hugues who took my virginity.' The girl's eyes filled. 'I told him no but that just encouraged him and you know we have no choice when the Lord decides. We're his vassals. But I might as well have said yes to the carpenter's boy when he asked and I wanted to, if I was only going to part with my treasure anyway!'

Damn Hugues! thought Estela. But at least he had not broken his word to her, as far as she knew. And he was hardly the first young lord to make free with the serving maids. Like it or not, that was how things were.

'All right,' she said finally. 'But only once. I will not be party to continuing trickery with different men.'

'I promise, my Lady. This will be my real, only, first time with a man.' Her eyes gleamed at the prospect and Estela almost envied her. The first time, with a man you loved. What a sweet combination of desire and duty. Or an illusion.

The Trotula offered many ways of restoring virginity. Estela mentally reviewed the ingredients to hand and chose ground holme oak for constriction. She measured a suitable amount of the powder from one of her jars into an empty one, added some rainwater and stirred till the ground bark dissolved.'Dunk a clean cotton cloth in this and put it in your vagina.' She could see the girl had no idea what the medical term meant. What on earth did such girls call their private parts? She tried, 'Inside your tunnel of Venus. To make it tighter.'

'Oh,' the girl nodded understanding.

'Keep it there until one hour before intercourse.' The word was obviously new to Maria but the meaning was clear enough to work out. 'Make sure all is removed before you lie with your lord,' Estela warned.

Maria took the jar but her face fell. 'But he won't believe it unless there's blood.'

Now comes the hard part thought Estela as she went to a stone ledge and took the leather cover off the bucket. 'They like to be cool and they can stretch out so thin, you'd be surprised what holes they can get out of and into,' she remarked conversationally as she scooped a couple of leeches out of the bucket and popped them and their water into one of her jars, 'so keep the cover on when you're not using them and make sure the holes stay tiny, needle-pricks, like they are now.'

She tied string round the jar and handed it to the ashen-faced girl, who held it like it was plague-ridden, rather than health-giving.

'You're sure you want to seem a virgin?'

Maria nodded, gulping, unable to speak.

'Then you need to insert the leeches into your vagina – your tunnel of Venus – tonight. Not too far, mind you.' Maria nodded, her eyes never leaving the jar in her hands.

'That should make enough blood for a clot that will break up nicely tomorrow night. Take them out first thing in the morning and use the holme oak the rest of the day.' Estela reviewed her instructions. Trota hadn't suggested using the two methods together but there were no contra-indications and *The Trotula* was particularly insistent on the efficacy of leeches.

Oh, yes – there was one more thing. 'I want my leeches back, mind. There are other patients need them, for serious health reasons.'

Maria seemed eager to leave, one jar in the pouch she'd brought, the other clutched firmly and held as far in front of her as she could.

'She must really love him,' Estela muttered to herself as she closed the door. Then she dismissed the matter and concentrated on her latest syrup. If only sugar were cheaper, this soothing potion, made from a thyme tisane, would benefit so many people. Her great hope was that the syrups would keep long enough to use them in the winter from herbs picked in their summer season. Now that would be amazing progress.

After hours of boiling, measuring, noting and labelling, Estela decided she'd had enough. She put everything back in its place, removed her sackcloth and wiped her face as best she could, using her reflection in a copper pan. She smoothed her hair and reached for her blue scarf, which she'd removed to keep it clean. It wasn't on the books, where she thought she'd left it and she couldn't see it on any of the shelves, stocked with neat ranks of jars and boxes.

Maybe she was confused and it was the day before that she'd worn that scarf. She frowned. She had other blue ones but that was Dragonetz' favourite and she'd planned to wear it to the tourney. Perhaps she'd treat herself to a new one at market the next morning.

She locked the iron-bound oak door and took the key personally to Malik, just to make sure there was no subversion of messengers possible, no way Dragonetz could ever have access to the poppy, if he weakened. She'd even labelled it 'devil's rosemary', so nobody but she and Malik could find it on the shelf.

Sweating and sleepless, Dragonetz lay in bed, fighting his demons. He wanted to spare Estela this weakness that came over him, especially in the middle of the night, from just the thought that the poppy was within reach. Sweet, trusting Estela, who really thought she'd hidden the poppy where he could not get it. No doubt she'd put it on a high shelf in the dispensary where she worked her magic. She'd probably labelled it 'Not the poppy' or some such thing, in Latin or Arabic, to throw him off the scent. He smiled.

The problem, my dear Estela, is that de Rançon only gave you a small portion of his stock in the first place. We both know, he and I, that I only have to send a messenger to him, any time of day or night, and I can get relief from this craving, sleep, heal... and awake worse than ever. Knowing it is one thing, dealing with it is another. The poppy, within reach.

Nights were the worst so Dragonetz had done his best to put the poppy out of reach. The hawk's perch barred the door. To leave the chamber and send a message, he would have to brave an unhooded Vertat in her foulest of moods. He had been keeping her lean, hungry, ready to attack. Her hood was tied to the perch, within her reach, and each morning, he had to be quick enough to grab the hood without the hawk reaching him.

At night, such acrobatics were difficult enough to stop the thought in its tracks. To put the poppy out of reach. To help him say no to the messenger who knocked on his door, saying, 'My Lord de Rançon wondered if you needed anything?'

'No,' he shouted. 'Go away and don't come back!' making up in communication for what he lacked in grace. The sound of the pageboy running away echoed along the corridor.

Vertat stood watch between Dragonetz and all comers, keeping his nights safe, if sleepless. He stayed sane in his accustomed manner, through music and poetry. He reached for the memory of voices that mingled in unearthly harmonies, the music that had come to him across the water, in his poppy dreams. He'd vowed that he would transcribe it one day and he felt closer to that goal, memorising the sections that felt right and re-working others.

Verses by Ibn Zaydūn soothed his cravings, setting his days in the context of a purpose bigger than he could imagine, beyond his control. Poetry sang in his head and let him sleep.

Elsewhere in Les Baux, another man lay awake but his cravings had no connection with the poppy. Geoffroi de Rançon was alone in bed but did not expect to remain so for long. To calm his anticipation, he reviewed his successes to date and felt he deserved congratulations. Tormenting Dragonetz could not have been more nicely judged: having the desired effect while keeping Estela's trust – he must not pursue that line of thought or anticipation would not be calmed.

He forced his distracted mind back to his projects. By recounting the news from the north and entertaining his noble audiences, he had also managed to gain status in this court that see-sawed between Les Baux and Barcelone. He wasn't yet sure how to make the most of the resulting position on Dragonetz' team but it had potential.

Why then, having achieved more than he'd hoped, did he not feel happy? He imagined Dragonetz lying alone – now that thought did give him some satisfaction – fighting the poppy addiction. De Rançon had frequented some of the more unsavoury quarters in Acre, Damascus and Jerusalem, and had seen the consequences of the poppy. When he'd known Dragonetz was doomed to such a fate, he'd found out what he could. Nothing had prepared him for the sharp-eyed Commander he'd met again in the Great Hall of Les Baux. There was no trace of the wild-eyed lunatic from Jerusalem days.

But no mortal could ever be *that* indifferent to the poppy, once dosed as Dragonetz had been. Especially when kicked in the gut by a double blow from home. An unfair blow, the kind that left slow poison, making a man wonder, 'How could she believe such a thing of me.' A wound that must fester, even if the future exonerated Dragonetz – as of course it should. De Rançon had no doubt of the knight's honesty and loyalty. Irony indeed. Dragonetz' father and liege readily believed him too proud or too headstrong to obey the order to go north and yet de Rançon had never once thought Dragonetz disloyal. He knew his enemy. However, he was more than happy to accept fate's contribution to his plans for Dragonetz.

So, the question remained. Why did he feel no satisfaction? He pictured Dragonetz, ill and sweating, wanting the poppy – or giving in and slumping into drugged sleep, the road to oblivion. He replayed the disbelief, the hurt on the other man's face when the messages from Aliénor, from Lord Dragon, were announced to the whole court of Les Baux. De Rançon imagined the blade being twisted in the wound as Dragonetz read those letters of contempt. The humiliation that his mother loved him 'despite' all he'd done.

Yes, Geoffroi had been thorough in completing the task he'd set himself years back, when Dragonetz had broken de Rançon Senior and made the family name a byword for disgrace. Death was too good for such a man and Geoffroi had repaid his father's debt in kind, destroying Dragonetz in body, mind and reputation. And yet he was still standing, offering the challenge to fight to the death 'with honour'. How could a man who'd been a crusader still hold such a notion? Geoffroi himself had seen 'honour' diminish daily in his father's shame and rages, self-pity and whoring; in the moment Geoffroi's mother gave up and left them. And yet, he felt no satisfaction at the damage he'd caused Dragonetz. Not even at the prospect of killing him.

His unruly spirits only rose at the thought of the tourney, of the pleasure in fighting with and against such opponents, of doing what he did best – behaving as a knight. In battle, even mock-battle, he could forget the letter from his own father. How well he understood all that Dragonetz was suffering! *An unfair blow,* he thought, *the kind that leaves slow poison, making a man wonder, 'How could he believe such a thing of me.' The kind that left a man wondering what to do with his life.*

A soft knock at the door interrupted his bleak thoughts and his heart thumped like a boy's. Naked, his welcome evident, he opened the door and let the woman slip into the chamber and into his arms, willing.

'Estela.' He buried his face in her hair, breathed in her scent, musk and oriental spice, a unique blend that she'd worn since their trip together to the Holy Land. 'You won't need this,' he murmured, loosening the scarf around her shoulders, kissing the golden skin revealed.

'Geoffroi,' she whispered, 'I have waited such a long time, for you, only for you.'

This too he shared with Dragonetz: Estela.

CHAPTER TWENTY-SEVEN

Diamond is of such great hardness that no other hardness is able to overcome it. It scratches and bores through iron. Neither iron nor steel is able to cut into its hardness. It is so strong that it neither gives way nor breaks before cutting into steel. Because this stone withstands his power, the devil is hostile to diamond, and so, at night as well as during the day, the devil disdains it.

Physica, Stones

Estela wiped a strand of sweaty hair back from her eyes as she opened the door to her dispensary. Good. The girl had remembered to return the leeches, although she still held them as far from her body as possible. Strange prurience given the work the little creatures had done. Maria sighed with relief when Estela took the pot, lifted a corner of the leather cover and slipped her healing aids into the container with their fellows.

Maria perched on a stool, glowing with secrets.

'You followed instructions and have no ill effects?' enquired Estela with delicacy, in a doomed effort to avoid too much romantic detail.

Unfortunately Maria's aims in conversation seemed to be the reverse of Estela's. She glossed over the treatments and dwelled on her prospects. 'I won't need those things again.' The shudder was genuine as she glanced toward the leech container and back, as was the pride with which she announced. 'An' I had been a maiden, I'd not be walking today, so keen was my Lord on his pleasures. Three times inside and once without. I pretended I was too sore, the better to show my skills.'

Estela winced and wondered whether Malik would be treated to such a consultation. She remained standing, hoping the girl would take a hint. 'I'm glad all went well and that you have no further need of *my* skills.'

'I just want to thank you. He loves me and he said so. And I have never been happier in my life. All those bad things, before – there must have been a reason for them. God's given me a chance for a new life as a lady.' The pretty face lifted to Estela's was without guile. 'He says he'll marry me.'

Estela opened her mouth to say something cautionary. 'That's wonderful,' she said, with as much enthusiasm as she could muster. Perhaps Maria *would* become a wife and a lady. Estela was both, and neither, depending which way she held her own situation up to the light. Was she actually envious of the girl?

'He says he shall make me a diamond ring and till then I shouldn't show it to anyone, for fear of robbers. But I shall burst if I don't show somebody and you can be trusted with anything because you're a doctor.' A sudden shyness. 'That's right, isn't it? You don't tell?'

'That's right. But you don't need to tell me anything you don't want to. If it's not medical, you can always confess to a priest if you need to unburden yourself.' Over something like feigning virginity, say, for instance. Estela chided herself for such vinegary thoughts. She knew full well the impossible situation Maria had been in and if anybody was culpable in the eyes of the Almighty, it was she, the professional who'd enabled such deceit. Yet she did not feel guilty and had no intention of confessing to some priest her actions with any patient. She had learned in Narbonne to mistrust the representatives of the Church.

'Oh no, it's nothing like that, although if I need your help to bear children, I will come back. It's too soon to say yet.' Maria was prattling away. 'It's just that my Lord wants me to keep this secret for my own safety, until I am his lady in the eyes of God and the world, protected by his men. Look.' She pulled a gold chain up from her bodice to show a locket suspended. 'Open it,' she commanded.

Curious, Estela prised the clasp open and gasped as light rainbowed from a gemstone, a diamond. 'That is indeed a jewel fit for a princess,' she said, snapping the locket shut quickly. Your Lord was right to tell you to keep such a gem quiet!'

'I know.' A cat with cream, bee in clover, pig in a wallow: all smug contentment. 'He is going to have it made into a ring, when we go back to his homeland.'

'I have only ever seen such diamonds once,' said Estela. A dozen of them remained in a velvet pouch that Dragonetz kept hidden, but she had no intention of saying so. 'In the Holy Land.'

'Yes, that's where my Lord came by this one, in the Holy Land. He told me so. And he had it polished to be a gift for his lady one day.' She beamed as her new status surprised her again. 'For me. I *am* his Lady. And it was the blood that made the difference.'

'The blood?' prompted Estela.

'From losing my maidenhead. When he saw the proof on the sheet, he went all strange and said he would make everything right. So I knew he meant marriage. And he searched through his things. I didn't know what he was doing and worried about some perversion – you hear such things, don't you? But he was sweet as could be and brought the diamond to me. Said something about my blood cleaning it, making it sparkle again. He talks so fine, like poetry. Stands to reason he didn't come by a diamond like that without blood on his hands, is my guess, and now he feels better, that it's a love-gift.'

It did stand to reason that diamonds from the Holy Land had blood on them. Estela shivered.

Maria remembered the ostensible reason for her visit. 'And I want to reward you, from my own purse. Not with the diamond.' She laughed. 'But my Lord has been generous and I can show you my appreciation.' She slipped the purse-string off her wrist and drew it open.

Estela stopped her. 'I will not take your money. You can't tell your

Lord that you paid the doctor for leeches and potions or he will want to know why. But you can make me a gift, as one lady to another.'

After a moment's thought, Estela said, 'As we will be spectators at the tourney and wearing the same colours, Dragonetz' blue, perhaps you would choose a new scarf for me. Mine seems to have gone missing.' Maria looked down at her pouch as she pulled the string closed again. 'Yes, if you could choose a new scarf for me at market tomorrow, that would do very well as a thank you. I suspect you can find a poor family who would benefit from your coin…' There was no need to say that she had Maria's own family in mind.

'You shall have three scarves, my Lady. And I know you shall like them because I have studied your taste, to help me improve and be more a lady.'

'Thank you, Maria! That is quite a compliment.' Estela was certain that studying Lady Sancha would further the girl's ladylike ambitions better than imitating someone who spent her time mixing potions or plucking a lute but refrained from saying so. She noticed that Maria had copied her own way of plaiting and coiffing her long, black hair, so that from behind, they looked quite alike. A compliment indeed.

Geoffroi was sitting on the cold stone, his gaze taking in neither the view through the window nor the letter on his lap as light faded from the horizon. He didn't need the candle-light in his chamber to know the contents of the letter. The words had him by heart and they wound themselves into his confusion. Satiated from the night before, aching to repeat the experience, he wondered what on earth or hell he was doing. For he had surrendered his chance of heaven on the long, shameful journey back from the Holy Land with his disgraced father. Instead of heaven, he had discovered a purpose in life, revenge instead of crusade.

What if he'd stayed with his brothers? If he'd died fighting the Infidel, the Pope had promised that his soul would be cleansed of all sins – so few and boyish in those days! Wasn't that his duty, to fight in

God's army, for his Liege Aliénor, alongside men like Dragonetz? His father had been found wanting, not him!

Yet he'd accompanied that broken man into perdition. And now? The missive had been addressed to *Geoffroi, hereto known as de Rançon* and he'd known before he read it that his father had finally lost his mind but he would never have guessed why, nor how the circumstances would allow no appeal.

Your mother has died.

Three years in a convent, refusing all contact with her son after she'd fled her husband's violence.

In her last moments, she begged the sisters to tell me of my true heir, your younger brother, Geoffroi de Rançon, born after she went to the convent. She told me that this baby was conceived in pure thoughts and blessed by the nuns. She confessed that your conception was by an incubus in my guise and that she committed the sin of lust. This is why you brought evil on our house. Your devilish spells made me fail in my duties as Aliénor's commander and led to my disgrace.

Once God revealed the cause of my behaviour, your mother pardoned me and bid me exorcise you from our house, so that the good name of our family be restored as if you never existed. She named the baby Geoffroi de Rançon and she did penance for her own part in bringing such an ill-begotten changeling into the world.

Now I understand the cause of all my woes, I too will do penance and protect my heir, Geoffroi de Rançon, from all evil. Do not come within one hundred miles of Rançon or I will have you tried by the Church for the sorcery you inflicted on this family. Seek employment or damnation elsewhere.

Formal repudiation of your rights to inherit has been lodged with our Liege, Aliénor, Duchesse of Aquitaine and Queen of England and with the Clerk de Rançon.

. . .

No signature, just the seal. In pity and respect for his service, Aliénor had sent Geoffroi on this mission and told him he could rejoin the company in England. If he did, it would be as a knight with no name. He heard the whispers, saw men crossing themselves behind his back.

He had vowed before God to avenge his father against the cause of their downfall, Dragonetz, and all he had left was his knighthood and that vow, plus the worldly goods he had accumulated. These were sufficient for his upkeep but no compensation for what he'd lost. Nor help in understanding what he'd gained.

He had a baby brother, growing up in the Rançon estate, its precious heir. Falling and skinning his knees on the gravel around the walled potager. Being shushed and cuddled by his nurse while he cried. Geoffroi felt the warmth of a woman's arms soothing a little boy's pain: his nurse – sometimes even his mother.

But this child was motherless and so was he. His mother's last act had been to kill her elder son. Worse than killing, she had taken his life and his name, given them to another, and left him breathing still.

Perhaps he should kill the Geoffroi usurper. He tried to imagine running his sword through the toddler, even gave the babe their father's eyes to stir up a rush of heat. After all, he'd done worse, for less reason, and enjoyed it. And yet, he couldn't do it. He could not change who he was and he had never betrayed his family, or rather what used to be his family. All he wanted was to make good the family name, protect this new member, teach him dice games and take him to his first drink, his first woman, his first fight.

Unclenching his fist, he studied his hand, saw a small fist curled in his, heard a baby's laughter. He would have been so good as a big brother. He could be such a good father too, he who knew the worst of parenting. What future was there now for any child his woman might bear.

Had he really pictured himself a ruddy-faced lord in Rançon, Maria and a brood of children beside him, accepting what life allowed him instead of seeking what was impossible? Hadn't Dragonetz himself found solace in some Damascan woman, even after he'd realised she was not Estela?

Never before had Geoffroi taken a woman without feeling disgust. He could not name, even to himself, the sweetness that had swept through in bed with this girl but he had dared to imagine that the future could be re-written. That he and the bloodied diamond could both be cleansed.

'An ill-begotten changeling'. He clenched his fist again, would have smashed it into the stone but for the knowledge that tomorrow was tourney day. Here, he was still Geoffroi de Rançon, stronger and more devious than Dragonetz los Pros and fighting beside him in the field. There was much to consider and he wanted all parts of his body at fighting strength. He remained a knight.

'Eschew false judgement and treason; honour and aid womankind. Thou shalt never slay thy lord, lie with his lady or surrender his castle. He murmured the words spoken over his making, when he had sworn fealty to Aliénor, as had Dragonetz. And look where they were now.

A soft knock on the door announced his evening visitor and the moment she was through the door he buried his face in the girl's long, black hair, twining it through his fingers like a safety rope. He kissed her silent, swept her to the bed, trying to be gentle. So soft, so sweet. He felt the wave of pleasure, surging too soon, tried to hold back. The pressure built like a thunderstorm, crashing up from his loins to the back of his neck and into his head, where it exploded like the wrath of God in pain such as he'd never known before.

'My Lord? Are you all right?'

Rainbows zigzagged in front of his eyes. The girl crushed beneath him split into three concerned faces, as she wriggled to breathe more easily. His head thumped with a headache worse than the time he'd caught a mace blow on his helm.

He rolled over, controlled his breathing as if in full armour under desert sun. Gradually, the thumping reduced to bearable pain.

'My Lord?' Frightened this time.

He reached for her hand, heart pounding to match his head.

'I'm all right,' he lied. 'Too much pleasure, too quickly. Go to sleep.' Perhaps his mother had been right. Damned in this world as well as the next. Why had God chosen to punish him for lust, just at the moment he was ready to atone for worse? Maybe this was a warning, a reminder. As he lay there, recovering, a sleeping girl's hand clasped in his own, he vowed that he would make it good, all of it. He would make the pilgrimage to Sant Iago de Compostela and complete it on his knees. He would marry his bedmate, bring children into the world and be a good father. His lashes were wet as his headache receded and he fell into dreams of storms and rainbows.

CHAPTER TWENTY-EIGHT

If someone is bruised on any part of his body from a blow or a fall, he should
take old fat, and mix with it equal amounts of sage and tansy. He should press
prasine into it, then heat it in the sun or near a fire. Then he should place all
this, with the stone, so heated, over the place where it hurts, and it will be
better.

Physica, Stones

Dragonetz could still hear the echo of seven voices blending, the gift left to him from his poppy dreams. While the singing lingered, he knew an inner peace. 'Inshallah,' he murmured. One day, he would find the voices to bring his music to the world. He had tried, had sent messages to abbeys and monasteries famed for their plainsong, but the reply was always the same. The notion of multiple voices singing different melodies was not possible. How many times in his life would Dragonetz be told something was 'not possible'? When he could hear the music of the spheres! One day, he told himself. One day, he would find the voices and teach them to interweave the pattern of his dream.

'My Lord Dragonetz?'

'Raoulf.' More cause for guilt. Dragonetz had barely wished goodday to his loyal lieutenant since they'd come to Les Baux. Barring some curt words over Raoulf's dispute with Gilles regarding Prima, conversations had been little more than instructions and yet Dragonetz had grown up with this bear of a man always at his side. Such a history, and the loss of his son, gave Raoulf the right and, in his own eyes, the duty to say what nobody else dared.

'I've not spoken to you since de Rançon's message –' Raoulf began.

'– Then don't.' Dragonetz cut him short.

'Your father, and the Duchesse, will see they're mistaken…' persevered Raoulf, flinching at the black-eyed glare he earned.

'Have you checked horses, armour, weapons?' Dragonetz asked, pointedly ignoring the comment.

'Of course, my Lord!'

'And is Hugues really recovered enough in your view?' The very question was intended as a salve to Raoulf's pride, a reminder that his opinion counted – on military matters.

'Put it this way: if he comes unseated, his arse will be sorer than a pair of unblemished buttocks would be. But between us, I wouldn't cry over it. And he's champing at the bit to have at the enemy – whoever he might decide that to be.'

Dragonetz smiled. 'Astute as ever. There will be a few on both sides having at their enemies, whoever they might decide fits the name. Walk with me and tell me what you think of a wheel formation to begin the tourney. If we have the young Comte as standard-bearer and Malik beside him, of course, then each of us rides as in a spoke at his jousting partner, do you think that would work?'

Raoulf sucked on the coarse hairs of his black beard, discovered a breadcrumb and disposed of it, chewing on the idea. 'Maybe,' he said cautiously. 'I like the formation itself but you're hoping they'll form a loose outer wheel, riding around until each selects his target?'

'Not hoping,' replied Dragonetz, a glint in his eye. 'relying on it.'

Raoulf sighed. 'Inside information.'

'Of course. So?' Dragonetz prompted.

'It's the best way to protect the young Comte,' Raoulf conceded, 'and it makes the one-to-one combat better organised than your average melée. But it gives them three advantages; they'll already be moving into the joust and they'll be picking who fights whom.'

Dragonetz shook his head. 'Hugues and I've agreed that each of his men turns and stops, then charges in turn, on the signal. That's time enough for us to do likewise. And it means we'll all move from a standing start.

As to the partnering – Hugues and I have decided that already. And of course Barcelone will be doing all he can to protect the young Comte too,' Dragonetz pointed out, 'so he'll work to keep our formation in place, even if he's on the other team.'

Raoulf's eyes widened. 'It wasn't Barcelone who…'

'I'm saying nothing,' grinned his Commander. 'Besides, Hugues is the opposition leader, not Ramon.'

'And you know fine well that any seasoned general can direct Hugues, simply by telling him what he mustn't do,' observed Raoulf.

'The third disadvantage?' pursued Dragonetz.

'They'll be charging at our standard-bearer – your precious young Comte – and we'll be charging towards a precipice.' The plateau might be flat and easy-going underfoot, especially in summer drought, but on three sides there were sheer cliffs.

'Motivates our men to control their horses well. Practising in a manège doesn't offer the same discipline.'

Raoulf wisely bit back whatever he had started to say. Instead, he asked, 'The rules are unchanged?'

'All as agreed. First contact with the lance, one attempt only, to avoid damaging other contenders. If one is unseated, he yields. If neither or both, the combat continues by sword until one yields. The men have been told we want no deaths and there is no shame in yielding but glory in fighting with honour.

We expect chivalry.' Dragonetz shrugged. They both knew how men behaved, once roused to a fight. 'Those taken prisoner are honour bound to go and stand with the Master of Horse. He has a vested interest in seeing that any riderless horses are removed from the scene by his hands and cared for properly.

We want to avoid any serious bloodshed. I had an idea that we could make blunted lances for such an occasion but all tell me 'it's impossible'. There will be a lot of excitable men and horse in a small space, even with the plans for formation. Bloodletting will be useful but I'm hoping we can stop at that.' One day, he told himself, blunted weapons would be in use at tourneys. Another project that would prove not only possible but practical, in the future.

Another hesitation from Raoulf before speaking.

'Spit it out, man,' Dragonetz told him. 'I'd rather know before-hand than after I've missed something.'

'It's just… there are a lot of men in this with good reason to kill each other.'

'That's what makes it entertaining!'

'And if Hugues de Baux manages to kill his young liege under cover of sport? You'd not find that so entertaining!' retorted Raoulf.

'Neither would Ramon,' was the reply, serious now. 'But you underestimate Hugues. He values his reputation as a man of honour too much to choose the assassin's route. If Etiennette were on the battlefield, now that would be a good question!

I've even wondered about Ramon,' he confessed. 'Whether he might take the opportunity to rid himself of Hugues. But I think El Sant is hoping to win Hugues over, not kill him, or he'd have done so long before. And on a more practical note, killing Hugues would only leave three younger brothers to follow, each more vengeful than the next, if Etiennette has her way. No, Ramon's main task will be watching over his nephew and no doubt arranging some sword-play for him to feel like a man.'

Raoulf was sucking on his beard again. 'Ay, there's another thing. If the young lordling is out of combat as standard-bearer, does that mean they're doing likewise? Keeping a man out of play? Where will he be then? First man to win a joust could take their standard early on?'

Dragonetz shook his head. 'It's more complicated. Malik is out of play too, protecting the standard. Neither he nor Ramon would allow the boy to join in otherwise. We have the extra man with de Rançon, they're keeping standard-bearer and one guard, the rest are paired in combat.

Some of the pairs I know; some I don't but I can guess. They don't have the same constraints as we do so maybe the standard-bearer will roam. But you're right, it's always good for morale to capture the standard, so if we can, we will.'

His grin was boyish, infectious, as he teased his lieutenant. 'Keep that in mind when you've won your bout.'

It was Raoulf's turn to shrug. 'What can go wrong?' he asked, with gloomy scepticism. He refrained from pointing out that charging over a precipice could be considered bloodshed by onlookers. Or indeed by the knight who found himself riding through clouds. War was tough. Training was practice for war.

'What indeed?' Dragonetz' smile would have warned anyone who knew him that the tourney would unleash all the wild energy hiding within the nickname 'los Pros'.

Striped canopies and banners in silks of all colours protected the spectators from the sun and many a lady wore her heart on her sleeve in red or blue favours. Pinned by a small gold dragon to the fashionable ruches, Estela's blue ribbons fluttered proudly from an azure gown. Her hips were girdled by a plaited navy leather belt, fastened with her Pathfinder Brooch. Was it only two years ago that she'd worn the Viking rune-gift to another tourney, when Dragonetz had misinterpreted her attire as support for another? She would give him no cause to doubt her this time.

In the same stand as Estela, but seated as became her status, the Lady of Les Baux sported a red scarf embroidered with the new house blazon, the sixteen-pointed star of her ancestor Bautasar. Estela smiled to herself at the birth of a legend and made a mental note that she would pay another visit to the Gyptian on her own behalf, to extract more details about her own mysterious discovery.

Red ribbons and scarves decorated the ladies like poppies in a field but there was no shortage of azure. Anticipation turned to anxiety as the spectators watched an empty battle-field and waited. The trumpeters sounded a fanfare. Then another.

'I feel faint,' murmured a familiar voice beside Estela, the woman's face hidden behind a makeshift fan, wielded more energetically than should have been possible by a damsel about to sink to the ground.

'Imagine how *they* are going to feel,' Estela rebuked her friend, noting that Sancha was wearing rather hideous blue and red stripes. 'I'm betting on three breathing casualties and two pricked by swords.'

'You have no sensibility.'

'No, none at all,' Estela responded cheerfully. 'And you have no allegiance.'

Sancha gave a helpless shrug. 'What would you have me do? My Liege is red and my lover is blue. Look, Vinse is wearing my ribbons!' And sure enough, one of the anonymous knights in the procession from the castle had ribbons tied round his arm.'

'They're all wearing ribbons,' pointed out Estela drily as the knights passed them, playing to the audience with half-bows and prancing horse-steps.

'Yes but those are mine,' insisted Sancha, blowing a kiss in the general direction of her gaze, then colouring and looking at the ground. 'That was too bold for a lady, wasn't it?'

Maria pushed her way past them to the front of the stand, leaning out to catch a red rose tossed to her by a knight who passed close enough to see the gleam of sweat on his horse as a neat side-step twisted rider and horse back towards the centre. Flowers. Estela's daily gift of flowers had stopped a few days earlier, causing her to wonder why. Should she have done more to acknowledge them?

She'd worn one each day but Dragonetz had said nothing. In fact, he'd seemed more trouble-ridden when he'd seen her, not comforted. Of course he was busy with his men, being a Commander, but it would have been nice to have a token, like Maria had been given. A romantic gesture. She sighed. Foolish, girlish thoughts.

Last of the riders wearing blue came one on the blackest of pure-bred horses. Sadeek. Estela's heart flipped at one curt nod of the helm, in her direction, one little dance of hooves, for her, then Dragonetz followed his men to their warm-up exercises. This was what he did, was who he was and she was overwhelmed anew that such a man loved her.

She and Dragonetz were a partnership, as much as he and his men, whereas Maria and her mystery knight were at the start of a love affair, all heat and no substance. Von Bingen would have prescribed a steam bath with cooling herbs to work against the madness known as being in love.

Estela had wondered who Maria's knight might be but she still couldn't tell. Blue, so one of Dragonetz' men. Maybe Raoulf? But she'd have recognized the bulk of Dragonetz' lieutenant even in armour. She glanced around the plateau and yes, there he was, unmistakeable in his battered armour. She even imagined strands of his unkempt black beard poking through his visor. No, Raoulf had not left Prima for a pretend virgin. That was hardly his style anyway. His approach was that of a rough soldier who took his pleasure lightly, left easily and supported the bastards he'd fathered, without worrying about their future.

Estela flinched from the word 'bastard' and sought out Maria's knight on the battleground. Barcelone was easy to identify, his helmet sporting a gold nose-piece and eye-slit; his mount smaller than all but the jennets of his nephew and Malik. The young Comte was easy enough to identify, carrying the leader's standard with its silver dragon on an azure field. All credit to his training in horsemanship, he managed his task with aplomb. The third small, nippy horse must belong to Malik, who would have been unmistakeable anyway with his spiked Moorish helm and sabre.

Still trying to distinguish the other individuals within the team, reciting an aide-memoire, a mix of riders and mounts: 'black legs, pointy helm, skinny roan, left-arm-ribbon...' Estela was distracted by the Lady des Baux jumping to her feet and clapping. The three younger sons who'd been banned from taking part were even more enthusiastic, as their older brother led out his men.

Each of Hugues' team wore a red tabard emblazoned with the white sixteen-point star and Estela had to admit they looked magnificent. How the sewing-women had made such attire in the time available was a miracle worthy of Bautasar!

'Bravo, Les Baux,' she murmured, then looked around to check nobody had heard her who could report back to Dragonetz. Sancha looked back at her, smug.

They watched the red tabards weaving among the riders with blue ribbons, like an army of metal-carapaced beetles, sun glinting on their freshly-oiled armour.

'If I had a blazon,' Estela mused, 'it would have to be a star, for 'Estela de Matin', the morning star. Eight points, I think, and a silver star on a gold field.'

'Gold is good,' approved Sancha. 'For the morning and for a bright future. But you need to learn the right terms.' That was the sort of thing Sancha *would* know. 'Background first. So yours would be 'Or, for gold, on a star argent.' I think you should make it quarterly gold and azure, to link your blazon with Dragonetz.'

Estela contemplated this but found it less exciting than having her own blazon. 'No,' she decided. 'It would be only gold. What would you have as a blazon?' Sancha was looking towards her blue-ribboned knight as she opened her mouth to speak and Estela insisted, 'For yourself, for what you are, not to proclaim your affections.'

Sancha closed her mouth again and thought. The knights were quite obviously hurling pre-tourney insults at the opposing team as they passed each other. The words were lost in the dust and warm breeze but, from experience, Estela had a good idea that they featured 'your mother, your sister and your lady' with reference to whores, dogs and sexual activities.

At least opposing Christian sides would understand each other's insults. In the Holy Land, Estela had been bemused at seeing the traditional Christian insults of the Saracens. What men like Malik made of gestures that suggested they wore beards and were literate, she could not imagine. The Moors did indeed wear beards and many could read, but it was unlikely that being reminded of this would reduce their confidence in a battle. But those were the benefits of travel, Estela supposed. Heathens turned into human beings and allies could sometimes seem very silly.

Still, men would be men, and Estela had visited enough taverns to know that insults could raise a man's blood in a manner likely to enhance fighting strength. Judging by the quantity if not the quality of insults, the men's blood was simmering nicely and Dragonetz could be relied on to bring it to boiling point at the right moment. Van Bingen had remedies for that too. Estela sighed. Her skills might well be called on afterwards but there was no chance of prevention so she might just as well enjoy the show. And it was going to be quite a show.

Barcelone and Dragonetz in one-to-one combat was the climax everybody had been waiting for, including, Estela suspected, the two protagonists. She could hear cautious bets being laid around her in the stand, with nobody certain of the outcome. Apart from her. General he might be but, sainted or not, Ramon would be no match for Dragonetz, and if Barcelone had caught even a glimpse of the devilment in his opponent's black eyes, he would know that.

'Argent on a fess sable – that's a black stripe – one needle between three pansies azure,' declared Sancha finally.

'Most apt,' was Estela's judgement. 'One of your talents, certainly, and blue is the colour for truth. The pansy because you want to show thoughts? Friendship?'

'No. Just because I think they're pretty.'

Estela sighed. Ladies. Perhaps it was just as well only men had blazons. The fashion was growing and even those who already had symbols were changing them for ones they liked better.

On the field, the colours were separating, blue ribbons retreating to the centre, around their standard, red tabards forming an outer circle. Estela suddenly noticed, 'They have no standard-bearer!'

'They don't need one if they're all wearing blazoned tabards. Nice tactic. Takes away the vulnerability of the standard-bearer...'

'... and gives them an extra man!'

'It will even things up. The blues had an extra man,' Sancha pointed out, revealing the sharpness that Estela loved. The demure exterior hid many talents. When they'd first met, Sancha had been one of Dragonetz' court spies.

'But Malik's sworn to protect the young Comte! So we are a man down before we begin. I don't like this one bit.'

The blues had formed a cluster round their standard-bearer and his guard, each of the men facing outwards, waiting. The reds found their places in a great wheel around them, each man stopping to face his tourney partner, as if along the spoke of a wheel. With one man in red, riding free.

With a growing premonition of disaster, Estela watched the wheel turn clockwise, move as one to a different partner.

'Why would they do that?' she asked.

'To unsettle the blues. They thought they knew who they'd be fighting. Now they have somebody different. And no time to re-think whatever strategy they had planned.'

The trumpet sounded and the first bout commenced, the two riders building up speed from a standing start to clash lances in the middle. Both were unseated and they'd barely staggered to their feet and drawn swords when the trumpet sounded again. The next pair charged, kicking up dust, lances high. One of the loose horses reared in fright, about to bolt, but a stable-hand caught its reins in time and ran it to safety, while one of his brave fellows rescued the other mount.

'No!' Sancha shrieked and gripped Estela's arm. 'He's going to get hurt!' Her knight, in the second bout, had been unseated and flew in an undignified arc to land firmly on the parched ground. 'I can't look.'

'And you're in favour of Les Baux going to war,' Estela pointed out to her friend, sotto voce. 'You can look now. I think there are some rules and being unseated is a loss. Your knight is leaving the field.'

'Thank God,' was Sancha's verdict, somewhat lacking in team spirit.

As the pairs launched in turn, round the clock, Estela had already guessed that Dragonetz would be last but, as she fixed the players in her mind – 'skinny roan, left-hander' – she suddenly realised what Hugues had done. 'He switched!' she said, outraged.

'Who switched? Switched what?'

The fourth pair didn't wait for the trumpet, the fifth pair started at the fourth trumpet call, then the next two pairs charged simultaneously. What with the dust and noise, horses charging and clashing weapons, the spectators could only infer what was going on from occasional sightings of a red flash, a loose horse or some blue ribbons. All formation had turned to chaos, with riders and men on foot chasing each other through clouds of dust.

'Hugues.' Estela was indignant but there was no mistaking the solid Barcelone general on his horse, roaming free, intervening in the fight only to haul out a reluctant loser – on either side – and send him on the march to the ever-growing number of prisoners in the Horsemaster's care. Ramon was pulling out loose horses too, whirling them away from men enraged by the fight, long lost to reason. 'Hugues replaced Ramon, to fight Dragonetz!'

Sancha laughed. 'Was Barcelone too scared to take him on?'

They watched Ramon riding into the thickest clouds of dust, judging a combat over whether the men in it thought so or not, dispatching justice and saving lives.

'No.' Estela could see the pattern Ramon made, as he rode, an inner wheel. 'He's protecting his nephew without shaming him! He won't let the fighting get too close to the standard-bearer and if a man's beaten, but won't surrender, he's declaring the fight over. No, it's not Ramon that worries me. It's Hugues taking Dragonetz!'

'If Ramon had little chance against Dragonetz, Hugues has less!'

'But you don't know…' Estela began. *You don't know how much hate Hugues is carrying and neither does Dragonetz. De Rançon, where are you now? Dragonetz needs you.*

CHAPTER TWENTY-NINE

Chalcedony (calcedonius) develops when it is past eventide, when the sun is almost gone and the air is still a bit warm... That stone turns infirmities away from a human being and gives him a mind which is very strong against wrath. He will be so tranquil in his ways that almost no one will be able to find a way to provoke him to wrath which is justified or harm him unjustly.

Physica, Stones

Disregarding the ever more frantic bugle, Dragonetz turned his head and peered through his eye-slit, analysing what he could see through the dust clouds. Sadeek snorted and pawed the ground, sleek muscle quivering with anticipation.

'Assuau mon amor, easy my love, easy,' he murmured, but neither he nor his horse were reassured. All turn-taking had been abandoned and Dragonetz readied himself, eyes fixed on the spot where Barcelone had been motionless, waiting till the others had all launched themselves into action. He and Ramon would unseat each other in the joust, spar, make some impressive moves without hurting each other and then enact a suitable finale. When they could see each other through dust, and men hacking at each other.

A red tabard was forcing a blue waistcoat across Dragonetz' jousting path but there was no point shouting at them. Even if they heard, they wouldn't take any notice. That just about summed up both teams, Dragonetz thought gloomily. Perfect simulation of battle; men who'd completely forgotten why they were there but tried to kill each other anyway.

In the distance, a blue waistcoat was walking to the prisoner's stand and a couple of horses were being rounded up by the stable hands. The pair fighting moved out of Dragonetz' line of sight and he brightened. The knight facing him across the terrain raised his lance slightly and lowered it again, a courtesy that Dragonetz had no time to appreciate as his partner spurred his horse into action. *Not Barcelone* registered in Dragonetz' mind as he automatically tucked the lance firmly under his armpit and let Sadeek fly. *Hugues. Keep to the plan and see what happens.*

A solid hit took Hugues from his horse and, stirrupless, Dragonetz let himself be carried off too. The thwack had been good enough to look convincing to the spectators – and to Hugues. Les Baux honour must be protected at all costs or the day was a failure. Landing without harm and recovering fast, Dragonetz thumped Sadeek on the rump with his gauntlet, ordering him 'Home!'

The riderless horse showed no fear but side-stepped anything that shone, shouted or waved a weapon. Black silk streamed in the wind as he moved from a walk to a gallop. Dragonetz didn't need to watch to know that Sadeek had gone straight to the Horse-Master, receiving a well-earned peppermint from his master's stock. After all, they'd been practising this very exercise since the moment Dragonetz came to Les Baux and the Horse-Master accused him of bragging about his horse. No doubt there would soon be a huge demand for peppermints in the world of horse-training, and another boost for trade with the supplier Oltra Mar.

Hugues staggered to his knees and Dragonetz was glad his smile couldn't be seen as he remembered Raoulf's words. Still, whatever the wound to his pride or his derrière, the young man didn't lack pluck. His new blazon was very attractive, on his shield as well as his tabard. Clearly, he had exercised his right as leader to fight against the leader of the opposing team. Dragonetz would make sure that the Lord of Les Baux would earn respect for that.

Dragonetz shifted his right hand further up his sword blade and flexed, ready to close in and push Hugues safely back to the ground, where they could wrestle a bit for show. The moment he met the other man's eyes, he realised that the plan would have to change. This was no partner but a serious opponent.

Murder in his eyes, sword mirroring Dragonetz' hold but with the point aimed at the eye visor, not at the chest, Hugues advanced, his footing sure now.

'Hugues?'

The reply was muffled behind the padded mail chin section of the hauberk but Dragonetz caught the gist. 'You shall not be my father!'

Cursing himself for an unobservant fool, Dragonetz caught the blade with his flat and punched Hugues backwards with his fist, a mere delaying tactic that allowed him to say, 'I have no intention of being your father! Or of replacing him. In any way!'

Rage overtaking battle-sense, Hugues landed useless blows on his opponent's armoured back, one for each word, and Dragonetz just let him. 'My – mother – asked – you – to – marry – her! I *heard* you both!'

There was no way to be honest and tactful, least of all while being beaten with a sword, even if it was no more dangerous than being lashed by hailstones.

Dragonetz caught Hugues' sword against his shield then grabbed it, forced Hugues into eye-to-eye contact. 'I told her no. Now look to your men and we will continue our bout when you remember how to conduct yourself.' Spoken like a father, he thought grimly, as he dropped Hugues' sword, backed through a cloud of dust, turned and ran in what he thought was an outward direction, away from most of the fighting so he could get out of the dust and see what was happening. Whatever Barcelone was doing, he and Malik would keep the blue standard-bearer safe from harm. But what about the rest of the men? And where in God's name was that snake, de Rançon?

There was no vantage point on the flat terrain but once he'd walked far enough out towards the northern cliffs, Dragonetz could see the spectators' pavilion and stands to his right, the red and blue of prisoners mingling with the recaptured horses. There must be some way of protecting a man's face in battle without him having to turn his head like an owl, he thought, irritated. Maybe something that swung open and closed, hinged like a door. No doubt the armourers would tell him that was impossible!

Turning his head and limited vision back towards the melée, he saw a man on horse – Barcelone – circling west, intervening in a duel where the winner had not stopped – or the loser had not surrendered. Men with battle-lust! Whatever had been said, no doubt involving a mace applied to the head, a blue knight was heading round the outside of the fighting, to the prisoner's stand. Dragonetz could see Hugues walking past men, checking who they were, running on, seeking him.

Then all Dragonetz could see was dust as he took a boot to the back of his knee and dropped, smashing face-first into dry earth. *Idiot!* He rolled, spitting out a mouthful of dust that merely dribbled down inside his mail aventail. He didn't think his nose was broken. If he were lucky, he'd find out later. Jumping to his feet and ducking sideways, he took in the main facts before trying to work out who'd attacked him from behind.

Red tabards, of course. Two of them. No, make that three. That hadn't been part of the plan either.

'Congratulations,' he shouted. 'Looks like the reds are doing well. Do you really need another one?' He readied himself.

'No,' one said. *The ringleader* Dragonetz noted, trying to identify the voice. Was that a band round the man's arm? Not a token from a lady but his own blazon? A pair of tusks on yellow background?

'No, we don't need another blue. But we're having you, *ferryman.*'

A prank come back to bite him in the bottom. Dragonetz sighed. 'Porcelet. Such a grudge-bearer. Go on then. Do your worst. One at a time, of course, in all honour…'

'There was no honour when you cried 'Forger' on John Halfpenny and then played his rescuer.' Dragonetz' protests of innocence were ignored as Porcelet nodded to his companions and all three rushed their victim. Boot, fist, sword and shield took the first onslaught but it wouldn't take his three attackers long to realise that all they had to do was force him back. The sheer drop would do the rest. Would they really murder him for some paint on their hands?

Dragonetz manoeuvred sideways, hoping to be driven towards the centre, to reach Barcelone's mediation but he saw recognition dawn in Porcelet's eyes. 'Go round the other side,' he ordered one of his cronies. 'Block him. Force him that way. We'll see how well he dances with air beneath his feet.'

Before the men could move to trap him, Dragonetz felt the rush of air as a sword tip whistled past his ear, from behind. Hugues? Who would not allow such a breach of chivalry, however irritated he was with his mother – and Dragonetz.

Holding the sword like a lance, under his armpit, the newcomer knocked Dragonetz to one side as he lunged at Porcelet, piercing the mail by his ribs as the latter turned to avoid the blow. Blue. The newcomer wore blue.

'In all honour, Dragonetz! You have my oath!' shouted de Rançon and moved so the two of them were back to back, in the strongest position of brothers-in-arms. The way they'd fought on crusade, two young knights from the same region, with de Rançon Senior as their Commander. But that was a defensive position, a way to postpone death while waiting for help. De Rançon was too fine a swordsman for them to need help.

Dragonetz stepped forward, turned his sword hilt first and whacked a bemused attacker on the nose-plate, then in the chest. The man stumbled and Dragonetz hit him again, made his nose run then winded him once more, forcing him in the direction of the cliff-face. 'Three steps,' Dragonetz warned him. 'Any last words?'

'Mercy, my Lord,' the man stammered, dropping to his knees.

Dragonetz pulled him up roughly, span him around while the man screamed and then jogged his dizzy prisoner enough towards the centre of the field that he could continue staggering towards Barcelone and his just desserts.

De Rançon had just booted Porcelet between the legs, to judge by the latter's response, and was battering the other attacker with his shield but was finding it difficult to use his sword to finish either.

'Don't feel constrained to keep them alive,' Dragonetz drawled as he joined in. He was met by eyes that danced, reflecting not just the sun. *Partnership. This is what we do.*

Dragonetz turned his attention to the leading Porcelet, the one wearing a blazon on his arm, but he was disappointed. No finesse, he thought as fended off a weak thrust with his shield, and drove his sword hilt into the same spot de Rançon had weakened with his boot. Winded, Porcelet dropped to his knees and was begging mercy before Dragonetz had even threatened him with a further blow.

'You know the way. Don't look back!' Dragonetz told the quivering merchant. He watched long enough to ensure he didn't get another surprise from behind then rested on his sword to enjoy de Rançon's skills. And they were a pleasure to watch.

He drew things out a bit for Dragonetz to enjoy, remarking, 'Missed that opening didn't I,' as he exposed all the vulnerable places on his opponent while goading him to continue.

'The man has some gumption, I'll give him that,' Dragonetz teased. 'He's making you work.'

'Think so?' De Rançon grabbed the other's sword, allowed his to be grabbed in return, so that they were eye to eye. Then de Rançon twisted neatly so the swords crossed and in the confusion he took them both and held them with the points an inch from the attacker's eyes.

'Mercy?' he suggested.

'Mercy, my Lord,' stammered the vanquished red tabard and was allowed to run off towards the prisoners' camp.

Dragonetz clapped de Rançon on the back, 'That was fine!'

De Rançon took off his helm, shook his curls free from the mailed hood and breathed heavily, his face flushed, his eyes glowing like a boy's. 'I think we've lost,' he pointed out the numbers of red tabards still on the field.

'I do hope so,' Dragonetz grinned, 'but we have done it in style. Let's go and console our standard-bearer and congratulate the winners.' He started to remove his helm but de Rançon stayed his arm.

'I should wait, if I were you,' he warned Dragonetz.

Advancing on them was a red tabard, determination in every stride. 'Dragonetz,' the knight shouted. 'We haven't finished, damn you!'

Before his would-be opponent drew near enough to swing a blow, Dragonetz dropped to his knees. 'Mercy, my Lord Hugues,' he pleaded. De Rançon stood relaxed beside him, making no move to replace his own helm. His eyes danced with light, catching his grin and throwing it back to his partner in blue, whose own smile was luckily hidden.

'You can't surrender before we fight! I demand satisfaction!' Hugues' outrage did not lead him as far as attacking the man who knelt in front of him, so he'd obviously calmed down a little. Dragonetz cursed himself again for not realising the cause of Hugues' moods, swinging towards him as a comrade and away from him at the idea of a stepfather, taking not only his father's place but his own title. He stayed still, waiting, considering his words.

De Rançon rescued him, lancing Les Baux's hurt pride neatly and cleanly. 'I think he has earned the right to surrender, my Lord. There is no dishonour for a tired man who spares his victor an uneven fight.' In a few words, he told Hugues of the attack by three reds and who they were.

As soon as he heard the name 'Porcelet' Hugues' frown disappeared. His mood swung back to the easy camaraderie that Dragonetz had been at such pains to create. 'Oh get up, Dragonetz. I accept your surrender. We said those whoresons would take their chance to make mischief and that it would be more difficult for them to take me if they were on my team, but I never thought they'd go after you! And three of them! Truly, men without honour.' His mouth set to a grim line. 'Well, it shan't go unpunished.'

Dragonetz stood, not jumping to his feet this time. He'd need some treatment from Estela for bruising and stiffness, and he suspected his nose would swell as if bee-stung, but if that was all the harm, he'd come off lightly. Thanks to de Rançon. The understanding between them still lingered, like an invisible handclasp.

As always, the task was to restrain Hugues. 'It would be easy enough for you to punish them,' Dragonetz allowed, 'and not without entertainment, but what if you test Barcelone instead?'

'The Porcelets are his men, aren't they. So it would be a good test of his justice to see what he does.'

Hugues took the point. 'And whatever he does will weaken his side and not affect my standing at all. Masterly, Dragonetz!'

The three men had walked to the centre of the field, where three riders awaited them, two blue and one red, and one blue knight on foot. The rest of the combatants had walked over to the stands, where they'd find wineskins and debate over what they should have done, rather than what they did.

Dragonetz bowed first to his standard-bearer, still holding aloft the silver dragon on blue. However proud his bearing, the boy's eyes gave away his disappointment, cloudy as the terrain.

'Bravo, my Lord.' Dragonetz met the youth's gaze full on.

'We lost.' Then the brown eyes did fill with unshed tears.

'Did we?' Dragonetz queried softly, with a barely perceptible glance at the scene beside them. Barcelone had dismounted and thrown his arms round Hugues, who returned the embrace with vigour, shouting, 'We won! Dragonetz surrendered!'

'Winning a battle is easy. Winning hearts is harder.' The boy nodded, understanding but not yet accepting. He would learn. Dragonetz glanced at Ramon, probably the finest general he'd come across, playing the lieutenant, hoping to avoid another war.

'Say it, Dragonetz,' yelled Hugues.

'I surrender,' repeated Dragonetz, 'and may the honour of both teams be sung in halls across Provence!'

'All but three,' muttered de Rançon.

'Three?' queried Malik, still mounted beside his young lord. Dragonetz knew full well why the blue standard had never been captured; Malik and Barcelone. If any man had tried for that prize, no man had – or could have – succeeded.

271

'Dragonetz?' prompted Raoulf, who'd clearly won his combat at the cost of being unseated and a few flesh-wounds. It was just as well his women apparently found his scars attractive.

De Rançon filled them in on the details as the group made their way back to the stands, accepting the spectators' cheers for the winners. Special applause for protecting the standard from capture cheered up the young Comte enough to ride twice past the spectators, making his mare perform a neat little bow to the crowd in thanks. The spectators loved him, shouting out his name as he waved to them. *Winning hearts* thought Dragonetz, checking Hugues' reaction, but he needn't have worried. Hugues was basking in the success of his own team and any lesser glory reflected on a youngster was all part of the glorious success of *his* tourney.

The heralds played a few notes that were almost in unison. Hugues spoke to Ramon, the latter nodded and sent a messenger to the stand where the Master of Horse still guarded the prisoners; seven red and ten blue. Three of the men in red shambled reluctantly towards the men on horseback, who waited for them in front of the stand where Etiennette held state, waiting for the moment she could formally congratulate the winners.

The three knights in red tabards dropped to their knees in front of Ramon Berenguer, Comte de Barcelone and the spectators shushed each other loudly, finally dying to an expectant silence. 'These men have behaved in a cowardly manner during the tourney, seeking to overcome one knight by attacking three against one. Their reputations are tarnished and that of Lord Dragonetz los Pros glows only brighter.' The name 'Dragonetz' was whispered round, with much confused bickering as to whether those who'd bet on him had won or lost.

'I hereby demand their spurs from men who do not deserve their knighthood.'

The townspeople who'd come to watch found a target for the rotting fruit they'd brought for just such an opportunity and nobody prevented them hurling it along with some abuse for good measure.

Shamed, Porcelet and his companions gave their spurs to one of Barcelone's men and trudged back to the keep.

'My Lord Dragonetz' team might have lost the tourney this day...' More cheering. 'But there is no loss of honour when men like Lord Hugues des Baux lead the opposition.' More cheering. The townspeople responded to the praise of their own Hugues. If they were to be believed, every single one of them had personally contributed to the upbringing of Etiennette's eldest boy.

'But I have to single out one man in the field, who stands for all that is noble and right, who showed chivalry and courage, skill and restraint. Who told his tale in all modesty, claiming no virtue in his own deeds.' Speculation was whispering through the crowd like flames in dry grass. Dragonetz, most were sure, but the speech had been oddly phrased. His nephew? Mere nepotism then, surely.

'My Lord Geoffroi de Rançon, for the part you played this day, and the manner of it, accept this gift with my admiration and respect.' Ramon took off his own swordbelt, studded with jewels and engraved in silver. His man removed his sword, returned it to Barcelone, and then presented the belt to de Rançon, who was dumbstruck. He looked towards Dragonetz, shook his head in disbelief, in denial.

'It is merited,' Dragonetz told him, throwing an arm round him, pushing him to accept, whispering in his ear, 'It is customary to express thanks – and don't forget Hugues, for God's sake.'

Recovering, de Rançon made a pretty speech, flattering the opposition leader and his strategy so that all were in good humour when they mounted again. It was Etiennette's turn to congratulate the combatants and to present gifts of armour and weapons to the winners. Then it was over. Officially.

De Rançon wheeled by the spectators, close enough to snatch a kiss from a pretty black-haired girl in blue scarf and gown. For one heart-wrench, Dragonetz thought it was Estela but no, his lover was there, looking steadily in his direction.

In his turn, he rode right up to the stand as Estela fought her way to the front. A summons, a squire and some manoeuvring attached his gift for her to the point of a lance, which he swung over two screeching women to reach her sure hands. She slipped the token off the end of the lance and looked as beautiful as the day he'd first seen her, dazzling him, an addiction without cure.

'Thank you,' she mouthed, and he knew he'd chosen well. The token and the lady. She added something, a mischievous lift to one side of her mouth. He could tell she was teasing him but he had to ask her to repeat the words, over the hubbub.

'It makes up for three days with no flowers.' She laughed. 'I thought I'd grown boring.'

He smiled back at her, indicated that he was heading back to the keep, to tend Sadeek, to change clothes. To ponder the fact that he'd not sent her any flowers at all, and that his bright day had just turned to ashes.

CHAPTER THIRTY

And so, precious stones are born from fire and water; whence they have fire and moisture in them. They contain many powers and are effective for many needs. Many things can be done with them – but only honest actions, which are beneficial to human beings; not activities of seduction, fornication, adultery, enmity, homicide, and the like, which tend toward vice and are injurious to people. The nature of these precious stones seeks honest and useful effects and rejects people's depraved and evil uses, in the same way virtues cast off vices and vices are unable to engage with virtues.

Physica, Stones

When Sadeek and his rider had vanished from sight, Estela opened her palm and studied the small object Dragonetz had given her. Hand-carved in oak, oiled to a shine, the wooden dog had a definite air of Nici about him, from the hint of shaggy coat and curved tail to the open jaw. No master craftsman would have whittled two rough fangs to represent a full collection of teeth but Estela loved the little wooden dog on first sight, knowing who'd made it. She imagined Dragonetz, wakeful by candlelight, sweating in need of the poppy, controlling himself with a knife and some wood. Better than flowers, much better.

Her heart was still pounding from the tourney, beating to the rhythm 'He's alive.' It had been difficult to follow the action with so many men fighting and so much dust but she kept track of her knight, worrying as he moved further away from the standard, from the protection of Malik and Raoulf.

Her jaw ached from gritting her teeth and when she saw the three red knights converging on Dragonetz, time stopped. Maria screeching, 'Dragonetz is going over the cliff'; spectators disagreeing, 'Foul play!' or 'It's only one at a time'; 'Now we'll see how good he is!' was the remark that nearly led to fighting in the stands but Sancha laid a cool hand on Estela's arm, murmuring, 'He's come through worse,' and then de Rançon joined his friend.

Maria's screeching increased but Estela no longer minded. This was how it had been with Arnaut, Raoulf's son: a bright partnership of sword and spirit. Even from this distance, the swordplay could be appreciated and few spectators were defending the red knights' behaviour now, as the two blues demonstrated their skills. For the first time, Estela saw the deep friendship of which Geoffroi had spoken so much and Dragonetz not at all.

'Like Roland and Oliver,' murmured one of the more cultured ladies, watching de Rançon dispatch a red knight. Estela could only agree. Like the famous friends of song, Dragonetz and Geoffroi fought together against the odds, Roland's wild courage tempered by Oliver's realism. Yet it had been Oliver who was killed. As Arnaut had been. *The past does not shape the future* Estela told herself firmly, as the third red knight stumbled towards the Horse-master and the prisoners' camp.

Dragonetz kneeling to Hugues drew much disagreement from the crowd as to whether it showed chivalry or defeat. Estela would have preferred to watch her lover take the young Lord of Les Baux across his knee and beat him with the flat of Talharcant but she appreciated that there were important issues at stake. Still, it would have been the perfect end to the tourney. If there was a Charlemagne on this field it was *not* Hugues des Baux.

Indulging in such pleasant fantasies, Estela let the speeches wash over her and waited for the only moment that was important. The moment when he looked at her. *He's alive* her heart commented. And her hand clutched a little wooden dog, proof of life and love. Dragonetz had ridden back to the keep but his token was here in her hand. Her face smiled. Her whole body smiled and she had no control over it. People smiled back at her. Geoffroi smiled back at her, soothing his horse, who stamped impatiently at being restrained so long beside these noisy people.

'Thank you,' Estela told him. 'You were magnificent.' His eyes were diamond-bright, radiant, reflecting happiness.

'Dragonetz was magnificent,' he corrected her. 'I would follow him to the ends of the earth.'

'Yes. So would I,' she said. They both laughed.

'You were the best knight on the field,' Maria said staunchly. 'Everybody says so.'

'Then it must be true, my Lady,' Geoffroi teased her. Maria was a good influence on him, thought Estela, despite the difference in intellect and status. Some men preferred women who were not their equals, women they could impress and who would be ever grateful.

'I must give thanks for this day, where it is due, so I don't become a braggart,' Geoffroi told them. 'And confirm our marriage arrangements with the priest.'

Estela waited for the predicted screech to finish then asked, 'When shall it be?'

'As soon as possible,' smiled Geoffroi. 'You will be the first to know.'

'Second,' pointed out Maria, without really seeming to mind.

'Second,' he agreed, bowing to her and the other ladies before riding off towards the citadel.

'That is an admirable knight,' commented Sancha, following de Rançon with her eyes.

'Yes,' agreed Estela. 'But I thought your heart was taken? Should Maria be jealous?' Sancha's obvious pleasure at her own knight's acknowledgement of his lady had not gone unnoticed.

Sancha didn't dignify the jibe with an answer.

Dragonetz tracked down de Rançon, finally catching up with him in the chapel. His sun-bleached curls glowing cherubic in the candlelight, the knight knelt in prayer, the hilt of his sword a cross held out in front of him. Just as Dragonetz himself must have looked all the times he had come here to think, to seek guidance. This was not the place for what must be said but Dragonetz steeled himself. With de Rançon there could be no excuses.

'Dragonetz.' The tone calm, joyous, as de Rançon responded to the clatter on the stone flags. He opened his eyes but remained on his knees.

'You sent flowers to Estela,' Dragonetz stated baldly, hand on his sword hilt. Even though he could never draw Talharcant in a place of sanctuary, he could make his intentions clear.

The other man's limpid gaze did not falter or change. 'I did,' he owned. 'But that was before. I have given her up.'

'She was never yours to give up. Whatever might have happened on the journey to the Holy Land.'

'Nothing happened,' de Rançon swore, then, perhaps glimpsing the lie reflected in Dragonetz' face, he amended, 'I kissed her. I should not have but I did many things I should not have.'

He was still kneeling, which Dragonetz found disconcerting. ''That was before. I am going to marry Maria and she can give me everything I need in a woman. I have changed. You *know* I've changed. You *know* what we shared today was real. It cannot be counterfeited. Do you remember crossing Germany? The times we tried to protect the villages?'

'And failed.'

'Byzantium? Louis being fooled as much by his host as by our own sweet Duchesse?'

Dragonetz remembered Byzantium, the double-dealing and wasted months. He also remembered his own relationship with their sweet Duchesse Aliénor all too well. He had changed. Was it possible that de Rançon had changed too? Left behind the obsession with vengeance? 'I was in love with her,' he admitted.

'We all were! I'd have followed her to the ends of the earth! Who among us wasn't in love with the fiery queen, the amazon we called liege.'

'Your father too?' Dragonetz risked naming the cause of all friction between them.

De Rançon's face tightened but he did not duck the question. 'I expect so. My father is not somebody I understand.'

Dragonetz weakened. Fathers and their shortcomings, their effect on children. What would Musca say about him one day? Every man carried so much guilt. The brotherhood forged in battle between him and de Rançon was an invisible chain between them but Dragonetz didn't know whether it bound them for good or ill.

He tested the tempering. He was only testing, he told himself but his voice shook. 'We've been through a lot. I need to think, to sleep properly. Can you give me some poppy? Just a little. Just for tonight?' Was he pleading? He gripped Talharcant tighter.

The same steady gaze met his, a trace of pity quickly hidden. Dragonetz felt a surge of fury before even hearing the reply, 'No, my friend.' Talharcant was half-unsheathed to force compliance when the flickering light caught the hilt. A cross. A sanctuary. A man kneeling. Sweating, Dragonetz sheathed his sword, nodded, joined de Rançon on his knees. Prayed hard.

So it was that Maria found them both, kneeling together, each in silent meditation.

'You've been here for hours, my Lord!' she chid Geoffroi. 'That's no good for your joints, kneeling on stone floors like that.'

De Rançon got to his feet. 'And it suits you to keep my joints flexible,' he flirted.

Dragonetz stood too, the anger and need passing, leaving him exhausted from the vigil. It had helped to have company. He tried to make polite conversation with Maria. 'I hear you are to be married. My felicitations.'

Her face alight with the day's contagious happiness, she babbled,

'Thank you, yes, we're ordering dresses and linen but we don't need to wait for all that if the priest has chosen a day to bless us then we can go right ahead – Geoffroi, did he name a day?' She barely paused for a shake of her knight's head before a thought struck her.

She reached down her bodice, pulling up something on a chain as she chatted. 'And Geoffroi's going to have this made into a ring because it is so beautiful and he says it will wash all the blood off it that came from how he got it I suppose it was like that in the Holy Land though always bad things happening and you had to kill all those men... but you shouldn't... feel... it... was... your... fault...'

She tailed off as she realised that something was wrong. Geoffroi's move to stop her had come too late and he stood pale, helpless. Dragonetz was also standing, rigid, his face stone.

Maria held out the diamond towards Dragonetz, stammering, 'It's a diamond. Isn't it beautiful?'

'Go back to my chamber, Maria.' De Rançon's eyes never left Dragonetz, his tone leaving no room for question. She left.

The two men remained more than a sword's distance apart and Dragonetz had not moved to draw Talharcant again. He was beyond rage. He was white fire, ice heart, diamond.

'Muganni's diamond,' he stated.

De Rançon did not lack courage. He had never lacked courage. Except perhaps when he murdered a small boy. 'Yes,' he said.

'He's dead. You killed him.'

'Yes. I'm sorry.' Dragonetz fought the urge to ask how, to ask where. He was experienced enough to know that details did not make grief easier. He knew all he needed to know and that was already too much to bear.

'Your life is forfeit. I will not take it here in church. You will meet me alone, tomorrow, at dawn, at the far end of the plateau. Only one of us will return.'

'Estela will never forgive you. She will never believe you, as to why.' He too was merely stating facts.

'But what must be done, will be done, all the same.'

'And if I win?'

'Then Estela will never forgive *you*. But you won't win.' Dragonetz turned to leave. 'Make your peace with God. I'm sure that's more grace than you gave Muganni.' Saying the boy's name was a knife through the heart. 'There can be no peace with me.'

Dragonetz had no option but another night with Vertat. Estela would be disappointed but she would assume he needed to recover after the tourney. He could not be with her and hide what he knew or what he must do the next day.

There would be no sleep this night and the only love would be in his tears for the child whose rescue had been so short-lived. The child who had sung like an angel in the court of Jerusalem, thanks to Dragonetz.

And who had never reached his beloved mountain home. Who had died, thanks to Dragonetz. It was going to be a long night and the heavy air threatened a thunderstorm.

CHAPTER THIRTY-ONE

If someone is regularly tormented by false dreams, he should have betony leaves with him when he goes to bed, and he will see and feel fewer false dreams.

Physica, Plants

Geoffroi had spent three years planning how to avenge his father and make Dragonetz pay. Three years wasted. Lives wasted. He'd relished the prospect of Dragonetz' pain on learning what had happened to Muganni, and who was responsible. Now the moment had come, he tasted only ashes. He'd made the morrow's duel inevitable but he no longer wanted it. He was sorry that Maria would not have her wedding but she was well provided for. Amid all that he was sorry for, Maria's disappointment figured small.

His will had been made a year ago and lodged with a notary in Poitiers. He saw no reason to change his requirements. His request might seem strange but should pose no problems in these times when bodies were often prepared in the Eastern way, to travel long distances home, without putrefaction. The only part of his dead body that mattered would be taken where it truly belonged. If he no longer existed in his parents' eyes, the manner of his leaving this world was of no concern to them. Or to the new little heir, the replacement Geoffroi de Rançon. Maybe this was how it was meant to be.

He took the copy of his will from its place alongside the letter from his father and sent it by messenger to a lawyer in Les Baux, along with coin to compensate for knocking him up at night to receive a scroll 'in case of need'.

Perhaps he would win the duel. Neither he nor Dragonetz knew who was the better swordsman. The only time they'd fought in earnest, they'd been interrupted and Dragonetz hampered by the effects of the poppy. De Rançon thought he could win, knew he had different techniques and skills from his taller adversary. However, unlike that adversary, he knew his own biggest weakness, the one most like to kill him. He didn't want to win.

He had stopped planning. He did not recognise the man he'd been since he joined his father in disgrace. He knew the man he'd been today, remembered him from the past and would never part from him again. Maybe instinct would take over in the duel and fight for him. Maybe not. He rolled a word around on his tongue and liked the sound of it. *Inshallah.*

'Geoffroi? Did I do wrong? You told me not to show anybody but I thought it would be all right to show your friend, now we are to be married.' Maria was already in his bed, anxious and pretty, like *her* in looks only. Yet Geoffroi had told the truth in that too. He had given *her* up. In the real world at least and a man's bedchamber fantasies were his own business – and Maria's. As she well understood.

'You did nothing wrong, dear heart,' he reassured her, removing his tunic. 'I am but roughly washed after combat,' he warned. 'The buckets had too many men wanting their use and not enough boys fetching them. Even the horse troughs were already taken. And Dragonetz is quite right – the lack of water is the castle's weakness. It could never withstand a summer siege.'

If Maria had been an Estela, she would have noticed his naming of Dragonetz; like a man mentioning his mistress to his wife, an inflection of new love, of guilt, of betrayal. Instead, Maria licked the sweat from his arm. 'Come to bed,' she said, as the thunder rumbled. 'You can wash clean in the rain afterwards, when the storm breaks.'

They were betrothed now and there could be nothing sinful in their union. Any child conceived this night would be blessed, Geoffroi was sure of it. He wanted to share his sense of peace, of rightness, of a new life, with this sweet girl who wanted only to please him.

He was especially tender with her, taking his time, giving her license to play, to invent. She was a fast learner and they were both lathered with sweat in the gathering pressure as he gave way to the storm. The pleasure-rush was more intense than any he'd known, driving him to scream, 'Estela!' before the second wave overtook him, pain crashing into his head without mercy, breaking him into a million pieces with no name, split open by lightning.

The storm outside broke and daggers of rain slanted through the window but the sudden cool brought no relief to Geoffroi de Rançon. Maria began to wail.

A boy's sweet soprano opened the hymn and all hearts, his Latin accented with Arabic. Dragonetz knew he should work on this, correct his pupil but he found it endearing.

> 'O ignee spiritus laus tibi sit
> qui in timpanis et citharis operaris'

> 'Praise be to thee O spirit of flame
> who speaks through lyre and tambour...'

A soul opened in joy, through song, the very essence of a hymn. A moment of bliss. Then the other voices took up the lyric, at war with each other, jarring – again! Dragonetz was hoarse from shouting instructions. Didn't they feel the music?

The harmonies? How could they sing like frogs when the music they'd been given was heavenly! They should chime in with the boy's sweetness, cherish it, move through the lyric from love to justice. *This* was the verse that should be strong, ominous, some minors. The verse when the boy's voice should fade.

'Quando autem malum ad te gladium suum educit
tu illud in cor illius refringis
sicut in primo perdito angelo fecisti
ubi turrim superbie illius
in infernum deiecisti.'

'When evil draws its sword on you,
you turn it back into its black heart
as you did to the fallen angel
in the beginning
hurling his tower of pride
down into hell.'

The boy, lost, drowned out by those who were stronger. Angry tears streamed down Dragonetz' cheeks, unchecked, pooling in streams at his feet as he conducted the invisible, inadequate choir. Water rose into a whirling tower, whipped his naked body. Hell's thunder crashed into the lyrics, pounding, regular.

Dragonetz woke, sweating and confused, convinced the stones moved and the castle was tumbling. There was barely a second between a deafening roar from the skies and the lightning, forking the room vivid pink. Vertat bated in the wild light, then cowered on her perch, shivering and mewing. As his eyes recovered from the blinding flash, Dragonetz saw the door open a crack, then quickly close again at the hawk's angry reaction. The regular pounding began again. Not thunder but somebody thumping on the door.

'Dragonetz? For the love of Allah, move that bird and let me in.'

Malik. 'I'm awake. Give me a moment.' Dragonetz fumbled a candle alight, sheltered it from the storm gusts behind his clothes-coffer. He threw on the tunic discarded by the bed the night before and he weighed up the distance between his gloves, an outraged hawk and her hood.

'When I yell 'Now' open the door a crack to distract her and I'll hood the hawk,' he called to his friend. Then he waited out another blast of thunder. There was no point trying to hood the hawk while she bated, especially given the exercise required to reach gloves and hood. He cursed his efficiency in making the manoeuvre so difficult.

'Now!' he called. The door opened, the hawk screeched at the intrusion. Dragonetz dived, briefly aware of the parts of his body exposed to claws and beak. Gloves; hood; covered; tied. Complaining more quietly, quickly reassured by the familiar darkness, Vertat clutched the perch as Dragonetz shifted the wooden stand enough to allow Malik into the chamber.

He must have taken in the arrangement; the hawk's stand blocking the door but he made no comment. Unlike Dragonetz, he was fully dressed, in white robe and neatly wound turban, and carrying his box of medicines. He sat down on the bed. Dragonetz sat beside him and they waited out the next burst of thunder. There was a longer pause this time and less violence in the jagged spear of light.

'Geoffroi de Rançon is dead,' Malik said. 'I was called as physician. I wanted to tell you myself. I am truly sorry that you have lost your friend.' *Another friend*, he meant.

'How?' asked Dragonetz, his mind still reeling from song and storm. This time he wanted to know how, in detail. And then to understand why.

'Maria was there. She is too shocked to make much sense but it seems he had some kind of seizure. He had been complaining that the storm was inside his head.'

Dragonetz had to ask. 'Do you think he might have… by his own hand? Poison perhaps?'

Malik glanced at him, taken aback. 'I have no reason to think so. Everybody knows how much honour he gained from today's tourney and it's obvious how much he cares for you, how good you are together on the field.' He corrected himself. 'Cared for you.' He hesitated. They too were good together in the field. 'Dragonetz, is there something else?'

The urge to speak, to share the terrible burden with a friend was stronger than poppy addiction but Dragonetz controlled this too. What was it Malik and Estela always told him, about the physician's creed? First do no harm.

'Estela,' he said at last. 'De Rançon and she were close. This will be hard for her. I don't know whether it will come better from you or from me but she should be told by one of us before she hears passing gossip.'

Malik nodded. 'You're right. I will go to her now, and stay with her until you return. As his only friend in this court, somebody who knows his family, I think you should check his affairs, see if there's anything personal that needs to be done, before the formalities begin. Talk to Maria.'

Not willing to explain why he was the wrong person, Dragonetz accepted the duty. As Commander of Aliénor's guard, he had arranged a man's effects often enough. One more letter to write, notifying family. One more tearful woman, to be given food and shelter. One more set of last wishes to make a man aware of how little we all are, how little we can truly call ours. A ring, a lock of hair, a wooden dog. By such stuff are memories kept alive.

Fully dressed in leggings, tunic and tabard, Dragonetz followed the page and flickering lantern to de Rançon's chamber. Maria was not there, for which he was grateful. He would assure her welfare in the morning. He let the boy light and take a candle then dismissed him, closing the door on all but himself and a ghost. The lantern burned strong, throwing light on the meagre possessions of a travelling knight.

It didn't take Dragonetz long to sort through the contents of the coffer and re-pack everything for Maria to keep or distribute. The signet ring, he would send to de Rançon's parents, with a letter penned by Dragonetz and signed by Etiennette. It was unlikely that de Rançon Senior would take kindly to any missive from Dragonetz, let alone one informing him of his son's death. The leather pouch, Dragonetz kept till last, hesitating as to whether he should read its contents or not.

Finally, only this one task remained and he sat, contemplating de Rançon's private letters. It was unlikely that Maria could read so, even if the judgement of such a woman could be trusted, she could make no sensible decision about the letters. A man had the right to his last wishes and they might be expressed in one of these letters. Somebody should read them in private.

But this was his enemy's lair. What if there were details here about Muganni's murder? How could he read such things and bear to continue living? What if Estela saw them?

He could just burn them. Too bad if there were last wishes that went unread – Muganni's last wishes had counted for naught. But de Rançon was Aliénor's official messenger. What if there were orders or news here that might make a difference to Aliénor's campaign? Dragonetz still felt the allegiance he no longer owed. He certainly wouldn't risk any damage coming to Aliénor from these letters getting into the wrong hands.

Decision taken, he started reading. And continued. He read the letter from father to son twice, then put it in the fireplace, touched a candle to the lantern and set the paper alight. He watched the paper flare and turn to ashes, singing softly.

'tu eam citius in igne
comburis cum volueris'

'your fire purges all ill
as is your will.'

In the dark fireplace, Dragonetz saw two young knights eager to fight a holy war for their beloved Aliénor; saw fathers and sons; saw hate that festered and ate its own young like a pelican. He heard Geoffroi's light baritone in duet with Estela and was no longer jealous listening; they were two people who had travelled far together, in friendship. Both had risked their lives to save his.

The fallen angel in his tower of pride: de Rançon or himself? Or all men, one way or another. He could not forgive but he could almost understand. Their paths had too much in common not to feel the pain of his comrade's tortured choices. Dragonetz let all his ghosts sing to him in the darkened fireplace as he waited for his decision to come to him. Some accused him as he accused de Rançon; others offered him only love and these were the ones who hurt him most. But he listened anyway, until he was sure. The last words that rang in his mind, after all the others faded, were, 'I'd have followed her to the ends of the earth.'

Dragonetz could find no will or last words, no further letters that would call de Rançon's honour into question, though it sounded like his parents were like enough to do that without help. Or maybe the new Geoffroi de Rançon would grow straight and tall, without the crippling of spirit suffered by his brother. In the end, Dragonetz had not been called upon to judge. He would not do so in the absence of the accused. 'What a waste,' murmured Dragonetz as he left the room to go to Estela.

He found her red-eyed and white-faced but she made the effort to smile weakly at him. 'That green tabard with yellow hose makes you look like an Italian herald,' she told him, her eyes filling up once more. 'I can't speak of him.' She buried her face in his shoulder and he hoped she took comfort in his arms.

'Geoffroi would have hated my poor taste in clothes,' he observed, seeking to lance the wound, and assuming that more crying was a desirable effect. He was dry-eyed, a gnarled black lump for a heart. He could feel the solid, poisonous weight of it. He looked over her head at Malik, who was still there, true to his word. 'Maria had gone, no doubt to her family. I found no last words or will. I'll make provision for Maria and send word to Geoffroi's family tomorrow.'

Malik nodded. 'I need to send for the laying-out boards and notify the sextant. The sooner a grave is dug the better. It's too hot to wait.'

'A day and a night, for those who wish to keep vigil?'

'There is only you.'

'Then don't wait. I have made my peace this evening.'

'Your peace?' Estela picked up on the odd phrase, looking up at him, her golden eyes red-rimmed.

'Peace with his death,' he told her gently. 'There was nothing anybody could do to save him. And today he shone bright. He will not be forgotten in Les Baux.' Her sobs stopped any further investigation of his feelings but he knew that was temporary and he must prepare his words better.

Malik slipped out and Dragonetz took Estela to bed, found comfort in her warmth. The rain was now steady, clattering on the cobbles below and the wind had eased. Somewhere far away, the thunder still rumbled. 'Are you awake?' he whispered.

'Yes.'

'I have decided.'

'About Provence?'

'Yes.'

'Because of the tourney?'

'Partly.' The tourney seemed a lifetime ago. 'Mostly because of Geoffroi. Something he said helped me decide.'

'Whatever you do, wherever you go, I will be there with you.'

A tremor, some tension in her voice told him she was afraid of what she might have to face, being there with him. Something from earlier in the day nagged at him, something that affected Estela but he couldn't quite bring it to mind.

'I hope so,' he said. 'I need you with me.' And then he told her what he had decided. Her reaction was unexpected.

'I thought you were going to marry Lady Etiennette.' Her voice was barely audible.

Hugues. The accusation, the resentment. Of course, if Hugues had heard snippets of conversation then so had Estela.

'Why didn't you tell me she'd asked you?' Estela asked.

'Because it didn't matter. It was just a complication not a possibility.'

'You should share things with me.'

'Yes, I should,' he agreed, the black lump in his heart calcifying. He reconsidered her words. 'You would stay at my side, even if I marry Etiennette.'

'I would *have*,' she emphasised, 'but I've changed my mind. You missed your chance.'

CHAPTER THIRTY-TWO

When the pelican first sees her chicks hatch from their eggs, she thinks they are not related to her and she kills them. When she sees that they do not move, she is sad and lacerates herself, resuscitating them with her blood.
Physica, Birds

De Rançon's honour and tragic death grew in the telling as word spread through the castle, with Dragonetz given a supporting role in both; Roland and Oliver not only in battle but with Geoffroi dying in Dragonetz' arms. Whatever Maria thought of this version she did not come out of her refuge to contradict it.

In his role as physician, Malik notified Lady Etiennette of the death and she sent word to all the officials required to conduct a Christian burial. When a notary came bustling up from the village, red-faced and waving Geoffroi's last will and testament, this too was passed on to the appropriate authorities.

Estela found talk of the tourney even more painful than plans for a splendid funeral. Her first instinct was to seek out Maria and see if she could help the girl but Malik suggested it was too soon. She could not sit and cry all day but she felt guilty at doing anything else, surrounded as she was by the business of a grand death. She had to get away from the castle so she would pluck up courage and pay one last visit to the beekeeping Gyptian, while she still could. Perhaps she could wring some truth out of the wretched woman regarding the cloth that was supposed to show her 'ancestry.'

It would be easier to dismiss the Gyptian's ramblings if none of them had come true. Yet, against all possible prediction, Dragonetz was dishonoured, accused of disloyalty. The prophecies weighed like curses on her and Estela wasn't sure whether she wanted them removed or explained. If Maria had come to her dispensary talking of such superstitious nonsense, she'd have laughed in her face. And yet. Estela fingered the Pathfinder rune that she wore for protection, for guidance, for reassurance in this crazy quest.

The Pathfinder medallion was her only protection. She preferred to go alone on such an errand, with the mysterious cloth in her saddle bag. She had no problem slipping away unnoticed and picked her way slowly and carefully down the sodden track, past the place where the white rocks narrowed and on to the hidden cave opening.

Tying up her mare, she walked through the large entrance, surrounded by water drips and plopping echoes, the night's rain seeping through the rock and sliming walls. She stumbled, caught herself against a wall and quickly pulled away. It was like touching an eel.

'Dame Fairnette,' she called, the 'nette' echoing through the caves and back to her, mocking. She entered the woman's private sanctuary but nobody was there. The hearth was cold and yet in her state of health such a fierce night must have been chilling. The bee veil was on the cot. Not down at her hives then.

Rather than return to Les Baux, Estela continued down towards the river and the vineyards, where she and Gilles had met the farmers. She glanced idly towards the beehives as she passed and then stopped in her tracks. The flamboyant mix of fabrics and patterns in all colours, draping a hive, could not be mistaken. She had been wrong: Dame Fairnette was indeed with her bees, whose anger clouded the air above their keeper.

'Dame Fairnette!' called Estela, not expecting an answer, and not getting one. She turned her horse, rode back to the cave, grabbed the veil and four scarves, then forced the increasingly reluctant horse to return to the beehives. Stopping at what she hoped was a safe distance, Estela dismounted, tied up her mount once more and donned the veil. She folded her dangling sleeves over her hand, tied her skirt with scarves to make a hobble – vulnerable but better than nothing and she took tiny steps towards whatever she might find at the centre of bee attention.

Amidst increasing noise and growing numbers of scouts, who pinged against her veil, she approached the beehive until she could clearly see the Gyptian's body draped over a broken top, face down amongst all the enraged occupants. The sound grew ever louder and more threatening but Estela kept walking towards it. She noticed a kitchen knife on the ground beside the hive, long strands of wicker stuck to it and she turned the body until she could what was left of the old woman's face, too swollen to be recognised. Dead.

More inhabitants poured out from their damaged hive, joining the black cloud that already impeded Estela's vision, ever more deter-mined as they attacked her veil. Estela could do nothing for Dame Fairnette and risked joining her if she didn't move fast and far. Twisting in tiny footsteps, hobbled by her skirt, she swore as the first stings came through a scarf round her hand and on her ankle.

It was as if the whole swarm became further maddened by the stings and she was chased by the whole black mob almost the whole field's length, until the noise diminished and she collapsed, panting. She tore off the veil and scarves, hitting her head wildly at imagined attacks. She suffered one more sting on her arm from a straggler who'd stayed with her, then she was safe.

She'd headed away from her horse, afraid the bees would never give up, and now she walked a wide circle to rejoin the mare. Murmuring sweet nothings, as much to calm herself as the mare, she rode back to Les Baux, running over and over in her mind what she'd seen, what it meant and what she was willing to say.

By the time her horse was stabled, Estela was desperate to get to her dispensary and make up a rose-water poultice to soothe the pain from the bee-stings. Van Bingen was curiously silent on bee-sting treatment but an older Arab tome offered a recipe which Estela had used before on others. She sent a stable-hand to tell Etiennette that a peasant was dead by the beehives and then she rushed off to her own domain, confident that the Lady of Les Baux could organise the burial of one of her own peasants.

Estela sat on her stool in the cool dark of the dispensary, amid the scents of dried thyme and lavender, rose and wormwood, that bitter herb which was the closest to cure-all that Estela knew. The poultices had brought instant relief, followed by a gradual return of a duller form of pain. There was already some swelling round the stings she could see but she'd removed the one tiny arrow left by a striped warrior. The second day was always worse than the first but she was confident the treatment was working and her thoughts returned to the dead woman.

There was no chance now of finding out what the Gyptian had meant about the cloth and Estela's ancestors. Nor was there an opportunity to shout at her for prophecies that twisted words, that had meaning only after the events which they foretold. Estela had been right – Dragonetz had not broken oath! And yet the words had indeed contained some truth. And never would she betray Dragonetz! The Gyptian had spoken hurtful lies when she'd seen another man lying with her! She should have had the chance to tell the woman so! But Dame Fairnette was beyond Estela's questions and recriminations.

Malik had taught her to look for symptoms and to consider what a patient said as only one of those symptoms. A doctor should never accept a patient's self-diagnosis but observe and analyse. What had she observed? A dead body surrounded by bees. So many stings would kill anybody. Perhaps the beekeeper had rushed out in the storm, worried that the hives would be damaged. She'd found one knocked over or broken, tried to right it. But then she'd have worn her veil. Unless she was somewhere else first, maybe in a farmer's cottage, in the other direction. It was possible. If Estela were asked, that's what she would say.

But she just *knew* that was not how it had been. What else had she observed? Not just today but previously. Dame Fairnette was coughing blood, showing signs of pain, refusing treatment. She'd turned down Estela's offer of treatment, suggested she could treat herself and said something strange; 'the girl can't do what's needed for me but I know those who can'. The malady was obviously getting worse and the Gyptian was not young. She gave every impression that her own life was over, apart from her dreams for her people and her desire to join them.

The wicker beehive, hacked. The knife, trailing wicker threads. And something else Dame Fairnette had told Estela; storms make bees mad. Even before the storm breaks. Were the bees 'those' who could do what she needed? Had the beekeeper known exactly what she was doing when she'd gone to the hive, probably before the storm. Had she cut off the top of the hive, lain across it? Estela shuddered, scratched at her own stings. If she were right, then Dame Fairnette's body should be buried without ceremony and her soul condemned to hell. So it would be, if Estela spoke up.

First, do no harm. Surely, the bees were God's creatures? Dame Fairnette could not be held responsible for their actions and Estela had no doubt that the Gyptian had died from bee-stings. It was not for the doctor to judge what a suffering patient might do or to offer mere speculations to those who made such judgements their business. No, Estela would not even talk to Malik about this troubling death. A physician needed to carry such burdens alone, to keep the patient's confidences secret, even beyond the grave.

Dame Fairnette's death might have caused lurid stories in the servants' quarters but went unnoticed amid the preparation for Geoffroi de Rançon's funeral. If the vigil over his body had been brief and ill-attended, there was no lack of enthusiasm for the rites themselves, the procession, speeches and feasts. While the Gyptian's body found a pauper's grave, de Rançon was allowed a place in the Pons crypt, in honour of his prowess during the tourney. There was much debate as to whether this was appropriate, given that he had died rather disappointingly of some malady rather than in the height of battle, but Etiennette insisted. Dragonetz had stated categorically that Geoffroi's remains were not to be returned to his home estate, and it was too good an opportunity to show off Les Baux's renowned pageantry.

Etiennette was deeply disappointed that neither Estela nor Dragonetz was willing to sing at Geoffroi's funeral feast but she recovered quickly when a cousin from Aurenja accepted her invitation. Estela had not seen Raimbaut d'Aurenja since leaving Die and, in other circumstances, would have appreciated the chance to hear this reputed troubadour once more. She'd last heard him in the court of Narbonne and his reputation had grown since then – rightly so, she judged. It was no surprise that her friend and ex-patron, Béatriz of Die, had succumbed to his charms.

But Estela and Dragonetz were both too heavy-hearted to enjoy the funeral pomp and they excused themselves whenever possible. Estela retreated to her dispensary to grieve, packing those items that could travel. Dragonetz endured emotions with no name. Unable to bury them with de Rançon, he merely continued with his duties. He tried to make up for the past months by sharing his plans freely, but in confidence, with Raoulf, who approved wholeheartedly. That would not be the case with others and, when the funeral was over, Dragonetz must speak to five people. It would not be easy.

'Barcelone has announced publicly that he is going home,' Estela told him.

'Yes.' They both knew what that meant. 'I have an audience with Etiennette this morning.' Estela kissed him, not needing to say more.

The ante-chamber was draped in its new décor, sixteen-pointed stars on red fields, visible everywhere fabric could be displayed, even on tasselled cushions.

Etiennette smiled ruefully, noticing his expression. 'I know but it makes Hugues happy. And the name of Les Baux deserves some fame abroad. *Au hasard, Bautasar* suits us well, don't you think?'

'Perfectly. The name of Les Baux will be a byword for courage throughout the world,' replied Dragonetz, kissing her hand.

'Barcelone is leaving,' she stated, knowing it was not news. 'We can build up our forces again while he takes care of his own land. Hugues will carry on with your training methods here and draw in new recruits. Once Barcelone has left, we can win back those he swayed. I am confident we have more than half of Provence with us already.

There is time for you to go to Arle, oversee the mint, produce all the gold we will need to go to war again. We will need coin and this time I want our money. I know you won't marry me for foolish reasons.' Her eyes flashed again. 'But you will come back to Les Baux when we declare war and lead an army. And it will be my head on the gold we use to fund it. I don't want to see a Barcelone head on anything but my battlements!'

Dragonetz lost any hope that Etiennette might have softened. 'You signed a truce…' he risked saying.

'I had no choice!' she spat back. 'My husband murdered, my sons threatened – and Provence all but taken from me! Besides, Hugues was too young to know what he signed. He will wage war, not I.'

'You have been the perfect host these last months,' murmured Dragonetz. 'Barcelone has nothing but praise for your hospitality.'

'Of course.' Etiennette drew herself up with pride. 'This is Les Baux. We know how to conduct ourselves with courtesy. And how to wage war with honour.' Her eyes flashed. 'Once Barcelone and his lordling leave, they are no guests of mine. Whether it takes one year or twenty, I will have my father's lands back!'

'My Lady, if you love Provence, don't tear her in two.' Dragonetz knelt so as not to tower over this indomitable widow. Never had he felt so strongly that she'd been wronged. 'Please. Give it up. Accept an overlord and rule Provence in his name, as you always have. Be the power, not the name.'

'Never,' she said. 'I will never bend the knee to some foreigner.'

If Dragonetz thought it equally unlikely that she would bend the knee to some local, a Porcelet for instance, he was wise enough to hold his peace. But he had reached the moment he knew would come.

'I won't help you tear Provence apart. I do believe your cause is just. I have done everything I can to teach Hugues leadership but some qualities are within, not learned. *You* still lead here. And if you choose war, you choose death for brother against brother, friend against friend. Barcelone soldiers will die, yes, but the people in Barcelone will carry on farming and going to market, while the people of Provence see their crops burned, their wells poisoned and their children murdered by their neighbours!'

White-faced, Etiennette said, 'I will not yield.'

'But I will,' Dragonetz told her. 'I will not help you turn Provence red with blood. Ramon is leaving because I have sworn to go with him. He will keep the truce and leave because he knows you aren't strong enough to fight him without me.' Her stubborn lack of reason suddenly infuriated him. 'God's blood! Don't you *know* he could have wiped out your entire family and it's by his mercy you're alive at all, let alone governors of his province!'

'It's not his province.' Her voice small and cold, her fists were clenched, she held firm. And she hadn't hit him. 'It will take longer without you but we will go to war again.'

He shook his head, torn between frustration and respect. 'The courage of Les Baux. I make you one promise: should it come to war, I will never ride against you. I swear it and I am no oath-breaker.' He bowed farewell.

'Au hasar, Bautasar,' were her last words to him.

When he reported the conversation to Estela, she asked the very question that had crossed his own mind. 'Will she have you killed?'

'No.'

'Because?'

'It would not be honourable. Another ruler would have poisoned Barcelone and his family here while they slept.' They knew such rulers. Mélisende of Jerusalem, perhaps even Aliénor – there were rumours.

'Hugues?'

Dragonetz had gone straight to Hugues on leaving Etiennette. 'More complicated. Some days he seems to understand what war would bring to Provence. Other days he wants to lead his men into glorious battle, avenge his father and please his mother. The hero of song. At bottom, I think he's glad to get rid of me.' He teased her. 'Apparently I'm competition for all the women in the castle.'

'That would sum up the focus of Hugues' romantic attention,' was the dry reply.

'And Ramon?' That had been a happier interview. When Dragonetz had offered his sword to Barcelone, with his conditions, there had been no hesitation. 'He is a man I can follow,' he told Estela, de Rançon's words ringing in his ears. Ramon had proved his mettle a hundred times, in the field and in tactics, as a leader and as a man whose judgement was tempered with mercy. El Sant indeed.

Malik's reaction had been even warmer than Ramon's and Dragonetz owned that it lifted his spirits to think of riding beside his friend, speaking freely with him again.

Estela hesitated, then named the last of the five. 'Sancha?'

'Turned her back on me.'

Estela said nothing but went on her own mission to bid farewell to their friend. Sancha did not flee her but stabbed at a piece of embroidery that was more in Estela's style than characteristic of her own neat work. She kept her eyes firmly on the victim of her mood, refusing to meet Estela's gaze.

'I don't want us to part like this,' Estela said, talking to cover the silence. 'We're leaving tomorrow, with Barcelone's party. Dragonetz has sent a pigeon to the villa and we're stopping to collect Gilles, Musca, Prima and Nici. Then we'll go to Marselha, sort out our business affairs – I have to visit the baths so the ladies have access to funds and know what to do with treatments. I've written notes for them.

Then we'll go to Arle and catch up with Barcelone's party. Dragonetz wants to see the mintmaster. He's sent a pigeon there too, has some idea that the man might come to Barcelone and work there. Etiennette will probably forget about him as there's nobody who can run a mint now Dragonetz won't do it. He'd have been good at it too. I think it's the one thing he regrets about going…' she broke off, realising that her chatter had taken her in a direction that was unlikely to help matters.

'I don't care,' Sancha told her. 'Baths, money, pigeons. It's all a game to Dragonetz. And to you.'

'That's not fair,' Estela retorted. 'You turn faint at the sight of blood. You had to hide your eyes during a tourney! Yet you want Dragonetz to start civil war here again, your own people killing each other.'

'They all ought to fight for Les Baux,' Sancha said weakly.

'I don't want our last words to each other to be an argument. We're not going to agree about Provence but you should know that Dragonetz is going to Barcelone to keep the peace here. We understand Etiennette's rights but that's not the point any more. The point is not to kill people. And I'm going to miss you!'

'Really?'

'Really!'

'But you'll have Dragonetz and Musca...'

'Dragonetz will be training men and Musca can't say much more than 'Icky'. I'll miss intelligent company. I'll miss *women's* conversation.'

'There will be women in Barcelone.'

'They'll all have strange accents and believe that babies arrive in baskets.' They laughed and some of the ice thawed. Estela told Sancha her plans to pursue her medical profession and establish a dispensary in Barcelone. At first they'd be living with Malik's wife and children. The prospect of living with strangers, who were also Muslims, was a little frightening but also part of the adventure. And she had no doubt that it was going to be an adventure.

Finally, Sancha accepted a hug and a tearful goodbye, and said she would wave to them when they left and check the message that came back by pigeon from Arle, to know they'd arrived there safely.

Estela had not realised how empty her arms had been until they were full of wriggling toddler. Musca cried when he saw the strange woman who wanted to grab him but after seeing Nici greet her in somersaults of joy, the little boy allowed himself to be cuddled. Stories collided as Gilles asked whether 'the witch' was dead yet;

Estela asked whether Musca was eating vegetables; Raoulf wanted to know how many horse and guards were at the villa and Dragonetz wanted a pigeon count.

Large quantities of food and wine eased the conversation and after dinner, Dragonetz found himself in a quiet moment with Gilles. Although there had been no open animosity, there was obviously tension between him and Raoulf with regard to Prima, who seemed blithely unaware of her current lover's protective glares.

'It goes well?' enquired Dragonetz, delicately.

Gilles understood. 'She's a good lass and we're suited.' Then it was his turn to probe. 'De Rançon turned up. Did he try to kill you again? Did you tell her about Jerusalem?'

Gilles was the only other person who knew, who'd been there and seen for himself. He could tell Gilles about Muganni, share the burden, have one other person who knew his real grief. But he'd already made that decision, when he thought of telling Malik. 'No,' he said. 'De Rançon intended malice but didn't follow through. Even saved my life.'

Gilles looked sceptical. 'He's a fancy enough swordsman but looking to run you through from behind no doubt.'

'No. I think something changed him.'

'I doubt that very much.' Gilles was clearly not overwhelmed by the notion of redemption so Dragonetz didn't pursue the issue. 'Have you told her?' Gilles repeated. Nici was barking furiously somewhere near the entrance.

'No. Even if I did, she wouldn't believe me. And now?' He shrugged. 'Where is the good?'

'She should know,' persisted Gilles stubbornly.

'No. the subject is closed. Estela has lost a dear friend and is hurt enough.'

Gilles humphed again.

'Dragonetz?' Estela was calling him. 'There is a messenger...'

Pinned to the spot by a large white fury was a messenger attired in the sort of colours for which Estela had criticised Dragonetz the night of the storm. He and his horse looked rather more portly than was the usual case in such an active job. Nici was doing his best to impress, barking manically, hackles raised, snapping if the man moved but otherwise causing no real threat. Those who knew him well could see that he was enjoying himself. His upward curve of a tail thrashed the air like a feathered sabre.

The messenger did not know Nici well, to judge by the stain on the front of his hose. 'Good boy,' he stammered, further delighting the dog.

'Icky!' Musca said sternly and the dog looked at him, wondering for a moment, then dismissing the idea of obedience.

'Nici!' commanded Estela and this time the dog considered it to be more than an invitation. He stopped barking but stood ready to pounce, staring at the stranger.

'I had word, in Marselha, that you'd come back to the villa, and I've a message for you, my Lord. Only I couldn't deliver it because I was attacked and robbed by a gang of twenty men. They left me for dead and I was rescued by a good Samaritan, a landlord, who nursed me back to health. As soon as I recovered, I sought to deliver my message but you had left the villa so I was too late. I put the word out that there would be a reward for whoever told me you'd returned. I'm sure you'll repay me the reward, my Lord?'

Dragonetz bit back all the words that came to mind. There were ladies present. 'The message?' He already knew what was coming but he listened anyway.

The messenger shut his eyes and recited, "By this token, I, Aliénor, Duchesse of Aquitaine and Queen of England, command you to come to me with all speed, lead my men against Louis's armies, protect your Liege and keep your oath.' And she said I was to give you this.'

If Estela hadn't put a hand on his arm, Dragonetz would have hit the man but he restrained himself and took the note from him. He broke Aliénor's seal and read the words she'd scrawled, 'I need you, Dragonetz. Come now. I trust you.' And he had not gone.

Raoulf stepped forward and hit the man's face with a mailed fist. Estela winced and gripped Dragonetz more tightly. Reeling, the messenger said, 'Thank you, my Lord, thank you.'

'Enough.' Dragonetz cautioned Raoulf, even though he couldn't find it in himself to be sorry. 'You owe me a message. You and your nag are well-fed and well-rested; you start for Aquitaine tonight and you ride until you find first the Duchesse and then my father Lord Dragon. You deliver two messages.

Tell Aliénor you never reached me, I never received her message in time and I am more sorry than she will ever know but I am no oath-breaker. You have that?' the man's lips moved as he repeated and memorised the words. He would not be Aliénor's messenger if he did not have at least that capacity so Dragonetz trusted his memory if nothing else.

'And the message for Lord Dragon?' the messenger asked, relieved that he'd been given work and no worse.

'Tell him I am with the only family I care about and he may go to hell.'

The messenger lost any colour he'd regained and looked perilously close to vomiting.

'If you survive the two messages, we are quits,' Dragonetz told him. 'If you don't deliver them, you will never know a night's rest again because I will find you, wherever you may be and I will rip out your coward's liver so you may watch it fry while you're still alive!'

'Thank you, my Lord,' the messenger managed to say, before backing towards his horse and galloping away.

The sombre mood lasted until Musca said hopefully, 'Evvybody happy now?' and his father laughed, threw him in the air, replied, 'Everybody is very happy now!'

The next day, Nici was bored. His favourite people had gone somewhere without him. So when he caught sight of another stranger walking onto to his territory, he took great pleasure in repeating the previous day's behaviour.

The man was carrying some object in front of him, which he waved above his head as Nici warned him to stay where he was. This time, there was nobody to help Nici defend his family's home so he added a few menaces to his routine barking and snapped a bit closer to the man's legs.

This was very effective. The man shrieked, dropped what he was carrying and ran back to the horse he'd tethered at the entrance.

Nici let him go, more interested in the leather bag on the ground. Underneath a top note of mint, citrus and a spice new to him, his perceptive nose detected the mouth-watering smell of decay and dead things.

The dog lay down and held the package firmly between his paws. He chewed on the leather for a while, sucking the flavour out. One part of the bag gave way between his teeth and he investigated the interior with his tongue, then tore the bag a little more. Some parchment rolled out but smelled of little interest.

The musty smell was stronger though so Nici ripped apart more of the bag until he could pull out its contents: a small wooden box. The smell was inside the box so he chewed on it for a bit but the wood resisted his teeth.

So he did what he always did with a carcass that needed to mature. He kept it for later and buried it between the roses.

When his family came back from their outing, Nici's world livened up again and he had so many treats passed to him under the table as they dined, that he completely forgot the one he'd buried.

The next day, he was anxious to see preparations for travel again and he chased his tail, worried at spending another day unable to guard his people. When he was summoned to join them, and allowed to run alongside the wagon, his tail nearly lifted him off the road in excitement. This was new!

It was too good to be true so he checked again. Everybody he loved, his whole family, was under his guard. He could see Dragonetz, a squawking bird on his shoulder, riding up and down the train, giving orders to Raoulf, and to other men, who didn't matter; Estela riding her palfrey beside Gilles; Prima and the two little boys in the wagon.

Nici settled into a lope. He could sense this would be a long journey. He was many lopes from home when his stomach reminded him of pleasure postponed but it was too late now to dig up the box and bring it with him. He forgot about it and kept running.

In all the packing to leave for Arle, nobody had noticed the small parchment scroll carried by the wind to catch on a thorn, waving from a rose bush like a small pennant. Only the breeze read the message before the rain washed it away.

Dearest Estela,
My heart is yours, in life and in death.
Geoffroi.

EPILOGUE

One fine day in 1152, Petronilla, the sixteen-year-old Queen of Aragon, gave birth to the baby boy who was expected to unite Barcelone and Aragon into the most powerful state of northern Al-Andalus, a counterbalance to the recently united kingdoms of Castile and Léon, further south.

Little Pedro had been conceived twelve years earlier by Petronilla's father, Ramiro, 'the Monk', and her husband-to-be, Ramon Berenguer, Comte de Barcelone, 'the Saint'. All that remained was for Petronilla to grow up and give flesh to their conception.

Bells rang; two kingdoms rejoiced at the birth of the little king, and everybody agreed that Petronilla had fulfilled her destiny. What the midwife said to Petronilla, as she passed the squalling baby to his mother, was a little more practical.

HISTORICAL NOTE

Dragonetz and Estela are fictional characters living in real 12th century events, which are set in the region now known as southern France. In this period, hunting, hawking and tournaments are not yet turned into the rituals they become in the 13th century and later. Coats of arms are also in their early stages as highborn families 'discover' their ancestors and emblems. I took the liberty of bringing forward the known appearance of the Baux motto, coat of arms and legendary ancestor, to suit my story, but there is nothing to prove that my version didn't happen.

The basic family tree below shows some of the difficulties in research. Multiple dates (if any) are recorded for a birth or death; the same name is passed on for generations; Ramon Berenguer II is actually the nephew of Ramon Berenguer IV and heir to a completely different region. Names are spelled according to language and humour, so Ramon could also appear in research as Raymond, Raimon, Ramun; sometimes hyphenated, sometimes not.

I have tried to be consistent within the series and to give a flavor of the Occitan, French, Latin, Arabic and Jewish languages which were commonly used, without rendering place-names obscure. Marselha is Marseille, Ais en Provence is Aix en Provence and so on.

I hope you enjoyed your visit to 12th century Provence.

HISTORICAL CHARACTERS APPEARING IN THE SERIES SO FAR:

- *Aaron ben Asher* – Jewish sage, who annotated the sacred Torah known as the Keter Aram Sola/ the Aleppo Codex
- *Abd-al-Malik* – the last King of Zaragoza, grandfather of my invented character Malik
- *Aliénor of Aquitaine/ Eleanor of Aquitaine*, Duchess of Aquitaine and Queen of France
- *Abraham ben Isaac/ Raavad II* – Jewish leader in Narbonne
- *Alphonse*, nicknamed 'Jourdain'/ 'Jordan', Comte de Toulouse, father of Raymond, killed by poison in Caesarea in 1148
- *Alphonso*, King of Castile, Emperor of Spain – died in 1144 leaving his estate to the Templars
- *Amaury* – younger son of Mélisende
- *Archbishop of Narbonne*, Pierre d'Anduze – brother of Ermengarda's husband
- *Archbishop Suger* – royal prelate in Paris, adviser to King Louis
- *Baudouin*, King of Jerusalem – Mélisende's son
- *Bèatriz* – the future Comtesssa de Dia/Comtesse de Die and famous troubairitz
- *Bernard de Clairvaux* – advisor to Louis, abbot leading and reforming the Cistercian order
- *Bernard d'Anduze* – Ermengarda's titular husband, brother of the Archbishop of Narbonne
- *Bernard de Tremelay*, Templar Grand Master 1151
- *Chirkhouh* – Nur ad-Din's general, killed Prince Raymond of Antioch
- *Constance* – widow of the Prince of Antioch, Mélisende's niece

- *Conrad* – Holy Roman Emperor, ruler of the Germanic peoples
- *Dolca* – Etiennette's sister, heir to Provence, grandmother to the young Comte, Ramon Berenguer II
- *Ermengarda/Ermengarde* – Viscomtesse of Narbonne
- *Etiennette/Stéphania* – widowed Lady of Les Baux-de-Provence
- *Everard des Barres*, Grand Master of the Templars during the Second Crusade
- *Foulques*, King of Jerusalem by marriage to Mélisende – died 1146
- *Geoffroi de Rançon* (the father), Commander of Aliénor's Guard 1148
- *Geoffroi de Rançon* (the son) – possibly more than one
- *Guilhelm de Poitiers* – married Bèatriz
- *Henri d'Anjou, King of England* – married Aliénor (2nd husband)
- *Hodierne*, Comtesse de Tripoli – sister of Mélisende, Queen of Jerusalem
- *Hugues des Baux* – Lord of Les-Baux-de-Provence, son of Etiennette
- *Isoard*, Comte de Die/Dia – Bèatriz' father (very little known about Bèatriz)
- *Ismat ad-Dhin* – Nur ad-Din's wife, Unur's daughter
- *Joscelyn*, Comte d'Edessa – deserted and lost the city to Muslim forces, starting the Second Crusade
- *Jarl Rognvaldr Kali Kolsson* – Prince of Orkney
- *Louis VII* – King of France, married to Aliénor
- *de Maurienne*, Comte – uncle and adviser to Louis VII
- *Maimonides* – Jewish philosopher
- *Manuel Komnenos/Comnenus* – Emperor of Byzantium
- *Manassés* – Constable of Jerusalem
- *Mélisende* – Queen of Jerusalem
- *Mujir ad-Din* – ruler of Damascus, 1151

- *Nur ad-Din* – Muslim Atabeg (ruler and general), uncle of Saladin
- *Pope Eugene III*
- *Petronilla* – Queen of Aragon, married to Ramon Berenguer IV
- *Porcelet* family – (First names are my invention)
- *Pons* family – the rulers of Les-Baux-de-Provence
- *Ramon Trencavel* – brother to Roger and Comte de Carcassonne on his brother's death in 1150
- *Ramon Berenguer IV* –'El Sant', Comte de Barcelona, Prince of Aragon and Regent of Provence
- *Ramon Berenguer II* – Comte de Provence, nephew to 'El Sant'
- *Raymond V* – Comte de Toulouse
- *Raymond Comte de Tripoli*, Hodierne's husband and relation of Toulouse, killed by Assassins in 1152
- *Raymon/Ramon/Raymond, Prince of Antioch* – Aliénor's uncle and rumoured lover, killed by Saracen troops in 1148
- *Raymond and Stephanie (Etiennette) of Les Baux* – rulers in Provence
- *Raymond de Puy* – Hospitalers' Grand Master 1151
- *Roger Trencavel*, Comte de Carcassonne – died in 1150
- *Saint Paul/ Saul of Tarsus* – famously converted on the road to Damascus
- *Salah ad-Din/Saladin* – Muslim leader during the Third Crusade
- *Sicard de Llautrec* – ally of Toulouse
- *Unur* – Muslim general, defended Damascus in the Second Crusade
- *Zengi/Imad ad-Din Zengi* – father of Nur ad-Din, murdered in 1146
- *The Hashashins/Assassins* – the Isma'ili Muslim sect
- *the troubadours* – Jaufre Rudel, Marcabru, Cercamon, Peire Rogier from the Auvergne, Raimbaut d'Aurenja/Raymon of Aurenja, Guiraut de Bornelh

- *Persian poets* – Omar Khayyam, Sanai
- *Medical authorities* – Galen, Nicolaus of Salerno, Trota, Hildegard von Bingen
- In charge of the Templar Commandery at Douzens – Peter Radels, Master; Isarn of Molaria and Bernard of Roquefort, joint Commanders

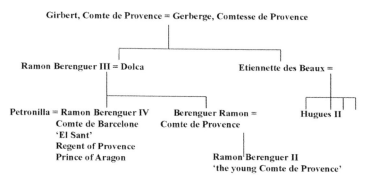

Key players in the Baussenques Wars, who appear in 'Plaint for Provence'

Girbert, Comte de Provence = Gerberge, Comtesse de Provence

Ramon Berenguer III = Dolca

Etiennette des Beaux =

Petronilla = Ramon Berenguer IV
Comte de Barcelone
'El Sant'
Regent of Provence
Prince of Aragon

Berenguer Ramon =
Comte de Provence

Hugues II

Ramon Berenguer II
'the young Comte de Provence'

ACKNOWLEDGMENTS

Many thanks to:

my editor, Lesley Geekie;
my critical friends, especially Babs, Claire, Jane, Karen C, Karen M
and Kris for your invaluable input and support.

A huge thank you to Monica Green and Priscilla Throop for permission to use their work on medieval medicine, which is an essential part of Estela's story.

Excerpts from *The Trotula*, translated by Monica H.Green. reprinted by kind permission of *University of Pennsylvania Press.*

Excerpts from *Hildegard von Bingen's Physica*, translated by Priscilla Throop, reprinted by kind permission of *Healing Arts Press*

Historical sources that were particularly useful were:

Les Seigneurs des Baux –Pierre Conso
La Provence, Enjeu des Guerres Médiévales – *Pierre Conso*
The Art of Medieval Hunting – John Cummins
Medieval Hunting – *Richard Almond*
The Chronicle of San Juan de la Peña, translated by Lynn H. Nelson
(University of Pennsylvania Press)
Poems of Arab Andalusia, translated by Cola Franzen *(City Lights Books)*
Chivalry – Maurice Keen

ABOUT THE AUTHOR

I'm a Welsh writer and photographer living in the south of France with two scruffy dogs, a beehive named 'Endeavour', a Nikon D750 and a man. I taught English in Wales for many years and my claim to fame is that I was the first woman to be a secondary headteacher in Carmarthenshire. I'm mother or stepmother to five children so life has been pretty hectic.

I've published all kinds of books, both with traditional publishers and self-published. You'll find everything under my name from prize-winning poetry and novels, military history, translated books on dog training, to a cookery book on goat cheese. My work with top dog-trainer Michel Hasbrouck has taken me deep into the world of dogs with problems, and inspired one of my novels. With Scottish parents, an English birthplace and French residence, I can usually support the winning team on most sporting occasions.

www.jeangill.com

facebook.com/writerjeangill
twitter.com/writerjeangill
instagram.com/writerjeangill
goodreads.com/JeanGill

SONG HEREAFTER

1153: HISPANIA AND THE ISLES OF ALBION

If you enjoyed *Plaint for Provence* don't miss the thrilling conclusion to the story of Dragonetz and Estela in *Song Hereafter, Book 4* of *The Troubadours Quartet*

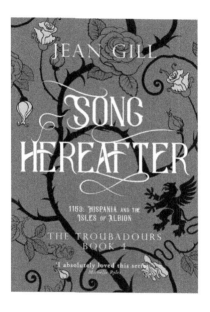

CHAPTER 1 SAMPLE

SONG HEREAFTER

Usually when El Rey Lobo bared his teeth, everyone in his line of sight wondered whether to do likewise and call it smiling, or to wait and pray for invisibility. Men had been killed for doing either. He had earned his nickname 'the Wolf King'. The men in front of the king today were not, however, his courtiers but his Christian neighbours of Barcelone: Ramon Berenguer and two of his commanders. They were not currying favour but seeking an alliance.

Ramon was sombre. 'Without the King of Murcia, we would have the Almohads in our gardens. I hear they make a virtue of killing.'

'And of dying, too. In order to *'purge'* this land.' the king replied. At the mention of the Almohads, El Rey Lobo's face darkened beneath his turban, and his mouth pursed as if accustomed to spit at the name. His swarthy features, oiled beard and flowing robes gave no sign of his Christian ancestry and it had been many generations since his family had converted to the Muslim faith of their overlords.

He continued, 'They will not rest until all our people are dead. All of our faith who have made this country our home for generations. We have 'sinned', we are 'unbelievers' and the penalty is death for me, for our wives, for our children, for men like your commander Malik. They will make slaves of Jews and Christians but us, they will kill.

They are superstitious barbarians from the hills of Africa! They shave their heads before battle. What pious man would do such a thing? And their black slaves thump on great drums the size of cartwheels. When you hear the beat of their war-drums, you hear your own death. This is what my men must face! Their own hearts beating in fear!'

Dragonetz listened intently to his Liege and the Wolf King, sifting courtesies from nuggets of information. They were all waiting for the king's terms.

El Rey Lobo dismissed the Almohads with a defiant gesture and began the bargaining. 'The Almohads are not causing me a problem today. If you want to solve the problems I have today, go and find me a mintmaster and an expert in siege warfare.' He paused for thought, then held up a third finger. 'And somebody who will repair a paper mill. These are the problems that take up a king's time! When you take away these headaches, we can talk about protecting boundaries and Almohads!'

He laughed.

Each responded to the flashing teeth in his own manner, until the nervous echo died out.

Then, shocking in the silence, Dragonetz' laughter rang out, unforced, echoing against the stone walls of the Wolf King's antechamber.

'You find my problems entertaining, Dragonetz los Pros?' growled El Rey Lobo. He gave a sarcastic twist to Dragonetz' nickname los Pros, meaning 'the brave' in Occitan.

Dragonetz looked to his Liege, received a nod of consent, and responded directly to the king. 'Forgive me, Sire, but you said we would be hard put to respond to your needs unless we were mintmasters, paper producers and siege specialists. I expected your opening requests to be more difficult.'

'And I did not expect the Prince's man to be a braggart.'

'Show him, Dragonetz.' Ramon's voice carried without strain.

Printed in Great Britain
by Amazon

42138881R00189